LIVING PROOF

LIVING PROOF

Kira Peikoff

TOR®

A TOM DOHERTY ASSOCIATES BOOK

NEW YORK

This is a work of fiction. All of the characters, organizations, and events portrayed in this novel are either products of the author's imagination or are used fictitiously.

LIVING PROOF

Design by Mary A. Wirth

A Tor Book
Published by Tom Doherty Associates, LLC
175 Fifth Avenue
New York, NY 10010

www.tor-forge.com

Library of Congress Cataloging-in-Publication Data

Peikoff, Kira.
Living proof / Kira Peikoff.—1st ed.
p. cm.
"A Tom Doherty Associates book."
ISBN 978-0-7653-2930-1
1. Obstetricians—Fiction. 2. Gynecologists—Fiction. 3. Multiple sclerosis—Patients—Fiction. 4. Stem cells—Transplantation—Fiction. 5. Government investigators—Fiction. I. Title.
PS3616.E3535L58 2012
813'.6—dc22
2011025190

First Edition: February 2012

0 9 8 7 6 5 4 3 2 1

To my parents,
with love and thanks for always believing in me

And to Matt,
whose passion gives me courage

PART ONE

ONE

One number flashed in Arianna's mind: *464*. She didn't have much time.

Dr. Arianna Drake stepped into the deserted hallway, listening.

It was 7:30 A.M.—still too early for the man to arrive. No matter her dread, their appointment could not be adjusted or canceled, even if a patient went into labor before her eyes.

In the silence, Arianna could hear her own pulse drumming in her ears. She hurried toward the locked door at the opposite end of the hall, her heels clicking across the linoleum floor. The corridor was narrow and painted an antiseptic white, made starker by the fluorescent lights overhead. Nothing about the place stood out from any other private clinic in Manhattan; Arianna had made sure of it.

She stopped at the end of the hall, thumbed through her keys, and inserted one into the lock. Pushing the handle down, she leaned into the door and slipped inside.

The lab was neither hot nor cold, and breathing suddenly seemed easier, like stepping into an oxygen tank. On the left side of the room, a black floor-to-ceiling freezer spanned about ten feet wide, with multiple doors opening to different compartments inside. A green digital display across the front read *-78°C*. It hummed quietly next to a liquid nitrogen supply tank. Along the back of the room was a row of electron microscopes hooked up to computer monitors. Facing the freezer, on the right side of the room, was an incubator set at 37 degrees Celsius.

She yanked one of the freezer doors open. Cool air billowed out. Inside, several hundred slender glass tubes lined the shelves in rows, appearing to contain a hardened red liquid. Murmuring numbers under her breath, Arianna shivered as she counted the tubes, her finger hopping up and down the rows.

A pins-and-needles sensation suddenly surged in her right ankle. The tingling slid into her foot, tickling her veins from the inside out. Afraid of losing count, Arianna pressed on, stressing every fifth number aloud like a musician keeping time. When she at last reached the final tube—number 464—she shut the freezer door and sat down in place, breathing hot air onto her frozen hand. For a moment, she closed her eyes, appreciating her aloneness in the lab and the way everything in it functioned. But her foot was waking from slumber, twitching with little stabs of pain. She pointed her toes and traced a few circles in the air, wincing as the pain dispersed. Was the numbness starting to last longer, she wondered, or was she just more aware of it?

It was quiet enough to hear the seconds tick on her watch: 7:50 A.M. Ten minutes to showtime. She swallowed uneasily, considering whether she had time to count the tubes once more, just in case. But there was no need; she had counted them last night, after hours, and arrived at the same magic number. Better to be sitting at her desk, composed and ready. She breathed in and stood up slowly, avoiding a rush of blood to her head. Before letting herself out, she threw a loving glance at the incubator. Sometimes she wondered if she was capable of forgetting what preciousness lay inside—or whether that knowledge stood like a pillar in her mind, with every other thought swerving around it just to get by.

The hallway was still empty, but she heard the low rumble of Dr. Gavin Ericson's voice in the office next to hers. It was a comforting sound, the reminder of an ally. She paused at his door and knocked.

"Arianna?" he called.

She opened his door a crack and peered inside, seeing he was on the phone. Gavin and his wife, Emily, who together constituted the rest of the clinic's staff, were among her closest friends, dating to medical school a decade back.

Everything okay? he mouthed, one hand cupping the phone.

She smiled and nodded. "Good to go," she whispered, and pulled the door closed.

Inside her own office, she sat down at her desk, straining to hear any sounds from the clinic's front door. Nothing. She turned to her computer and pressed her index finger to the middle of the screen. After two seconds, the screen lit up and unlocked. A floating message in a box read, WELCOME, ARIANNA. NOVEMBER 1, 2027. 7:57 A.M.

It was impossible to concentrate on real work, and Arianna knew better than to try. She wondered who the man would be this month—but there was no way to know ahead of time. She looked up at her wall, which was covered with pictures of newborns swathed in blue and pink, next to a bulletin board of cards from grateful parents. In the middle of all the pictures hung a flat screen that streamed live video of the entrance to her clinic. Now it showed an empty sidewalk, occasionally a passerby, and a tree-lined street littered with yellow leaves.

For a few tense minutes, she watched—and then, just as she turned back to her computer, she heard it: the creak of the front door. She felt her body stiffen.

Neon red light burst from the screen on the wall, followed by an earsplitting whistle. She swiveled fast to face the screen. Between flashes of red, she could make out a man in a suit. Shielding her eyes, she grabbed a remote from her desk drawer. As she clicked off the alarm, the high-pitched whistle faded, leaving a ringing in her ears.

She stared at the screen, which preserved a snapshot of the intruder. This one was a stout older man with a raised knee, captured the moment he entered the clinic's waiting room. He wore a black suit and a stern expression, also a gun at his waist. Arianna's stomach clenched as she recognized him. He was the most senior inspector at the New York Department of Embryo Preservation.

Even though each month it happened the same way—the creak, the alarm, the snapshot—Arianna still felt jolted. She felt even worse for patients who happened to be in the waiting room when a man with a gun swaggered in. But DEP inspectors, as Arianna would explain, had magnetic passes that let them swipe into any fertility clinic whenever they wanted, which set the alarm off every time.

With a sigh, Arianna walked to the waiting room to greet the man. He was standing in the center of the room, looking starkly out of place next to the bright yellow couches and *Babytalk* magazines. His gaze steadied on Arianna, revealing no emotion as she stepped forward to shake his hand. Pinned to the lapel of his suit was a thin gold cross.

She forced a cheerful smile. "Good morning, Inspector Banks."

He shook her hand firmly, saying nothing. The man was a professional judger, she thought: too shrewd to show his contempt. So they had one thing in common.

"Follow me," she said, turning on her heel back to the hallway.

In the narrow corridor, they walked uncomfortably close to each other. His breathing was slightly strained, as if the bulk of his extra weight sat on his lungs. She slowed down so as not to outpace him, keeping her arms crossed over her chest. They passed the five examining rooms that made up her modest clinic, along with the three offices that belonged to her, Dr. Ericson, and Emily, the clinic's embryologist and nurse. At the end of the hallway, they stopped at the locked white door. Banks still had not said a word.

He took a printed form from his briefcase.

"It was a busy month here for in vitro, wasn't it," Arianna said as she put a key into the lock.

"Yes, it was," he responded, clearing his throat and looking down at the sheet. "Unusually busy. According to the department's tally, you should have four hundred sixty-four unused embryos this month from thirty-one couples."

"That's exactly right," she said. The state-run Department of Embryo Preservation mandated that all fertility clinics "preserve the soul of every embryo." In keeping with the law, the department required that clinics report, once a month, the number of embryos left over from every patient's attempt at in vitro fertilization—a number the inspectors verified with their visits. To ensure accurate reporting, the department periodically conducted random audits, during which it obtained access to a year of the clinic's original records, complete with all patients' contact information. Women could always be counted on to remember exactly how many eggs were taken out of their bodies, and how many embryos were later put back in—so their memories often proved to be the department's greatest resource in corroborating a clinic's reporting. If even a single unaccounted embryo came to light, it meant serious consequences for the clinic: probation and heavy fines.

But if a destroyed embryo were discovered, then the clinic would be shut down and the doctor charged with first-degree murder.

Six weeks prior, the department had questioned dozens of her own patients in a random audit, but all the women had reported the correct numbers. The clinic passed easily, as Arianna had known it would; her real patients knew nothing.

"Something about fall this year," she said as she swung open the door to the lab. "It feels like spring, so everybody wants to have babies." She laughed shrilly. *Don't make small talk,* she thought. *You don't know how.*

The inspector grunted as he stepped past her into the lab. She followed and closed the door, leaning against it. The oxygenated air filled her lungs like a calming agent as the inspector pulled on a pair of gloves.

"Let's see here," he said, opening one of the freezer doors labeled OCTOBER 2027. After the whoosh of cold air dissipated, Banks surveyed the rows of tubes inside and looked over his shoulder at Arianna. "That's quite a lot you got here."

Arianna felt her heartbeat do a drum roll. "I know, right?"

Banks turned back to the tubes and painstakingly lifted each one, examining its label as he counted. The label on each tube disclosed several facts: the names of the couple whose egg and sperm had joined in a dish; the date that embryo had been frozen; and its place in the couple's leftover batch, such as ANNE AND MIKE SMITH, OCT. 10, NUMBER 5/16.

For the in vitro procedure, Arianna would surgically remove about eighteen eggs from a woman's lifetime supply of three hundred thousand. Then Emily would mix the extracted eggs with sperm, and after five days of growth in the incubator, Arianna would implant only two or three of the strongest embryos back into the woman's uterus, to lower the chance of multiple births. This routinely left about fifteen excess embryos per couple to be frozen, suspended in the first stages of growth forever.

Arianna waited as Banks counted the October flasks; he paused after each one to mark another tally on his sheet. The minutes dragged on. When he finally reached number 464, she had to keep herself from noticeably exhaling.

"Perfect," she said, gripping the door's handle behind her.

"Let me count those one more time to make sure."

Her stomach dropped; she didn't know how much longer she could stand to be trapped there, watching him.

"Of course," she managed. "Take your time."

Monotonous counting ensued. She stood by, willing herself not to fiddle or twitch. At least his rounded back was turned. What was he thinking, she wondered, when he cradled the flasks in his hands? As the embryos' legal guardian, was he overcome with a desire to protect them? Or did he enjoy the power he held over helpless lives, including her own?

"And that, again, makes four sixty-four," he said at last, turning around to face her. "Now let's make sure you're preserving them properly."

She smiled. "Which ones would you like to see?"

"I would *like* to see all of them. But unfortunately, I only have time for a sample. Let's see these."

He turned to the flasks and randomly pointed to several dozen of them. Arianna placed each one carefully on a tray and carried it to the electron microscopes in the back of the room. One by one, she put the flasks under a microscope, and a camera underneath captured and transferred the images to the adjacent computer screen. Almost immediately, pictures showed up of circles with vague clumps of cells inside. The inspector squinted at the images, nodding after each one.

"Fine," he announced after scrutinizing all the images. "You can put them back now."

He scribbled his signature on the form as she eagerly replaced all the tubes in the freezer. Sweat dribbled onto her upper lip, salty and warm. She licked it away before he could notice any sign of nervousness.

She thought he was walking back to the door when he paused next to the incubator, grabbed the chrome handle, and pulled it open. Arianna sucked in a silent breath; that wasn't part of the protocol.

Banks peered at tiny petri dishes carefully spaced on the shelves under heat lamps. On the bottom shelf, a cluster of dishes was pushed to one side, under a label marked only with a sad face.

"How are they doing so far?" he asked with a general wave toward the dishes.

"It varies," she said. "They're still less than four days old. We don't know which of them we'll use yet."

"Then what about those?" He frowned, pointing to the cluster of dishes under the sad face.

"Oh, those." She winced. "Those just aren't doing well. They'll likely be frozen. We need to differentiate the strong ones from the weak."

Banks nodded. "I assume those will count for November's EUEs, then."

Extra-uterine embryos—the politically correct term for "leftovers."

"Yes." *Don't flinch,* she willed herself.

He eyed her for a moment. Indifference glazed across her face.

He looked down at his form. "Well, none are missing. They look to be properly preserved. Sign here."

She took the paper from him that was headed in bold, **NEW YORK DEPARTMENT OF EMBRYO PRESERVATION**, and signed under her clinic's name—WASHINGTON SQUARE CENTER FOR REPRODUCTIVE MEDICINE—next to the number 464.

"Good, so we'll see you next month," she said, turning to open the door. She stepped out into the hallway and exhaled shakily, as if she had just stumbled off a carnival ride.

"Me or one of my colleagues," he replied.

"I'll show you out," she said, not wanting to leave him alone in her clinic for a second. She walked briskly back to the waiting room as he trailed a step behind. Saying good-bye always felt like an awkward moment to her. Was she supposed to thank him? Act gracious for the interruption that threatened to undermine her life's biggest project?

In the waiting room, a slender woman with auburn curls was sitting on the couch, drumming her fingers on her lap. She grew still when she saw the inspector enter the room with Arianna.

"Hello!" Arianna exclaimed, and then, remembering, evened her tone. "I'll be with you in a moment, ma'am."

Turning back to the inspector, she nodded and casually extended her arm toward the front door. "Have a good day," she said.

He muttered, "Same to you," striding to the door. She watched it swing open and slam. And just like that, she thought, they were safe for another month.

With a giant grin, she turned to the woman on the couch, who sprang up and embraced her.

Arianna hugged her tightly. "Thank you so much, Meg."

"Of course," Megan said, stepping back. "But first I want to know: How the hell do you stand that guy?"

Arianna shook her head. "It's easier if I pretend he's just a handyman coming around for a checkup."

"With a gun?"

Arianna shrugged.

"So how are the good souls doing?"

"Pretty nippy," Arianna said with a smile. "But they're not lonely, that's for sure."

Back in her office with the door shut, Arianna thought how much they resembled each other. Both were tall, thin, and pale, thanks to their grandfather's side of the family. They shared thick hair, though Arianna's was nearly black. And unusual dark blue eyes. As kids, they used to pretend to be sisters—each wanting a sibling that never came. But it didn't matter: to be cousins, growing up side by side, was enough to give each the companionship she craved, without the rivalry. Still, being part of a small family had its downsides: With Arianna's parents dead, Megan's living far away, and neither woman yet married, they were each other's Thanksgiving gatherings,

Christmas mornings, and faithful standbys through every difficult time when family was indispensable—like now.

As soon as they sat down, Megan's face contorted with worry, as if she suddenly remembered why she was there. She stared at Arianna with the same determined hope as any other woman about to undergo ovary stimulation. "I want to think my eggs will help."

Arianna reached across the desk and took her hand. "They will."

"But what if they don't? What if they just turn into more failed attempts?"

Arianna shook her head. "Whatever happens, it won't be a complete failure. The whole thing is trial and error, so we need all those errors to get us closer to the answer."

Megan sat back with a frown. "Do you—do you think they're getting closer?"

Arianna looked away. "You know I would tell you."

"And there's nothing else I can do?"

"Meg, you're doing plenty. More than I could ever ask for." Arianna picked up a chart that lay next to her computer, feeling the steeliness of her professional training cut through her own fear. "All your vitals look good. We can get started if you're ready."

Megan grimaced, running her hands through her hair the way she often did when she was nervous. "You know how I get around needles. It's so embarrassing."

An injection of follicle-stimulating hormone into Megan's rear once a day for ten days would make her ovaries produce about eighteen eggs for the month, instead of the usual one. Then Arianna planned to surgically remove all those eggs, as she did for any patient undergoing in vitro. Except this one had no child in mind.

Arianna smiled. "It will barely even sting, you big baby. Just think about me doing C-sections all day long."

"But a shot every day for *ten days*?" A sobering thought must have entered Megan's mind then, because her expression changed. "It's fine. I can do this."

"I know you can, sweetie. You'll do great. Just imagine how you're going to spend the five grand."

Megan glared at her. "It's insulting that you're paying me."

"That's ridiculous. I'd pay more if I could."

"And you promise no one's going to arrest me, right?"

Arianna flashed her a conspiratorial grin. "What for? You're just a bighearted egg donor."

"What about—?" Megan's voice lowered. "What about all the other donors? You trust them all right?"

"Completely. I handpicked every single one of them. No woman who puts her body on the line for science has any interest in destroying it."

Megan nodded and then sighed. "Let's get the damn shot over with already. I can't stand the anticipation."

Arianna smiled, thinking of the childhood nicknames their family had fondly given them: the worrier and the warrior. The irony struck her that their old roles still had not changed. Yet something between them had evaporated over the last few months, something precious, and just when they needed it most: lightness.

"First things first," Arianna said as she stood up.

Megan groaned. "What?"

"You have to pick out the father," she deadpanned.

"What?"

"We have a wide collection of donated sperm on hand from every race, age, creed, you name it. Widens the gene pool for the research. You can flip through the book and decide who you think your eggs would like best."

Megan laughed in spite of herself. "If I didn't know you that well, Arianna, I'd think you might be having fun with this."

Arianna grinned. She was about to respond, determined to regain the tone of their old banter, when she felt herself inadvertently sway. Her office walls rolled into one another with quickening momentum as the pictures of newborns blurred around her, a spinning spread of faces and colors. Shutting her eyes, she sank to her knees in front of her desk and thrust one palm onto the ground. Her forehead dropped to the floor, sweat against cold. She was anchored. With her eyes closed and her body still, the spinning room began to slow down.

"Oh, Christ." Megan's voice hovered somewhere above her head. "Perfect timing. Do you need anything?"

Arianna didn't dare shake her head, just as the world was coming to a halt around her. "Time," she murmured into the floor.

She felt Megan's hand stroking her hair. "Okay. Take your time. You know I'm in no rush."

Arianna pressed her forehead harder into the ground, as if to prove the stability her senses refused to accept. She heard Megan stand up next to her.

"I'll just go out and run an errand. Call me when you're ready."

" 'Kay," Arianna muttered. Around anyone else, she would have been mortified. At least, she thought, Megan knew enough not to make a fuss. Her footsteps fell away, and then the door opened and shut. Arianna breathed in, grateful to suffer alone.

Megan stepped outside onto Washington Square South. In her mind, she replayed the frightening way Arianna had just sunk to the floor like a dummy. What if she were really in trouble?

But she did what Arianna had long ago instructed: walked away. "Just let me be," Arianna told her sternly the first time it happened in her presence. "I don't need any help."

Megan marveled at her bravery: How could she handle so much, so well? It just reminded her why she had looked up to her fearless cousin since childhood, when Arianna had ridden her bicycle without hands, approached popular boys she liked, dragged Megan onto her first upside-down roller coaster. Nothing ever seemed to faze her, while even as an adult, Megan panicked over the slightest medical problem. And now—

"Excuse me," came a man's voice behind her.

Megan turned around, holding her purse close to her body. The man looked a little older than she, in his mid-thirties. He wore faded jeans and a button-down white shirt and held a small notepad. A Yankees baseball cap covered his face in shadow, and when she looked at him, she understood why he wore it. Orange and brown freckles dotted his face with the frequency of pores; they lent him a juvenile quality that made him seem harmless.

"Can I help you?" she asked.

"I hope so," he said with a tentative smile. "I'm actually a reporter on the health beat. My name's Jed. I noticed you walk out of the fertility clinic right there, and I was wondering if I could ask you about it for a minute."

Megan's brow knotted. "Ask me about what?"

"Well, for starters, are you a patient at the clinic?"

"I am." *And how is that your business?* she almost snapped, but didn't.

"What made you choose to go there, out of all the clinics in the city?"

She stared at him. "Excuse me?"

"Sorry to be nosy," he said, but his tone was urgent.

"Are you doing a survey or something?" she asked. *I'm a patient,* she thought. *I'm supposed to want a baby.*

"A survey? Kind of. You could say that. I'm trying to figure something out."

"Well," she said, "I decided to go there because I got a great recommendation about the doctor. What are you trying to figure out exactly?"

"I'll tell you," he said, stepping closer. "See, I got this tip that a bunch more women than usual are going to this one clinic all of a sudden. It's such a small clinic, too. Maybe my mind's overactive, but I thought it sounded like there might be a story there. See if the patients know something I don't."

"I see. Where'd you hear that?"

He shrugged with polished nonchalance. "A tip from a source. So, have you noticed anything? Off the record."

Megan shook her head and tried to look puzzled. "I don't know anything about that. But I will tell you that the doctors there are really top-notch, even though the clinic's small. I've already recommended them to a lot of friends, and I'm sure others are doing the same. What kind of story are you doing?"

"I don't know. That's what I'm trying to figure out."

"Who do you write for?"

"I'm a freelancer. Got to depend on my own instincts to find stories. What do you do?"

"I'm in real estate. And I'm sure there's lots more interesting things happening in New York City," she said, and then added, "Good luck," for fear of seeming rude.

She started to fish her sunglasses out of her purse. When she found them, he was still standing there.

"You couldn't even point me in the right direction, at least?" he asked, raising his eyebrows.

"Sorry, I don't have a clue what you mean," she replied, and crossed the street toward Washington Square Park. *Don't run,* she thought. *Don't look back, and don't touch your phone yet.* She ambled through the park, forcing herself to concentrate on the sunset-orange trees, the park's glorious fountain, and a nearby acrobat who had drawn an impressive crowd. She eased among the chanting people, pretending to watch the man doing backflips over a row of tin cans. When she had inched into the first layer of people, she knew the reporter could no longer see her, so she withdrew her cell phone from her purse and called Arianna.

It rang twice before she picked up. "Hey, I'm okay now—"

"Arianna, I think somebody might know something."

TWO

Trent Rowe looked at his watch and sighed—12:35 P.M. Four hours and twenty-five minutes until the weekend. For the second time that day, he thought how oppressive it was that his office did not have a window. If only he could see the sky, or the sleek façade of another building, even a sliver of daylight. The headquarters were in the heart of Midtown: *mid-Midtown*, he thought wryly. Midway up the building, midway through the day, midlife crisis well under way. He was only thirty-six, though he felt much older. Not a sense of maturity, it was more a lack-of-freedom-until-he-could-retire kind of old.

He glanced up at the only picture on the wall where he would have liked his window. Framed in imitation gold, it was the famous portrayal of the Crucifixion. Blood dripped from Jesus' nailed palms, and his head hung forward limply, crowned with a ring of thorns. It was a gift from Trent's supervisor, Gideon Dopp, when he had started the job three years ago. Dopp, a former priest, explained that Jesus' suffering was a daily reminder of why their work mattered: the modern-day version of catching heretic killers like those who murdered Christ. That the crimes now lacked visible gore made them no less violent. Trent's job offered the chance to stamp out these sins, serve justice, and uphold morality.

Trent Rowe was an agent at the New York City bureau of the Department of Embryo Preservation.

"Trent," spoke a voice in his doorway.

He closed the game of solitaire on his screen, which luckily faced away from the door, and looked up. Dopp's square shoulders reached both sides of the doorway. His eyes were intense, and he had the perfectly straight nose of a nobleman. One side of his mouth dipped down when he smiled, yet it seemed entirely genuine. That was one of the reasons Trent admired him: He was no phony, and on some level, Trent knew that he himself was.

"Hi, boss," he said.

Dopp clasped the doorframe. "We're starting in ten minutes. Are you ready?"

"All set." Trent's lips spread into an ashamed smile; he had forgotten about his presentation. "I think you're going to find it very interesting," he added hastily.

"Good. Banks and Jed are both back."

When Dopp left, Trent returned to moving red on black, black on red, letting his eyes blur over the colors.

All week, he had been researching one fertility clinic. It was an arduous task, but Trent knew Dopp would be happy with his research. Trent had first noticed this certain clinic's unusual spike in popularity while going over routine reports, and now Dopp would be even more pleased with the surprising results of his digging. Maybe it would help propel him out of this office and into one with a window.

The thought of a promotion filled him with superficial warmth, like drinking froth instead of coffee. A promotion would confirm that he was right for this job, a validation he desperately wanted, and it would show the world what a success he was, so maybe the fact that he didn't feel like one wouldn't matter. He looked at the painting of the Crucifixion, convincing himself that he had every reason to feel successful: His work was more worthy here than it had been at the newspaper. Here he was able to defend the tenets of Christianity, help the helpless, expose the corrupt, preserve human life.

But sometimes he wondered what his life would be like if he had stayed at *Newsday*, Long Island's biggest paper, where he had worked the investigative beat. There were thrilling moments, to be sure, such as when he had single-handedly uncovered a money-laundering scheme at one of the biggest churches on the Island. It had taken guts to ingratiate himself with the priests, to draw out answers to the right questions under a guise of harmlessness. Oh, how he basked in the respect of his editors when his front-page series on the fraud had even earned him a spot as a Pulitzer finalist, his proudest moment to date. But despite his success, that story had crushed his religious consciousness. Later, there would be more such stories—the worst being gay priests who preyed on little boys—that made him privately question God's very existence. It was too dangerous a precipice, and Trent had pulled back swiftly before looking down too far. His editors were devastated when he told them he was leaving to join the DEP. But here he could restore his damaged connection to God, with no doubts about false leads or wasted time. Here he had finally found meaning; so how could his dominant feeling be boredom?

With a sigh, he walked down the hall to the meeting room, with its oval table and downtown view. Jed, Banks, and Dopp were already there.

"We were just talking progress," Dopp said, "or lack thereof."

Jed nodded, his lips tight. His orange hair looked flattened. Trent had never seen him wear anything but a suit and tie, but now he had on jeans, which Trent eyed enviously.

Jed reluctantly explained that none of the patients would talk to him, and Banks reported that the clinic had passed the inspection.

On the table, Banks dropped a form with a slanted signature—*Arianna Drake*. "There weren't any embryos missing or damaged, but the numbers are quite high." He paused, wagging his hand in the air as if to summon the right words. "There's something about that woman, the doctor. I can't explain it, but I don't like it."

"What do you mean?" Dopp said.

Banks's lips curled up. "Some people give off bad vibes, and she's one of them."

Trent smiled to himself. He could not have hoped for a better lead-in.

Dopp's thick brows knotted. "That's something to consider. But we need facts." He turned to Trent. "What do the numbers tell us?"

"Let me show you what I found." Trent rose, shutting off the lights, and slipped the disc into the projector. "This slide shows six bar graphs representing the number of infertility patients at each of these six clinics over the past year. The clinics are all similar in size and location." He clicked through the next six slides slowly, each of which showed a large graph mapping a single clinic's data. "These six clinics all show a steady, relatively fixed influx of IVF patients each month. Some months are more popular in all the clinics, but none show especially volatile shifts. With minor variations, they all tend to get busier in the summer and slower in the winter. But now, look at this graph."

With a flourish, he clicked to the next slide. Across August, September, and October, the bars on the graph rocketed off the chart.

"This is a graph of the Washington Square Center. For the first nine months, the graph is like the others. But over the past several months, this clinic has been treating *double* the number of patients, leading to over four hundred EUEs each month. It's inexplicable. The clinic has not hired a new doctor, increased their advertising, offered any new services, or lowered their rates. There is no reason for this spike that we know of." Trent paused, relishing the perplexed faces. Oh, how he was going to blow them away.

"There's something here," Dopp said, frowning. Trent noticed that when his boss was upset, his features drooped, as if his face had emerged from the side of a melting candle.

Trent looked away. "There are a few more facts that you might find interesting."

"Go on."

"I did some research on the doctor who owns the clinic, Arianna Drake. Her father, who's now deceased, was one Edmond Drake."

Trent clicked the slide so a newspaper article filled the screen.

"When I started researching her, I didn't find anything much right away, but one thing led to another, and I finally stumbled across this op-ed by her father in a small Brooklyn newspaper that folded over a decade ago. Here is the first paragraph. I won't make you read any more of it."

HOW THE DEP IS DRAGGING AMERICA
BACK TO THE MIDDLE AGES

By Edmond Drake

In outlawing the destruction of human embryos, the newly formed DEP is, in essence, freezing science itself, tucking it away in the same liquid nitrogen that freezes each embryo. How long it will remain confined there depends on the courage of future thinkers left untainted by today's religiosity. It will be up to those minds—in a decade, a century, perhaps longer—to break the ideological stranglehold on this country and use those embryos to carry on the scientific revolution that we are now ending.

The men stared.

"That's right," Trent said. "Edmond Drake was a dissenter. He wrote this article while his daughter was in college at Columbia. No doubt, she picked up on his radicalism, because she became a cheerleader for a biochemist at the school who was later found to be spearheading illegal research. She organized protests each time a DEP investigator visited the campus."

"How do you know this?" Dopp demanded.

"Digging deep into the campus library's archives. Columbia ended up firing the scientist, a Dr. Samuel Lisio, and her group held a sit-in for two days."

"Disgusting," Banks muttered. "It's unbelievable how young people can be brainwashed like that."

"I tried to track down Lisio himself," Trent said, "but he disappeared after he got out of jail."

Dopp's pen stopped moving across his notepad. "What else does she do now, besides work? Any clubs, groups, associations?"

"I don't know. She hasn't been in the news or published anything except in medical journals. She could still be a rebel, but we can't be sure."

"Exactly," Dopp said. "We need to dig deeper. Her embryo count is always perfect, every inspection, and she passed the audit six weeks ago. We can't find fault with her clinic, and we can't swing enough fact-based suspicion to get a warrant for a wiretap. But I can feel something is off. How often do people like her find their way back?"

"What are you saying?" Banks asked with interest.

"I'm saying, this could be exactly what we need." Dopp leaned in, his eyes lit with eager suspicion.

The three men nodded. Trent was sure they were all thinking the same thing: *a shutdown*—a legal permanent closing of a fertility clinic for ethical transgressions. For every shutdown, the state allotted more money to the department. There hadn't been a shutdown in two years, and though no one had stated it, it was becoming more of a priority than ever: the department was struggling to defend its very existence. The liberals in the state assembly were gaining strength for the first time in a decade, and they were shouting that the DEP was a waste of taxpayer money. The department's fate would be decided during the budget negotiations in January, when its conservative advocates would have to fight to show why it was still relevant.

But even within their own party, the battle was stacked. Some conservatives felt that the DEP was sucking tax dollars away from its sister division of the state health agency: the Department of Embryo-Fetal Protection. This department, which operated out of the same building, monitored all pregnant women in order to protect unborn babies until their birth. Upon learning she was pregnant, a woman was required to register with the DEFP, where she was assigned a caseworker. The caseworker scheduled regular visits throughout the pregnancy to assess whether the woman was taking her vitamins, exercising regularly, and going to all doctor appointments. This important measure of oversight had helped to prevent countless illegal abortions, premature births, and malnourished babies. Fines for not cooperating were steep, and if the fetus was found to be harmed as a result of improper prenatal care, the mother could be charged with manslaughter.

With so many pregnant women to monitor, and relatively few fertility clinics, some conservatives were arguing that the DEP should be drastically downsized; damaged embryos were hardly ever discovered these days, so why maintain such stringent oversight? Besides, how many scientists today even remembered how to research stem cells, so what was the point of destroying embryos? But Dopp knew that it was crucial to maintain oversight of fertility doctors, many of whom didn't even believe an extrauterine embryo was a person. So Dopp knew it was up to him to prove that threats to EUEs still existed—thus keeping their department afloat.

"We have two whole months," Trent said, trying to sound positive.

Dopp looked around the table gravely. "Only two months."

"I don't get it," Jed piped up. "Any conservatives in Albany with a brain should be fighting for us tooth and nail. It's obvious that EUEs will always need our oversight. Why should a shutdown change anyone's mind?"

Dopp sighed. "Up in Albany, they don't operate on principles. They're pragmatists. So we need to show them that our department is still necessary. One big shutdown could mean a difference of millions of dollars in our budget next year. And—" He paused. "—lots of jobs."

Trent couldn't help feeling some pity for them all; fear was the new receptionist that greeted them every morning, a reminder of the outside world's power to obstruct their mission.

"Back in the old days," Banks growled, "I never would have believed it would come to this."

"How was it then?" Jed asked quietly.

"It's not over," Dopp snapped. "Far from it."

With a look of nostalgia, Banks explained that the department used to do shutdowns every few months, and regularly busted scientists who had smuggled embryos into their labs.

"But we haven't found a stolen embryo for five years," Banks said. "Sometimes I give tickets for missing or damaged embryos, take away medical licenses, things like that. But nothing sensational."

Trent remembered the last isolated shutdown two years ago—an elderly doctor had been destroying embryos for no reason other than to spite the department.

Trent looked at his boss. "So where do we go from here?"

"We need to catch her in action, whatever she's doing with all those embryos," Dopp said. "Yes, they're all stocked at the end of the month, but where are they *before* that?"

"Are you saying she could be cloning and replacing them?" Trent asked, astonished. Harvesting embryos on the sly—to cover up their mass destruction—was nearly unprecedented. It was akin to genocide, the twenty-first-century equivalent of Hitler's ovens.

Dopp half shrugged, lifting his eyebrows. "The technology is still out there, and we can't tell the difference between an original embryo and a clone. But the logistics would be very complex. She'd need biochemists who remember how to do it, not to mention instruments, a private lab space, money, and bottom line: a lot of embryos. It would be a major conspiracy. I didn't think people would have the gall to try that anymore, but who knows."

"You mean—running secret labs to get embryonic stem cells?" Jed asked, his voice pitching on the last words.

Dopp blinked. "Yes."

"But only adult stem cells are viable," Jed cried. "Embryonic stem cells never helped anyone even when they were legal!"

Trent shook his head in sympathetic frustration. Adult stem cells, as he had learned from his job training, were undifferentiated cells—blanks—found in specialized tissues such as heart or muscle. These blank cells, which were used regularly in bone marrow transplants, could grow into the type of specialized cells found in the tissue of origin and possibly other types, though adult stem cells were harder to find and extract than the embryonic type, which were blank cells found in five-day-old human embryos. Those could give rise to any cell in the body, making their therapeutic potential unlimited. And they were easy to obtain—but that meant killing an unborn child. Before the embryo rights movement put a legal end to the barbarism, not one sick or paralyzed person benefited from embryonic stem cells.

"I never understood how people could claim those cells would help anyone," Jed said, "without any proof of it at all."

Trent nodded, though he wondered about his colleague's choice of the word *proof*. A vision of the infamous stem cell heart popped into his mind—the first human organ that had been created purely out of embryonic stem cells more than twenty years prior, when the research was still a dangerous open highway. He wondered, had that been proof of something beyond depravity?

Dopp's mouth was one steely line. "Criminals can find ways to justify anything. This situation must be looked into."

"How?" Trent asked. "We need proof."

"Secrecy breeds the need for secrecy," Dopp replied. "Trent, I'm impressed by your digging."

Trent smiled modestly. *Finally,* he thought. *Window office, here I come.*

"How would you like to do some undercover fieldwork?" Dopp asked with a friendly smile.

Trent stared. "What?"

"This whole case was your idea, so you should follow it through. You have the people skills and the discretion from your reporter days."

"Wow. I wasn't expecting . . ." He trailed off, amazed at this turn. "So, um, what do you have in mind?"

"Arianna Drake seems too smart to make any errors in execution. We've got to come at her from the side, undercover, where she isn't expecting it. That's our *in,* God willing. I'll help you devise a strategy to get her to talk. I think you'd be a natural for this kind of work."

"Thank you, I think," Trent said, pausing. "Does that mean you think I'd be a good liar?"

Dopp's lips stretched up, defying the drag of his face. "Only for the sake of the truth. You're an agent of the DEP, Trent, but really, you're an agent of God. This is the kind of assignment that you could look back on as your life's work."

"Then I'd be mostly out of the office, just coming back to report to you?" *No more suit,* he thought. *No more walls.*

"This will be your focus. If you hit it big, I'll move you out of that little room, closer to me."

Trent smiled at the irony that only a half hour before, he had been craving his old investigative beat. Not to mention that Dopp's office was on the side of the building where glass walls were set dramatically against the edge of Central Park.

"I'd love to do it," Trent said, looking out at the park. From the seventeenth floor, they were practically parachuting over the treetops.

"Good. Now, remember, as an undercover agent, you cannot tell anything to anyone, strictly *anyone,* under penalty of expulsion and legal action."

"Of course not."

Trent glanced at Jed, whose delayed smile betrayed a hint of envy, while Banks looked on with new respect.

"Trent, start brainstorming strategies for how to approach her. You've only got one shot."

Trent nodded, his reporter's mind already working angles.

Dopp closed his eyes for a moment. When he opened them, he stared directly into Trent's eyes. "I have faith in you, as does God. He will guide us to the answers."

Trent nodded again, unsure whether he felt privileged or intimidated, or both.

"Just remember," Dopp went on, "however you get to the truth will be the right way. Everything happens for a reason."

THREE

As a doctor, Arianna understood that symptoms do not arise without a cause and that her sudden dizzy spell was significant. Sometimes, in her darkest moments, she saw her medical knowledge as a curse; she knew too much to chalk up her fall to an imbalance of the inner ear or to that catchall diagnosis, stress. At the same time, she knew enough not to be surprised, which allowed for a quicker recovery—she had managed to lift herself off the floor and plunk down into her chair before Megan returned.

She was much less worried about that pesky reporter. Megan had fended him off just right. As she reasoned, he would move on from her clinic after he found no story. There was no crime in having a busy practice.

The next day, Saturday, she preoccupied herself in the kitchen, preparing dinner for two. The problem was that her guest did not know he was invited. Give him much notice, she had learned, and he would find an excuse to decline, so she waited to call until she could smell the food cooking. Years of solitude had left him friendless. She had taken on the task of injecting some happiness into the dead realm once known as his personal life; often, though less and less, he resisted her efforts.

After she prepared the steak in the broiler, she punched a number on her speed dial. It rang several times.

"Hullo," said a raspy voice.

"Hi, Sam. A little slow getting to the phone," she teased. "Don't tell me you have company."

"No one dates at my age, Arianna."

"Why not?"

"They're either widowed or dead. What can I do for you?"

She smiled. "I made too much for dinner."

"I already ate."

"Today?"

He sighed. "What did you make?"

"Filet mignon."

"You don't have to bribe me with food."

"Oh, and here I thought a steak would make all the difference."

He grunted. "I'm too cranky to be company."

"A cranky genius? I don't believe it."

"All right, all right."

She chuckled as the phone clicked off. He seldom said good-bye. But Sam Lisio's rancor didn't faze her anymore; she understood why it had seeped into his persona, like a diseased cell that had multiplied. It was such an inexorable part of him now that it was hard to remember what he used to be like before, when his tone was not married to scorn and when his smile dazzled students and professors alike. Instead of being repelled by his negativity, she knew it was defensiveness: *Don't get too close,* said the words behind his words.

He was a reclusive workaholic. When she called, he had probably been poring over his notes. Although they rarely mentioned it, the grim context of their association touched every word they exchanged. As Arianna had come to understand, sarcasm kept that knowledge at a distance and reshaped it into something palatable.

She wondered how his work was going. If he had any news, she would of course find out first, though it was torture to keep from asking. Nor did she want to leave the impression that her goal was to mine him for information; it saddened her to imagine that he might ever suspect an ulterior motivation in her warmth. That was not the case at all—their quest had united them in business, but left them friends.

Her thoughts were interrupted by the buzzer.

"That was fast," she said as she opened the door.

His lips quivered as he smiled at her, as if those muscles were stretched past their comfort zone. He was an old sixty-seven, with hollow cheeks and a gaunt frame, withered by injustice as much as by time. Strands of white hair lingered on the top of his scalp, too few to comb—not that he ever would. Despite his obvious age, though, she was sometimes surprised by the wrinkles around his green eyes and the frailness of his bones, because his mind showed no signs of senescence; its sharpness seemed only to have increased over time.

"Here," he said gruffly, handing over Napa Valley merlot from 2015.

"Aged twelve years!" she marveled.

"It's a decent red, but I don't like it. Too dry."

"Then why'd you bring it?"

"For you. I'll take the usual."

Arianna smiled and led him back to the circular glass dining table. "Rough day?"

His expression hardened, but he said nothing as he sat down at the table.

"What's wrong?"

He sighed. "Oligodendrocytes are just such a goddamn mystery."

She swallowed, concentrating on pouring his drink from the fifth of vodka she kept for his visits. "But it only took you guys four months to figure out how to get to the neuroprogenitor stage. . . ."

"And that's like turning a frog into a kid when what you really want is a prince."

"Little by little, right?"

"There's so much damn error in trial and error."

"You did it with the rats, though," she said over her shoulder as she poured her own wine.

"It's trickier with human cells, obviously."

"Look, Sam," she said, facing him, "you guys have already come a long way." She stared at him, daring him to deny it. He snatched up his drink and took a swig.

"Maybe you just need a few days' break for perspective," she added, as she sat down. "What do the others think?"

He exhaled an acrid breath. "You'll hear tomorrow. They're both just as fed up." He squinted at her. "How do you get off being so cavalier about it, anyway?"

She squinted back, mocking him with a grin. "Hey, I'm not the one that has to figure out anything. My part isn't nearly as hard."

"Cheers to you," he said, lifting his glass in her direction. Arianna shook her head good-naturedly as she chewed a mouthful of salad. Sam twirled linguini around his fork and smothered it in bloody steak juices before shoving it into his mouth. Hunger and worry usurped her need for mental stimulation, and the lull in conversation went unnoticed.

"How was work this week?" Sam asked eventually.

"Fine," she replied. "Except for yesterday."

"Because of that nosy bastard reporter?"

She scoffed. "That guy couldn't touch us."

"So you're not going to do anything?"

"What's to do?" she said. "We're just getting more popular, right?"

He looked skeptical.

"Come on, Sam, we've got the whole thing down pat."

"The execution of it, anyway."

Arianna rolled her eyes.

"So what was wrong yesterday, then?" he demanded.

She looked away. "One of my patients just found out *she* has MS. All she wants is a baby, and now she has to decide whether she wants to skip her crucial meds for nine months or give up having a child. You can't believe how much heartbreak people go through because of this goddamn disease."

"I think I can," Sam said, watching her.

"And to think that what we're doing . . . It blows me away. I just wish I could have told her there's hope."

Sam nodded, saying nothing.

They ate in silence for a few minutes, contemplating the weight of her words. Arianna felt a familiar rush that came whenever she pictured Sam at the moment of a breakthrough, as if envisioning it would somehow coax it into happening. A thrill ran through her as she bobbed her head to the beat of the music pulsing from her kitchen's speakers.

"Megan and I are going dancing tonight," she volunteered.

His eyes narrowed as he chewed his pasta.

"What," she said, "you don't think I can dance?"

"Don't you need a man to lead?"

"Nah. Plus, do you see any men around here?"

He made a face of mock hurt.

"Seriously, Sam. I doubt you would take me dancing if I paid you."

"And why would I? It's just two people trying not to step on each other's toes."

"You're right, it would be more fun to stay home."

"Just like me, right?" he said, forcefully chewing the last of his steak.

"Sometimes I feel like I'm babysitting you," she said lightly. "It's like a study in tantrums."

She saw a smile on his lips, despite his mouthful of food. Their plates, she noticed, were empty. She stood up to clear them, but he reached for hers.

"Thanks for cooking," he muttered, carrying the plates to the sink.

"Sure." She moved beside him, putting a hand on his back as he rinsed their dishes. She could feel the blades under his skin like knife edges.

"So . . . ," Sam began, not looking at her. "How is everything?"

She withdrew her hand and crossed her arms. "Everything? Well, let's see. My painting is going well. . . ." She saw him scowl. "Oh, you were talking about something else? Why didn't you say so?" A note of annoyance floated on her teasing words. "I like dancing, but not around reality."

He nodded sheepishly, still scowling. "Fine. What's your latest health status?"

"It's *eh,*" she responded matter-of-factly. "Are you trying to do a time check?"

He nodded, reddening. She turned off the faucet and looked at him. It was not a question that required contemplation; the answer was like a billboard in her mind, inescapable on the way to other thoughts.

"I would say at least a few months, but I'm not that kind of doctor. When I see my specialist soon, I'll find out more exactly."

"So you're going dancing all the time," he said softly.

She nodded. "I'm going to dance until the day they strap me to a wheelchair."

His paper-thin lips tightened. "Damn them, whoever *they* are."

"The fates, I guess."

"I don't believe in fate," he retorted.

"Neither do I." She smiled and walked him to the door. "Have a nice evening, Sam. See you tomorrow." She paused for effect, and the solemnity of her voice did not match her smile. "At church."

"See you at church," he said, shaking his head. "Our irreverence never fails to amuse me."

She chuckled. "Me either."

"Good night," he said. She closed the door and leaned against it.

One of Sam's earlier sentences, spoken with quiet frustration, had tempered her spirits like a thundercloud: *There's so much damn error in trial and error.* Was she naïve to think three men could solve the unbelievably complex mystery of regenerating life through life? She frowned, feeling her heart quicken in that panic-stricken moment of doubt. On cue, her mind fed her the reassurance reel: *The best and the brightest—if anyone can do it, they can—they have everything: knowledge, purpose, supplies, space—the best and the brightest . . .* The pattern continued for several sentences until its triumphant conclusion: *So they will do it in time.* She summoned the words so often that their familiarity calmed her more than their meaning. A mantra, an obsession, a dream, hope—whatever their name, she clung to the words, for without their promise, soon she would have nothing.

When her breathing slowed, she realized that something was wrong; it took her a moment to realize that she had not heard Sam's footsteps in the hallway. She spun around to face the door, and froze. Through the peephole, she saw the familiar slouched figure standing still, hands in the pocket of his slacks, staring at her door. She wondered if he had forgotten something, although at least a minute had passed since his departure, and he hadn't brought anything except the bottle of wine. Keeping her eyes trained on the peephole, she grabbed the brass doorknob and turned the cool metal. As if he were a puppet controlled by its movement, Sam straightened, turned, and ran down the stairs with surprising agility. Arianna swung open the door, but the hall was empty. His footsteps echoed below.

She did not follow him. Instead, she thought of her late father, who, when she was a teenager, used to watch her from their second-floor window whenever she left their apartment at night. Rather than suffering adolescent embarrassment, she had always felt safe in his gaze, as if its protection alone were enough to fend off danger. Sam, she thought, must harbor a similar fatherly inclination. It made sense based both on their ages and the responsibility he carried regarding her life. A symbiotic pair they made—she, fatherless, and he, childless. Of course, he would deny tenderness toward anyone, so she wouldn't humiliate him with her realization. That was one major difference between Sam and her father, who used to tell her he loved her with the regularity of the tides. But despite Sam's misanthropic bent, she was glad to see he was still capable of fondness. With a little smile, she opened her shoe closet by the door and slipped on her dancing heels.

Trent wondered if he would ever meet a woman who was impressed by his job. Some of them blanched and bolted when he told them where he worked. That Saturday night, he bore the full shame of the stigma. The girl at the bar was stunning—her eyes were sea-glass green and her blond hair slid over her shoulders, skimming the tops of her breasts.

"So, what do you do?" she asked after a minute of flirty banter. "Let me guess, but if I get it right, you have to buy me a martini."

"Okay."

She tilted her head. "I bet it's something brainy. I'd say you're that cute teacher the students are totally obsessed with."

He chuckled nervously. "Not quite." An incongruous mix of pride and doubt laced through what felt like a confession. "I work for the DEP."

"As in the Department of *Embryo Preservation*?"

"Yeah." He tried to smile, despite sensing futility. "But I'll buy you a drink anyway, since you never would have guessed that."

"You're right," she sneered. "I never would have pegged you as a religious freak."

"I'm not." *And that's part of the problem,* he thought.

But she slid off the barstool without giving him the consolation of a second glance.

He had expected his job to strengthen his faith—that had been his goal in taking it—rather than being humiliated by it. Thank God he wasn't part of the DEFP, at least. Women in New York reviled that department even more than his own. It was a wonder that any single men there ever got dates.

The next morning, over brunch with his parents, he vented his frustration.

"Oh, Trent," his mother sighed. "It's so much easier to date someone with your values! Think of the women at church!"

"Right," he muttered, thinking of the devout, humble women who prayed beside him on Sundays. "Wife material, maybe, but no good for a night out."

Even though his parents had been married thirty-five years, they still held hands and even flirted. Trent saw them as the model for the relationship he wanted one day—though one day was turning into anytime now. He was thirty-six and single, his prospects as slim as the pickings, with a dull job that was supposed to be his life's work. Yet his parents had been together since high school, and by age thirty, both had developed fulfilling careers.

"So what's the secret?" Trent asked them as his father kissed a spot of whipped cream off his mother's lips. "You make it look so easy."

"What?" his mother asked.

"Life. Love. All of it."

"Life—that's one thing. But there's no secret to love," his father said, putting his arm around Trent's mother. "It's easy."

She grinned. "Actually I think that *is* the secret," she said. "Finding a person who makes it easier to be with than without."

"Now you're just rubbing it in," Trent said. He said nothing about it for the rest of the meal, as he listened to them talk about their busy social life.

But as they finished eating, his mother tilted her head at him. "Hon, this isn't like you. You hardly ate anything."

He looked down at his plate, where scrambled eggs were pushed around, and felt a slight irritation at her prompting.

"Is something up?" his dad asked.

He hesitated a moment too long. He didn't really want to talk, but at the same time, he wondered if it would be a relief to confide in the people who cared most about him. Then again, how could he explain a problem he didn't understand?

"Now you have to tell us," his mother prodded.

"Well," he began, "I've been feeling kind of off lately."

"What do you mean?"

"Just something in my life, Ma. I don't know what it is, and that's the whole problem."

She eyed him. "Then how do you know it's there?"

"I feel weirdly . . . unsettled," he said, struggling to explain, "like I can't be myself in my own life."

Her skepticism took on a tinge of worry. "Are you trying to tell us something?"

"I'm trying to understand something."

His father looked dubious. "You're a bit young for a midlife crisis. Is it something to do with your job?"

"I—I think so. I don't know. Maybe."

"Honey, you've got the best job around," his mother said. "You know that."

Trent almost rolled his eyes. Just because a job had the society-approval stamp didn't make it automatically fulfilling or fun. And maybe that was part of the problem.

"What higher calling could there be?" his father chimed in. "If they had had the department up and running back when I finished school, I would have worked there in a heartbeat."

"I know that, Dad. You tell me all the time," Trent said, trying to keep his voice even. His father was an accountant who had once dreamed of being a policeman, though he hadn't the courage. Trent could see that his own job would have been his dad's perfect compromise between protecting others and inviting danger. "Hey, I changed careers," Trent said. "Why can't you?"

His father smiled. "It's enough that I can watch you succeed there. Father Paul told me just this morning that the big man—Dopp, right?—well, he told Father that he's real happy with your work lately."

His mother beamed, while Trent gave a tight smile. "That's great, but it still doesn't solve my problem."

"Oh, Trent," she said, "everyone feels restless sometimes. Do you think you're just overthinking it?"

"Maybe I'm not thinking enough," he said quietly.

A mischievous smile spread across her face. "I know what the problem is. You need a girlfriend, that's all." She paused, treading carefully. "You do want one, don't you? You haven't had one in ages."

He looked at her with exasperation. "I didn't realize you were keeping track."

"You know what you should do," his father said. "Come home and talk to Father Paul. He's always helped you."

His mother nodded. "Whenever I doubt something, I know it's time to get closer to God."

Trent knew she was right, but her advice troubled him more. Trying to get "closer to God" had felt like a futile exercise to him ever since his crisis of faith three years ago, from which he had never fully recovered.

He had been working at *Newsday* and was becoming increasingly disillusioned with the Catholic Church after a series of sex scandals involving local priests. He was overcome by conflict, as if he were stuck at the bottom of a deep chasm between the ideals he was raised to believe and the reality he reported on every day. If God was the ultimate leader of the Church, how could He have let it get so out of hand?

That painfully uncertain time reminded him of his childhood

frustration with God, the incident when he first experienced grave disappointment. The memory was vivid, and one of his earliest.

His back was to his house; he was crouching in its slanted shadow, fanning his palms over the prickly grass. One of the blades, he knew, was alive. It had jumped, nudged by the unwitting touch of his hand. The grasshopper's legs rubbed together like a chorus of zippers, taunting him to follow. He inched his feet toward the sound, but it faded when he reached a tree with low branches. The early-morning sun splintered through the leaves and he sat back, lifting his face toward the warmth. Behind a cluster of leaves, a patch of red caught his eye. He stood up and craned his neck to see the robin.

"Hi, little birdie," he said, waving a chubby hand. It chirped and jumped to a closer branch. He stared at it, mesmerized by its breathless twitter.

"Trent!" his mother's voice called from the doorway to the backyard. "What are you doing? We're about to leave. Trent Aidan Rowe!"

He stood immobile, focusing only on one sound. His mother hurried over the patchy grass toward him, pinching her fitted black slacks at the knees.

"You're making Mommy ruin her clothes. C'mon, we're going to be late for church."

Trent did not turn to look at her.

"What are you doing out here, honey? Let's go."

"Mama, what is the birdie saying?"

"It's saying you need to come inside with me so we can go. We have to leave in five minutes."

He did not move.

"Hello?" his mother said, putting a hand on his shoulder and whirling him around. "Look at me when I'm speaking to you, young man."

"I'm not going," he muttered, glaring up at her.

"Of course you're going."

She grabbed his hand and started to pull him toward the house. He stayed rooted to the ground.

"Okay, Trent. We don't have time for this. Why don't you want to go?"

He stared at the ground. "Because I hate God."

His mother's eyes widened and she put her hands on his shoulders. "You must never say such an evil thing. Look at me. That is very, very wrong. Why would you ever say that?"

"Because He took Grandpa away. And you told me to pray for him but God didn't listen. So now I hate Him."

His mother took a deep breath and knelt down to his level. She seemed about to scold him again for his impiety, but then her expression softened. "Honey, I know it's hard for you to understand why Grandpa had to go away with God, but God knew it was the right time to take him, and we have to trust His decision."

"Why do we have to?"

"Because God knows what is best for everyone."

"Even me?"

"Yes, sweetie, especially you. He is always taking care of all of us."

"But what about Grandpa?"

"He took Grandpa to a much better place, and you will see him again one day if you are a good boy. I know you will be."

Trent was quiet for a moment.

"So if I go to church, God will let me see Grandpa again?"

"That's right. One day. Be good to Him and He will be good to you."

"But is it too late now?" Trent asked, scrunching up his face in anticipation of crying. "Because I said I hated Him?"

She smiled easily. They really were about to be late. "No, honey, as long as we go to church right now, God will forgive you."

Trent nodded, his brown curls bouncing. "Okay, let's go," he said.

His mother kissed his forehead and stood up, stretching out a hand to her son. As he grabbed it, he looked up.

"Bye, birdie," he called, but the streak of scarlet was gone.

That incident had marked the origin of his disillusionment, neatly contained by his mother, until the church scandals two decades later dredged it up again. During the worst of it, he had briefly considered leaving the investigative religion beat altogether by switching to the newspaper's science section; it seemed like the opposite of corruption and scandal, just hard facts and straight reason. But he knew it would just be a distraction from his internal dilemma.

Reassurance had come in the form of Father Paul, who offered the helping hand that pulled Trent out of the chasm. Brushing aside the church scandals as sabotage perpetrated by the Devil, Father Paul reminded Trent of the importance of faith in God at all costs, and told him that the only way to feel right again was to strengthen that faith.

"But how do you know when to be faithful and when to be skeptical of something?" Trent had wanted to know.

"You must always have faith in Christ, no matter what," Father Paul responded.

"But how do you know to draw the line there?"

Father Paul looked exasperated. "If you come at it scientifically like that, you ruin the whole experience of faith!"

Trent persisted. "But how could He have let this hypocrisy take place within our own church?"

"You're right, the Church isn't perfect, but that's because it's run by men. Remember the whole idea of faith, Trent: Let go of reason and give in to God's higher plan. We can't question Him, we can only follow."

"I guess so. It's just hard when I'm so torn."

"No wonder you're miserable, Trent. If you think about yourself and your problems all the time, it only depresses you because deep down you know how selfish you're being. Think of Jesus. You need to learn how to sacrifice your own desires in order to do something that will help others. That's the only way to come out of this. Let the Lord guide you back to grace."

Father Paul had recommended him to his old friend Gideon Dopp, and Trent had gratefully accepted the position he offered, moving away from Long Island and into a (much smaller) studio apartment in the city. He felt better for the first six months, set on the path of a noble mission instead of burying his pen in the Devil's smut, but the novelty of his job had soon worn off. Instead of lofty goals, he saw inspection reports, clinic statistics, and bureaucratic forms. And walls.

And now, three years in, here he was—faced with the prospect of crawling back to Father Paul for another helping of religious meat and potatoes. A neglected sense of rebellion pricked him. He wasn't that settled: no wife, no kids. The excited feeling of his youth surged weakly within him, the feeling that the best was yet to come. He could still pick up and go—maybe travel the world, write about it, sell his stories to magazines, and . . .

"I could not believe how many people showed up," his mother was saying to him, recounting the latest charity drive she had run. "It was the most . . ."

He smiled and felt common sense kick in, the unfortunate side effect of fantasy. Traveling as a way of life wasn't realistic; he knew he could not run away from guilt. So maybe he should accept his self-doubt as a personality flaw, like a permanent sunspot in his eyes, and simply wait until he didn't notice it anymore.

With a stab of remorse, he remembered Father Paul's warning: constant introspection was a selfish habit, a dangerous source of unhappiness. Even now, pretending to listen to his mother, he was indulging in it.

He picked up a steaming mug of coffee and guzzled it. The scorching pain in his mouth and throat shocked him back to reality, and he coughed.

"Are you okay?" his mother asked, interrupting herself.

"Fine," he said, wiping his watering eyes. "Sorry."

Suddenly a doctor's name popped into his mind—he could envision her slanted signature on Inspector Banks's form. What a chance Dopp had given him! How could he have forgotten to mention it? "By the way," he said with delight, "I can't tell you much about this, but I got a huge assignment at work. . . ." He trailed off, reveling in the contagion of his own smile. "I wish I could tell you more, but it's confidential."

His parents looked at each other wide eyed; the need for secrecy implied his work was important and therefore impressive.

"Look at you," his father said. "Before we know it, you'll be all the way up the ranks to supervisor."

Trent shrugged, as if that were his plan all along.

FOUR

Right away, Dopp spotted two problems with the inspector's report on his desk: the actual embryo count did not match the records, and there was no signature from the head doctor as required. It was from an inspection conducted that very morning at a clinic on the Upper East Side. At the bottom of the page was a scrawled note:

> ATTN BOSS: *9 missing, but Dr. locked himself in office and refused to sign. Case for you.*

Must be an old-timer, Dopp thought, shaking his head. Few remained—doctors who stubbornly thought their seniority would allow them laxer oversight, or who were still clinging to the days of zero regulation. Dopp shuddered, unwilling to imagine how regularly embryos had been destroyed in those days, and for the sake of what? The justifications chilled him: Savage experimentation? Shelf space? It was unfathomable, a clear violation of the sacred right to life.

And how many had been lost? No one would ever know, since it was before the government kept such records, but the question haunted him. Hundreds of thousands, he guessed, if not more.

He glanced up to look at the thing that calmed him: A digital picture frame propped next to his computer spun through dozens of family pictures, a slideshow he often updated. He picked up the frame, pausing it on a photo of his two-year-old daughter, Abby, splashing in an inflated Jacuzzi in their Long Island backyard. She was too young to know it now, but one day she would understand how much his work related to her own existence.

After nine failed attempts at in vitro fertilization and more than $100,000, his wife, Joanie, had become pregnant naturally with Abby. Despite the Catholic Church's disapproval of in vitro, when four years of trying had worn out their patience, Dopp had reluctantly given in to Joanie's desperation to try the procedure, and God had made them pay the price. But everything happened for a reason, and Dopp knew that God wanted them to endure those years, which could hardly be summed up by the word *struggle;* no, it was closer to an all-encompassing feeling of failure that strained his marriage and his confidence, an ordeal that thrust him into a pattern of empty reassurances, holding Joanie and stroking her belly as she wept, while he whispered in her ear, "It's not your fault, sweetie, it will happen. . . ." Crusted underneath his words like hidden grime was a private guilt—he was fifteen years older than she, and surely not as potent as a younger man.

God's reason for their agony, as he interpreted it after Abby's birth, was to show him the true nature of fertility doctors: They were swift in cashing their payment after each time Joanie did not get pregnant, and swifter still in urging her to try the same, costly, difficult procedure again. But what he resented the most were the pictures of the doctors' own babies in their offices: eight-by-eleven-inch portraits of tender faces that mocked him and Joanie with their own inability to conceive. He had been angered by the doctors' insensitivity and their lack of compassion in displaying the photos. It was only after he and Joanie stopped trying with the doctors that God had blessed them with Abby, just as He had blessed them seven years prior with Ethan. And, as if to reward their patience, God had smiled upon them once more: elated and incredulous, Joanie was now, at age forty-one, pregnant again.

Yet Dopp understood that there was a darker reason for their struggles to conceive, and he knew that Joanie knew it, too. Their suffering was God's punishment for Dopp's abandonment of the priesthood. Fifteen years ago, right after the DEP had first formed, Dopp was a revered priest at a large Catholic Church on Long Island. As a younger, idealistic man, he had hardly flinched at the vow of celibacy, believing that pleasures of the flesh were only a sinful distraction from God's work. Though the work was spiritually fulfilling, he became crushingly lonely. It was a feeling he alternately discounted and wrestled with, never reaching a solution.

At about the same time that he began to sink into a depression, he noticed a beautiful young woman sitting in the front pew of his congregation; her green eyes watched him intensely—erotically, he thought—as if he were the only person there. She was slender like a dancer, and just as graceful, with limbs that seemed to exert no effort when she came up to take her Communion. Those moments were the closest Dopp came to her, the moments he began to look forward to. If only for a few seconds, he could smell her perfume and admire the way her dress straps fell against her white collarbone. She always sat alone at the service. The first time she caught him watching her, she had smiled a strange mocking smile, as if extending a forbidden invitation. Looking back, Dopp would realize that their relationship had begun then, and that the months they exchanged glances over the heads of the congregation had been not a prelude to courtship, but the main act, a deliciously public trespassing. To Dopp, Sundays had become like dates, each seemingly more intimate than the last. It was both an ecstasy and a torment to feel such temptation. They had not exchanged a word, but what they shared was enough to sate his desire, more pleasure than he had ever expected from a woman. At least he told himself it was enough.

And then one Sunday, she didn't show up. Or the next, or the next. Dopp lost focus. Each week, he watched the back door of the church as he delivered a halfhearted sermon. Later he would find out that she had forced herself to stay away, that she knew she risked ruining him. She fought for him valiantly by remaining scarce, not knowing that he was ruined either way. After three weeks, Dopp insisted to himself that her absence was for the best, that his loneliness had probably blown the whole thing out of proportion. That maybe it was God's way of letting him off gracefully.

But after six weeks, she returned.

He stopped her after the service for the first time, as the other churchgoers were leaving. She didn't seem surprised.

"Where were you?" he asked before any introduction.

"I didn't know you took attendance," she replied. She smiled up at him with a look of pain: *I've given up, so here I am.*

"It would help if I knew your name," he said.

"Joanie," she replied, extending her hand. "I think I already know yours."

As soon as he clutched her hand, Dopp knew he had surrendered the priesthood. It was the quiet death of a life he could no longer uphold. Their affair quickly grew physical—a step neither of them even pretended to fight—and Dopp officially left his post within a month. A brief uproar ensued, as the scandal seemed to envelop their neighborhood, but Dopp knew. His instinct had never failed him; as counterintuitive as it seemed, this was what he had needed all along. The gossip eventually subsided as the new priest urged forgiveness, but Dopp and Joanie moved to another town anyway. They married a year later.

Dopp became resigned to the fact that he would always be a sinner in God's eyes. It was a trade-off he had struck the moment he first touched her. As selfish as it was, he would rather die now than live without his wife, and so there was only one thing for him to do: spend his life making it up to God. Working at the DEP seemed a good place to start, and over the years, he had risen steadily to chief. But whenever some fate turned against him, as with their struggles to have a baby, Dopp knew why. He was not angry; he only wished that Joanie did not have to suffer for his heresy. Yet God, working in His mysterious way, must have known that any pain Joanie endured was a thousand times worse for Dopp than his own.

After Abby's birth, Dopp had thrown himself into his work, hoping it would prove his true devotion to God, and thus spare his family any further hardship. Seeing himself not only as an embryo advocate, but also a patient advocate, he pushed for a new department initiative to leverage doctors' monetary motivations against them. It was his idea to set doctors' pay contingent upon their patients' appraisal of their compassion during treatment. Although patients could technically lie and underpay, Dopp assumed that people who were satisfied with their treatment would want to pay for their doctor's services; however, this initiative would be impossible to implement and monitor without greatly increasing the DEP's budget. Keeping it steady for next year was already his foremost worry, as the liberals in the state assembly were anticipating the upcoming budget negotiations with glee, knowing that for the first time in a decade, they were equal in number to their foes: just plentiful enough to pose a threat to the conservative agenda.

Dopp took a deep breath, kissed the picture of his daughter's smiling face, and set the frame down on his desk. Then he picked up the inspector's report with the missing signature and studied it again. He would have to face the rogue old-timer directly, and the sooner, the better.

He pressed a button on his desk phone that connected him straight to his driver.

"Hello?" came a familiar voice.

"Hey, Mark," Dopp said. "Got some time?" It was their running joke; Mark's full-time job was to stay on call for him.

"I think I can squeeze you in."

"See you in five."

Trent sat riveted to his computer screen. He was staring at the profile of Arianna Drake on NYfaces.com, a ubiquitous social networking website. Dopp had instructed him to search for a way to base their initial meeting on what would seem to be a common interest, to make it appear unplanned. So Trent had turned to scrutinizing her profile for details he could use.

He had seen the page before, when he was compiling background information on her for last week's presentation, but this time her picture was new. She was sitting on a swing that was dashing forward like a whooshing pendulum. Her head was thrown back and her black hair reached her waist, flying in all directions. The picture captured her mid-laughter, eyes squeezed shut. Beneath a yellow sundress, her tan bare legs stretched up to the sky.

Her joy was like a fistful of mud flung into his face, but he could not wrench his gaze away from the screen. He stared at her curves, coyly outlined under her dress. She had no right to be beautiful, he thought irritably. And he had no right to think it.

He became further frustrated by the relative lack of personal details she provided on her page. This assignment required him to be secretive himself, so in preparation, he had erased his own profile page, and Dopp had erased his name from the department's website. As a government agency, it wasn't difficult for them to have their contacts at all the major search engines get rid of any leftover web crawl data relating to Trent in his current capacity. There was no longer an online trace of Trent Rowe, agent, only Trent Rowe, ex-reporter. His trail stopped after the last article he had written several years earlier. Dopp had decided it was safer for him to use his real name and cover only his current path, rather than invent a fake persona that would be risky to sustain: This way, they wouldn't have to worry about her seeing his driver's license, credit cards, or mail.

On Arianna's profile page, the fields of home address and contact information were left predictably blank. She listed herself as single, which made his strategy clearer. At first, he had considered becoming a regular sperm donor, so as to establish a patient–doctor relationship that he could then try to exploit. But that route would be slow, since he could go in only once a week to donate, at which time, he would have little contact with her. Dopp convinced him it would be faster, albeit riskier, to approach her as a potential beau, since apparently she did not already have one. If she fell for him, Dopp reasoned, perhaps she would confide the truth about her clinic. It was a one-shot gamble, though; if she rejected him, they would have to give the case to another undercover agent. Trent had decided not to worry Dopp by telling him about his recent track record with women; he also realized, with relief, that he would not be telling Arianna about his job, the one handicap he most encountered. If only it were so easy in his own life to assume an alter ego with no qualms about truth or lies. Blessedly zero guilt about ethics applied to him now—this was a mission, and his Machiavellian mentality was not only logical; it was necessary. He remembered Dopp's words, delivered with the conviction of a judge: *Secrecy breeds the need for secrecy.*

Trent continued to study the rest of Arianna's profile. Under employment, she listed her position as founder and head doctor of the Washington Square Center for Reproductive Medicine. Under the section labeled "activities," the information was mostly too vague to help him: "dancing, painting, cooking, biking." There was only one specific revelation. For "favorite books," she wrote: "anything by Aaron Dakota." Dakota was the rare mystery writer whose books were also critically esteemed, a one-two punch for popular culture.

Trent leaned forward in his chair, typing into a search engine. Dakota was on a book tour promoting his newest hardcover, *The Found Link*. In two nights, he would be stopping in New York City. That would give Trent time to buy and read the book, and then approach Arianna at the signing as if he were a fellow fan.

But how would she know to be there? An idea wormed into his head, and before he had fully contemplated it, he was already creating a fake profile on NYfaces.com of a bubbly, professional-looking woman in her twenties, whose picture he stole randomly from a website of personal assistants. He invented a common name and a few generic hobbies. Under the employment section, he wrote: "publicist for Aaron Dakota." Then he quickly typed a message:

> Hi there! I noticed you're a fellow fan of Aaron Dakota and I just wanted to let you know that he will be signing copies of *The Found Link* this coming Wednesday at the Barnes & Noble at 66th and Broadway at 7 P.M. This special event is not to be missed, so we're trying to spread the message to all of his New York fans. Hope to see you there and happy reading!

Without hesitating, he sent the message off into the oblivion of the web, hoping Arianna would check her profile in time. Everyone he knew checked the site at least once a day; their generation had grown up on it. Then he rushed to Dopp's office and told him the plan, aware that he sounded more confident about her expected presence than he had reason to be: even if she did check her messages, what if she was already busy that night?

"Good," Dopp said. He rose and opened the safe next to his desk. He withdrew his pistol, a Glock 23, and secured it in his holster. Wearing the gun, a show of police powers—and the urgency of their work—meant that Dopp was leaving to go into the field. Thank God, Trent thought, his own turn to get out was coming.

"Right now," Dopp added, "I want you to accompany me. There's something I want you to see. Don't ask questions yet. Just watch and learn."

Trent nodded, surprised. He followed Dopp into the Lincoln Town Car waiting outside.

The driver, a round-faced man, turned and smiled.

"Hi, boss. What's doing?"

"Hey, Mark, how was Kristin's birthday party yesterday?"

Mark grinned. "It was a blast. All the kids loved the piñata, but the water slide was the biggest hit. I can't believe she's already six."

"That's great, man," Dopp said. "Yeah, they grow up so quickly. Just enjoy every minute of it. I was joking to my wife yesterday about when we're going to have the next baby after this one comes."

"Number four, eh?" Mark whistled.

"It's really not up to us, though," Dopp replied. "Anyway, we're off to Sixty-eighth Street. Between Park and Lex."

The car lurched forward. As Trent looked out the window at the slideshow of buildings, he felt a surge of goodwill toward his boss. He marveled at Dopp's ability to establish a rapport with all his employees; no wonder he was such a popular boss. Even the cynic in Trent was impressed: Dopp could be counted on, with the consistency of an atomic clock, to make those who worked for him feel worthy of his respect.

"Here we are," the driver said, pulling up in front of a glass door.

Trent and Dopp slid out of the backseat and walked to the door, which was almost inconspicuous between a pharmacy and a hardware store. Trent saw that white painted letters read FAMILY FERTILITY SERVICES above a smaller name, DR. BRIAN HANSON, OB-GYN. Next to the doorknob, there was a tiny block about the size of a sugar cube. Most people probably never noticed it, Trent thought.

Dopp turned to him with his lips pressed together. "Want to do the honors?"

Trent smiled nervously and reached into his suit jacket for a shiny gold badge splashed with the hologram DEP: the magnetic all-access pass to any fertility clinic in the city. He waved it in front of the cube. A pinpoint green light flashed, and the lock audibly clicked open. Dopp pushed the door, and Trent followed him inside as an alarm began to shriek. What were they doing here, anyway?

Holding their ears, they walked into the waiting room, where two pregnant women shrank back, gaping at Dopp's gun, eyes darting around for help. The alarm was quickly silenced, and it left behind a perceptible ringing in Trent's ears. The women leaned hard against the cheerful yellow couches. Feeling like an intruder, Trent almost blurted out an apology, but before he could speak, a worried-looking nurse rushed toward them from an inner hallway.

Dopp flashed his DEP badge at her, and she slowed as if to keep her distance.

"How can I help you?" she asked coldly.

"I think you know who we want to see," Dopp murmured. His quiet voice was even more compelling than a barked order, Trent thought.

"The doctor is in with a patient," the nurse retorted, though Trent could see her resolve weakening as she glanced between them.

"Tell him it's an emergency."

She took a step back. "One moment."

She turned around and scurried away. Trent looked at Dopp with an eyebrow raised, but Dopp held up a hand. Trent glanced over his shoulder at the women sitting on the couches. Their faces slipped behind pink *Parent Talk* magazines.

Dopp turned to them. "Sorry for the interruption, ladies." He held up his badge. "My partner and I are here to take care of some state business."

"Is—is everything okay?" one of them stammered.

"That's what we're here to make sure of," Dopp said.

The women shifted anxiously, set the magazines down, and rubbed their stomachs. It reminded Trent of being on a turbulent airplane, when the pretext of normalcy disappears.

The nurse returned, escorting an elderly man in a white coat with thin hunched shoulders. She kept her hand on his elbow and whispered to him in the hallway as they approached. When they reached the edge of the waiting room, she hung back. Trent watched the doctor shuffle forward.

He stopped in front of them and looked up tiredly through wire-rimmed spectacles. "Didn't take long for you to come," he muttered.

"Do you know who I am?" Dopp said evenly.

"You're DEP."

"I am the director of the New York City bureau, Dr. Hanson."

The doctor looked stricken.

Dopp continued: "Are you aware that you can be fined a thousand dollars for not cooperating with one of my inspectors?"

Dr. Hanson's gaze swept around the waiting room: his patients were not bothering to hide their interest.

"Can we take this into my office?" he asked, a pleading note in his voice.

Dopp frowned. "I believe your patients here have a right to know about this, before they continue to pay for your flawed services."

"The numbers were mistaken," the doctor said. "We must have mixed up the reports we sent in. I swear that we have not misplaced any embryos, I swear it on my practice!"

"I have only the evidence in my hand," Dopp said gravely, extending an inspector's form with a handwritten note at the bottom. "After receiving your monthly report, my inspector came this morning to count your embryo stock and found that there were nine missing. And you know what else is missing? Your signature on this form, right here underneath the inspector's."

"That's because we didn't do anything wrong!" the doctor cried. "I refuse to acknowledge 'missing' embryos that didn't exist in the first place. I told your inspector, there must have been a simple error in data entry when my secretary sent you the report. That's all this is!"

"So the story changes," Dopp said. "Was it a report mix-up or an error in data entry? At least stick with one excuse, Dr. Hanson."

The doctor shook his head in exasperation. "What would I want with nine embryos? And even if I did want them—which I assure you is not the case—don't you think I would have just underreported?"

Dopp stared into his eyes. "Perhaps you know all too well the consequences of false reporting and you rightly fear the random audit—much more often these days, isn't it? Especially for you now, I would think."

The doctor's white hairline glistened. He reached up to rub the back of his neck, looking away. Trent could not help feeling a twinge of pity for him.

Trent thought that Dopp must have felt it, too, for his tone softened. "I'm just doing my job, Dr. Hanson. How are we to know whether those embryos existed or not? I'll waive the fine this time for not cooperating"—the doctor looked up hopefully—"but I really have no choice but to do this."

Dopp reached into his briefcase and pulled out a square pad the size of a coaster. After scribbling on it, he ripped off the top page and handed it to the doctor, who took it from him, closing his eyes. Dopp glanced around the room. "That," he announced, "is a forty-five-thousand-dollar ticket—a five-thousand-dollar fine per missing embryo. This clinic is officially on probation for the next year. That means a surprise inspection can take place at any time. I would expect your records to be audited very shortly, Dr. Hanson. I trust you are aware that in the event of another so-called error, the department will have to revoke your medical license."

The doctor grimaced at the last few words, and one woman gasped.

Dopp walked over to the doctor, who was pinching the ticket, and placed one hand on his shoulder. "I understand this is an awful setback for you, but God will still have mercy on you if you—"

The old man squirmed away. "Scare off my patients, fine me, but if you actually value human dignity, don't you dare preach to me."

Dopp matched his defiant stare before retreating to the door, motioning to Trent to follow. As they walked out, Dopp turned back around. Trent stepped aside, relieved not to be the target of his boss's furious gaze.

"Bottom line, Dr. Hanson: Treat *all* your patients with compassion and respect, and we'll never have to see each other again."

He turned and walked out. Without looking at anyone in the room, Trent followed on his heels, letting the door slam behind them. On the sidewalk, the car was waiting as promised. After they entered the backseat and greeted the driver, Dopp turned to Trent.

"So, what did you learn from that?"

There was a feeling of awe in Trent's response: "That we have a lot of power."

"A lot of power *for good*. That's the beauty of it."

A gnawing question forced its way out. "But, well, what if the doctor didn't do anything wrong with the embryos, and it was just a simple numerical error like he said?"

"That's his fault, not ours. He must take the responsibility for it. Imagine if you fell asleep while you were driving, and then you crashed into a pole. You wouldn't say to the police, 'Oh well, don't punish me for it, because I didn't kill anyone.' This was a wake-up call: I guarantee those embryos will never be disturbed now. We're the only advocates for those souls, Trent. We owe it to them not to let any mistakes slide."

Trent nodded in earnest. The words imbued him with a new intensity of purpose, like a faded painting regaining its color.

"Now," Dopp said, "this slap on the wrist is nothing compared to what we could do if we happened to get a confession out of Arianna Drake about stealing EUEs."

Trent knew he was referring to a clinic shutdown, which could happen only if the department found proof of a doctor destroying embryos for scientific research; biotech cannibalism was a felony and would entail a murder trial and an almost-certain jail sentence.

"But," Dopp continued, "I wanted you to witness, on a smaller scale, the importance and the effect of our work. Whenever you get frustrated, remember the exhilaration of knowing that you did right, that you are defined by your conscience and not your own desires. I want you to be able to feel that, too."

"I want to, boss," he said, and a deep-seated admission escaped him. "I want to know my life has a meaning." Speaking the words stung. He was aware his painful uncertainty existed, but it had been repressed, buried like a splinter.

Dopp did not respond right away, and Trent smiled uncomfortably, trying to mitigate the weight of his own words. But when he looked into Dopp's eyes, he saw empathy.

"Your life does have meaning, Trent," Dopp said. "The meaning is in your pledge to do whatever it takes to help others. And I know you have made that pledge, because you are here right now. If it isn't clear to you yet, it's because you haven't seen the direct effect of your work. You see the data and you analyze the reports, but you're not out there taking action. That's why I want you to have a go at this assignment. And if you're successful, we can talk about moving you to fieldwork permanently."

Trent's head snapped up. "Really?"

"You miss being a reporter, don't you?"

He was taken aback; how did Dopp detect something he had barely admitted to himself? But it was true—he craved interacting with people and hitting the streets for a scoop, blissfully far from an office.

"Sometimes," he allowed. "But I know my work here is more important."

"Well, it doesn't have to be one or the other. Maybe you're not as well suited for an office gig."

Trent couldn't have asked for more incentive. "I think you read me right."

Dopp chuckled. "We may just be more alike than I thought. I understand where you're at, son."

The fond slip made Dopp smile; it was clear he relished his position as a mentor, something he had given up when he left the Church. They were almost back at the office, and as the car made the last turn around a corner, Trent was convinced he did not have to seek guidance from Father Paul, as his parents had suggested at brunch the day before. Everything he needed to see and hear and emulate was an arm's length away.

"You won't be disappointed," he said, grabbing the door handle. "I will crack this case." His own confidence surprised him; he wasn't used to feeling so sure about anything. And then he realized that he did have faith in the outcome, based on the strength of his own motivation. Though he wondered briefly if that was really faith, if it was based on reason.

The car pulled up in front of their building's towering black façade, and Trent jumped out, remembering what he had to do.

"In a hurry?" Dopp called.

"Yeah," he said, jogging backwards on the balls of his feet. "I've got a book to read."

FIVE

Trent thumbed through the last hundred pages of Dakota's novel, barely concentrating on the words. Tonight was the night. Would he flub his approach? Would Arianna brush him off? Would she even be there?

It was late afternoon when he finished the book, a mystery with a seemingly ambiguous ending—the kind he would have enjoyed pondering if he were not so distracted.

"You'll be in God's hands tonight," Dopp reassured him before he left the office.

Trent wanted to draw comfort from the words, but somehow they sounded like a preemptive excuse for whatever might happen: *If you fail, it was never meant to be.* The words also seemed to carry the subtext that if you succeed, it was due to God's help, not to your own skill. Either way, he walked home feeling like a pawn of a higher force. If he did conquer the case, he wanted to believe that he was responsible for the triumph. But that was selfish, he thought, and silly. Who was he to steal credit from the Lord? And to even resent His help? Trent laughed out loud, feeling better. And then a brilliant thought clicked in his mind. To destroy his inner monster of egoism was simple: All he had to do was laugh at it.

When he reached his apartment, at Seventy-third and Columbus, his anxiety about the night was gone. He whistled as he showered, shaved and dressed, taking care to gel his unruly hair and iron a red button-down shirt. Wearing comfortable washed-out jeans and black sneakers, he felt more like himself than he ever did at work. He left for the bookstore an hour early, even though it was only seven blocks away.

But as he neared it, an unexpected sight made his heart thump: A line stretched from inside the store down Broadway, looping around Sixty-sixth Street and out of sight. Would Arianna take one look at it and decide it wasn't worth the wait? He scanned the crowd, restlessly searching for her face as the line inched forward for a half hour.

Just as he started to convince himself that waiting in the rest of the line was a waste of time, a ringlet of black hair edged into his peripheral vision. He glanced to the right and saw the woman's profile: It was Arianna. At first, he just stared. She was clutching the book and chatting with another woman off to the side of the line, where liter bottles of soda were arranged next to cups on a white plastic table. She was taller than he had expected, which somehow made her seem like a more formidable foe. She was dressed in slim-fitting jeans, low-heeled sandals, and a white blouse that made her olive skin seem darker. He couldn't hear what she was saying, but she was gesturing and pointing to a page in the book.

A light tap from the person behind him sent him scooting forward, as the line had cleared five feet ahead of him. How had he planned to approach her? He tried to remember, but the line was moving so fast, and all he could focus on was keeping her in sight. Out of the corner of his eye, he watched her talk, begging God to keep her going. If he left the line now to go up to her, it would look bizarre—he was almost at the front. A slow minute ticked away before he reached Aaron Dakota, a gruff-looking man with a gray beard and a permanent slouch who was sitting behind a plastic table.

"What's your name?" Dakota mumbled as he took Trent's book.

Trent told him, and added, "Great mystery." The book's cunning was indeed a feat, the most enjoyable research for the DEP that he had ever conducted. Arianna, felon or not, had stellar taste in literature.

Dakota smiled after he scribbled his signature, but to Trent's relief, he had no interest in conversing; he was already eyeing the next person in line. Clutching his copy, Trent walked—slowly, he told himself—to the drink table and poured himself a cup of Coke. Pinned to the wall above the table was a banner with words the color of spilled blood: WHO KILLED MARY FLETCHER?

Trent opened his book, pretending to study a passage while waiting for Arianna's conversation to wrap up. Her back was to him, but he could overhear what she was saying: "There's no way the murderer was the sister! How could she have done it if it was mentioned in the fourth chapter that she was taking a shower at exactly that time—it was just one sentence, but look, just wait, let me find it."

"Hmm," mused the woman standing across from her. "But if it wasn't the sister, then it had to have been the boyfriend, who was so likable. . . ."

Arianna shook her head as she opened her book and started flipping through the pages.

"It wasn't the boyfriend either," Trent cut in, sidling up to them. "Hey, I couldn't help but overhearing."

They both stared at him expectantly, as if it were natural that a fellow reader should jump into their discussion. He swallowed, realizing that he had hardly contemplated his own theory about the book's puzzle.

"What I think is," he said, "that whether the boyfriend seemed likable or not, it would have been arbitrary for him to commit murder with no motive. Dakota's a better writer than that."

"I know!" said the other woman, whose blond hair was pulled into a tight bun that made her powdered face seem pinched. "So who do you think it was, then?"

Arianna looked at him; did he detect amusement on her face? Was he saying something idiotic? Yet it was too late to backtrack. He cleared his throat.

"So," he said, "Think about Max. Even though he was a minor side character, he was a shady guy who had subtle feelings for Mary. He had a motive, then—he couldn't have her, and if she was dead, no one else could either. And where was he at the time of her murder?

Dakota distracts us with the family's revelation. So we completely switch focus from Max, just like Dakota wanted."

"What did I tell you?" Arianna said, snapping her own book shut and turning to the woman. "If it was Max, that's the only way all the unconnected clues in the later chapters make sense. I can't find them all now, but go back and you'll see." She smiled at Trent, seeming to take him in with a fresh perspective. "Impressive."

"What," he teased, "you thought you were the only one who got that?"

She smiled, but the woman frowned.

"Just because you two happen to agree doesn't mean you're right. The whole stupid book is just about getting people to argue so it will sell."

"Maybe," Arianna said. "We're just saying we think the answer is there, that's all."

We.

"Well, I don't think it's that simple." The woman turned on her heel and walked out, with a pointed glance at Trent.

He looked at Arianna with an apologetic shrug, but underneath her raised eyebrows, she was struggling to hide a smile.

"I think we scared her off," she said.

Trent nodded, feeling his shoulders relax. "Hey, sometimes the truth is hard to handle." He smiled.

"The funny thing is," she said, shaking her head, "that woman started the whole discussion with me, and then she ends up complaining about how the book makes everyone want to argue."

He chuckled and sipped his Coke. Up close, with her black hair pulled into a long ponytail, all the slopes in her face seemed more dramatic: her straight nose, her pointed chin, her cheekbones protruding like tiny rounded cliffs. Nothing about her was soft—as a woman should be, he thought. The intensity of her steel blue eyes reminded him of a man's.

He pulled the cup from his mouth and extended his hand. "I'm Trent."

She shook his hand firmly, as he expected. "Arianna. Can you believe the turnout here?"

"No, the line was ridiculous. But it was worth it, to meet Dakota."

"Yeah." She looked in the author's direction. The line was still snaking through the store. "I love his stuff. I wonder if all these people got the same message."

Trent's heart pounded. "What message?"

"Oh, I got this note from his publicist on NYfaces. Otherwise, I wouldn't have known to come."

"Oh, really? I walk past here to go to work every day, so I've been seeing his name in the window for a while."

"Where do you work?"

"I rent some office space in Midtown," he said, not missing a beat. "I'm a writer." This he had prepared; he could not think of a career easier to stretch in terms of when, where, what.

Her lips spread into a genuine grin. "Is that the hardest profession like everyone says?"

He shrugged. "Depends what day you ask me."

"What kind of writing do you do?"

"Fiction," he said. The kind that lets you make up anything.

"God, you must have a great imagination. I wouldn't even know where to start. I'm a doctor."

"Oh?"

"An OB-GYN. I specialize in reproductive endocrinology."

"Ah," he said, "well, I doubt my work is harder than that."

"So do you write short stories? Novels?"

"I'm on my first novel," he said. "I used to be a reporter on Long Island, but I left to do something more creative."

"What's it about, if you don't mind me asking?"

"It's about—well, it's a thriller, complicated to explain on the spot." He drew back with a shy smile and sipped his Coke.

She nodded. "So you must really be able to appreciate all the techniques Dakota uses. I think he's a fantastic writer."

"Absolutely."

A brief lull ensued, and he scrambled for words to keep the conversation flowing. All around them, people were talking loudly.

"It's so crowded in here," he said lamely, soon regretting it.

"Yeah, I have to get going anyway." She started walking toward the exit, and he followed her outside. The unusual fall heat was like a furnace blast after the air-conditioned bookstore, and at once, he recognized another opportunity.

"Man, I should have ridden my bike here," he remarked. "It would have been so much faster to get home in this heat."

"You bike? I do, too, though I should go more often."

"I've been trying to go more also," he lied. "I need the exercise, since I just sit at my desk all day." He paused, and then, as if it had just occurred to him: "Hey, would you like to go together sometime? Maybe in Central Park?" His mouth was dry; he glanced down at his sneakers, waiting for her inevitable response—if only he could stay in this exact moment, before the cards toppled, he could tell Dopp he'd lived up to the plan.

"Sure," she said. "I sometimes go for a ride after I get off work, when the air is cooling."

"Great." He grinned.

"When do you want to go?"

His mind made a quick calculation: Let a few days pass so as not to seem pushy, but don't waste time. "How's Friday at seven?"

"Okay. Oh, wait." She winced. "I have something Friday."

"What about the weekend?" he asked, praying he didn't sound desperate.

"Hmm." She paused. "I think that might work. How's Saturday morning, nine A.M.? It shouldn't be too hot then."

Oh no, he thought, *an early riser.* "That's perfect."

He withdrew his silver cell phone from his pocket, a finger-sized slat of plastic with a black sensor on one side. She took it out of his hand and waved her own similar phone in front of his.

"There you go," she said, handing it back. "Call me Friday to confirm."

"Will do," he said, slightly taken aback at her directness.

"Nice meeting you." She waved and turned to walk south on Broadway.

"See you in a few days," he called.

Then he turned around to hide his disproportional elation in case she looked back. The seven blocks to his apartment passed in a blur of buildings and pedestrians and cabs, a backdrop to the feeling of accomplishment that radiated inside him. He wished he could report to Dopp immediately, but also relished the anticipation of delivering the news tomorrow morning. The case had sparked an enthusiasm he hadn't felt since he was a reporter: that of a face-to-face challenge. Maybe God really had been watching him tonight; perhaps this was even His plan all along: to allow Trent to use his reporting and information-gathering skills for a more honorable purpose.

But one thing is sure, he thought with a wry smile. *I need a bike.*

Hunched over metal handlebars and seated on a hard wedge, Trent pedaled on his new street bike—$320 that Dopp had gladly told him to expense to the department. The shiny metal spokes in his wheels glinted in the sunlight as he rode. He was one block away from the designated meeting spot of Central Park West at Seventy-second Street, and two minutes away from being late.

Through his sleep-crusted eyes, he was surprised to discover that the world had a tranquillity this morning that he missed when he rushed to work during the week or to church on Sundays. Drops of dew on the grass glittered like strewn gems. The absence of traffic lent the air a pristine sweetness, and the only remnants of the bustling streets he usually navigated were lone joggers or other bikers. Encouraged by the lack of cars, he swerved into the middle of the road and peddled hard over the crunch of gravel, leaning forward to compensate for the pavement's incline.

Tightening his grip on the handlebars with his right hand, he removed his left—the bars wavered slightly—and glanced at his new watch. It looked foreign on his wrist, unlike his other watch, a black titanium ode to sleekness. This one had a white circular face with roman numerals and a brown leather band that said old-fashioned elegance. The stiff band was secure around his wrist. Good. Dopp had promised him it looked classy, though Trent thought it just looked old. But then again, that was the point.

When he looked up, he saw Arianna ahead, standing next to an electric blue bike in gym shorts and a tight zip-up jacket, with a backpack slung over one shoulder. Her hair was again pulled back in a long ponytail. They exchanged waves and he jumped off his bike, wheeling it toward her. As he neared, he could not help noticing the curve of her breasts under the jacket.

"Hey," he said, stopping in front of her. "Hope I'm not late."

"Is it too early for you?" She smiled, but he couldn't see whether her eyes were friendly or mocking behind her black sunglasses.

"Nah, I'm good."

"Then let's get going," she said. "What path do you usually take?"

He blinked. "The main one."

"The big loop, you mean? I know a better one, less crowded. Follow me."

He exhaled as she swung her leg over her bike and pushed off with the other foot. He did the same, wobbling behind her. *A job that comes with a workout,* he thought. A surprise perk.

Twenty-five minutes later, he was just beginning to break a sweat, relishing the cool wind on his perspiring forehead and the comfortable exertion of his legs. But when he looked over at Arianna, she was standing on the pedals, pushing left foot, right foot, coaxing her body to keep up with him. The asphalt path she had taken him on was one for only the fittest riders; there was no respite from the upward slope, and although it was minor, Arianna looked like she was climbing a mountainside.

"You okay?" he called over his shoulder.

"Fine," she gasped, motioning for him to keep going.

Trent reduced his edge, pedaling more slowly to match her pace. They barely exchanged words—her lungs were busy enough. Trent felt strangely satisfied; the physical challenge had morphed into a competition in his mind, erasing any worry that she could outpace him. But just then, he glanced up to see her black hair flying in the wind, her tanned legs pumping the pedals as she stood, gliding past him. *I will take you down,* he thought. A surge of might invigorated his muscles, and he pedaled faster, harder, until he quickly gained a few yards on her.

"Hey," she panted from behind. "I didn't know we were racing!"

He slowed down to let her catch up. *Enough,* he thought. There was work to be done, the tough job of getting to know each other. "Water break?" he suggested.

"Please."

They both dropped their feet to the ground, skidded to a stop and dismounted. His shoulders found relief in his straightened posture, but his legs felt hot and rubbery. Arianna turned off the asphalt to a dirt path lined with trees, and he followed her single-file until it opened to a grassy patch with a few oversized rocks. They withdrew water bottles from the holders on their bikes and stood drinking; she stopped after every few sips to catch her breath.

"I told you I needed to do this more often," she said, wiping her lips. "How did you get so fit?"

"Well, thanks," he said modestly. "I'm afraid it's easier for men, or so I'm told."

"It's true. Nature two, women zero."

"Two?"

"When you've seen as many labors as I have . . ." She trailed off, shaking her head with a smile.

"Right. Another reason God must be male."

"Or so I'm told."

He wasn't sure what she meant, so he said nothing as she unzipped her jacket and threw it to the grass on top of her bike. Then with a gesture, she led him to the rocks. He lagged behind her, carefully watching her bouncing ponytail. With the slightest nudge from his right pointer finger, he slid the metal knob on his watch down a millimeter until it clicked into place. Then he joined her on the smooth boulder, sitting on her right and leaning back on his hands as she was. Before he could direct the conversation, she spoke.

"So how's your novel coming?"

He gritted his teeth.

"Look, I'm terrible at small talk," she said. He noticed she did not seem apologetic.

"Me, too," he said. "My novel's going okay. Sometimes I get stuck."

She nodded sympathetically. "The creative process is painful. I paint, and it's always a choice between colors and strokes. Sometimes I have no clue how to choose."

"It's like that, but with words," he said, and went on before she could reply. "So if you're the creative type, what got you into medicine? The money?" *Shouldn't have led the question,* he thought. It was the first rule of reporting.

She shook her head with a glance that told him his assumption was clichéd. "Once you get to know me, you'll see that that's the last reason I would pick a lifetime endeavor."

"Why's that?"

"Well, for one thing, I was lucky enough that money wasn't a factor. My parents were both successful bio professors who told me that the only criterion for my career was to do something I loved. So I figured I would end up doing research like them, since their work intrigued me so much."

Trent's heart knocked harder, set off like a giant church bell by that key word. "But you didn't end up a researcher." The word slurred off his tongue, as if uttering it might tip his hand.

"No. I love biology and I loved studying how the body works on the molecular level, but the appeal of practicing medicine won out. Research can be so tedious and with no guarantees of any success. With medicine—"

"But research can be exciting, right?" Trent interrupted. The bell clanged frantically in his chest. "If you discover something big?"

"Sure, if," she said.

"Did your parents?"

"My dad did once. . . ." She trailed off, looking wistful, and Trent remembered that he had read her father's obituary in *The Times.* As his sensitivity battled curiosity, he decided not to prod her. Instead, following a reporting technique, he let the silence prolong into awkwardness so she might feel obligated to elaborate. She did not. He waited.

"Anyway, as I was saying," she said, "with medicine, I'm constantly doing hands-on problem solving and seeing results. It's very satisfying, although I respect scientists to no end, and if I had been born with more patience, who knows."

Trent could see she was about to ask him a question, so he cut her off.

"So why reproductive medicine, then? Doing risky IVF treatments and all that?" His heart beat faster, a warning that he was veering into a dangerous zone. Most men probably had no idea about in vitro fertilization, he realized; why would he? "I don't know much about it," he added, "but I bet it feels great to help people have kids who can't."

She nodded. "It's pretty amazing what we can do today—even beyond IVF, we can finally do a full genetic screening of any embryo before we implant it, basically guaranteeing a healthy baby."

"Really? Wow." Trent seemed surprised but knew she was talking about a technology called PGD—preimplantation genetic diagnosis. And he knew more than just the name; he remembered the controversy precipitated by the department shortly after he started working there, when PGD had made the news: In May of 2025, scientists figured out how to use the technique to screen all twenty-three pairs of chromosomes in a five-day-old embryo, leaving no diseased strand undetected. While most commentators hailed the progress as a boon to future generations, Dopp and the others had warned the media about eugenics, doctors playing God, and discrimination against genetically inferior EUEs.

"Yes," she said. "And there's no happier place to be, most days, than in the delivery room. I wouldn't trade my job for anyone's."

She beamed at him. He had seldom seen people discuss their work with that expression—it was the kind of unreserved flow of happiness he associated only with sex, and even then, he often felt guilty for feeling it. Or felt he should, anyway.

She was looking at him thoughtfully. "What do you love about your work, Trent?"

He paused, caught off guard. The possibility of drawing his answer from his current job didn't cross his mind. But before he could reply, her cell phone trilled in the front pocket of her backpack, at the foot of the rock.

She hoisted it up and unzipped the pouch. "Excuse me," she said, looking at the caller ID, "I have to take this. Hello? Hey . . . From the injection last night? . . . How swollen? . . . Well, don't panic, I'll swing by now and check it out. . . . Bye."

When she closed the phone, Trent was studying his watch. The second hand ticked around the blank white face, a poker face if he ever saw one.

"Sorry," she said, "but I should get going. My cousin's having surgery in a few days, and she's having some trouble with her medication."

"What kind of surgery?"

She looked at him a little sharply.

"Sorry," he blurted. "I'm just really interested in medicine and science. I don't know much about it."

She brightened. "No, it's okay, I didn't realize you were interested in it."

"Oh, yeah. I'd love to talk more about it sometime." *Like what kind of research interests you most.*

She laughed and he grew embarrassed.

"What?" he said, aiming for a playful tone. "Something wrong with that?"

"I just never hear anyone say that. I'm usually the nerdiest one in the room."

"Well, maybe not anymore," he said, recovering with a grin. "I would actually really benefit from some biological knowledge for this section I'm writing soon. But it's so easy to get lost in all those textbooks."

She stepped off the rock, putting a hand on her hip in mock frustration. "Well, why didn't you say something earlier? I could talk about this stuff for days. We could meet up again for another bike ride and then chat some more if you'd like."

"Great. That would be perfect," he said, rising and walking with her across the grass. "What's your schedule like?"

"Well, I never go into the clinic on nights or weekends. If anything, I'll get called into the hospital for a delivery, but usually I work normal business hours. I also have a prior commitment on Sundays and some weeknights. Let's see."

It was like dangling aces in front of an underage gambler: He had to restrain himself from asking what kept her so busy. *Back off,* he reminded himself. *You're not a reporter anymore. And it's only the first meeting.*

"I think next Tuesday might work, depending on how my schedule works out. Let's talk in a few days. You have my number." She stopped and turned to him, crossing her arms, but her tone was light. "By the way, I'm happy to chat and bike, but I can't date you, if that's what you're here for."

He smiled at her bluntness, unsure how to react. She really did like being direct. Maybe it was a social flaw, but it could also be a huge plus, if he maneuvered correctly.

"Hey, I'm fine with just hanging out, working out, whatever. I recently got out of a relationship, so I'm not looking for that right now. Just good company." *And your trust.*

"Fine. As long as we're on the same page."

What's your reason? he wondered. But he said nothing and she offered no explanation.

No matter, he thought. *Eventually, you'll tell me everything I want to know, and you'll think it was your own idea to do it. May God help us both.*

SIX

Thank God it's raining, Trent thought as he waited on a bench near the fountain in Washington Square Park: his umbrella was an excellent facial shield. The sky was a sopping gray sheet overhead. College kids scurried past, guarding books under their arms. Nobody seemed to find it odd—amidst the twenty-four-hour chess players in one corner of the park and ever-present drug dealers in another—that Trent was sitting outside in a mild storm, apparently doing nothing. But he was watching a specific brown door on the south edge of the park. He was far enough away to remain unobserved by those who passed through the door, but close enough to distinguish their faces. It was 5:15 P.M. on Monday, the twelfth of December. Where was Arianna?

Just over a month had passed since their initial bike ride, with regular rides once a week, and lately, every few days—opportunities shrouded in the guise of workouts. He wondered why she took him on such difficult roads when it seemed she struggled to keep up, but when he suggested as much, she shook her head defiantly and pedaled harder. Meanwhile, her clinic had passed the December 1 inspection, to no one's surprise. The embryo count remained inexplicably stratospheric, and Dopp's encouragements to patience were fading. Trent inferred that he would lose his chance at the case if he didn't make significant headway soon. He also knew they had limited time to continue regular bike rides, as the weather often threatened rain that would too soon become snow.

But the task of building trust was arduous. He lugged his patience around like a stone block, slowly stacking the base. As he and Arianna cooled off after their rides, they shared basic aspects of their pasts. It was simpler to keep his as truthful as possible.

He told her about growing up an only child—a rarity they had in common—on Long Island, with his still-married parents and his dog, a black Lab. Skateboarding after school, eating home-cooked dinners, camping with his family in Maine. His was a childhood that had not known adversity. In his most rebellious stage in high school, he had tried smoking marijuana. It lasted a month; he'd quit after his mother found the plastic bag in his sock drawer, a gram of ziplocked sin. Instead of reacting angrily, which would have been easy for him to combat with defensiveness, she told him that she was disappointed in him.

Two years later, he had moved into the dorms at Hofstra University, fifteen minutes away. After graduating with a degree in journalism, he moved to a studio apartment near his childhood home, and began writing for their local newspaper, the *Long Island Post*. Eventually he made a name for himself and moved on to the biggest Island paper, writing high-profile stories. But it wasn't satisfying enough. So at age thirty-three, he moved to his current apartment in the city at Seventy-third and Columbus and—here, he fudged—began writing creatively and freelancing on the side. For three years, though, the freelancing had taken up more time than he expected and sidetracked him from his creative pursuits. Now, finally, he was focusing on his novel. His savings, he said, would last several years—long enough to finish and publish the book, if all went as planned. If not, he told her he could always fall back on journalism. In his crafty mind, his improvised life plan seemed well thought out, and she did not appear to disagree. The past he painted for her was like a Monet: sweeping brushstrokes that provided enough information to understand the whole, but omitted key specifics, like the devoutness of his upbringing. It was the major detail he left out, so as not to alienate the daughter of two scientists.

What he had so far gathered from her was mostly insignificant. She had grown up in NYU faculty housing, raised by her father alone after her mother's death in a car accident when she was sixteen. She attended Columbia University for both undergraduate and medical school, NYU for residency, and then established her small fertility practice with several colleagues in Greenwich Village, along the border of the park that tethered her to the nostalgia of home, across from the fountain she had splashed in as a child. She spoke of her mother fondly—in two decades, her mother's memory had eased into a beloved recollection, rather than a traumatic one—but rarely mentioned her father. Trent learned why after he asked one day what had happened to him. She responded in a strained voice, her topaz-blue eyes watering, that he had died unexpectedly from colon cancer two years prior. Although Trent felt certain that her father's influence somehow tied in to the case, he did not mention it again.

They talked about books and movies and music only if she had an opinion to share. It was time Trent considered wasted, although Dopp told him it was not. It reminded Trent of practicing scales on the piano: nothing enjoyable came of it directly, but it would enable fluid playing later. He couldn't always manipulate the conversation back to her interest in biology, but when he did, she would discuss only cutting-edge research in fertility treatments that affected her practice. He encouraged her to tell him more about her practice, but she never hinted at anything unusual, so he tried another approach; when he asked for a primer on biochemical research for his "novel," she directed him to a textbook, explaining that research was not her field of expertise, though she did offer to guide him to certain sections that would be clearer for him to understand. Her graciousness frustrated him; she was so willing to help him that he half doubted she might be hiding something from him relating to exactly that topic.

But a curious incident yesterday had kindled his suspicion again.

Squirming on the wet bench now, with the rain driving tiny pellets into his umbrella, he moved the knob up on his watch to listen to their short, perplexing exchange from the day before. They had just been mounting their bikes when her phone rang.

Their voices emerged from the circular face—hers abrupt, his surprised:

"Hang on, I have to take this call. Hello? . . . Uh-huh . . . hmm . . . Okay . . . Soon. Bye." Her phone snapping shut. *"I'm really sorry, but I have to go."*

"What do you mean? Where? We haven't even started—"

"Something came up."

"What happened?"

"Look, I can't— Call me later, okay?"

The recording clicked off, and in the ensuing silence, he recalled her wheeling her bike to the curb and then hailing a cab. He played the exchange for Dopp this morning. They listened to it several times, trying to detect nuances in her tone. But beyond an obvious impatience and a slight excitement, they could glean no substantial clues from the recording except for one: The watch had picked up the low-frequency grumble of a man's voice coming from the earpiece of her cell phone.

"What does it mean?" Trent demanded. "She can't *what?* Stay? Tell me where she was going? And who was so important that she dropped everything for him?"

"I don't know," Dopp had said, lifting his pointed chin. "Have you mentioned her off-nights yet?"

Arianna always scheduled their bike rides around certain evenings, telling Trent she was busy then. Otherwise, she never mentioned those nights, let alone offered an explanation for her whereabouts. The nights had no consistent pattern—one week, she said she was busy on Monday, Wednesday, and Friday, but the next week, it was Wednesday and Thursday.

"No," Trent said. "I feel that it's not my business."

Dopp had been standing sideways at the window, his nose and chin a jagged silhouette against the light. But at this remark, he turned to face Trent, and the room seemed to darken with his expression.

"That is exactly what it is, Trent." His voice was deeper and softer, as if it were emerging from a cave in the back of his throat. "I want you to find out, however you can, where she is going. That's your job. Do it." He spoke evenly; his lips were the only part of his face that moved. There was no trace of anger in his tone, yet Trent felt the hot rise of intimidation tempered by resentment. Then Dopp's lip lifted, stretching one corner of his mouth up: *I have faith in you*. It was the parentheses to his command that reassured Trent he was still in his boss's good graces.

He had marched out of Dopp's office, cell phone in hand, and called Arianna to schedule another bike ride for today after work, ostensibly to make up for the previous day's foiled ride. But she had declined without an excuse.

"I'll call you," she told him, though her tone was not unfriendly. She said nothing about her sudden exit, and despite his determination to learn more, Trent could not bring himself to ask about it. He returned to Dopp ashamed, unable to push the boundaries of propriety. And his control was sliding; she had swiftly seized the upper hand for their future planning.

"If you can't call her right away, and you can't ask her where she's going," Dopp said, "then watch."

The window behind Dopp's head was streaked with rain; the storm had just begun. Trent saw his advantage: the umbrella was a lucky tool in a last-minute arsenal of disguises.

Now he brought it low over his forehead, just above his eyes. Where was she going to go when she left the clinic? Not home, he hoped. If he could find out even just an address, then he would have a location to investigate.

Rain could not have been her reason for declining to bike, he realized, since this storm had started within the last hour. He sighed impatiently, bouncing his knees and staring at the door of the squat, old building that housed her clinic. It was squeezed (ironically, he thought) next to the university's Catholic Center, which peaked much higher than its neighbor. Adding five feet to its height, atop the center stood a gold cross. On sunny days, the clinic dwelt in its thin, elongated shadow. Trent's eyes wandered up to admire the cross, and then a peripheral movement on the ground tugged his focus back.

The brown door had swung open, and in the moment before a purple NYU umbrella bloomed in front of her, Arianna's face was visible. From Trent's distance, he could not pinpoint her expression, only her distinctly tall figure. She pulled her umbrella down over her head and started walking east, away from Trent. Her stride was quicker than usual, despite her slightly uneven gait.

A strange limp kept some pressure off her right leg. Maybe she had sprained her ankle, and that was her excuse. But why wouldn't she have said so? He kept his eyes on her retreating figure. Trent knew from their conversations, and had confirmed it with a public record search, that she lived at Fifth Avenue and Eighth Street, just one block north of the park. If she was going home, walking due east, she was certainly taking a roundabout route.

He waited until she reached the southeast corner of the park before he jumped up from the bench. He walked briskly with his black umbrella touching his head, so the canopy completely blocked his face. Her purple umbrella stood out on the drab street, so when he lifted his own periodically, he caught sight of her. She continued walking east for six blocks until reaching Broadway, and then crossed the wide street and started walking north, without slowing her step. Fifteen seconds behind her, Trent neared the crosswalk. The red hand flashed at him in vain: His eyes were riveted to her figure across the street with such focus, he was almost surprised she did not turn around to acknowledge it. At the threshold of the curb, with his umbrella hoisted above his eyes, Trent sized up the situation: four lanes of cars lined the crosswalk; beyond the intersection, Arianna was nearing the block's first corner, hugging the sidewalk's edge as though she was about to turn out of sight.

His feet made the decision for him, hitting the asphalt a second before the light dropped to green. He reached the middle of the intersection before the honking started—an angry cab swerved around him, forcing him to straddle the white line of one middle lane; behind the first cab, another driver honked and glared when he saw Trent, frozen amidst the flow of cars. The honking swelled to a cacophony of dissident pitches sustained in annoyance. More than fear, Trent felt frustrated by his trap, and he looked past the traffic to regain his focus on Arianna. As she turned the corner, he saw her lift her umbrella to look back, no doubt to assess the commotion he had caused—

He pulled his own umbrella down so quickly, it slammed his head. But seconds later, he dared to lift his makeshift tent and saw she was gone. *At least she didn't see me,* he thought; if she had, she would have backtracked over to him. As the green light sucked away precious seconds, Trent kneaded the white line with his toes to keep his feet from dashing in front of any other cars as they continued to honk and swerve around him. The rain was pounding merciless bullets on his umbrella, as the windshield wipers of the cars swished furiously back and forth. When he saw red brake lights reflecting off the glistening street, he raced to the sidewalk and rushed up to the first block. So determined was he to find her that he didn't notice he was drenched, sprayed from the cars zooming around him.

The heaviness of his soaked jeans slowed him down as he rounded the corner, wheezing from anxiety and suspense. He stared down the sidewalk as far as he could see, wiping away the raindrops sliding through his eyelashes. But that bright lure, her bobbing purple umbrella, had vanished.

The next day, Trent sat in Dopp's office, brainstorming strategies to proceed. Next to Arianna's file on the desk lay a copy of *The New York Times*. The top of the fold showed a photo of New York's governor, Warren Vance, ducking into a black car with a grim expression, surrounded by a gaggle of reporters who were thrusting their recorders at him. The headline read, STATE BUDGET NEGOTIATIONS COLLAPSE AMID REVELATIONS OF VANCE'S IMPROPRIETY. Trent picked up the article and read:

> ALBANY—New evidence, including e-mail and phone messages retrieved by *The New York Times*, appears to reveal that Democratic Gov. Warren E. Vance channeled state funds in an attempt to tarnish the reputation of Senate majority leader Chuck R. Windra, the state's top Republican, who has opposed the

governor on multiple issues during preliminary budget discussions. The budget has been tabled indefinitely, pending investigation by the state attorney general.

Trent looked up and rolled his eyes.

"This is why I hate politics. It's so full of this corrupt crap." He threw the newspaper back on the desk and it slid toward Dopp, who stopped it with one hand.

"I've never liked Vance so much as I do today," Dopp said.

Trent raised one eyebrow incredulously, then both.

Dopp leaned forward, putting his elbow on the newspaper. "With all of his corrupt crap, Vance has done us a huge favor: He's bought us time. As long as the budget talks are stalled, we have that much more time to crack Arianna, and then bring her down in a very public way." Dopp raised his eyebrows, and Trent knew he was thinking of certain lawmakers' claims that they were a black hole of tax dollars; but if they could loudly bring down a nefarious doctor, they might be granted an extra life during the budget talks.

"I just need to get her to feel close enough to trust me," Trent said.

They discussed ways to ease her into socializing with him in a way that was more than a workout but less than a date, which she clearly did not want. If Trent suggested that each bring along a friend to a group dinner, it would shake off the romantic vibe. All the better if his "friend" was someone privy to the mission—like Jed—who could vouch for Trent's strength of character in front of Arianna.

"How else to deepen her trust, but to have someone reassure her?" Dopp said.

"I'll set it up," Trent promised.

"On another note, besides finding out where she's going, I want you to get her to invite you inside her apartment, so you can see if there's anything unusual going on there."

"Unusual, you mean, like a home lab? Nobody's done that for years."

"It's still possible. If she is doing something illegal with those embryos, she needs to have a space to do it, and it's not her clinic—that's covered. No judge will give us a warrant to search her apartment at this point, so it's up to you to get her to let you in of her own accord."

"Which basically means getting her to trust me."

"Right. It's like a hammer and a nail; see, right now they're lined up straight, and now you've got to whack it in. Might take a few swings before you get there, but just keep trying."

But why else would she invite me in, Trent thought, *unless she wanted sex—and then what?*

Throughout his twenties, while his friends were indulging their sexual appetites, he had prided himself for his restraint, always waiting to sleep with a woman until they were both ready, whether it was two weeks or two months—a behavior that usually impressed women rather than insulted them. Whenever the priest at church would speak of abstinence before marriage, though, Trent would feel a guilty tightness in his abs, knowing it was the one teaching of Catholicism he could not follow, a reflection of his too-weak convictions and too-strong desires. Once he had broken the rule at age eighteen—in his freshman dorm, single bed, first love—he rationalized that it was too late to be abstinent anyway.

I will not use Arianna, he thought. *But what if she wants to sleep with me?* The possibility of needing to escape gracefully from such an awkward situation intimidated him.

But she won't, he thought, *she doesn't even want to date me.* A pause as the tide in his mind swept over this reassuring voice, carrying it away. What swept back was a conundrum: *But if she doesn't want me, she won't invite me into her apartment. . . . So how in the world am I going to get in?*

The frosted martini glass in front of Arianna was nearly empty. She picked it up, swirled the magenta liquid, and then drained it all into her mouth in one tart trail of cranberry vodka.

"That," she announced to Trent and Jed, setting the glass down, "was the perfect martini. And I'm not even a drinker. What did you guys slip in there to make it so good?"

Across the booth, Trent and Jed exchanged pretend conspiratorial grins. All three leaned back, sated with food and drink, soaking up the ambience of La Lanterna. Live jazz ricocheted off exposed brick walls. In the fireplace, flames crackled and shivered. The restaurant was a Greenwich Village staple of classy nightlife, just one block away from her clinic—the reason Trent said he had invited her to come along.

When he had called the other night, she was scrutinizing the clinic's records for errors, methodically going over pages of patient information alone in her office. The numbers were blurring on paper like hovering black insects. Frustrated by her degenerating optical nerve, she had squinted her eyes until she saw white behind her lids, and that was when her phone rang. She'd been meaning to call Trent about rescheduling their bike ride, and apologized for what must have seemed like the cold shoulder. But he wasn't offended. And luckily, she thought, he was confident enough to call her. His invitation to join him and a friend for dinner at La Lanterna, extended to Megan as well, had sounded like an antidote to her stress and an easy way to make up for putting him off.

But to her disappointment, Megan would not be able to join them; she had opening-night theater tickets, a treat for successfully undergoing her egg-retrieval surgery the month before, despite a minor complication from the hormone injections. Trent seemed eager to keep their plans regardless. Anyway, she told herself, the presence of his friend implied that it was not a date, so he could not have any expectations.

Jed, a freelance reporter, and Trent were entertaining company, lively without being draining. They teased her about her low tolerance for alcohol (little did they know why she hardly drank), and after she asked them how they met, they amused her with anecdotes about their college fraternity, releasing tension from her mind, much like the joy she found in dancing, painting, and her own friends.

She wasn't sure quite how Trent fit into her social life, but she knew that seeing him gave her a much-coveted escape to normal life, one in which dinner and drinks and skilled saxophonists were their own end, pleasure for the sake of pleasure, and not just a distraction from pain. Her frenzied week—keeping the group fully stocked with embryos, manipulating the records, scheduling new donations, and seeing her actual patients—began to recede in her mind. She noticed the dimple in Trent's chin when he cracked a joke. He was the only person she socialized with who did not know about her condition, and so felt comfortable teasing her. "What's the problem, slowpoke?" he had shouted once from the top of a hill they had biked up, relishing watching her huff in his wake. She had merely smiled, granting his victory with a thumbs-up.

Across the room, the drummer in the jazz band was playing a solo, and they turned to watch.

"He's got amazing chops," Trent said. Arianna nodded; she had lately regretted never learning an instrument.

Jed elbowed Trent's arm, smiling at her. "This guy was a rock star in a different life."

"What makes you think I'm not now?" He laughed, and in that moment, he seemed contentment personified; but rather than envy, Arianna felt drawn to his effortless smile. She recognized a mirror of her own nature in that smile—a pure delight in life and living that made her think, *Suffering is only an interlude to this, and not the other way around. If only we had met sooner.*

A woman's shrill voice from a table nearby distracted her from her longing.

"No, Harry," the woman was shrieking, "I will not allow our daughter to go on a field trip to a creationist museum!" She slapped the table, making their glasses quiver. "Does anyone even hear the illogic of those words together anymore?"

The man across from her looked mortified as diners at several other tables, including Trent and Jed, glanced over to them.

"Deb," he coaxed, "it's just a stupid field trip. Kids don't pay attention to museums anyway."

"But it's a fucking *public school*!"

"Can't you just relax—?"

"You want me to relax while Elizabeth buys straight into their goddamn propaganda?"

The man's embarrassment flushed his face. "Okay, okay, we'll pull her out of school that day, all right?"

The woman looked appeased and lowered her voice, blending back into the din of the restaurant. But her indignation was contagious; Arianna turned to Trent and Jed, eyes flashing.

"She's right. That museum is crap, people are totally apathetic, and that's why it's gotten so bad."

Trent and Jed said nothing, so she went on.

"I really think we are at a crucial fork in our history. The separation of church and state is breaking down all the time. First the line was blurring, and now it's all but indistinct."

She swallowed the words that dangled from her tongue, threatening to expose her fury toward the DEFP and the DEP. *Don't even go there,* she steered herself. *You barely know them.*

"Remember when we were in college," she said instead, "they called it the Information Age? Well, now we're in another era altogether. I'd call it the Contemporary-Medieval Period, and who the hell knows how long it will last." She laughed ruefully, feeling her blood pressure rise. "You'd think it would be a contradiction in terms."

There was a silence, and her breath caught; had she gone too far?

"Don't even get me started," she said, flicking her wrist.

"No, it's good to be passionate," Jed said.

Trent seemed contemplative, rubbing the stem of his glass between his thumb and forefinger. Then he looked at her. "I wish I saw more people care, too."

"Thank you, guys," she replied, settling back into the leather booth. She didn't realize she had been leaning forward, pressing her palms to the table.

Trent scooted out and stood up. "You scared me off," he joked. "Restroom, be right back."

As he walked away, Arianna took a deep breath and cast her full attention on Jed. She wondered if he would later offer an appraisal of her to Trent, even though that didn't matter.

"So," Jed said, "Trent tells me you are quite the cyclist."

"Oh, really?" She chuckled, wondering what else he had said about her. "He's faster than I am."

"Sounds like you're getting him into shape, then."

"More the other way around." She paused. "And it's nice to have the company."

"Sure. He's a great guy." Jed paused to sip his gin and tonic. "He's been an incredible friend to me."

He looked eager, almost proud, so she prompted him to go on. "How so?"

He proceeded to tell her about a time in college that Trent refused the advances of Jed's then-girlfriend, whom Trent had long desired. But their friendship—and his integrity—came first.

"I'm sorry," Arianna said. "That must have been so painful."

"Yeah, it was," Jed replied, nodding across the room at Trent, who was returning to their table.

"You guys look sad," Trent said, sitting down. "Don't tell me you missed me that much."

"I was just telling her about Ashley," Jed said.

Trent frowned. "That's ancient history."

"So what happened to her?" Arianna asked.

Trent and Jed exchanged a look that she could not read: Had she stumbled on forbidden territory?

"Well, I obviously broke up with her," Jed said, clutching his glass. There was a silence, pregnant with tension, and Arianna wished she had not probed further.

"Thank God for this guy," Jed said, nudging Trent. "I don't know how I would have gotten through it otherwise."

She smiled. "Sounds like you're pretty solid." She looked at Trent and felt some sort of tacit understanding pass in his glance, like acknowledgment of her compliment and perhaps something more. He looked away first, at that old-fashioned watch on his wrist. "What do you guys say we call it a night?"

Outside, they waved good night to Jed as he walked away. Arianna tightened her coat and took a deep breath, inhaling the cold night. The breeze was like an atmospheric cocktail shaker, mixing the scents of alcohol, cigarettes, and pizza. MacDougal Street was in its prime, with drunken revelers laughing loudly and crossing the street from one bar to the next. Ahead in the park, several shadowy figures moved close to one another, and then scattered.

"Let me walk you home," Trent said. Vodka floated on his breath, the culprit of his slightly messy enunciation. "Please."

It's only three blocks, she thought, but did not protest.

"It's only three blocks," he said. "It's no problem."

"All right, thanks."

They fell into step along the edge of the park. She walked quickly, out of habit, but soon realized she was in no rush.

"So when can I read your novel?" she asked, moving closer to him in the darkness. The hair on her arms prickled, sensing his body heat.

He was a beat slow in responding—the alcohol, she thought. "It's not gonna be done for a while." Then he blurted: "But you know what I really wanna do sometimes? It may be silly, but I wanna travel the world and write about it. That'd be so cool. Have you been to Italy? I wanna go there first."

She chuckled at his drunken ramble, recognizing an unguarded confession of his dreams. "That's not silly. It's beautiful there. Why don't you go? You can write your novel anywhere. You work for yourself. Take advantage of that freedom!"

"Nah." He inhaled sharply, and when he let out the sobering breath, he seemed steadier. They rounded the park's corner, and her apartment building came into view. "Maybe later."

"You should," she said. "It sounds like something you really want to do."

He nodded as they crossed the street. Her building's bright lobby spilled a moat of light onto the sidewalk.

She stopped at the edge of the darkness, intoxicated by a desire that made more sense than her will to ignore it. He stopped next to her. But before he could say good night, she lifted a hand to his cheek, satisfying a curiosity she had felt all night about the texture of his stubble. The rough bristles prickled her fingertips. Her hand cupped his chin, pulling his unresisting face down to hers. Their lips met, surprising her with the tenderness of a kiss she had not expected.

The scent of vodka on his breath, sour and intrusive, prompted her to pull away. She watched him open his eyes. For a second, they stared at each other. *Shit.*

"What's wrong?" he asked.

"I'm sorry, I don't know what I was thinking." She bit her lip, tasting the wetness stamped there.

"It's okay," he said, smiling cautiously. "Don't apologize."

"No, you don't understand. . . ."

"Understand what?" His words seemed sharp. But what could she say? If she explained, he would never tease her again; their rapport would be lost, and she would inevitably become the grudging recipient of his pity.

"I can't date you," she said. "Well, I guess I could see you, but I can't commit. It's not anything about you. I just can't be in a relationship."

"Hey, that's fine. You're getting ahead of yourself."

"The thing is, Trent, I really do want to keep seeing you, but I need you to know it's not serious. Is that okay?"

He smiled. "I think that would make most guys' night."

"Including yours?"

"Sure. And I want to keep seeing you, too."

She sighed with relief, pleased that he did not press her for a reason.

"How about tomorrow after you get off work?" he asked. It would be Friday.

"I can't," she said. "How about Saturday, we'll bike that path on the West Side we were talking about? And then grab lunch?"

"Sold. I think we can get away with a few more days before the first snow."

"Let's hope." She stepped back from him into the moat of light. On her cheeks, two red orbs smeared outward to her hairline, worry tinged with desire. Then Trent's lean figure in the shadows seemed to move back and forth before her eyes, disorienting her by turn—until she realized it was she who was swaying. She took a careful step backwards, but tripped over her foot and grasped the lobby door with a flailing hand.

"Whoa, there, drunky," he said, stepping into the light. "You got that?"

She flashed him a smile, as carefree as she could manage. "See you later," she said. Then she swung open the door and hurried inside before he could respond.

The next afternoon at 5 P.M., Trent returned to his discreetly positioned bench in Washington Square Park. As he waited, the weak sun shone down. No umbrella would shield him today. He would have to be extra cautious. As he watched the clinic's brown door, his mind drifted back to their parting last night. Arianna's hand on his cheek—and the kiss that so naturally followed—had caught him off guard, as did her cryptic reaction. Guilty warmth seared his face as he thought that the kiss had not been entirely unpleasant—in fact, it had thrilled him (though that was just the alcohol talking). Of course, he omitted that part when he told Dopp about it. His boss was ecstatic, hailing his "clear progress" as a sign that God was helping their mission.

"We must be on our way to a confession," Dopp had said. "You're doing great. Oh, and Jed told me about her little outburst at dinner. I'm surprised you forgot to mention it—that was pretty fantastic news."

Trent froze for a moment, and then deduced what he meant. "The creationist museum. Yeah, she got all worked up about it."

Dopp looked pretty excited himself. "Jed said she called it 'crap.' It just confirms what we've thought all along: She still has an evil agenda."

Trent nodded slowly. He remembered her lecture about the separation of church and state, but out of some strange reluctance, had decided not to discuss this tidbit with Dopp.

Dopp wagged a spindly finger. Trent almost apologized before realizing the gesture was not meant for him. "That woman is up to no good. Write up the transcript. And keep following her every chance you get."

"Today," Trent said. "She said she was busy today after work."

"Keep on her this time."

"I will." Trent paused, hating to diffuse Dopp's hope. "But she could be going anywhere. . . . I don't know where. . . ."

"Exactly," Dopp had responded, emphasizing each syllable.

• • •

The pulse of the park was dying with the afternoon light: Children dismounted from swings, guitarists packed up, students hurried past the fountain as they wrapped cheap scarves around their necks. A few like Trent sat on benches, clutching plastic coffee cups. Near him was a small-dog run, a fenced-off spread of dirt the size of a subway car. He pretended to watch the critters scamper around, trembling in glove-sized jackets, while he kept his peripheral gaze on the clinic's door, yards away.

A visibly pregnant woman hurried past him just as her yellow MetroCard slipped out of her pocket and landed near Trent's bench. He jumped up to grab it and ran after her, shouting, "Ma'am!" She turned around and smiled as he held it up, then froze as she caught sight of the DEP identification card still clipped to his belt; he had forgotten to take it off. Her hands flew to her stomach, and she grinned widely, nearly grimacing.

"Thank you," she said. "I was actually just on my way to meet with my caseworker. I—I'm so sorry for missing the last appointment, but I just got caught up with work, and I—"

Trent held up a hand, feeling his pulse quicken for some reason. "It's fine. I don't work for the DEFP. That's a different department."

"Oh." The woman looked down as her brow relaxed. "Sorry. Bye, then." She turned and rushed away.

Trent returned to the bench, again focusing his gaze on the clinic's door. But a part of him was horrified. The fear in that woman's face was disturbing: fear of *him*. He felt like a criminal or a dictator, someone with a deficit of compassion and a surplus of power. But that was absurd; there was nothing wrong with him. Or the department. Just the opposite.

The door opened then, and Trent forgot his discomfort because the first emotion he felt when he saw Arianna wheeling her bike through the doorway was betrayal. She lied, he thought. She said she couldn't go biking today. When she mounted the bike and began cycling east, traveling a seemingly familiar route, his hurt morphed into intrigue. He rose from the bench, half-jogging to keep up with her, while maintaining a fixed distance; although to his relief, he realized it would be more unlikely for her to turn around and spot him now.

At Broadway, she stopped at the curb to wait for the light, planting one foot on the sidewalk. He lingered a block behind. When the cars stopped at the crosswalk, she charged across the street with her black hair rippling in the wind, beckoning him. He followed, crossing the street in the same light. Up ahead of him, at the first corner, Arianna turned a familiar right. His heart thudded, propelling his legs to match her speed. *You won't lose me now,* he vowed. He rounded the corner and saw her pedaling two blocks ahead. Where before he had been thwarted, now he was going to see—

No one was near her when it happened. Trent watched in disbelief as Arianna stuck her right foot in the spokes of her front wheel, missing the pedal by inches. He could see her body tighten, as if clenching her muscles would forestall the blow, as her front tire stopped short and the momentum hurled her over the handlebars. Even from his distance, he heard her shriek—a useless cry wrenched out of a voice he had never heard lose control. She flew forward, arms stretched out, clawing at the air in vain, as the bike collapsed underneath her. Onto the unforgiving pavement she crashed, skidding on her forearms, bouncing on her chin. With a smack, her knees followed. The momentum dragged her a foot until friction interceded. Then, facedown, she was still.

"Jesus Christ," he breathed. *She could be dead.* Panic and restraint wrestled within him, keeping him in limbo at the edge of the sidewalk. His urge to run over to her was growing dangerously compelling—but then she let out a moan and turned onto her side, bringing her knees up to her chest. Several passersby rushed toward her, yelling to one another to call an ambulance. A motherly-looking woman crouched and held her hand, while a man collected her bicycle from the middle of the sidewalk. The last thing Trent saw before more people gathered around her was the blood streaming from her kneecaps, scarlet rivulets of pain.

He waited on that corner, an inconspicuous onlooker, until an ambulance arrived four minutes later. Even after she was placed on a stretcher and loaded into the back, and the siren wailed on, Trent remained standing. He watched the ambulance squirm and twist through the traffic until he could no longer see or hear it. He thought of calling the hospital to ask about her condition, but then he realized he didn't know where she was going. Instead, he grabbed his cell phone from his pocket and dialed Dopp's office. No answer. He dialed Dopp's home. No answer.

By default, Trent started to walk north, as if a magnetic pull was dragging him to the one place he had no interest in going: home. It was more than sixty blocks away, but he passed the subway in Union Square that would have accelerated his trip, unable to bear standing still on a packed rush hour train. Moving his legs provided a release of his escalating energy and gave him a sensation of purpose. As the sky deepened to indigo dusk, he walked on, passing store owners pulling down metal fronts, closing their clothing boutiques, pet shops, used bookstores. Trent took no notice, insulated in a mental world by thick walls of concern, coated with dread. His body reacted appropriately to stoplights and traffic, although later he would have little memory of the journey home. After twenty blocks, he began to tire, but pushed on, ignoring his chilled bones, blistering heels, and grumbling stomach. He had not eaten for six hours. As he walked, he recalled his boss's words: *Don't hesitate to call me at home if you get anywhere significant this time.*

Trent snorted as he considered the last few words. What if they were forced to close the case because of *significant* injuries to the targeted party? That was certainly not the outcome his boss was expecting. And how would he explain the accident to Dopp? He imagined how their exchange might go:

"She fell off her bike."

"How come?"

"Missed the pedal."

"Was she going very fast?"

"No."

It doesn't make sense, Trent thought. Nothing was in her way to distract her. Suddenly he remembered that she had been limping several days before, but it had not been severe enough to hamper her speed, and he hadn't noticed it when they walked home last night.

Though he hadn't been too steady himself. Then he remembered their plans for tomorrow morning and cringed: They were supposed to bike the path on the West Side. . . . He was supposed to call her tonight to confirm. . . . So that's exactly what he would do. It gave him a perfectly innocent reason to call her.

The starless sky was now navy blue—as dark as the city of infinite night-lights would allow. Soon Trent noticed that the blur of stores around him was beginning to assume a familiar pattern, and he saw he was only four blocks from home. He stopped by a corner pizza place, then went up to his apartment with one goal flashing in his mind: *Talk to her.*

His studio apartment on the seventh floor looked like the physical form of an afterthought: it was halfheartedly decorated with a tan sofa, a futon with a black bedspread, a small wooden table with two chairs, and a bookshelf. Across from the sofa was a Yamaha keyboard waiting for its daily dose of attention. A nineteen-inch flat-screen television hung on the wall. Near the head of his futon, overlooking Seventy-third Street, there was one window. Maroon curtains hung from either side, the one touch of color in the room. He liked the fiery glow they emitted in the mornings, making it seem as if he were tucked into a cozy den lush with color, rather than a sparse room, alone.

He walked to the window and called her. The phone rang as he contemplated the possibility that she might not be able to answer at all. He paced over the wood floor, pressing the phone hard against his ear. One, two, three rings passed.

"Hello?" came her voice, scratchy and soft.

"Hey, Arianna," he said, his tone chipper. "How are you? I just wanted to see if we're still biking tomorrow?"

"Actually, no. I'm in the hospital."

"What?"

Her voice was flat. "I had a bike accident. Had to get six stitches on my chin, and my knees and elbows are all ripped up."

"Holy shit, are you okay?"

"Luckily, that was about it."

He exhaled a breath he did not know he was holding. "Thank God."

Silence.

"Arianna?"

"I'm here."

"What's wrong?"

She sighed a long breath, and when she spoke, even her voice sounded deflated. "I guess it's only fair to tell you."

"Tell me what?"

"Look, Trent, I owe you an apology. I haven't been completely honest with you."

"Okay . . ." In spite of the irony, his heart began to race; was this the moment of her confession? He hadn't imagined it like this—with his opponent bandaged and broken, a suddenly weaker match—but why would she tell him now about a secret lab?

"I have malignantly progressive multiple sclerosis. I lose my balance sometimes, and my limbs go numb out of nowhere, like today. I shouldn't have been riding anymore, but I hate letting it interfere with my life. Which is also why I didn't tell you. You may not mean to, but I don't want you to start treating me like I'm some cripple. Because I'm not. Maybe it's only in my mind, but I'm not." Her voice rose, lifted by self-respect. "And if you still want anything to do with me after this, you'll have to get that straight."

Trent's mind swirled with a montage of instantly linked events: her limp, her stumbling into the lobby, her foot thrust into the spokes of the wheel. He had never known anyone with MS, had no idea what it involved or implied.

"Jesus, Arianna. I had no idea. . . . I can't believe you were still biking, when you knew the danger—you're a doctor, for God's sake!"

"Oh, and don't even dare patronize me. I will live my life however I choose and take whatever risks I want. If I decide to skydive tomorrow as my last life's wish, then you can either wave to me from the ground or—"

"Your last life's wish?" he interrupted. "What? What are you talking about?"

"It's malignantly progressive. Soon I'll be in a wheelchair, and after that . . ." After a pause, her voice dropped to a hard note. "I like you, Trent, but you'd be wasting your time to date me."

He took a deep breath, trying to loosen the shock that was lodged in his throat like a clot. "I don't care," he said, trying to sound brave and supportive, and not as rotten as he felt. "I still want to keep seeing you for as long as I can."

"You do?"

"Yes. But isn't there any treatment that could help you? Any drug?"

"There are some drugs that slow its progress," she said. "But no, right now, there's no cure."

No cure.

Right now, there's—

And then, flabbergasted, he latched on to the wildly glaring connection— *Can it be?* His head began to throb as if from an ice freeze, oversaturated with information.

"I don't know what to say," he finally said.

"I need to go, anyway. You probably need some time to digest this. You can call me later if you want. And needless to say, we can't bike together anymore."

He closed his phone and stared out the window, barely perceiving the dark treetops below. Time passed—a minute or ten—before his hand mechanically dialed a number on his phone.

Dopp's voice sounded incongruously normal, even pleasant, when he answered. "Hey, Trent, how did it go?"

Something deep within him, unacknowledged and unwanted, recoiled against his words as he answered:

"I think I found her motive."

SEVEN

Arianna dropped her cell phone onto the starchy hospital sheet as Trent's voice dissipated in the silence. She closed her eyes, trying to retain the timbre of his voice, but its distressed tone magnified her worry. *I won't be surprised if I never hear from him again,* she thought. *In fact, I would completely understand.*

Her throat clenched for tears, but she knew that indulging in self-pity was its own side effect of MS, and one that was more detrimental than a numb foot or a wave of dizziness. Even though some other doctors denied it, she believed that attitude played an important role in the rate of a disease's progression—a staunch belief that compelled her to focus on the joyous aspects of life, and to savor even its smallest pleasures, like crisp air invigorating her lungs.

She breathed in deeply, expanding the tightness in her throat, but the air was stale and reeked of disinfectant. She surveyed her surroundings in dismay, glancing from the paper blue curtains hanging dismally on either side of her bed to the tiny television mounted on the opposite wall that betrayed its age by its DVD player.

She tried to swing one leg onto the floor—and was stunned, not by the expected shock of pain, but by the sensation of nothing at all. Her leg had not moved. She threw off the faux-wool blanket, thrashing her bandaged legs until she felt a viciously sweet pain pulse in her knees, hardly noticing the screech of the curtain as it was yanked along its steel rod.

"Arianna!" exclaimed a voice. "What are you doing?"

The kind face of her own doctor, an MS specialist, instantly stilled her.

"Oh, Dr. Morris, thank God! My legs just went completely dead. I thought for a second . . ."

He nodded knowingly. His wire-rimmed glasses perched on the bridge of his nose like a filter of emotion: the only one that ever showed was calm.

"But you can move and feel them now?"

"Yes."

How much easier it was to remain calm when you were the one at bedside and not in it, she thought. But she knew that it made her a better doctor, at least. Sympathy was the crux of the job at times, as barren couples cried in her office, and understanding the depth of their suffering was a trait that seemed to inspire more goodwill than her degree from Columbia.

She swung her legs over the edge of the bed, and he tested her reflexes with a small hammer. Her feet kicked up weakly.

"I saw a copy of your admit report. You must have taken quite a spill." His words were not judgmental; if anything, his tone was sympathetic. It was one reason why she had stayed with Dr. Morris since her diagnosis two years ago: He understood her fundamental need to lead a normal, active life at whatever the risk, never scolding her for testing the limits of the disease.

"I know what you're going to say," Arianna said. "And I guess I have to agree."

"The Novatrone drip is the right course of action at this point, Arianna," he said gently. "And I think we should get you started on it as soon as possible, since your legs are already showing symptoms of preparalysis. We'll start it with a course of antibiotics to prevent infection in your cuts. It seems that the shock to your system from falling is expediting the degeneration of myelin in your lower spinal cord."

She nodded reluctantly. *I took what I wanted and I'm paying for it,* she thought. The key to the progression of her disease was myelin: the fatty protective membrane layered around nerve fibers in the brain and spinal cord, which increases the speed at which impulses are conducted. The thicker the myelin sheath, the faster impulses can travel. Arianna's own body had inexplicably begun to attack her myelin, disrupting the electrical impulses conducted to and from her brain, resulting in nerve damage. As more and more areas of myelin scarred, it felt like watching herself drown; soon she would be left paralyzed.

Novatrone was a last-resort drug, a powerful immune-suppressing medication to delay paralysis in rapidly worsening patients, and Arianna was more aware of its risks than most: It could be tolerated by the body for only a limited time before causing heart damage.

"Let's do it," she said, wishing more than ever that she could confide in him.

She had hinted at her secret a year ago, when the group was first coming together, but Dr. Morris had been skeptical of its potential for success. Even worse, he had scoffed at her remark that she wished to be the first human trial.

"Rubbish," he had said, "it's a nice fantasy, but first of all, if any scientist ever got that far today, it would be like a monk decoding the human genome in the Middle Ages."

"I know of a certain monk who was the father of genetics," she had retorted.

"Mendel was in the nineteenth century, not exactly the Middle Ages! But look, even if some genius managed to discover something without going to jail in the process, it's almost certain death to be the first trial. Stem cells could be rejected by the body, or lead to tumors, cancer . . ."

But what other choice do I have? she had thought. *I'd rather die trying to live than live waiting to die. And Sam said there are theoretical ways to get around those risks. . . .*

"Arianna, be careful, whatever you're doing," Dr. Morris had added. "And don't tell me. If the DEP ever questions me . . . But I wish you the best of luck. . . ."

How she wished to tell him now about Sam's rats, which once suffered from autoimmune encephalomyelitis, an animal model of multiple sclerosis characterized by almost identical scarring and symptoms. Today those rats scampered around their cages and spun madly on metal wheels. Arianna thought of the plump little creatures often, even lovingly, despite knowing that the complexity of human cells made the same progress so much harder.

Instead of mentioning the rats, she propped herself up on her bandaged elbows and stared into Dr. Morris's eyes without fear. "Tell me one thing straight," she said. "With the Novatrone, how long before my legs go?"

"About a month."

"And after that, how long before—before it's not worth living?"

"Hopefully, another two months . . ." He knew better than to deign to apologize or persuade her to accept existence in a vegetative state, one which neither of them would term *life*.

"Thank you." She took a breath of stagnant air. "Can you give me a minute?"

"Of course. I'll go see about starting the drip." He ducked behind the curtain and she heard his rubber soles squeak across the floor.

This really could be my last winter, she thought, suddenly recalling the winter break during her senior year of college, when she and Megan had jaunted around Europe, savoring "the last winter" before the onslaught of graduate school and jobs. With three days left of their trip, on a delicious whim, the cousins had taken a night train from southern Italy to Florence to see Michelangelo's *David*. The most stunning sculpture in the world, they had decided, would be the perfect last stop to their trip. But when they arrived, the museum was locked—a sign on the door read: CHIUSO PER RINNOVO/CLOSED FOR RENOVATION. Her disappointment that day had not been too terrible, as they shopped for handmade leather purses and gold jewelry instead; no doubt she would return to Florence in her lifetime. She had not.

I will, she vowed silently. She stared down at her bandaged knees and rolled her ankles for good measure. *I will,* she thought; *I will stand before that sculpture and marvel at the height of human achievement, and I will walk away from it on my own two feet, knowing that I, too, am the product of a genius.*

She grabbed her cell phone off the bed. Sam answered after one ring, his voice husky with exhaustion.

"What is it?" he grumbled. "I've been working all day in this damn basement and I'm too tired to talk."

"I just have to tell you one thing."

"What?"

"We have three months."

Trent had planned on calling Arianna back that evening, but after his conversation with Dopp, he felt sapped of strength. What Dopp told him was to be expected: As grim as her situation was, it helped their case in several ways. It yielded a surefire motive for embryo research, and it set Trent up perfectly to use her vulnerability to develop her trust. Soon, Dopp assured him, she would confess.

"But aren't we taking advantage of a sick person?" Trent had asked, desperate to expose this qualm darting around his brain like a trapped fly.

"It could look like that," Dopp said. "But I don't have to remind you what the stakes are. Don't believe she's weak just because she's sick, or it will throw you off."

"You think she's strong?" Trent asked with disbelief, although he knew that she was, in a way he could not entirely explain.

Dopp scoffed. "This is a woman who's completely selfish about everything she does."

Total self-reliance, Trent thought: Physical, emotional, intellectual—that was it. Suddenly a phrase from the Bible popped into his mind: *Woe unto ye who laugh, for ye shall mourn and weep.* Trent had always been haunted by it—had God really meant that? Must those who were happy and strong be cut down for those who weren't? It seemed to offend his deepest sensibility, the same sacrilegious part of him that respected Arianna.

Dopp sighed. "This line of work isn't always pretty, but it *is* always necessary. Remember who we're working for."

"Yes."

"You can call me whenever you need to, Trent. We're in this together. And God is guiding our hand, I'm sure of it."

Dopp proceeded to talk strategy about how to gain access to her apartment, while Trent scribbled notes. When he hung up, he fell back on his bed, intending to follow through right away. But the foam mattress sank under his fatigued muscles. As dawn began to penetrate the burning-red curtains, Trent's stomach lurched before he fully awoke. The sensation of dry plastic on his eyeballs reminded him he had not meant to fall asleep.

He jumped out of bed, peeled his contacts off, and jumped into the shower. As the hot water revitalized him, he tried to rehearse the new plan, but could not focus; the knowledge that had long been obvious to his body was now creeping into his mind. It was no use kidding himself anymore: Arianna had awakened something deep and uncontrollable inside him. Trent cursed, spitting out a mouthful of water. How did he get to this place? And where the hell did he go from here?

He wondered if he was in shock. Since her revelation last night, he had been possessed of a desire to protect her—and immediately recognized the painful irony. How could his instincts be so at odds with ethics? It was impossible to answer. Or maybe the answers were impossible to accept.

There was only one thing for him to do: push on with his job. How he felt—how amazingly alive she made him feel—was irrelevant. No one could ever know. He would continue to do the right thing, and what happened to her because of it was not his concern.

Arianna's obvious delight at his call that morning encouraged him to stick to Dopp's strategy. She said she was returning home after the administration of some IV drug, and then she would be resting all evening. It was the perfect segue.

"Do you need someone to help you get home?" he asked.

"Oh, thanks, but my cousin is going to help me."

He scrambled to recover, hoping he would sound kind and not

desperate: "Well, how about if I come over to your place later on and cook you dinner?"

"That's so sweet," she said. "Are you sick at all, though?"

"No, not at all."

"Okay, I just can't be exposed to any pathogens right now. And I don't look too presentable, but what do I care, I'd love to see you."

Yes, he thought, *that wasn't too hard.*

But the speed with which she had accepted his offer undermined his anticipation. If she were hiding a lab there, wouldn't she have hesitated before allowing him in? But maybe she had decided on the spot to show him, as a reward of sorts, since he had not abandoned her?

Leaving his apartment six hours later with a cooler of food, he sent an unspoken prayer up to God, or was it to himself? Either way, the hope was the same: *Let me be ready for whatever happens tonight.*

His heart did not begin to pound until he swung open the glass door of her lobby, making his imminent arrival feel real. He strode across the checkered floor to an open elevator feeling a spurt of guilt, as if he were sneaking in, and realized then how dangerous it could be for him to feel any guilt at all. *I'm just doing my job,* he countered. *And with any luck, it will get done tonight for good.*

He clipped his cell phone innocuously over the pocket of his jeans. A camera's eye peered out from its cover, furtively set to record video of her apartment. Come Monday, Dopp was counting on this footage for proof or clues. On his wristwatch, Trent slid the knob up.

The elevator opened to a hallway with white walls and beige speckled floors. He knocked on her door.

"Coming," she called. He heard her footsteps draw near, along with the sound of a cane hitting the floor. She unlocked the door and opened it several inches, keeping her face hidden behind it.

"Do you like blue eyes?" came her coy voice.

"Huh? Sure, why?"

"Good," she said, and swung the door all the way open, stepping around it with a flourish. "Ta da."

Trent gasped. The whites of her eyes had turned aqua, making her own blue irises seem diluted in comparison, like glass marbles floating in a fluorescent pool.

"What the—?"

"It's a side effect of the drug I got," she explained. "Pretty creepy, huh? Too bad I didn't need it on Halloween. Instant costume!"

Trent laughed weakly. "You're all bandaged up," he said, taking in her covered chin, elbows, and knees. She was leaning on a cane, wearing pajama shorts and a tank top. "How are you doing?"

"Good, now that you're here. Come in, let me show you my place."

His heart sped up. "Great."

"Thanks for doing this," she said, taking the cooler from him. "You don't have to make anything fancy. I'm not even hungry yet."

"No problem."

He followed her to the kitchen, glancing around the apartment. On the right, there was a small living room with a black leather sofa, a low glass table, a bookshelf, and a television. There was no room for a lab here, he thought with disappointment. His gaze lingered in the room, as if he needed only to look a little harder. Covering most of the living room floor was a white fur area rug. He stared at it, suddenly transfixed by a bizarre image of lying naked across it, feeling it tickle his bare back.

"Do you like it?" Arianna asked, seeing him looking at the rug. He whipped his head back to her, feeling sheepish. She was opening the refrigerator to put away the cooler, and he peeked inside to look for glass test tubes. The only contents of her fridge were butter, milk, a lettuce head, and a few apples.

"Nice place," he muttered.

She smiled and led him out of the kitchen to the sofa, hobbling with the cane. He didn't ask if she needed help, sensing her hard-nosed independence. Instead, he hung behind her, unsure if he should walk in front of her at a normal pace, pretending to ignore her disability, or allow her to keep the lead.

"Race you to the couch," she announced. He laughed genuinely, recognizing the woman he remembered.

"Last one there has to cook dinner," he responded, darting in front of her. Then, taking what he knew was a risk, he turned back around with a devilish grin. "Slowpoke."

She snorted as he plopped onto the couch. "You're lucky I can't kick you right now." A few steps later, she laid the cane down and gingerly sat back next to him. He put his left arm around her, making sure his wristwatch skimmed her shoulder.

"And I'm lucky you were free to see me tonight."

"I think getting stitches and intravenous drugs does a pretty good job of clearing one's schedule."

"True," he said, stroking her hair, "but you're always so busy. It's pretty admirable how you keep that schedule up."

"You mean my work?"

"Yeah . . . and after work. You never talk about it. Maybe it's the fiction writer in me, but I can't help being curious."

She smirked. "What, are you imagining I have some exciting double life? Doctor by day, superwoman by night?"

He shrugged. "You tell me."

"Well," she said, locking eyes with him, "it might come as a surprise, but I'm actually going to church."

He laughed at the utter improbability of those words escaping her lips. But her expression remained the same: slight smile, wide eyes.

"Why?" he blurted, as if there were more than one reason why someone might go to church.

"To practice my religion," she said; a strange amusement in her eyes made it seem as though she was joking.

"Well, what's your religion?" he asked, playing along to whatever punch line she was aiming at.

"I go to a Christian church, like most everyone else."

"Which one?"

"A small congregation in the East Village. You wouldn't know it."

The East Village, he thought with a start. *That* is *where you have been going. . . .*

"So wait, you're serious? You really go to church?"

"Yeah." She smiled broadly.

"Even midweek services?" he asked, unable to believe that she believed. They had hardly discussed religion before, and yet, somehow, her faith seemed contradictory.

"Yep."

"How about tomorrow morning?" He knew no devout churchgoer would miss Sunday morning Mass, except in the most extreme circumstances.

"I expect to be strong enough to go."

"Wow. I guess we have a lot left to learn about each other." He frowned.

She merely laughed. "What's wrong?"

"The thing is, no offense, but it just doesn't make sense. How can you be so passionate about science and be that devout?"

She chuckled, slid her hand around the nape of his neck and pushed his head toward her lips. As they kissed, he was distracted by his own bewilderment: *First she tells me she's a good Christian, and now we're making out?* She wasn't drunk, but maybe the drug she received was making her act loopy.

Her tongue sought out his, sliding into his mouth and setting off a tingling in his groin. *No,* his conscience scolded, *you cannot let her turn you on.* He slipped a hand underneath her tank top, caressing her flat stomach. *Stop this now!* the voice in his head shrieked. He leaned into her, wrapping her in his arms–

"Ow," she said, depositing the word into his mouth.

He jerked away. "What happened?"

"My ribs are really bruised from my fall." She sighed, leaning back. "This probably isn't a good idea right now, as much as I wish it were."

"You're right," he said as his sense flooded back, stinging as it scrubbed away his desire. "We should definitely wait."

She lifted a hand to her forehead, closed her eyes, and winced. "You know what, I'm sorry to do this to you, but I think I actually need to go lie down. I really did want to see you, but I need to rest."

He cringed as he watched another flash of pain wrinkle her brow. "Sure," he said. "You should do that."

"Thank you," she said, opening her eyes. "I owe you a dinner. I'm actually a pretty good cook when I can get myself together."

He smiled and got up, glancing past her into the hallway leading to another room, when a last-minute idea struck him.

"I'm just going to use your restroom before I leave," he said.

"It's in the hallway right next to my bedroom."

As he got up, she lifted her bandaged legs onto the couch. He walked around her into the hallway, which was plastered with old-looking pictures of her and her parents, and a painting of the Sistine Chapel.

Maybe she really is religious, he marveled. He stepped into the bathroom and saw that it was far too tiny to hold laboratory materials like a freezer, a laminar flow hood, or a centrifuge. As she reclined on the sofa, he tiptoed out of the bathroom and ducked into her bedroom. The room smelled floral, like her hair. It was simply decorated, with a dark red bedspread, lacy white curtains dangling over a window, and white carpeting. On top of an oak dresser stood an array of orange prescription tubes filled with pills.

Feeling foolish, he turned and walked back into the hallway. As he passed the Sistine Chapel painting again, a shocking thought stopped him short: *She could have found religion after college, and now she's not doing anything wrong—we could be suspicious for nothing. . . . She could be innocent!*

The possibility was so tantalizing that he felt a physical longing, a dull ache tug at his gut: the birth of hope produced its own set of pains. But just as quickly as it came, it vanished.

I am an agent of the DEP, he reminded himself, as if thinking it would properly align his loyalties.

He strode to the sofa, where Arianna was lying with her eyes closed. They fluttered open when he placed a hand on her shoulder.

"Good night," he said.

She pulled on his arm, and as he leaned down to her, she planted a soft kiss on his lips. "You're amazing," she whispered.

He swallowed and drew back. "You, too."

As soon as Trent closed her door behind him, he whipped his cell phone out of his pocket and called Dopp. He longed to hear the crystalline voice of reason, not the voice that had splintered in his mind, with each slice staking claim on a conflicting realm: logic versus emotion, right versus wrong, duty versus desire.

"No lab, boss," he told Dopp. "But we did have an odd conversation. . . ." He recounted what she had told him. "I don't know why," he finished, "but it seems like she was lying or joking about church. It just doesn't fit. Maybe she really is religious, though."

"How could she be religious if she was upset about a creationist museum?"

"Maybe she was just upset about the blurred distinction between church and state? I remember her saying something about that."

"I don't buy it. I bet she's lying and using the church excuse to cover something up. Tomorrow morning, go and poke your head into all the Christian churches in the East Village. We need to verify if she's going where she claims."

"And if she is?"

"Then find a way to ask her directly what she thinks of embryonic stem cell research—if she really is a good Christian, she'll reject it with disgust, and at that point, I would have to be inclined to believe her. A worshipful person has no reason to lie, because she knows God will have the final say. As far as her clinic's high numbers, I guess sheer popularity could explain them . . . although it would be bizarrely unprecedented."

"And we could drop the case if so?"

"I guess so. But let's not write her off yet. I want to see if she's going to church like she says."

"And if she's not?"

"Then find out where she *is* going, and the faster, the better."

"You got it," Trent said.

On the subway the next morning, Trent tried to ignore the tension in his gut that was keeping his abs in a perpetual state of crunch. Whether it was anticipation alone or mixed with the poisonous handle of hope, he did not care to learn. For hope—of seeing Arianna in a church, and of ending this pursuit—signaled a selfish investment in the case that could derail his judgment.

He studied the two printouts in his hand: one, a list of addresses of the six Christian churches in the East Village that had a congregation of two hundred or fewer; the other page was a map marking out fourteen blocks long and six avenues wide, the neighborhood of tattoo shops and bars, smoke shops and dives, peppered here and there with a sobering house of worship to repent for last night's sins.

He got out of the subway at Astor Place, right at the block where she had fallen off her bicycle two days earlier. The streets were littered with glass bottles and crushed cans, and the late-late-night stragglers who were only now heading home. Trent felt out of place in his formal suit, but he focused on his list. Calvary Christian Church was four blocks north and two avenues east. He walked briskly, crossing streets in the absence of traffic, until he came up to a building that was narrow and tall, with sharply pointed spires. The bronze door was engraved with a cross. He pulled it open, relieved when it did not creak.

Words bellowed throughout the modest chamber, coming from a pastor facing his rapt audience: "To serve Christ is to live for Him, even if it means losing it all. As we learn in John twelve twenty-five and eight forty-four, everyone serves something: Some serve themselves, and don't realize they're serving Satan. . . ."

Trent scanned the backs of heads along the pews, looking for thick black waves over dainty shoulders. Even before he finished looking, he somehow sensed she would not be there. Quietly, he slipped back outside, and headed four more avenues east and a block south to the next church, Saint Mary's Mount of God, which was nestled next to a Chinese restaurant and a cigar lounge. He had never walked so far east in this part of town, and it felt as if he were in a different, more dilapidated city. This church looked older than the first, with a crumbling brick exterior and a peeling wooden door. Inside was a surprisingly large hall lit only by candle chandeliers hanging from a high ceiling. A pastor, bowing his head, stood at the pulpit underneath a life-size painting of the Crucifixion. The room of about 150 was silent, filled with the fervor of prayer. Feeling like a voyeur, Trent quickly examined the rows—to no avail.

He exited as noiselessly as he could, feeling strangely criminal, as if he were getting away with something. As he walked toward the third church, he realized why: It was the first time he had walked out of church in the middle of a service. For a moment, he worried that he was not observing Sunday Mass, the earmark of his religious life. *But I have Dopp's permission,* he thought. Certainly a former pastor had the authority to dismiss him. It was a free pass, redeemable this morning only, to skip church—and it was guiltily liberating.

At the sight of a peeling cross on a door that was several steps up from the sidewalk, Trent stopped. Stained glass windows on either side of the door were smashed in. The handle of the door was green with rust and grime. He climbed the stairs and seized it. The door didn't budge. Peering inside the broken windows, he could see empty pews and stray cats milling around. He stepped back, wiping years of accumulated filth off his hands, and glanced at the street signs. He was at Avenue C and East Tenth Street, one block north of the actual third church on his list, so he hurried down the steps, and walked on.

This looks more like it, he thought, walking up to a red-painted door with a polished gold handle and a sign that read DAMASCUS CHURCH OF CHRIST. He opened the door to the smallest hall yet, which set off a twinge of hope that she might be there. The pastor didn't pause in his sermon as Trent entered, but smiled welcomingly and continued speaking:

"Man has a natural inclination to worship—it is built into his faculty of thought to worship something. For some, it is the perverted call of the flesh, and others, the greedy call of the dollar, and still others, the hedonistic call of the bottle. The challenge is to worship God, for only He is worthy of true worship. Let us refer to the passage of John four twenty-four. . . ."

Trent felt, before he saw, that Arianna was not there. Something was off in this roomful of dutiful churchgoers. He recognized what he was accustomed to seeing and hearing in churches—in the preacher's tone, the content of his sermon, the deferential bowing of heads praying for redemption—and that was the problem. *She does not fit in here,* he realized, *because she is not like them—she is not subservient. But if it's true that everyone worships something, what does she worship?*

"What man worships," the preacher was saying, "is indicative of his very essence, for reverence is man's deepest form of love, one which holds the key to his soul."

Trent bit his lip, confronted by the rise of his own insecurities about life and truth, God and meaning, that he had managed to repress since focusing on the case. *I worship nothing,* he thought. *Journalism, traveling, music, nature, food. Nothing worthy enough.*

Suddenly he couldn't bear to stand in the back of the hall any longer. He turned and ran out, clutching the list he knew was useless. He stood on the cracked sidewalk, staring at the names of the last three churches, squinting to focus on anything but his own thoughts. The next address was only one avenue west; for the sake of activity, more than thoroughness, he trudged there. At that church, and the next, and the last, he sought her out in vain. *She is as absent as my faith,* he thought. *Now, where to find both?*

Leaving the final church, he called Dopp. "She wasn't in any of the churches that matched her description."

Dopp let out a low whistle. "I thought her religiousness was too good to be true."

"But why would she lie to me?" A voice of denial suggested that maybe she had not lied; she could have been too sick to attend church after all. . . .

"She's obviously hiding something and trying to get around it," Dopp said. "But I have a new idea."

"What?"

"Dealing with liars is tricky, and I'd be able to guide you better if I could observe her up close. I've never even set eyes on the woman."

"I'm listening."

"Next weekend is Christmas. I plan to have a family dinner with a few special guests: you, your parents, and Ms. Drake."

"What do my parents have to do with this? They don't know anything!"

"You can tell them now. I know from my friend Father Paul that they are honest Christians, and we need their help. You are going to be my nephew for the day, and your father will be my brother. It's going to be a simple family get-together, and she will be your date. Now that she's starting to fall for you, we need to push her to trust you, so we're ramping up the game."

Trent flinched at the last word. "Okay . . ."

"Introducing her to your parents will show that you care enough that you won't abandon her, despite her disease. And I'll get to observe her."

"I see."

"Call her right now to invite her—it's for next Saturday night, Christmas Eve—and then call me back to confirm."

"Okay. But wait, what if she recognizes who you are?"

"She can't."

"Why not? She could have seen your picture online, or—"

"Have you seen my picture online ever?"

Trent thought for a moment. "I don't know."

"You haven't. You know why? I've never allowed it to be published."

"Why not?"

"Do you think I want to run the risk of being recognized in the most liberal city in the country?"

"No."

"So call her."

When Arianna answered, Trent could hear voices in the background.

"Hey," she said cheerfully.

"How are you feeling this morning?"

"Better, thanks. Sorry about last night, but I really needed to sleep. What's up?"

"Actually, I, uh, was wondering what you're doing for Christmas Eve next weekend?"

"Nothing much, why?"

"Well, my family always has this dinner party on Long Island, and they—we—were hoping you could join us."

There was a pause, and her voice dropped. "Are you sure you want to introduce me to your parents? It's sweet, but aren't you—?" Her voice trailed off.

"I just want to enjoy the present with you," he declared, wondering desperately if that were a lie. "We'll deal with that when we have to. And my family doesn't know. All I told them was that I'm seeing an amazing woman. So they really want to meet you."

He felt her smile transcend their phone lines, from wherever she was. "Then I would love to enjoy the present with you as well," she said. "Let's do it. Besides, I bake a mean chocolate cake. That ought to win them over."

Trent laughed ruefully. "You don't have to worry about that."

A man's voice grumbled in the background, but Trent couldn't make out his words.

"Where are you?" he asked.

"I told you last night," she said. "I'm at church."

"You—you are?"

"So I can't talk. Thanks for the invite, though. I'm looking forward to it."

Trent pulled the phone from his ear and realized he had stopped in his tracks in the middle of the street. He crushed an empty soda can with his heel. The aluminum *crunch* of its destruction was so satisfying that he kicked it hard. For two blocks, he kicked it, until he reached the stairs leading down to the subway and the can was mangled tin.

One final call stood before him and the train.

Dopp answered after a single ring.

"She's coming," Trent said. "And she's definitely lying."

EIGHT

Arianna and Megan pulled up to Sam's Union Square West apartment in a cab, as the alternative fifteen-minute walk was too grueling an option for her. "He needs to remember how appreciated he is," Arianna said as they got out in front of an aquamarine glass skyscraper.

On the twenty-eighth floor, in the corner, solitary as its resident, stood a door with chipped black paint.

Arianna knocked. No answer.

She slapped her palm against the door.

"Who's there?" snapped a faraway voice.

"It's me," she called. She heard footsteps draw nearer as his voice got louder.

"I don't know any me's," Sam said, swinging open the door. His chin looked freshly shaved and his silver hair damp. He was clad in sweatpants and a T-shirt that hung loosely over his shoulders. At the sight of Arianna, his habitual scowl flipped into its opposite. "What are you doing here?"

Megan stepped out from behind Arianna and waved. His eyes narrowed slightly, as if she were an illogical sight.

"We're just dropping by to say hello," Arianna said. "Can we come in? Sorry we forgot to bring a peace offering."

"I'm not drinking for now." He turned around and receded into his apartment, apparently intending them to follow. Megan shot Arianna a look of curiosity.

"He doesn't trust himself with liquor when he gets stressed," Arianna whispered. "He's got a past."

They followed him through a narrow hallway that opened into a living room perched in the sky, bound by a sheet of curved glass. There were no lights on, and yet the room glowed with the light of nearby buildings, like a moon collecting the radiance of a hundred suns. The most brilliant was the Empire State Building straight ahead; alit in red, white, and blue, it was enough to make even the most jaded citizen feel patriotic. Glancing at it, Arianna wished she could feel the full force of that gale of pride in being an American, but her patriotism had shriveled like the myelin around her nerve cells, and for the same reason.

"Your view is stunning," Megan remarked.

"Distracts from the clutter." He sat in a well-worn chair next to a table littered with yellow legal pads and textbooks. Chinese takeout boxes lay steaming on various scraps of paper. Bits of rice and sauce were splattered on his notes like haphazard punctuation marks.

"Are we interrupting your dinner?" Arianna asked. "We can go—"

He shook his head, wiping up the fallen pieces of food. "Sit."

She and Megan sat on a two-seater couch facing the 270-degree view. It gave them the convenience of not staring at one another during the silence that followed.

"Stiff tongues, eh?" Arianna said. "I can prescribe something for that, you know. It's not a condition you have to live with."

Megan laughed a little. At her feet, a raggedy gray towel lay in a heap. "What's that for?"

"Oh, nothing," Sam said, getting up to grab it. "Just getting cleaned up before going back."

Arianna frowned. "You're going back tonight? Don't tell me you've started sleeping there?"

"So what. I got a cot at Kmart. There's a sink and toilet." He flashed her a challenging look.

She knew better than to argue. "So any improvement since Sunday?"

He cleared his throat. "We're getting low on embryos. I wish we could use yours again," he said to Megan. "Those were as robust as they come."

She grinned. "I'm glad. But Arianna says I can't donate again."

Arianna shook her head. "No, your ovaries need a rest. They were sensitive to the hormones."

Sam hadn't answered her question. She wondered if he had purposely ignored her. Of course, she decided. It was easier than confronting her with the grim reality. She looked at the patches of light scattered up and down the neighboring skyscrapers. Of all the people inside those rooms, how many like her were thinking of death?

"When are you bringing a new batch?" Sam demanded.

"On Friday," she said. "Don't worry, I've got donors lined up for at least the next five weeks."

"So interest is still good?" Megan asked.

"Better than usual. I got back in touch with some of the girls from the CPR club, Sam."

"Oh yeah?"

The CPR club, or the Coalition to Protect Researchers, was a group of about fifty angry Columbia students who united to protest the DEP's formation. Arianna, then a sophomore, had taken on a leading role in recruiting members. Most had been Sam's students.

"You might even remember some of them, Sam."

He shrugged, his expression hard. "I wasn't paying attention to much back then except one thing."

"By the way," Arianna said quickly, "did I tell you I'm going to Long Island on Saturday for dinner with Trent's family?"

Megan smiled strangely at her. "You told me earlier."

"Who is that kid, anyways?" Sam scowled. "Is he the one who phones you?"

"Yes. He's this sweet writer I met at a book signing." She paused. "I know the timing is terrible, but we hit it off really well."

"He doesn't know?" Sam's tone was snide: *Tell me you didn't tell him.*

"Not about you."

"About you?"

"I had to." She pursed her lips. "But we're going to enjoy the present together."

Sam grunted and turned to Megan. "Have you met him?"

"Not yet. I want to."

"I don't know," Sam said, wrinkling his overgrown eyebrows. "Men these days are swine. In my day, there were gentlemen, but not anymore—the feminists won't allow it."

Arianna raised her eyebrows. "My God, it's uncanny, Sam. You really are just like my father."

"What?" He seemed taken aback.

"In a good way," she reassured. "He was the best man I knew." She smiled. "And the most politically incorrect."

"You're not planning to tell that kid, right?"

"He's no kid."

"Well?"

"I wasn't."

"You weren't? Or you aren't?"

Arianna swallowed, wondering if she knew the answer herself.

"Who's she?" Megan interjected, pointing at a picture frame on the wall above Sam's head. Arianna glanced at it: a brunette was smiling playfully, as if sharing an inside joke with the photographer.

Sam did not turn his head. His voice came out strained. "That's my wife, Charlotte."

"She's beautiful."

"She's dead."

"Oh, I'm sorry," Megan murmured.

Sam stayed still, but Arianna could see an ominously bulging vein at his temple.

"You didn't tell her?" he said.

Arianna felt helpless knowing what was about to unfold, as it did every so often, but empathy kept her from trying to prevent it. He needed, maybe more than anything, a sensitive listener—someone to shoulder the burden of the pain if only for a few minutes.

"No, Sam, I don't discuss your personal life."

"Well," he said brusquely to Megan, "let me fill you in."

He rose and began to pace, barely looking at them. "Charlotte had diabetes since she was a girl, the worst affliction that could happen to a high-spirited kid like her. The day I met her in high school, it was after she had passed out in the hall from eating candy. I was the one who took her to the nurse. She thought she was invincible. But she still had to give herself five shots a day and check her blood sugar nonstop. Her arms were like leather from being pricked all the time. But that girl was the best sport there ever was. She saw it as a small price to pay to live.

"It was Charlotte who inspired me to go into biochemistry. My family used to say how nice it was that I wanted to research for her, but they had me all wrong. It was the most selfish career I could have chosen, to the extent that my happiness depended on her well-being.

"After I finished graduate school, we married. We moved to a small apartment near Columbia, where I taught and researched. She would have terrible mood swings out of nowhere, and she started getting tired and depressed. I worked like a fiend, but I wasn't even coming close. Then the genetic breakthroughs in 1998 finally gave us the map to the answer: human embryonic stem cells.

"I joined a group at the school that was doing all kinds of innovative techniques like gene splicing and targeting and regenerative organ growth. . . . We were doing so goddamned well, we never could have dreamed that religious politics would kill it all. It was sixteen years ago in February, the day when science died, when the DEP came into being. I didn't take those bastards seriously, I just couldn't. In less than a year, I was in jail. But how the hell could they have expected me to obey their stupid laws? Would you expect a starving man not to eat the filet mignon on his plate because it came from a fucking cow?"

"Sam—," Arianna cut in. His face scared her; it was the color of a heart attack.

He looked straight at her, breathing hard. "The DEP might as well have killed her."

"Sam—"

"Not only did they wipe out her chance for a cure, but the year I spent in jail, she just got sicker and sicker, and I couldn't take care of her. Do you know what it's like to sit in darkness while your wife's body rots alive, to know you had the chance to save her, but no, you're stuck in a wretched cell next to real killers, and you're alone with your mind. No one can save you from the torment, the guilt, the rage, not the alcohol or the drugs or the sick fantasy that deludes half the men who get out of prison alive—that goddamned farce known as God. There's nothing and no one to help you."

He went on, shaking: "When I got out, I was already destroyed, but watching her die . . . No wonder I became a fucking alcoholic!" He kicked the side of his chair and then stumbled away, limping.

"Sam," Arianna said, softer this time. She got up and walked over to him, expecting him to lash out. But he allowed her to touch his arm, and then to gently pull him back toward his chair.

He sat down forlorn, but when they locked eyes, he grabbed her hand. "For you," he said, "it's not too late."

She squeezed his hand with both of her own, overcome with a hope so fierce, it sucked her breath away.

"As long as we all keep pushing," he said. "I should go back right now. . . ."

Her heart filled with tender warmth, and she kneeled down to his level. "Your mind is exhausted, Sam; your soul is worse than that. Sleep here tonight and start fresh tomorrow."

He looked down.

She lowered her voice. "There was nothing you could have done about any of it."

After a second, he closed his eyes, but whether in defiance or acceptance she couldn't tell. She decided to let him be. Something about their exchange needled her: the look on his face when they locked eyes. It was pure adoration. Arianna knew he probably thought of her as a daughter, but their dynamic was delicate. He was risking his life to save hers. His ferocious work ethic—sleeping at the lab, for God's sake . . . Could it be that she was unintentionally manipulating his affection to drive him to work harder? When she cooked him meals and charmed him with unannounced visits, was a tiny part of her pushing, pushing as much as she could get away with?

She had been told before that she sometimes had a coercive effect on people, though she was oblivious of it. But the thought that she could be exploiting Sam was too disturbing to contemplate. It was also preposterous, she told herself. She knew their friendship was sincere. And he wanted nothing more than to research embryos like the old days; hell, she had practically exhumed him from the liquor cabinet when they first regained contact. Giving him a private lab had been hands down the best thing she could have done for him. She searched his face as if for validation. His eyes glazed over from exhaustion.

She rose uneasily and glanced at Megan, who gave her a pleading look.

"We should go," Arianna said to him. "Are you going to be okay?"

"Fine," he mumbled.

Arianna smiled tentatively, and then bent down and kissed his forehead.

The gratified look in his eyes reassured her that he would, indeed, be fine alone.

"Good night," she said. "We'll show ourselves out."

He nodded.

"Bye," Megan called. "Sorry to have imposed."

Outside the apartment, Arianna turned to Megan and held up a hand.

"I know, I know. I didn't expect that. It's my fault. I should have warned you not to mention his wife."

"Yeah, thanks. But no wonder he's so bitter."

"Welcome to the Dark Ages," Arianna said as they stepped into the elevator. She spoke quickly, to distract herself from that needling worry. "But I think it's good for him to retain that anger, to feel it through and through sometimes, as long as he doesn't go overboard. It keeps his humanity intact—imagine if he just became this jaded shell. I've seen so many old people retire, and then slowly lose their memory and their reason. When the mind loses purpose, it withers. Passion keeps it alive. I just wish he would just direct less rage at himself."

The elevator doors opened, and they walked through the lobby.

"You should just be careful with him, Ar," Megan said.

Arianna's stomach clenched. "What do you mean?"

"The way you can be with people when you're ambitious. I know you don't mean any harm, but just be aware. You know how you used to be with your dad sometimes."

Arianna didn't have to ask. She had been famous in the family as a child for working her charm with her father to get what she wanted, and later as a teenager to get out of trouble. She used to marvel at how easy it was, without even really trying—but then she would feel guilty. The unintentional manipulation seemed almost natural, a bad habit she had to remember to rein in, like her craving for sweets. By now, she thought both had been under control for years.

"Trust me," she replied. "I'm aware."

"You want a lot from him," Megan said, as if she had to be reminded. "More than you've ever wanted from anyone. And he seems so vulnerable."

"I know that. But I'm not trying to push him. I swear on my dad's grave. I would never, ever do anything to hurt him."

Megan held up a hand as they walked into the shivery night and leaned under a nearby awning. "I believe you."

Arianna dropped her voice to a whisper, eager to change subjects. "By the way, how is our little investment doing?"

"Great. Turns out it was pretty undervalued."

"You're kidding. So you could make a killing."

"Me?" Megan smiled pointedly. "It's only mine in name."

"Oh, I'd let you keep any profits. Look how much you've done!"

Megan shrugged. "Buying and selling I do all the time."

"Plus your eggs . . ."

"Those were my gift to you."

Arianna chuckled. "Who would have thought, when we were kids, that one day I would be thanking you for your eggs?"

Megan smiled briefly, then turned serious. "I've been thinking about this new man of yours."

"Oh?"

"Are you sure it's the right time to get so involved?"

Arianna shrugged. "It's been a long time since I've felt this way about a man. Better late than never, right?"

Megan eyed her. "What are you not telling me?"

"Well, I know it sounds like a bad idea, but I wish I could tell Trent everything. It's so hard not to!"

Megan closed her eyes. "I was afraid of that."

"But, Meg—"

Again, she raised a hand. "Would you trust him with your life, Arianna? He could rat you out in a second—and make a quick grand. Don't be impulsive."

"I think he values my life more than a Vigilant Citizen Award," Arianna replied indignantly.

"Do you even know what he thinks of this kind of research?"

Arianna shook her head. "I've steered clear. Part of me doesn't want to find out."

"If he seemed the slightest bit suspicious, I'd move and change my number if I were you. Hell, even my name."

"Come on."

"You want to end up like Sam's wife?"

"No," Arianna said vehemently. "But you don't know Trent. He's been so good to me, even after I told him about my MS. And it's not just that. I remember to have fun when I'm with him."

"Talk about an elephant in the room."

Arianna hesitated. "I guess I should at least find out where he stands. But if he truly cares about me, how could he not support research that might *save my life*?"

"I don't know," Megan replied, feigning thoughtfulness. "Maybe you should ask the judge who threw Sam in jail. I bet he could tell you the answer."

As Trent watched Arianna step out of her clinic on Friday evening, he immediately noticed that something was different: In one hand, she was carrying a strange black case. Although the edges appeared rectangular, it bulged around the middle; the shape was unlike any carrier Trent had ever seen. Despite its bulk, it did not appear to be heavy—her fingers curled easily around the handle as if it were a Styrofoam lunch box.

Trent rose from his furtive bench in the corner of the park and followed her east on a now-recognizable path, as the people around him hurried to escape the city for Christmas weekend. He and Arianna were planning to leave the next day, but she had rejected his suggestion to stay in Long Island overnight, emphasizing the need to return to Manhattan for Sunday morning Mass on Christmas Day. Being fed her lies disgusted and even disappointed him, if he was honest with himself.

She was walking slightly faster now, as she had become more adept with her cane, but her pace was still below a comfortable walking speed, requiring Trent to maximize the distance between them. The rush hour crowd pounded the sidewalks, helping to obscure him in their midst. She kept walking east, crossing one avenue after another, with a purposeful stride and confident posture. It struck Trent as odd, despite her hampered gait, that she was considered handicapped: far from being a helpless woman, she projected self-sufficiency. Her attitude of strength seemed to negate her body's weakness, and he could not deny that it endowed her with even greater beauty. A beauty that he now thought was undeserved.

They crossed Fourth Avenue, and then Third, Second, First, like a straight arrow through the heart of the East Village. As he trailed her, Trent thought about his most recent instruction, one that unsettled and excited him: to divulge something to Arianna so that she would feel obligated to return the confidence.

"It's human psychology," Dopp had explained at the office that afternoon. "She will think you are trusting her if you open up about yourself, and will feel compelled to do the same. Make her think you are bonding in ways that are private and exclusive to your relationship."

It was a smart move, Trent thought, but one that required careful planning, and for now, he was at a loss. Better to focus on the present. Where in the world was she going? The farther east they walked, the more the streets were lined with decrepit buildings and stooped beggars. It was not a neighborhood Trent pictured Arianna frequenting, but she appeared unfazed by her surroundings.

At Avenue C, she turned left and out of sight. Far behind, Trent hurried up to the corner, dodging panhandlers, and peeked around it. She was turning right two blocks up ahead, at Tenth Street. He dashed there, charging across the shadow of a familiarly dilapidated church. He turned the corner just in time to see her disappear again, turning right into an alleyway between Avenues C and D. *Where the hell?* he thought—but he had no time to dwell on the bizarreness of her path: he poked his head into the alleyway, fearful for her to be venturing there alone. It was narrow, like an accidental crack in the city's grid. The backs of buildings on either side blocked out the sun's low rays, and the space was deserted, save for Arianna's silhouette receding into its depths, the black case close at her side.

Abruptly, she stopped, slipped her cane underneath her arm, and gripped a black railing on the right side of the alley. As Trent looked on, baffled, Arianna stepped down a staircase until he could see only her torso, her shoulders, her head. Like the sun dipping below the horizon, it was too captivating to turn away, despite the danger of watching. Then she was gone.

Trent stared at the spot where she had vanished beneath the street, racking his brain for an explanation. Was it an illusion? Where was he? What was happening? He put his fingertips on his forehead. A fleeting sense of disorientation made him glance up to the sky, but he never got that far. Instead, his gaze stopped on the steeple above the stairs she had descended.

NINE

So you didn't lie to me after all, Trent thought, wiping his hand across his forehead. *You are going to church.*

He stared at the black railing Arianna had clutched only moments before. What could she be doing at the bottom of those stairs?

He had not moved from the edge of the alley, as if walking into or away from it would lead to an irreversible error: either a premature revelation of his identity or a wasted opportunity to possibly catch Arianna mid-crime. *Careful,* he told himself. *Think.*

He knew he had to consider his options, but then he also needed to ignore the feeling of vindication pumping through him, rejoicing at the fact she had not actually lied to him about attending church. Did this mean she really was Christian? Maybe she was part of a fringe sect that held their services underground for religious reasons, although that seemed unlikely. Suspicious, yes, he thought. But criminal? Uncertain. *Do I have probable cause to go after her? No. Would following her down the steps damage any hope of solving the case? Possibly.*

He took a step back. *I'll wait to act,* he thought, *until I investigate this place later myself, and I'll wait to tell Dopp until I have it figured out; why get him all excited for nothing?*

Trent retreated from the alley and hailed a cab at the first corner. He strained to recall what, exactly, Arianna had told him about her religion and the frequency of her church attendance. That night in her apartment, her tone had conveyed a subtle sarcasm that he did not understand at the time, but now, he felt as if he might be on the verge of deciphering why she had laughed so easily at his disbelief.

The watch, he remembered, her words were on the watch! He looked at the device on his left wrist that managed to be both old-fashioned and high-tech, and rewound it to their conversation from that night. Then he listened:

"What, are you imagining I have some secret double life? Doctor by day, superwoman by night?"

"You tell me."

"Well, it might come as a surprise, but I'm actually going to church."

His shocked laughter. "Why?"

"To practice my religion."

"Well, what's your religion?"

"I go to a Christian church, like most everyone else."

Trent rewound the recording for a split second.

"I go to a Christian church, like most everyone else."

"Which one?"

"It's a small congregation in the East Village. You wouldn't know it."

Gaping, he stopped the recording and cleared through the fog of his own assumptions to recognize a fact that had escaped him:

She never said she *was* Christian.

His mind reeled from this realization for a few seconds before launching the next, inevitable questions: So what was really her religion? Why that carcass of a church?

He pictured her hobbled figure retreating into the alley.

And what was in that black case?

On the train ride to Long Island together the next day, Trent's desire for the truth was maddening. It sprang not only from professional determination, but also from the hope lodged in his heart like a stray bullet—unwanted and yet impossible to remove. Such a stubborn wish—for her to be as innocent as the embryos in her care—persisted against his better instincts.

He felt even worse for her genuine excitement about meeting his family. A homemade chocolate cake sat on her lap, covered in tinfoil. Trent pictured her limping around her kitchen, gathering all the right ingredients to please the people who meant so much to him. How could she know how pathetic an effort it was?

"Hey," he blurted after they left the train and got into a cab, "I know we haven't talked much about religion, but I thought you should know my family's actually pretty religious."

She looked surprised. "They are?"

"Yes."

"Oh. I didn't imagine them that way."

You weren't supposed to, he thought.

"Yeah. I just thought I should—" *Warn you,* he almost said. "—tell you, in case you weren't expecting it."

"I wasn't," she said, not unkindly. "I didn't think you grew up religious."

"Yeah. I'm not so much now," he said truthfully. "But they still think I am."

"Let me make sure I have everyone straight," Arianna said. "Your uncle Gideon is your father's brother."

"Right."

"And what does he do?"

"He's a retired consultant."

"What does he do now?"

"His wife is pregnant with their third kid, so he's staying home to help raise them."

"Wow, that's a big age difference between you and your cousins."

"Yeah. His wife is fifteen years younger." Trent smiled; this fact was true.

"Got it. And what are the kids' names?"

He swallowed, straining to filter this previously minor information from his memory. "Abby," he said, remembering her picture on Dopp's desk. "And Ethan."

The cab pulled up in front of a house on a cul-de-sac lined with basketball hoops and neat lawns. His parents' black sedan was already parked on the curb.

On the doormat, Trent noticed the Christian fish symbol next to the word WELCOME. His parents had a similar mat. He stepped on it as he rang the bell.

As he heard cheerful dings echo inside the house, Trent felt oddly removed, as if he were watching himself on the doorstep, watching the door swing open. . . .

And then Dopp was before them, burly and smiling. He wore a red collared shirt and khaki slacks, the first time Trent had seen him without a suit and tie.

"Trent, so good to see you!" he exclaimed, pulling him into a hug that felt uncomfortably close. Trent smelled tangy cologne on his neck and fought the urge to stiffen. Upon release, he inched back.

"Uncle Gideon, this is Arianna. Arianna, Uncle Gideon."

Arianna smiled and leaned in to kiss his clean-shaven cheek. "Nice to meet you."

Trent looked down, as if privy to a vulgar sight.

"Likewise," Dopp answered. "Merry Christmas," he added, looking only at her.

"Same to you," she said, extending the chocolate cake. "Thank you for having me."

"How nice," Dopp said, taking it. "Come on in. What happened?" He pointed to her cane.

"I had a bike accident last week," she replied.

"Oh, I'm sorry to hear that."

Arianna took off her coat, wearing underneath a red satin dress cut in a straight line above her breasts. No one could fault it for being too revealing, as it showed no cleavage, but Trent thought it somehow inappropriate. It teased her curves, exposed her naked collarbone.

He breathed in the house's warm, spicy aroma, like the inside of a cinnamon candle. The smell was pleasant, though his throat seemed unnaturally narrow. He took Arianna's hand as they followed Dopp through the foyer into a living room where his parents and Dopp's wife were sitting. His parents rose at the sight of them. Trent smiled tentatively and felt his nervousness escalate, the way he used to feel when he acted in front of his theater class in high school: unable to lose himself in the character, aware that everybody could see through his pretense anyway.

"Merry Christmas," he said to them, arms outstretched. They chorused it back, both hugging him. Trent noticed they looked stiffer than usual; his mother's embrace felt mechanical, and his father's smile—usually so genuine—was surely a veneer that concealed the wheels of judgment spinning behind his eyes.

"Mom, Dad, this is Arianna," Trent said. "Arianna, my parents."

"So pleased to meet you both," Arianna said. She leaned in to kiss his father's cheek. Dopp's wife rose with effort from the couch, and Dopp hurried to her side to help her up. She was heavily pregnant, and looked haggard, with stringy brown hair and swollen legs. She had a small oval face with chiseled features; Trent had seen a pretty picture of her before, but in person, he noticed the bags under her eyes and the effort with which she smiled first at him, and then at Arianna.

"Welcome," she said, giving Trent a one-armed hug and then shaking Arianna's hand. "I'm Joanie, Gideon's wife. Nice to meet you."

"You, too," Arianna said, glancing sideways at him, and then back to Joanie. "Are the kids upstairs?"

"Oh, no," Joanie responded. "They're at a kids' event at our church that's held every Christmas Eve. They look forward to it every year. Sorry you won't get to meet them."

"That's too bad," Trent said, contemplating the irony that the adults had banished the children for fear that honesty might disrupt their grown-up machinations.

Dopp smiled at Trent as though he could read this thought, and put an arm around his wife's waist. Like an airborne virus, awkwardness struck. They stood in a silent cluster, and Trent knew they were all wary of speaking first, paralyzed by the fear that the slightest slipup would doom them all. In the corner of the room, he noticed a twinkling six-foot-tall tree decorated in gold bulbs. Shiny boxes lay wrapped beneath.

"You have a beautiful tree," he remarked.

"Thank you," Dopp said. "I did it all myself this year."

"That's not true," Joanie said. "I put up a few of the lower bulbs."

"You weren't supposed to help," Dopp replied, kissing his wife on the cheek.

"When are you due?" Arianna asked her.

"January thirtieth."

Arianna smiled. "Just a few more weeks to go."

"Five," Joanie said.

"It'll go by before you know it."

"So is it too early to break out the champagne?" Trent asked.

Heads shook all around.

"I'm starving," his mother said. "Any chance the chicken is ready?"

Dopp nodded. "Just about. Why don't we all go sit down. Trent, would you like to help me serve?"

"Sure."

Joanie led Arianna and his parents out into the dining room, while Dopp escorted him the other direction into a large kitchen that smelled of rosemary.

"So?" Dopp said, setting Arianna's cake dish on the granite counter. "Any progress since yesterday?"

Trent thought of the deserted alley and the decrepit church.

"Not yet," he said.

A troubled look clouded Dopp's face. "Do you ever feel dirty around her?"

Trent nodded guiltily, surprised at Dopp's perceptiveness; lying had never felt right to him, even when he knew it was.

Dopp turned to face the sink and thrust his hands under the sensor-activated faucet. "Like after being with her, you can never be fully cleansed?"

Oh, Trent thought, *that kind of dirty.* He watched the water spraying off his boss's hands. "Yeah," he lied. "I know how you feel."

Dopp dried his hands. "So did you confess anything like we talked about?"

"Not yet." What could he confess to her?

"Do it tonight, after you leave."

"I will."

"Now, let's get back out there. I should get to know her a little better."

• • •

As soon as they were all seated with plates full of chicken, yams, and broccoli, Arianna lifted her fork to a table of watchful silence. Trent put a hand on her thigh under the table, and she set it down.

"Let us first say the Lord's Prayer," Dopp said. "If everybody would like to repeat it with me . . ."

They bowed their heads and began in unison.

"Our Father who art in Heaven, hallowed be thy name. Thy Kingdom come. Thy will be done on earth as it is in Heaven. . . ." Trent sneaked a glance around the table: Dopp's gaze had settled upon Arianna's barely moving lips. "Give us this, our daily bread. And forgive us our trespasses, as we forgive those who trespass against us. And lead us not into temptation; but deliver us from evil. For thine is the kingdom, and the power, and the glory, for ever and ever. *Amen*."

Heads lifted. Trent crossed his fingers under the table, hoping his boss would not seize upon Arianna's obvious disregard of the most famous prayer in Christianity. But to his relief, Dopp continued to speak.

"And on this Christmas Eve, let us all take a moment to remember the Lord Jesus Christ's ultimate sacrifice."

Dopp dropped his chin to his chest, as did everyone else. Ten seconds passed before Dopp lifted his head and cleared his throat.

"Bon appétit!" he declared.

Trent's mother and father echoed the words and lifted their forks. Arianna smiled at Dopp. "I don't know if you're a good cook yet," she said, "but it definitely smells like it."

Trent stared at the food on his plate, wondering what he could stomach in the absence of hunger.

"I hope so," Dopp replied. "So, Arianna, Trent tells us you're a doctor at a fertility clinic?"

"Yes," she said happily. "That's my baby."

Trent's mother gave a small laugh. "That must be such a rewarding career."

"It is," Arianna replied. "Most of the time. Speaking of babies, how's your pregnancy going, Joanie?"

"Surprisingly well for my age. Although not so much when I was younger. In fact, a few years ago, Gideon and I went to several fertility clinics, and they were all frauds."

Trent stared at Joanie. *At least pretend to treat her like a guest,* he thought.

Arianna chewed a mouthful of chicken and swallowed before she spoke. "I'm sorry to hear that."

Dopp shot a glance at his wife, who was watching Arianna.

"We believe only in the natural way now," Joanie said. "God didn't want us to interfere with all those drugs."

Arianna didn't respond, taking a sip of her Coke instead.

"Whatever works, right?" Trent said breezily.

"So, do you do abortions there?" Joanie asked. Trent's mother gasped, and Joanie turned to her. "Don't pretend we're not all wondering, Becky."

Arianna held Joanie's gaze. "Not since it was outlawed."

"But you did before that?"

"Yes. But I can see we have our differences, so I'd rather not discuss it, as it's been a moot point for a long time."

Joanie and Dopp both reddened, and Trent could see they were restraining themselves. His father pushed food around his plate, looking uncomfortable, and Trent felt sorry for involving his parents at all; manipulation went against their grain, though he knew they were happy to do anything in service of the DEP.

His mother piped up then, making an effort to dispel the tension. "Arianna," she said, "tell us why you decided to be a doctor in the first place. What a difficult profession, and the years of work it must have taken!"

Arianna smiled kindly at her. "Well, I grew up with two biology professors, so it was pretty hard not to find the body fascinating. And I love seeing a new life come out of my work—it's very gratifying to help give people the gift of a child. Although unfortunately," she said, glancing at Dopp and Joanie, "the science of eliminating infertility is not yet perfect."

"Children are the ultimate blessing," Mrs. Rowe said quickly. "I really do believe every one is a miracle."

Arianna turned back to her. "You both must be so proud of your son. I can't imagine any professions more challenging than the creative ones, especially writing. I don't know how he does it."

Trent's breath caught in his throat as he met his parents' eyes. They smiled curiously at him.

"Yes, of course," his father said after a pause that Trent hoped would pass unnoticed. "Trent has always been a talented writer."

"Have either of you read what he's working on?" Arianna asked.

"I haven't shown it to anyone yet," Trent cut in. "Not till it's done."

"Well, I'm sure we'll all look forward to that," Arianna said. "Excuse me. Where is the restroom?" She pushed her chair back, and Dopp pointed her around the corner, back toward the living room. "The food was very good, by the way, thank you," she said, picking up her cane and walking away. As soon as she was out of sight, the group uttered a soft collective sigh.

"Intermission," Joanie joked.

Trent almost rolled his eyes. Dopp's flush of anger had dispersed, replaced by his characteristic half smile; the director was satisfied.

"Well, we got what we came for, didn't we?" Dopp said in a low voice. "There is no way that woman is Christian like she told you, Trent."

"Seems that way."

"She refused to say the Lord's Prayer, for heaven's sake!" Joanie said. "Didn't you see that?"

"It was pretty pitiful," Trent agreed. But then again, he thought, she never did claim she was Christian.

Trent's mother and Joanie exchanged grimaces, while he made an expression of distaste, appearing to agree with their sentiment.

"Honey, are you paying the poor man overtime?" Joanie asked.

Dopp looked apologetically at Trent. With the prospects for the department's share of the state budget still looking poor, there was no way it could afford overtime. But Trent knew he would be well reimbursed if he cracked the case, for his success could resuscitate their hopes for more money.

"For having a disease, she doesn't look half-bad," Mr. Rowe

remarked. Mrs. Rowe just shook her head. He looked at Trent. "A writer, eh?"

"I was, once," Trent replied.

"You were a fabulous writer," his mother said.

"Soon," his father said, "I bet you'll be writing her a nice ticket."

"Oh, it will be much worse than that if we can peg her for something criminal, which she is clearly capable of," Dopp said. "She didn't even apologize after *admitting* she did abortions."

Joanie put her hand on the nape of his neck. "I couldn't help asking." Her face twisted. "Can you imagine what families like us go through to have a child, and there she is, cutting babies out of wombs, and then dumping them like trash."

Dopp caressed Joanie's globe of a belly. "She was totally unashamed, and that told me all I need to know about who she is."

Trent heard the sound of a cane hitting wood floor, and his stomach toppled over.

"To minimize the chances of anyone slipping up," Dopp whispered, "Trent, check out soon and we'll follow suit. And thank you both for coming," Dopp muttered to his parents. "We should get together some other time, for real."

His voice returned to its normal baritone as he addressed the table. "So who wants seconds?"

Arianna appeared and trudged behind Trent into her chair as everyone shook heads.

"I'm so full," Dopp said. "I think I'll have to wait on your cake, Arianna."

"I couldn't even think about dessert," Trent said, and before anyone could engage Arianna in conversation: "By the way, Mom, how was your charity drive this week?"

Trent leaned back and grabbed Arianna's hand under the table as his mother talked about what happened at the drive. For once, he appreciated her volubility, and he suspected everyone else did, too. At the first lull, he cleared his throat.

"Well, everyone, sorry to cut it short, but we should probably get going. It's a pretty long ride back." He looked at Arianna and squeezed her hand under the table. "We have a party in the city tonight."

Arianna nodded, and he sensed she was grateful for his exit strategy. "Thank you very much for having me," she said.

A chorus of pleasantries followed. As the group rose from the table, Trent's father offered to drive them back to the train station. At the front door, everyone exchanged handshakes and hugs and Merry Christmases, but Trent knew that they were all rushing to be through with one another.

When the door closed behind them, he let out a brief sigh. The feeling of goodwill that usually came over him like magic every Christmas season was missing, he noticed; all he felt was an understanding of the sense of dirtiness Dopp had described.

As they pulled up to the station, Trent saw that the train was already waiting with open doors, which expedited their good-byes. The train stood in the station for only one minute, and it had already been at least thirty seconds; with a sinking heart, he appraised the staircase leading up to the platform, knowing there was no way Arianna could rush up it.

"I have to do this," he said. "Hold on to your cane."

Then he lifted her into his arms, as she squealed with delight. "My dress!"

"No one's looking," he said, racing up the stairs two at a time. Then he ran across the platform and slid between the closing train doors. He let her down gently as the train groaned forward. She smiled at him with that same windblown exuberance he remembered from their bike rides.

"It's nice to go fast again," she said.

He chuckled and guided her to two open seats.

"So, what was up with that sly exit?" she asked, taking the seat next to him.

"That's about all I can take of my family at one time," he joked. "They get kind of overbearing when they're all together—I don't know if you noticed. . . ."

She snorted. "You said it first."

Trent looked down at his lap, recalling Dopp's instructions from their impromptu meeting in the kitchen. He sighed deeply.

"What's wrong?" Arianna asked. "I'm sorry if I offended you—"

"No, it's not that." *Won't it help if my confession is truthful,* he wondered, *since she'll see it's sincere?*

"The thing is . . ." Or was he just rationalizing Dopp's instructions so he could open up to her for real?

"Yeah?" she said, putting her hand on his.

He looked into her concerned blue eyes. "The thing is, well, I've actually never admitted this to anyone before . . . but for some reason, I feel like telling you."

"Okay . . ."

"I get this weird feeling sometimes, like something's wrong with me, but mostly just when I'm around my family." He swallowed, waiting for her brows to knot in confusion, for her lips to curve down in solidarity.

But her expression remained placid, save for the comprehension in her eyes. "I understand completely."

"You do?"

"I'll tell you my opinion as long as you promise not to hold it against me."

"No, please, tell me."

"Your family—particularly your aunt and uncle—they're just as judgmental as the God they believe in, and if you don't follow their ideas to a tee, they'll make their wrath felt. So I can see how they would make you feel uncomfortable if you ever diverge from what they consider good. Have you ever stood up to them?"

"Of course." He racked his brain, thinking of the only example he could recall. "Back when I was a journalist covering religion, I had this whole crisis of faith because of a bunch of church scandals, one after the next. It made me seriously doubt God. I told my parents I was done."

"And what did they say?"

"They were furious, and sent me to talk to our priest. . . ."

"And? Did he convince you to keep believing?"

"Yeah," he said, feeling sheepish for some reason. *So?* he wanted to add.

"Well, that was then. What about now?"

"I don't know. I'm still trying to figure it out."

There was a pause. *This is supposed to be about you,* he thought.

"And in the meantime," she said, "you feel guilty for not feeling as religious as you think you should be, right?"

Trent's eyes widened. "How did you know that?"

"I can tell they've put a lot of pressure on you to be a certain way. What do they think of your taking time to write fiction? I noticed they weren't overly supportive."

He shrugged.

"I bet they don't like it," she said. "Writing is the most selfish career of all, since it's mainly to challenge your own mind. No charity drives there."

He nodded weakly. At least investigative journalism had been a service to society, while personal writing was selfish, he realized, the very opposite of the self-sacrifice he had always been told was right.

He suddenly laughed out loud at the bizarre notion that she could be a murderer.

"What's so funny?" she asked, smiling.

For the first time, he seized her cheeks and kissed her, trying, through his lips, to communicate the one truth he could not disguise—perhaps the only truth of which he was certain—that he wanted her mouth, her body, her mind; to be close to her, to know everything about her, as a lover and not an investigator; to shed the skin of that person whom he had blindly impersonated for so long. His kiss was fierce as his fingers buried into her hair.

Stop, his mind roared. *Remember yourself!*

He pulled away with dogged effort, like a magnet repudiating its pole. "Maybe we shouldn't do this here," he muttered.

Arianna looked worn out from the exertion. "You wouldn't believe how wiped I am from this trip."

"It's the cold," he said quickly.

"And your family loved me like a daughter." She flashed him a glimmer of a smile. "Listen, I would invite you back to my place, but I need to sleep."

"That's fine," he said, feeling clashing tides of relief, disappointment, and guilt.

"I'm sorry," he blurted. "About my family."

"Don't be. You are not your family."

His smile quivered as he grasped her small hand—it seemed incapable of the forceful handshake he remembered from their first meeting. "I'm sorry you're tired."

"Me, too. Thanks for being so patient. I know most men aren't."

"No problem. I'm not in a rush if you're not up for it—that's not why I'm here."

She smiled gratefully.

At least, he thought sadly, it was the truth.

After they parted in front of Penn Station an hour later, anticipation quickened his pulse as he hailed a cab. He couldn't wait to get back to the alley, and twenty minutes later, he was standing at the threshold.

It was darker than before, blanketed in the shadows of adjacent buildings. No streetlights reached into its depths. Trent looked around—the only person in sight was a bum slumped across the street.

He stepped across the threshold, keeping his elbows close to his body. Though it was below freezing outside, the alley felt colder. He stopped and looked behind himself, knowing that he was being paranoid; Arianna was on her way home, not here. About thirty yards away, the church's tall steeple beckoned. He pulled out his phone and shone the electric blue light on the ground. Trash had pooled there: yellowed wrappers, cigarettes, decaying food. He tiptoed over it, shivering. The air was fetid with the scents of urine and dirt, and he held his breath until he reached the black railing under the steeple. Ten concrete steps led down to a steel door.

He scanned the empty alley behind him before climbing down the steps—large, steep blocks. He breathed in sharply when he reached the bottom. The stench had disappeared, replaced by floating dust he had kicked up on the stairs. Up close, he could see the door was scratched and dented, but no less impervious to being opened. Above and below a brass knob, there were two keyholes. Trent grabbed the knob and tried to twist it as hard as he could. It didn't budge. He let go. What was this damn place? Why was she hiding it from him?

With a grunt, he kicked the door, sending a shock of pain through his toes.

Why did he care so much?

Again he kicked the door, taking satisfaction in the release of incongruous emotions that had been mounting all night.

"Who's that?" growled a male voice from behind the door.

Trent froze.

"Hello?" prompted the voice.

Trent did not dare breathe.

"If you're a hoodlum, you better get lost," the voice snarled. "You don't want to deal with me."

Images of gunshots and slaughter skipped through Trent's mind with terrifying plausibility; he was unarmed, in the middle of a squalid alley, and alone with a threatening voice. He turned and scampered to the top of the stairs, tripping over the steep blocks as fast as he could, before sprinting back to the edge of the alley, stepping carelessly on the pools of debris. Under the streetlamp, the sidewalk gleamed with alluring beauty.

TEN

The confessional booth in the back of Trent's church smelled like musty wood. He closed the door behind him and knelt in the cramped space to avoid revealing his identity to the priest on the other side of the screen. Hammered into the wood above the screen was a bloodred cross. On the kneeler was a plaque with the Act of Contrition engraved on it. Trent skimmed the words, feeling guilt and despair mingling in his gut:

"O my God, I am heartily sorry for having offended Thee, and I detest all my sins, because of thy just punishment, but most of all because they offend Thee, my God, Who are all-good and deserving of all my love. I firmly resolve, with the help of Thy grace to confess my sins, to do penance and to amend my life. Amen."

Guilt, because the words meant nothing to him—despair, because he wished they did.

"Hello, there, my child," came the priest's gentle voice. "What is it you would like to confess on this Christmas morning?"

"Merry Christmas, Father." Trent paused, suddenly reluctant to confess anything at all. It was obvious what the priest was going to tell him—and who was he to dictate the terms of Trent's life?

"Merry Christmas to you, my son. What's on your mind?"

But whom else could he turn to? "I have a problem," he started.

"Go on. You are in the right place."

"Well, I'm confused about my work. I'm on a big case, a criminal case. There's a lot of pressure on me to solve it, but . . ."

"Yes?"

"I might be falling for the woman I'm supposed to be investigating." Trent bit his lip; speaking the words felt blasphemous, yet also relieving.

"That is a very big problem indeed."

Trent looked around the tiny space he was kneeling in, growing more claustrophobic by the second. He could barely stretch his elbows out. "I should go," he said, beginning to stand.

"Wait," the priest commanded. "Don't go. I know this isn't easy, but God sent you to me for a reason. He wants to help you. Please."

How do you know? Trent thought. *Are you God?*

But he knelt back down. "I don't know what to think," he finally said. "She's spun my head around. And I'm pretty sure she's no Christian. She might even look down on—" *Us,* he almost said. "—on religion."

"Oh, dear—"

"Plus, I know she's hiding something from me," Trent interrupted. "It kills me that it might be something heinous . . . and that she doesn't trust me enough to tell me."

"She sounds very dangerous. Recall the Lord's Prayer: 'Lead us not into temptation, and deliver us from evil.' It sounds like you need reminding of this verse."

Trent shook his head, his voice rising. "But how can you say she's evil when you don't even know her? She's also very sick. There isn't much time, and I feel like every second I'm not with her is a waste!"

The priest's voice grew stern. "If you feel you are incapable of doing your job in an ethical manner, you must resign and stay far away from her."

"Then I'd have nothing left!"

"You certainly cannot have both. If you must continue with your job, then I urge you to direct the temptations of your flesh elsewhere, toward a woman who respects the Lord and her fellow man, a good Christian like I know you are in your heart. But if you let your base desire for this one woman overcome your ethical sensibilities, that is a very grave sin indeed."

Trent raged silently; this was exactly what he had expected, and just what he didn't want to hear.

"Recall, my son, James one verses two to five and twelve to fifteen. 'Blessed is the man who remains steadfast under trial, for when he has stood the test, he will receive the crown of life, which God has promised to those who love Him. Let no one say when he is tempted, 'I am being tempted by God,' for God cannot be tempted with evil, and He himself tempts no one. But each person is tempted when he is lured and enticed by his own desire. Then desire when it has conceived gives birth to sin, and sin when it is fully grown brings forth death.'"

The priest's words rushed past Trent's ears and echoed around him in the small chamber.

"This verse should become second nature to you," the priest went on, "a fallback for your troubled conscience. May the Lord's grace guide you to eternal salvation."

"Thank you, Father," Trent mumbled.

The screen shut, and Trent rose, rubbing his sore knees. There was some truth in the priest's advice: If he could make himself forget Arianna, he might still be able to get his life back. There was no better time and place to start.

He approached the first woman he saw leaving church that morning who looked to be around his age. She looked delicately breakable, like a ballerina in a snow globe. With the confidence of necessity, he strode toward her with a forced smile and introduced himself. When she smiled encouragingly, he took a chance and asked her out to brunch, and to his surprise, she accepted.

They started walking toward a restaurant up the block. Emma, whom he vaguely recalled having seen before, admitted that she had spotted him for the first time at a service several months earlier.

"Why didn't you come say hello?" he asked.

She shrugged, smiling down at the sidewalk. "I don't know. Fear, I guess."

"Don't tell me I'm that good looking," he teased.

She blushed, and he got the distinct feeling that he had made her uncomfortable. At the restaurant, the hostess led them to a two-seater table by the window. Crystal wineglasses stood neatly next to silverware on a white tablecloth. A waitress came by and poured them champagne and water, and handed them two laminated menus.

"This is nice," she remarked sadly, as if she were watching from the other side of the window.

He nodded, wondering if she were unaccustomed to luxury.

"So how come you don't have any big plans today?" he asked.

"My family lives on the West Coast, and I couldn't take off enough time from work to visit them."

He groaned. "What do you do?"

"I'm a community outreach coordinator at a nonprofit. It's a volunteer ministry that encourages inner city kids to embrace Christ."

"Wow." He eyed her with a new respect. "Must be a tough job."

"It is."

"So you must have to really love it to be able to get up and do that every day."

"You would think." She cradled her elbows against her body. The creases in her forehead were like dry ravines stretching to her hairline.

"What do you mean?"

"I hate my job. But that's why it's right for me."

"Huh?"

"It's a sacrifice," she said, setting her elbows on the table. "I'm living my life to help others know God, just like Mother Teresa and Christ himself. My parents always said there were no better footsteps to follow."

"Well, if it's so honorable, then why don't you like it?"

"Do you think anyone dreams of walking into Spanish Harlem for a living with nothing but a Bible and a prayer?"

"What did you dream of?" Trent asked quietly.

"I was going to be a Broadway star," she said as the creases on her forehead deepened. "I was going to be Roxy in *Chicago*."

He did not smile, for he knew the slightest lift of his lips would discredit her dream as naïve.

"I know what you're thinking," she said. "It's so impossible. My parents thought so, too. But I was good. I even secretly went on an audition for the part once, ten years ago in college. I got called back, too."

"You did? What happened?"

"I didn't show up." She lifted her chin with a melancholy smile.

"*What?*"

She nodded.

"Why not?"

"I thought about Jesus, and I realized how selfish I was being. Singing was a waste of time, but I didn't think I would have the strength to turn down the part if they offered it to me. So I just never went back."

A pang of regret crumpled Trent's gut. "But you threw away your dream!"

"Don't you see how it's better this way? So many people are benefiting from my sacrifice and getting closer to God."

"But . . . aren't you unhappy?"

"So? I know the Lord will reward me in Heaven."

"With what?" he demanded, not caring about his impertinence.

She looked at him crossly. "Eternal salvation."

For a moment, Trent seriously considered the prospect of existing forever in some other realm that promised intangible paradise.

"What are you planning to do for all that time?" he asked, only half-joking.

She raised an offended eyebrow, a response she seemed to feel would suffice.

"So you don't know, then," Trent said, aware that he was pressing her for an answer she could not give him—that nobody could give anyone—and that the girl before him was a mirror of his future self, plunged irrevocably into a religious life she did not want—a living catalyst for the realization of a truth only his own reasoning mind could reach.

"She was right," he breathed. "She was completely right about me."

"Who was right about what?"

"I always did everything my parents and the priests said I should," he said, ignoring her question. "Until lately, I barely questioned whether it was right for me. Or even right at all."

"Well, only God knows what's right for us."

"But how do you know what He knows? Or that He's right? Or" —Trent suddenly thought—"even exists?"

She looked disturbed. "What are you talking about? What else is there?"

"I don't know," he said, feeling his heart start to hammer, signaling the precarious loosening of the linchpin of his belief: blind faith. "But I know this doesn't make sense. There has to be something else. . . ."

"I don't know what you're talking about."

"I have to quit the case," he declared, marveling at the liberty of allowing himself to listen to the flow of his own, independent thoughts—as if from a repressed underground, they sprang, softly at first, and then louder, demanding to be heard, drowning out the impostor ideas he had for so long tried to believe were his own. One thought clamored above the rest, resounding with certainty throughout his entire brain: *I love her.*

I could never love a criminal, he reasoned, *so there must be some terrible misunderstanding; she must be innocent, there must be a good explanation for everything. I'll quit tomorrow, and then we can spend the rest of her days together. . . . She will never have to know who I was. . . .*

"—you listening to me, Trent? I was asking what you do for a living?"

"I'm sorry," he said, noticing her pout. "I'm really sorry. I have to go—but listen, here's a hundred bucks. Get whatever you want and keep the change."

He withdrew his wallet and slapped a bill on the tablecloth as he stood up. "Merry Christmas," he said. "And do me a favor: Enjoy yourself."

"What? Where are you—?"

But he was already heading toward the door. Before he turned the corner, he looked over his shoulder at her bewildered face and knew there was no language he could use to explain—none she would understand. But he still owed her something.

"And Emma?" he called back.

From the table, she raised her eyebrows.

"Thank you!" he yelled, and hurried out.

The next morning at work, Trent walked to Dopp's office. He lifted his fist to the wood, silently rehearsing his excuse one last time. He could never tell Dopp the truth, which would mean expulsion from the department, immediate severance of pay and benefits, and probable criminal prosecution for sabotage. Exhaling a breath, he knocked.

"Come in," Dopp called.

From the high pitch, Trent could tell he was in a good mood. He felt an ember of worry spark; the fall would be even steeper now. With a grim expression, he walked in and closed the door. Dopp was typing, and it took him a second to look up.

"Trent! I've been dying to know what happened after you left our house. Did she say anything?"

"No, nothing significant, but . . ."

Dopp swiveled in his chair to face him. "But what?"

"I want to talk to you."

"Do I not look like I'm listening?"

"The thing is . . . I think I'm doing too well."

Dopp stared at him. "I don't understand."

Trent's carefully planned sequence of words burst like confetti in his brain, leaving him to grope for coherent snatches of explanation. He licked the dry roof of his mouth.

"The problem is, she's falling in love with me, and it's going too far. It's really making me uncomfortable; she's dying, for God's sake! And I think she would have confided in me by now, if anything was going on. But we still have no proof . . . maybe we should let this one go."

Trent swallowed hard, already starting to doubt the persuasiveness of his words. Dopp rose and turned away with frightening calm to face the wall. Five seconds passed. Trent wished he would speak, yell—anything but the ambiguity of silence.

Then Dopp's deep voice rumbled into the room. "Tell me, Trent, are you so incredibly fragile and important that you can't tolerate discomfort for the sake of *saving lives*?" He spun around, glaring. "Is that how you really feel? Because the Trent Rowe I knew would have gone out of his way to do the right thing. The Trent Rowe I knew would never *quit* a job because he got uncomfortable or impatient."

Trent looked at the floor, clinging to the hope that Arianna was not destroying embryos. Didn't he love her? So how could she be a killer?

"Look at me," Dopp commanded. "Do you think you are more important than the multiple innocent lives at stake?"

"No," he whispered.

"What?"

"*No.*"

"Do you think that her disease excuses her from justice?"

"No. But if there's something going on, why hasn't she told me yet?"

"When someone has something serious to hide, they don't spill the beans to the first stranger that picks them up. It takes time. You have to hold on until the end."

"Even though we still have no proof?"

"We may not have direct proof of a current crime, but now we have proof that she is capable of the worst."

"Because she did abortions?" Trent winced at the memory of this inconvenient fact.

"And she did them without remorse. It was scary, how nice and normal she seemed, and then to find that out . . . You would never see it coming from someone like her."

"I know!" Trent cried. "It seems impossible."

Dopp sat down and leaned forward. "Even after all these years, it's still shocking to wrap my mind around how good some people seem and how evil they really are. It's like trying to understand death, or the size of the universe—some things are on a scale that most of us can't register."

"Exactly," Trent admitted. "I guess it's easier to think she may have changed her ways than to think she's a monster."

"It's easier because it feels much safer. But that doesn't mean it's the truth."

Trent nodded miserably.

"This is the worst time for us to quit."

Trent knew the DA was set to issue his report about the governor's bribery in a few weeks, and after that, the state budget talks were to resume. The talks that could make or break their jobs.

He imagined Arianna's delicate hands covered in an infant's blood.

"We should keep going," he said softly. "I'm sorry."

"It's the right thing to do," Dopp replied. "Keep seeing her as much as you can to strengthen her trust—and keep following her. By the way, where did you follow her to on Friday? You never mentioned it."

Trent pictured the dented steel door. He still didn't know what was behind it. But if he mentioned it now, he would be setting his own trap; he imagined Dopp's likely response: *You knew she was going somewhere strange, and yet you still wanted to quit the case?*

"She went to a drugstore," he said. "It wasn't anywhere worth mentioning."

"I suspect that's not the whole story. Follow her every chance you get."

"I will," Trent said, resolving to wait another few days before mentioning the seedy church. In the meantime, he would investigate it better, and remember to bring his gun.

"And don't give me another scare like that."

Trent sighed. "Thanks for talking sense into me, boss."

"Anytime."

Trent turned away cringing, for Dopp's tone clarified his real meaning: *Don't let it happen again.*

Trent walked back to his desk, ashamed. How could he have blinded himself to her criminal capacity? Only last night, he had told her how much he was looking forward to seeing her again. Now, he would have to still endure the agony of lying—but for an honorable purpose, he reminded himself. And the agony lay in the possibility of what she could be doing. . . .

A red light on his phone was blinking: a message from her. He felt a swell of delight. *We are both sick,* he thought.

"Hi, Trent," came her cheerful voice. *"You're probably writing, so don't let me interrupt you. But let me know if you're free later today. There's somewhere special I want to take you."*

He stood in front of his desk, facing the picture of the Crucifixion. But he saw nothing except the phone buried under his white knuckles. He loosened his grip and fumbled with the buttons.

"I'm free," he said as soon as she picked up. "Where are we going?"

Trent hid his disappointment as he climbed the stairs to meet Arianna at the Museum of Natural History. What could she possibly want with him there?

"Hey," she said, using her cane for balance as she stood on her tiptoes and kissed him. "I'm really glad you could come." He noticed that her eyes, despite the levity of her smile, seemed serious.

The first thing Trent saw as they walked into the entrance hall was the eighty-foot-long skeleton of an *Apatosaurus* dinosaur, as dramatic as he remembered from childhood. Again, he wondered: Why were they at a museum that specialized in dinosaur fossils?

"So what's the surprise?" he asked.

"You'll see."

At the admissions kiosk, a short line of people waited, most with children. In front of the left wing of the museum, Trent noticed a handful of silent protestors whose signs read, WE ARE NOT APES and GOD IS THE CREATOR.

"Who are they?" Trent asked, pointing as he followed Arianna into line.

She gestured to the words high above the protestors' heads, painted in silver onto the wall: DARWIN HALL: EVOLUTION TODAY.

"I guess you haven't been here for a while," she said.

"Not since I was a kid."

"Those people have been trying to convince the museum to take down that exhibit."

"I think I did hear about that," he said, recalling a stir of controversy that he had experienced only through glimpses at online headlines. "But everybody knows there's proof of Darwin's theories now, with DNA analyses and all that."

The thought of evolving from monkeys had not unsettled Trent, as it had so many of his colleagues and churchgoing peers—once the proof was widely evident, he had dismissed their vitriol as unfounded. To Trent, a disciple of journalistic objectivity, their anger was akin to sulking about the bacteria invisibly crawling on one's hands: it was unpleasant to think about, even contradictory to the senses, yet ridiculous to deny.

"Well, you know their attitude toward proof," Arianna said.

Her words homed in on a deeper conflict within him, pointing out a paradox he had recently realized: Christians rejected the need for proof to support belief in God, yet dismissed proof altogether when it was there.

Suddenly a conversation with Dopp and his colleagues came rushing back to him, from a meeting months earlier: *I never understood how anyone could claim embryonic stem cells would help people,* Jed had said, *without any proof of it at all.* Now this response triggered a question that had not occurred to Trent then:

Did they have proof of God?

And if they did, would it be called God, or just a scientific fact?

"Part of why I love this museum," Arianna said, "is that they won't succumb to the pressure."

He nodded as they moved to the front of the line. After they paid, he turned to her.

"So now you have to tell me."

"I'll show you." She led him into an elevator, out on the third floor, turned right into a narrow hallway, and followed it around a corner. Fewer and fewer people passed them.

"Someone knows her way around here."

She smiled, walking past room after room of exhibits, turning left, right, left, until stopping in front of a plain black door. Trent glanced around the doorframe for a label; there was only a black rectangle the size of a piano key. No one was around. Arianna pressed her right thumb against it, and the door slid open.

"Whoa," Trent said. "What—?"

She pulled him inside, and the door closed behind them. "This is a private exhibit," she said. "Members only."

The room inside was small and dimly lit. On top of a pedestal in the center, there was a single exhibit: a glass box that appeared to serve as an incubator, with fluorescent lights glowing around a red fist-sized lump. With a start, Trent realized what it must be. He held his breath and walked up to the box, seemingly floating in the darkness, supported only by its aura of light. He peered into it. As he expected, the lump was beating in oddly steady contractions that gave life to nothing.

"This is the stem cell heart," he said.

"Yes."

"I didn't know it was still here."

"It's the other reason I love this museum," she said. "The main reason, actually."

"Really," he said, his own heart pounding.

He waited for her explanation, aware that they were suddenly at the periphery of his most crucial question about her.

"What, exactly, do you know about this heart?" she asked.

"Well, it was the first heart ever created using human embryonic stem cells," he said carefully, feeling the words pinch his tongue—the words at the very core of his pursuit. "Like twenty years ago, right?"

"That's right," she said, nodding. "And it was donated to this museum after stem cell research was outlawed."

"Right," he said, "and there was a big outcry that the museum even kept it on display. I thought they got rid of it years ago."

"Nope. The people at the museum weren't cowards, just smart. They moved it from the entrance hall to this private room. To be admitted, you have to be screened and invited by the board. There's also a security camera—" She pointed to a tiny bulb in the corner of the ceiling. "—and this box is made of an unbreakable glass called Quarx. All so no one can destroy it."

"Wow. How do you know all this?"

A proud smile broke her solemn expression. "Remember I told you when we first met that my dad was a researcher? And you asked if he ever discovered anything?"

"Yes."

"He was on the team that developed this heart."

"Wow," Trent exclaimed again, at once impressed, confused, and newly suspicious. "So was your dad famous, then?"

And, he wondered, *why didn't that tiny detail show up in my case research?*

"No," she said. "He had his name removed from the team after it became illegal. Back then, I thought he was a coward. But I came to understand that recognition wasn't worth the hate mail and threats, and this all happened shortly after my mom's death. He was still grieving, and it was easier on him to stay anonymous."

"I see. So why are you telling me this now?"

"I've been wanting to talk to you about this type of research, to see how you feel about it, and I thought this was a good place to do it."

A few seconds passed as Trent gathered his wits. "How I feel about it?" He paused, pushing away his actual concerns about immorality and focusing instead on what he knew she wanted to hear. "It's sad this heart is a relic in a history museum."

"I agree." She flexed her ankle, wincing.

"Are you okay?"

She waved a hand.

"I remember," he said slowly, "there was so much excitement."

"And for good reason."

He looked straight at her. "Do you think these cells really could have helped people?" *They never did when they were legal,* he thought.

"Absolutely. There just wasn't enough time to research."

Not like it mattered, he thought. Murder was murder.

"This heart makes me sure," she went on. "And this was twenty years ago. Imagine what could have been possible today. The therapeutic potential is endless because these cells can turn into any cell of the body."

"Still just a potential," he responded automatically, delivering the skepticism drilled into him by the department. What the hell was he saying? Risking losing her trust, along with the entire case? He configured his features to seem sad. "Maybe if things had been different, without the DEP and the DEFP. . . ."

"I can't tell you how many times I've thought that." Arianna leaned on her cane, shaking her head. "So many lives might have been improved, saved. . . . And what just makes me crazy is how many people today think that since this never helped anyone directly before, it's no great loss now."

"Maybe," said Trent, "they just need to see proof."

That word again.

She cocked her head, studying his face. "I can see you have a rational mind. You're just stuck in a society that sees that as a liability."

"What?"

"There's a deeper issue here that involves more than your opinions on theoretical science, which have to be backed up by some kind of ideology. But we haven't discussed your ideas, except for your family being religious and you, not as much. So let me ask you this: What do you believe?"

Trent felt a familiar uneasiness wriggling in his gut.

"I'm trying to figure that out. . . ."

"What do you know so far?"

He sighed deeply and began to pace. She looked so patient, so eager to understand him, that his words spilled out with little calculation. "I know that I was raised Catholic, but I've never felt at peace with the religion. I'm starting to see that it makes other people miserable, too, not just me, so there must be something wrong with it. . . . And it bothers me that nobody can tell me the black-and-white truth about God or heaven or eternal salvation."

Arianna lifted her eyebrows. "What do you expect them to tell you?"

Trent spun around to face her. "How can something unknowable be the goal of my existence?" He lifted his hands in frustration. "But what's the alternative? Nothing? What kind of life is it to hold nothing sacred?"

"It's no kind of life," she said. "But you can still hold something sacred without religion—in fact, I think you should."

"What?" He felt empty, like pretense personified and exposed.

"Your own happiness here on earth."

The image of Emma's defeated face popped into his mind; he nodded the slightest bit.

She took a deep breath and looked straight at him. "I believe that following your own happiness is what life is all about. What makes religion so bad is that it condemns you for caring about exactly that."

"But they say you should devote your life to others."

"And look where it's gotten you! Denying yourself is fighting yourself, sacrificing yourself, and for what? Nothing in the end."

"What do you mean *nothing*?"

Her tone softened. "People have faith, but no proof, no *reason*, to believe there is anything or anywhere to go after we die, so that makes our life here on earth all the more precious."

He shook his head. "Why do you think I've doubted for so long?"

"Why are you doubting your own doubt? When you abandon your reason for faith in God, you succumb to the notion that you're a pawn of some higher being. But you are the only one in control of your life—of what you love and who you love." She paused, looking up at him.

"That's all I've really ever wanted," he said honestly. "Not to need permission from anyone else to live my life."

"And you don't! They make you believe you were born a sinner and must spend your life making up for it. But the irony is that your only sin was belief in the first place. Which was hard for a mind like yours, and why you've felt uneasy for so long."

Trent stared at her as the words popped in his brain, exploding with clarity, shedding light on new roads he had only begun to glimpse.

"This is what I've been trying to understand," he said. "I've been trying to buy in to something that I always knew, on some level, didn't make sense. . . . That's my whole problem, and yet all these years, I thought there was something wrong with *me*."

She shook her head sympathetically.

"Everything you said makes perfect sense," he continued. "I've always worried deep down that God wasn't listening or didn't care, or even—didn't exist." Speaking the words—a fear he had pondered in his darkest moments—felt like heresy, and he automatically braced. But nothing happened, except for a deep ache that burned in his chest. He realized it was sadness. "All the time I spent at church, all the guilt over the years—for nothing."

"That's not true," she said. "It was painful, but you had to go through those years to get to where you are now—to your own understanding."

"I think I've been in denial," he admitted. "It's so hard to accept that much of my life has been a lie. . . ."

Her eyes glistened with empathy. "But not anymore."

"No," he whispered. She looked so gratified that the pain in his chest expanded until he felt he would burst. He backed away and began to pace. How could he have gotten so sidetracked from the mission? Damn his emotions for getting in the way, when he was so close to the truth.

He stopped in front of her. "I knew you weren't really Christian. But why did you say you went to church?"

And I know you're going there, but why?

She smiled as if he had whipped back a curtain on a private window, but one always meant to be found. "I wanted to test your real attitude toward religion, and that night, when you were incredulous that I could be a supporter of religion *and* science, I kissed you, because I saw you understood the issue. Now you need something from me. You asked for proof about the possibilities of embryonic stem cells; you just haven't had a chance to see what they can do."

His heart thumped wildly as he watched her take a breath, as though she were gearing up for a long-awaited announcement. She put a hand on his arm and stared up into his eyes.

"I will give you the proof you need to become committed to science, which far from making demands on your life, could save it one day, as it may save mine—"

He gasped. "What did you just say?"

She reached up and touched his cheek. "Yes—I've been wanting to tell you so badly. The truth is, I brought you here to screen your reaction to this exhibit and to have this conversation, because what I really want to do is take you somewhere else."

The mysterious steel door materialized in Trent's mind, along with the sinister voice behind it, and he knew—before they hailed a cab, drove in silent suspense to the East Village, and tiptoed through the dark alley—that she was finally taking him there.

PART TWO

ELEVEN

Arianna knocked.

"Well?" demanded a familiar male voice from behind the door. Trent shivered on the concrete slab next to her. In the shadows, she had become a silhouette, her cane appearing as a natural extension of her fingers. The air felt sapped of all warmth. Trent wrung his hands, knowing that the truth was imminent—a truth he didn't know if he wanted to know, but had no power to stop.

He saw her reassuring smile in the darkness as she answered the voice: "Sad face."

He was too distracted to process the random words as he heard three bolts unlock. Then the knob turned and the door swung back into the light of the room behind it. A wizened face thrust through the opening. At the sight of Trent, hostility set into the old man's eyes. A blue face mask hung around his neck by an elastic band.

"Who is this?" the man snapped at Arianna.

She didn't seem disconcerted. "Sam, I'd like you to finally meet Trent, Trent, this is Dr. Sam Lisio—one of the leading scientists working today."

Trent extended his hand, but Sam ignored it. There was something hauntingly familiar about his name, like a snippet of a common melody.

"Arianna, are you mad?" Sam rasped.

"Just trust me, okay? He knows what's at stake."

She pushed the door open, motioning Trent inside. Sam did not budge.

"Are you serious?" Sam whispered with a note of fear.

"Sam, I'm telling you, he's with us."

Trent blinked and nodded. He wanted nothing more than to turn and run back into the alley.

Sam shot Arianna a vicious glance as he stepped aside. "It's your loss more than ours."

Arianna ignored him and grabbed Trent's arm. Together they walked through the doorway. Bright light cascaded from the ceiling, assaulting his eyes. After his pupils adjusted, he saw that the room was about the size of a studio apartment, but with a much lower ceiling; if he raised his arms, he could scrape it. The first objects he saw were three microscopes on a counter at the back of the room, next to computer screens. Sitting on a row of stools, two men were staring at him with shock, but Trent took no notice. Seeing the microscopes was like witnessing the death of hope.

Claustrophobia overtook him as he realized he was standing in a reality that was exactly as Dopp had suspected. Unnerved, he glanced to the right: three white laminar flow hoods created a sterile environment on another counter, and across the room, a shiny black freezer stretched from floor to ceiling. Its green digital display read *-78° C*. Next to the freezer was an equally large incubator showing a steady temperature of *37° C*. Next to them stood what Trent recognized as a carbon dioxide tank, a centrifuge, and a shelf with various supplies including petri dishes, gloves, vacuum tubes, pipettes and guns, and inverted microscopes.

As Trent surveyed the room, he heard a strange squeaking noise coming from the corner. He walked over—despite Sam's protests—to a cage holding rats running on a spinning metal wheel. In another cage, more rats were crawling stiffly, if at all. One of the men near the microscopes asked him a question, but he wasn't listening; he couldn't hear. He turned back around to look at Arianna, who was shaking her head at Sam and gesturing. Behind them, next to a cot on the floor, was the black plastic case she had carried from her clinic.

He walked back toward them, feeling the remnant of hope slip away.

"What—what is this?" he stammered.

Arianna smiled as Sam glowered.

"It's a lab," she said. "And these are the scientists who are trying to save my life." She motioned to the two men to come over. They did so, slipping their face masks off, removing their rubber gloves, and stuffing them into the front pockets of their white coats. "This is Trent, the man I'm seeing, who I promise won't expose us, so don't feel threatened. Trent, this is Dr. Patrick Evans and Dr. Ian Kelly."

Patrick—a tall, bony man with lips as thin as his hair—lifted his head in minimal welcome. Ian, who was shorter and stockier, stared at him with dismay. Trent worried that his true identity was obvious, that he ought to just make a run for it. But no, he reassured himself. They couldn't know.

"Please, can you at least say hello?" Arianna said. "He's not a monster!"

The men grunted a greeting, which Trent reciprocated. He felt trapped in an ethical straitjacket laced tight with emotional strings, and for the first time in his life, he began to have a panic attack. His hands lost feeling and his throat seemed to close, as if his whole life force were withdrawing into his chest.

Just get the facts, he thought, coughing to cover up his nerves. "So how does this all work?"

"Well," Arianna said, "all of this is top secret—"

"Used to be," Sam interrupted.

"He's not going to do anything!" she exclaimed, whirling on Sam.

Trent shook his head in a vain attempt to reassure him.

"So," Arianna went on, "we have to be top secret to avoid detection by the DEP. It's a complicated operation, actually, but it's been working out for a few months just fine."

Trent looked down at his wristwatch as if conferring with a trusty sidekick; that was all he needed to hear. But instead of glory, he felt confusion; instead of rage, curiosity.

"So how does it work?" he asked again.

"For the past few months, I've been recruiting as many sympathetic women as I can to donate their eggs at my clinic, which we then mix with sperm to create embryos. Of course, for the DEP, I record their donations as attempts to get pregnant through in vitro fertilization. But the DEP doesn't keep track of pregnancies, only the leftover embryos, so they never know that these women aren't getting pregnant from all these so-called attempts."

"Clever," Trent said. So that was behind the clinic's sudden popularity, he realized.

"Once I have the embryos, I separate them from those of my real patients who *are* trying IVF. Then after about four days, when the embryos are at the right stage of growth, I bring the strongest ones in that case—" She pointed to the black case on the floor. "—which keeps them at the proper temperature until I drop them off here, for these guys to use."

To use, Trent thought. How mechanical she made it seem, like dropping off a wrench at a car garage. He felt the first belated prick of anger, but focused on what she was saying.

"This is where the record keeping gets a little complicated, and is the most worrisome part. We take out about eighteen eggs from each woman, which makes for eighteen embryos. But for IVF, we rarely implant more than three embryos so the woman won't give birth to too many babies."

"I think I see where you're going," Trent said. "So you bring the three strongest embryos per donation back here for research?"

"No, because that would be wasting valuable resources. What we do is take *all* of the strongest embryos from each batch—usually about seven—and use those, even though the records for the DEP say we only used three. It wouldn't be such a big deal if the DEP didn't send inspectors to physically count our stock of leftovers every month. But because of that, we have to make it seem like every embryo is there. If even one is missing, we'll rack up a huge fine and bureaucratic hell. So these guys clone the few embryos that we need to make up the difference for each batch, and I take them back to the clinic in that black case and put them in the freezer in time for the next inspection. There's no way the inspectors can tell the difference between an original and a cloned embryo on sight, so the clinic has passed every inspection perfectly. I still get nervous each time, but I think we've got it down."

Trent nodded as snatches of an early exchange with Dopp came back to him, from the day they first decided to tackle the case:

"Are you suggesting she could be cloning and replacing the embryos?"

"The technology is still out there. But the logistics would be very difficult for her. She'd need scientists, tools, a lab space, money. It would be a major conspiracy. But we've seen it before, years ago. . . ."

Trent recalled later asking Dopp if they could test the DNA of a whole stock of embryos to find out if there were clones. But Dopp had explained that such a process would require a prohibitively costly contract with scientists and a lab to test hundreds of embryos—and even if they did find genetic matches, how could it be determined whether they were man-made clones or merely identical twins? It was an impossible hurdle that Arianna must have understood in advance.

"Impressive," Trent said. "It seems very well thought out."

"Thank you. We all worked it out together." Arianna smiled at Sam, who looked away. The three men stood by like white-coated sentries, noting Trent's every move.

Arianna sighed. "So that's how it's done."

Trent tugged at the strap on his watch. "But if you know how to clone embryos, then why couldn't you just keep cloning the same embryo over and over for research purposes instead of using a bunch of donated ones?"

"It's possible in theory," Arianna replied. "But not in practice. If you clone an embryo, it increases the chance of tainting the cells, which could skew your experiments. It's the same problem with thawing frozen embryos. We also want a wide gene supply to ensure that the techniques will work the same way on every cell. So we need a constant supply of fresh new embryos."

One of the scientists cleared his throat. "Some of which are going to waste right now."

"Of course," Arianna said. "We'll get out of your way. Let me just show him the rats."

She dropped her cane to the floor and grabbed Trent's arm.

They walked to the cages in the corner, while Ian and Patrick grudgingly returned to their microscopes. Trent glanced over his shoulder, feeling the tingly wrath of a stare; sure enough, Sam stood by the door with crossed arms, watching him. Trent whipped his head back to Arianna, who was pressing her fingers into his biceps.

"I know you might have been skeptical about stem cells," she said quietly. "But this is the proof I wanted you to see in person, to show you I have a chance. See those rats that are barely moving? They have a similar disease to multiple sclerosis in humans, but for them it's called EAE—experimental autoimmune encephalomyelitis. But see those other rats running around like crazy? They had the disease, too, but my guys injected their spinal cords with stem cells, which restored their ability to move."

"Wow," Trent said, genuinely taken aback. "That seems like magic. How does it work?"

She beamed. "Let me try to explain. You have many different specialized cells in your body—for example: heart cells, bone cells, nerve cells, which all develop out of stem cells. Around your nerve cells, there's a dense membrane called myelin that transmits impulses to the cells, allowing movement. The thicker the myelin, the faster the impulses are conducted. But in multiple sclerosis, this myelin degenerates over time, so eventually you're paralyzed. That's why I'm walking so stiffly now, and will need a wheelchair soon. But if the scientists can trick stem cells to grow into myelin-producing cells, and inject those into my spinal cord, then theoretically they will replenish my lost myelin, restore my cells' ability to move, and save my life—just like these lucky rats."

"That's brilliant! So if they can do it with the rats, why can't they do it with you?"

"It's harder for humans because we have different genes. What Sam and the others are working on is trying to activate the right genes in human stem cells to trick them into becoming myelin-producing cells, which are called oligodendrocytes. But in order to activate the right genes, the guys have to use an exact—and so far unknown—combination of molecules to inject into the stem cells. This combination is the holy grail of the research, and the key to my life. Once—if—they figure this out, we'll be able to inject the right cells into my spinal cord, and hopefully, my myelin will grow back. It's just a matter of time, and lots of trial and error, but they're getting closer every day."

"So this is for real," Trent whispered. "This could really save your life."

"Yes."

Hope burst like a tonic within him, overpowering his anguish. He stared down into her blue eyes and saw the intensity of his own feelings reflected in them. A lump rose in his throat. He leaned in and kissed her lips so she wouldn't see the wetness in his eyes. All he wanted was to stand there and hold her, and to think about being able to do so for the rest of their lives.

Somewhere in the back of his mind, his conscience was shrieking.

He pulled back. "I still have so many questions," he murmured. "This is all so unexpected."

"I understand—it must be quite a shock. But a good one, I hope." She smiled. "What do you want to know?"

"Where are the embryos?"

In his years at the DEP, Trent had never set eyes on an actual embryo, the driving force behind his work.

"They're not too glamorous, but I'll show you." She tugged him over to the refrigerator and pulled open the heavy door. Gas billowed out. "That's the carbon dioxide that controls their environment," she explained. "And there they are."

Rows of thin glass flasks lined the interior of the fridge. Inside each flask was a red liquid. As far as he could tell, there was no life in there at all. And even though he knew to expect this, the reality seemed like a letdown.

"I told you they weren't that exciting," Arianna said. "At this stage, they're just clusters of cells that you can only see under a microscope."

"I see. Why are they red?"

"The red fluid is a culture medium that contains nutrients for the cells." She shut the door and turned to him. "We should go."

He nodded with relief.

"Bye," she called to Patrick and Ian, who lifted their heads from their microscopes but said nothing. Trent and Arianna crossed over to the door, where Sam remained seething.

"Sam." She patted his arm affectionately. "Please don't worry. I'll talk to you tomorrow."

"We should change the password," he spat.

"Okay," Arianna said, rolling her eyes. "Tell me later."

Trent waved awkwardly as he and Arianna walked out into the cold night air. The door shut hard behind them in satisfied riddance.

"Sorry about them," she said immediately. "Working in this kind of atmosphere makes them paranoid. But it's just because they don't know you—it's nothing personal."

"No, don't apologize. They—you—are taking a huge risk."

"This is true."

When they reached the landing of the stairs, he put his arm around her and guided her through the alley. "So why here?" he asked. "Of all places for a lab, a church basement? And how did you manage to set it up like that?"

"I know it's an odd place, and scary at night, but we couldn't risk using a known lab, because the DEP makes periodic sweeps. And you saw how much equipment is needed, so none of us had the space in our apartments. When we were talking about forming this group about a year ago—"

"Are there other members?"

"Two more, the other doctors who work at my clinic. They help with recruiting donors, keeping the clinic running smoothly and studying the embryos. So with the three scientists, there are six of us altogether."

"How did you find the scientists?"

"When I was an undergrad at Columbia, Sam was the foremost embryonic stem cell researcher at our school before it became illegal, and I formed a club that rallied to support him after the DEP got on his trail. He ended up going to jail, though—"

Trent barely contained a gasp, recalling that his initial research had yielded the same story, forever preserved in the campus archives.

"—and I found him all these years later, through some mutual acquaintances. I approached him cold, explained my situation, and of course, he remembered me. He was basically a recluse when I found him, but I managed to convince him to take on this project—he needed this in a way as much as I do. And he contacted Patrick and Ian, who he had worked with at Columbia. He actually contacted his whole team from back then, but only Patrick and Ian would have anything to do with the idea."

"Fear?"

"Yes. If the DEP ever discovered us, we would all go to jail, no doubt. But luckily a few others feel the same way Sam did: that someone has to take the risk, or else scientific progress will end. And I'm paying them, of course, since I commissioned the research."

They were standing at the threshold of the alley, but Trent could not wrest himself away from her, or stop himself from prodding. "It's very brave," he said. "Wouldn't you be putting your body in serious danger to be the first human trial, if it comes to that?"

"And I hope it does! Of course it would be very dangerous, but necessary, so the risk is meaningless." She looked pensive. "I feel like I'm reclaiming my life and my world. And if I happen to die in the process, well, then, I hope they learn something from my body. Then I'd die happy. But I refuse to sit around and wait for it to happen, with no struggle, no point, nothing whatsoever to be gained."

Trent drew a ragged breath. "So, you were saying, why here of all places?"

"Right. When we were talking about forming this group, I looked up foreclosure properties, and this abandoned church was available to the top buyer or it was going to be destroyed. So then I realized: What is the last place the DEP would look for a secret lab? In a church. Plus, I couldn't help but enjoy the irony. So, to be extra cautious, I put the money in a real estate investment trust where my cousin is a partner. Her company has a bunch of legit investors and buys a lot of properties in Manhattan, so the church slipped in under the radar. She bought it in her company's name, so the IRS has no reason to trace it to me. I purposely left it looking deserted so nobody would think anything had changed."

"Smart move, especially if the IRS decides to audit you. But how did you get all the lab equipment? And how did you get it in there?"

She explained that she ordered it from a manufacturer, who delivered it to a storage facility, and then she drove it in a rented U-Haul to the church in the middle of the night, with the group acting as movers.

"It's taken my whole inheritance and savings to afford the building, plus the equipment—which cost thirty thousand dollars alone. Then there are the salaries of Sam, Patrick, and Ian, and I also pay five thousand dollars in cash to each woman who donates. Basically, I'm working at a huge loss. But, of course, it's worth it."

Trent squinted down the deserted street. His reporter's curiosity had kicked into high gear. "How do you account for that huge loss of money to the IRS? Besides the investment in your cousin's company for the church?"

Arianna nodded. "It's an important question, and one that bothered me for months before this whole operation began. But I think I managed to get around it. Back in February, I took a trip to Europe and seemed to spend a fortune on MS treatments that I supposedly couldn't find in the U.S. Actually, I put that money in a Swiss bank account, even though the U.S. government thought I spent it. Then I used it to buy the lab equipment. And that's the cash I'm using to pay the scientists and the women who donate."

Trent nodded. "So you thought everything out."

"I had to. It would be too risky if the IRS could trace my money."

They stood in silence for a moment.

"Talk about reclaiming your life," Trent said. "You're exhausting every resource you have."

"Wouldn't you?"

He nodded, thinking of the seemingly inanimate flasks. It might be tempting to choose your own life over those, he thought, but not if the cost was mass infanticide. Such a horror could never be justified; and how could she pretend it was? But then again, were five-day-old embryos really—*really*—the same as human babies? The Church said so, but how good was its track record with truth?

Suddenly a bothersome memory hit him.

"Wait, didn't you say when we were at your apartment that you were going to church to practice religion?"

"I said to practice *my* religion," she corrected. "That of furthering and bettering human life here on earth."

He suppressed the words he itched to retort: *When does human life begin?* It did not seem like the type of question that could have an ambiguous answer. He thought again of what the Church said: Life began at conception. It seemed as straightforward as basic math.

Wasn't it? He had never thought to question it, but now everything he had learned there seemed subject to scrutiny. Yet what other answer was there? Life began at conception. It seemed like wondering about the shortest distance between two points. He studied Arianna's calm face and considered asking her, but thought better of it.

Instead, he vowed to research it the only way he knew how—on the Internet—as soon as he could. If anything was clear, it was that he had to be completely confident of the answer; for without certainty on this point, he could not move forward.

An unsettling twinge pulled him back to the moment. Something was still bothering him about their night in her apartment.

"But what about the Sistine Chapel?" he demanded. "The painting on your wall? Why would you have that if you weren't actually religious?"

She laughed. "You have an eye for details, don't you? Michelangelo's work is inspirational to me because it conveys the same sense I have about the beauty of life, in a way that has nothing to do with religion."

"Oh." He watched the puff of his own breath disperse.

Arianna leaned against his chest, rubbing her arms. "Got everything straight so we can go home? I'm freezing."

Everything, he thought, except the main thing.

It was a question he could not answer with any degree of conviction, and the only question that mattered.

• • •

Trent lay across his bed, racked by the thoughts rolling through his mind: *I'm destined to murder. Whatever I do, I'm going to help kill embryos or help kill her.* Somehow, somewhere, there had been a terrible mistake.

The clarity he had so briefly enjoyed in the museum was like a distant light overshadowed by a hailstorm. He pictured telling Dopp.

I know everything, he would say. Somehow, his mouth—a traitor to his heart—would form the words: *You were right.*

Dopp's face would light up with all the triumph of an innocent prisoner finally exonerated. *I knew it!* he would shout. Perhaps he would pump a fist or, in a moment of feverish excitement, throw his arms around Trent. Then the police would be called and they would all converge in the alley, force their way past the steel door if necessary, and storm the underground lab. What if Arianna was there when it happened? Trent pictured her face, frozen in shock at his betrayal, and at the realization that she was going to die in jail.

He moaned. He could not bring himself to do it, not until he had answered the question once and for all: When does human life begin? It seemed impossible to imagine a truth different from the one he had always accepted.

He lifted his laptop onto his thighs and typed the critical question into a search engine. A list of websites popped up: godnet.com, prolife.net, christiansunited.org, humansforhumans.com, alllife.com. The list was endless. He clicked the first site, knowing what it would say.

"The fusion of an egg and sperm marks the beginning of a new life with a unique genetic map never before created," read a statement posted on the site's homepage. "This is an inarguable fact, and, as such, God endows each embryo with all the dignity and the sacredness of every human being on earth."

Trent opened the next site.

> The moment of conception marks the exact moment of personhood and of the human body, which God injects with a soul. You are no different in your later incarnation than you were at that very moment. Therefore, unborn babies have the same right to life as you and I.

Was there any answer not tied to religion?

He typed in the website of the National Institutes of Health, the federal government's leading biomedical research organization. On the search page, he typed "stem cell research." A section of the website popped up labeled: "Adult Stem Cell Information."

Trent clicked on a list of FAQs: "How are adult stem cells different from embryonic stem cells?"

> Adult stem cells are undifferentiated cells found in specialized tissues such as heart or muscle tissue. Adult stem cells can give rise to the type of specialized cell found in the tissue of origin and may or may not be able to give rise to other cell types. Embryonic stem cells are found in five-day-old human embryos, and can give rise to any cell in the body.

So far, so good. Trent clicked on the next question in the list: "Why is adult stem cell research preferable to embryonic stem cell research?" The answer was one he knew well:

> Adult stem cells are cultivated from the developed tissue of already-born humans, so they do not involve compromising a life. They have been used for decades for procedures like bone marrow transplants and are being widely researched to find the potential life-saving gains associated with illegal embryonic stem cells.

He stared uncomfortably at the screen, realizing that the question was loaded.

On the sidebar of the web page, he noticed a tab that read "Archives." On a hunch, he clicked and navigated more than twenty-five years back to the year 2000. Then in the search bar, he typed "embryonic stem cells."

A list of old news announcements appeared: "First Symposium on Embryonic Stem Cells Calls Human Life-Saving Potential Unprecedented." Beneath that headline, there was another: "National Institutes of Health Answer: What would you hope to achieve from embryonic stem cell research?" A seventeen-page-long answer followed, outlining the specific hopes of each institute: Heart, Lung, and Blood; Dental and Craniofacial Research; Diabetes and Digestive and Kidney Diseases; Neurological Disorders and Stroke; Allergy and Infectious Diseases; Child Health; Eye; Aging; Arthritis and Skin Diseases; Deafness; Mental Health; and Human Genome Research.

Trent stared in awe at the broad array of hope for every part of the body, wondering why he had never researched the topic before, why he had never questioned it.

Because even though religion allows you to ask questions, he thought, *you're not supposed to question its answers.*

He changed the year in the archive to 2001, the first year that legislation against embryonic stem cell research began. More news announcements popped up, but the change in rhetoric was stark: "Congress Limits Embryonic Stem Cell Research to 64 Existing Lines," and "President Calls on NIH to Issue Grants Only for Adult Stem Cell Research."

With a sinking feeling, Trent changed the year in the archives to 2012.

"Supreme Court Bans Embryonic Stem Cell Research," read the news announcement. Trent remembered the decision well: it had sparked a giddy patriotism in his community—bumper stickers, flags, Republican campaign donations. The next announcement read: "Federal Government Allocates Funds for a Department of Embryo Preservation in Each State to Monitor Existing Embryos." He slammed his laptop shut and threw it to the foot of the bed.

But how could he pretend that a cluster of cells meant more than her life? He again pictured what would surely be her shell-shocked expression—and the terror of impending mortality in her eyes—and thought: *There is no way I could live with myself. I would rather go to jail than send her there to die. So that makes me a killer of innocents. I am a killer.*

He struggled to believe the words. Embryos were dying as he stood by, at this very moment. Shame overwhelmed him, even as he knew his decision was final. The swiftness of his descent into immorality was staggering, and it frightened him. How could he, a person who had once been so consumed by a desire to do good that it had landed him at the DEP—how could he have sunk to the most depraved rung of all?

But she stood there proudly. To live with herself, she had to be either inconceivably evil, or have a good reason for her peace of mind.

Trent jumped off the bed and rushed to the door, propelled by the turbine force of a single thought: *I have to know her reason.*

As he opened the door, he glanced down at his watch. It clung to his wrist like a barnacled spy, filled with incriminating evidence. He unhooked the leather strap and flung it against the wall.

"Trent!" Arianna exclaimed. "What are you doing here?"

She opened the door, motioning for him to step inside. He did not answer, but walked into the foyer and kissed her hard on the lips, those lips that he no longer had to fight, even if it damned him.

She laughed a little bit before gently pushing him away. "What's going on?"

"I can deal with being a criminal," he said, "but I have to know if that's how it really is."

"A criminal?" She frowned and led him to the couch in her living room. He sank wearily beside her.

"I'm no threat," he reassured her. "I could never rat you out. But this is what I can't reconcile: When does human life begin? The only answer I've ever heard is that life begins at conception. So does that mean killing embryos is killing a life? How do you live with yourself? And how can I?"

Arianna looked thoughtful but unworried. "I thought you might have absorbed that notion, but you never said anything at the museum, so I assumed it didn't bother you."

"All I know for sure is that no matter how much I should, I can't care more about an embryo than about you. But I hate to think that makes me a criminal!"

She took both his hands. "Neither of us are criminals—far from it. The problem is that you're asking the wrong question."

"I am?"

"Yes. This was a question posed by the Ancient Greeks: When does a potential human being become an actual human being who possesses the right to life? The issue is not when life begins—but rather, when does a potential become an actual? An acorn is alive, but far from the equivalent of an oak tree. It's clear that an embryo, which is no bigger than a grain of sand, is only a cluster of undifferentiated cells that have the potential to grow into a human being. But saying an acorn is the same as a tree is as ridiculous as saying a cell cluster has rights. The potential is actualized only when a baby is born and becomes an independently existing individual. Before this happens, it's a parasitic mass of developing cells dependent on its host. It's not sentimental, but it's a medical fact. Only religious mystics would assert that a cell cluster has a God-given soul."

"So you don't believe we have souls?"

"I believe that we have the power to think and love and hope—if you want to call that a soul—but not that it's an entity within our bodies."

Trent recalled Dopp's fury over her remorseless performance of abortions. "So if these cells are just a primitive mass, with no soul or rights, then early abortions are ethical, too."

"Yes. I used to perform them because I think a pregnant woman should be able to decide the fate of the cells within her own body. The religious right wing, far from being pro-life as they claim, would prefer a woman to sacrifice her life to an embryo within her, even if it threatens her health to give birth. They are the same people who would prefer me to die, rather than research cell clusters for a cure. I am pro-life, in the real sense of the term, and so are you. Human life *is* sacred, not because of a supernatural infusion, but because of the unique capacity of our minds to reason—to think, to love, to create. So your instincts were correct—my life is more valuable than an embryo. This makes the research moral, and it makes you rational, Trent, not criminal."

He closed his eyes for several seconds, feeling her words lift his guilt. All that remained was a fleeting regret for his self-torment. He opened his eyes.

"I couldn't imagine you as a murderer."

"That's one thing you don't have to worry about." She smiled and pulled him against her. "Now does it all make sense?"

He nodded. *And now my love for you finally makes sense*, he thought: *it's not wicked, but a response to what I have always valued most, but never realized—the joy of living, personified in you.*

"But I'm worried," he said. "You're taking such a big risk—"

"Oh." She waved her hand. "I don't think the DEP will find us. We just passed another inspection a few weeks ago."

He felt sick. "So this means that the whole DEP is a moral fraud."

"Completely. They're nothing but religious thugs forcing their ideology down science's throat."

Trent felt strangely disassociated from his identity, as if he were viewing himself from the other side of the mirror, judging actions he had never thought to judge.

"Do you think they are malicious?" he asked, fearing her answer. "The people at the DEP?"

"Somebody must be evil to prefer me to die, and the millions of people like me. But I think most of them probably believe that what they are doing is right, even as they destroy all the boundaries between church and state. At best they're misguided."

He nodded. "Let's forget them."

"Sounds good to me."

They stretched out under a throw and she nuzzled into his shoulder. He felt fiercely protective as he wrapped his arms around her, feeling the slow beat of her heart against his ribs. They lay inhaling parallel breaths, and he sensed that she did not often relinquish herself to the comfort of another's arms. To think that she was fighting a two-front battle, both with slim odds, was agonizing; but then—to think that he was her opponent! His heart squeezed with shame.

I'll quit tomorrow, he thought. *I'll never have to face Dopp again.*

He owed nothing; he could give two weeks' notice and let the door slam behind him. Then he could focus on making her life as enjoyable and full as she deserved—and maybe someday, hopefully long after she was out of danger from the DEP and from disease, he would tell her everything.

But wait. Even if he quit the case, it didn't mean *they* would.

Dopp wouldn't put the case to rest until he exhumed the gritty truth; so they would find another strategy without Trent—which would force him to tell her about the investigation. But then, if the stress didn't kill her, she might never look at him again. The thought of losing her as a result of his own unwitting betrayal made him groan. In his arms, Arianna shifted but did not open her eyes.

He mulled over his options, trying to steady his heartbeat so it wouldn't startle her awake. Even if she came to accept his initial lying, what if Dopp discovered his disloyalty? A traitor to the U.S. government—that would be the end of him. Not to mention that if he quit, he would be dangerously ignorant of Dopp's next move. . . .

No, he realized, *I can't quit. I can't let them get to you.*

His path—despite its perilous double deception—was clear. It was his only feasible option.

One day, he thought, *when it doesn't matter anymore, I'll explain; and you won't be angry, because you'll understand what I saved you from. . . .*

He kissed the top of her head, cashmere against his lips. She did not stir. Even the light of the living room couldn't hold off the exhaustion pulling his eyelids shut.

A vibration somewhere around his hips nudged him awake. She must have felt it, too, for her head snapped up, hitting his chin.

"Ow," he muttered, opening his eyes.

"Sorry—oh my God, what time is it?"

He shrugged, turning his stiff neck from side to side. Wan light streamed in, shining into Arianna's eyes. She threw the blanket off their legs and dug into her pocket for her cell phone. It was still vibrating.

"Hello?" she said, her voice throaty from sleep. A pause. "What? Right now? What time is it?" Pause. "Tell me what's going on." Her face drained. "I'll be right there." She snapped the phone closed. Trent saw that it was 8:15 A.M.

"What's wrong?"

She stared blankly into space.

"I have to run over to the lab right now. That was Sam. He said they're having some kind of emergency."

TWELVE

As Arianna hurried down the steps to the lab, the unmistakable sound of shouts emanated from the basement. A chill of apprehension cleared her nasal passages. She rapped on the door.

The din stopped, and she heard footsteps shuffling closer.

"Well?" came Sam's voice.

"You never told me the new password!" she yelled. "Just open up."

"Are you alone?"

She rolled her eyes. "Yes."

Sam swung it open, revealing his heated pink face crowned by a few strands of white hair. She walked in and shut the door.

"At least now you can use my batch," Ian was saying to Patrick.

"Don't pretend to twist this into something good," Patrick snapped.

They stood in the center of the lab, as if they had been screaming at each other. A jumble of emotions clouded their expressions: Patrick looked frustrated, muttering at the floor, while Ian hung his head, refusing to meet Arianna's gaze.

Her grip on the cane tightened. "What is going on?"

Nobody spoke.

"C'mon, Ian," Sam said, "don't make us do your dirty work."

Ian raised his head and looked into Arianna's eyes. "I'm quitting."

"You're *what*?"

"I'm sorry, Arianna, I don't want to do this, but after you brought that man here yesterday, I don't feel safe anymore. I can't risk going to jail—my wife would never forgive me. Last night, I told her about it and she was outraged. She . . ."

"She what?"

"She threatened to leave me unless I quit today. And the truth is, I understand where she's coming from—it's just not fair to her to put myself in so much danger. . . ."

"Ian. Trent is a *good guy*. I promise you he won't threaten us."

Ian looked unmoved, and Arianna felt her reserve of diplomacy begin to falter.

"A lot of good you did us," Sam said to her.

Arianna gulped a breath. "Ian, you are as safe here now as you were before." She held up a hand. "I swear on my father's grave that Trent poses no danger to us—we talked about the whole thing last night, and he is completely on our side."

Ian shook his head. "I'm sorry. I don't know anything about him—it's just too risky."

Arianna pulled her cell phone out of her purse and waved it in the air. "What do you want to know? I'll call him right now, we can all sit down and talk—"

"No, I promised my wife," Ian mumbled. "It's too late now. Maybe if I could have met him before . . . but you just sprung him on us." His voice turned hard. "It's really your fault, Arianna, not mine."

She glanced among the three men for an ally, knowing her poise was sliding. Her tone was a mixture of deference and fury: "I'm sorry, I should have warned you all before I brought him here, but imagine not being able to tell your partner that you have a chance to live. That there is reason to hope!"

Ian half shrugged. "You could have told him in vague terms. Why did you have to bring him here?"

Her eyes flashed as her blood pressure spiked. "This lab holds proof of concepts that are alien to the outside world—proof that this research can work! You wouldn't believe it either if you were raised the way he was—unless you *saw* it in progress. I trust Trent—why isn't that enough for you, Ian? Why don't you trust my judgment anymore? I arranged every detail of this whole project; don't you think I'd be the last person to upset it?"

Ian pursed his lips. "Love is blind."

"Not for me," she retorted, turning to Sam. "What about you, Sam? Don't tell me, you, too—"

Sam shook his head, but his expression was far from kind. "Even if you did screw up, I'm here to stay. What have I got to lose?"

"Thank you, Sam," she breathed. "Patrick?"

Patrick was standing with his arms crossed over his chest. He pointed a thumb at Ian. "This coward's got a point. It is riskier now, thanks to you. But I hope your judgment is as good as ever, because I can't bear to walk out." He looked at Ian. "We will never have this chance again."

Ian shrugged. "I know, but—"

"But what?" Patrick demanded. "The three of us might be the only scientists left doing this kind of research. Don't you think that outweighs our own worries? We could save Arianna's life, not to mention revive this field. . . . Yes, it's risky, but think about Copernicus, Galileo, Newton. . . . They weren't cowards . . . and what if they had been? Where would we be today?"

"I doubt we could be much worse off," Ian muttered. "They don't matter anymore, none of it matters—"

"Nonsense!" Arianna shouted. "Do you hear yourself? Patrick is right: You are a coward, you have no vision, you've bought in to all the fear they want you to feel—you think you're threatened by Trent?" She let out a bitter laugh. "It's people like you, who know better but have no courage, who are the biggest threat of all!"

Ian tore off his white lab coat, yanking his arms out of each slot. He pulled his elastic face mask over his head and stuffed it into the pocket of the coat. In his jeans and T-shirt, he looked like the outsider he was. He nodded at Patrick and Sam before walking up to Arianna. She didn't flinch as he stopped in front of her and handed her the coat. She took it. He opened his mouth, but any parting words died on his tongue as she narrowed her eyes.

"Don't," she said. "There's nothing to say."

He closed his mouth, but studied her face. With a chill, Arianna realized that he was trying to memorize her face for posthumous recollection.

"Get out," she barked.

He stepped around her and pulled open the door. Pale morning light streamed into the basement as he walked out and let the door slam. Arianna closed her eyes, but her lids were futile dams against her tears. She looked to Sam.

"Don't look at me," he said angrily. "You deserve most of the credit."

The urge to protest faded with her strength. She turned to Patrick. He was already walking pointedly back to his microscope.

Not knowing what else to do, she reached for the door. Sam said nothing as she stumbled out. Ian was gone. In front of her, the concrete stairs looked like mountains, requiring more energy to climb than she possessed. With a muted sob, she sank onto the first step and pulled out her cell phone.

At work, Trent felt jumpy; anxiety did more for his alertness than any espresso could. What emergency was she facing? What could he do to help? And could he actually outwit Dopp? It was beyond any risk he had ever taken, and he had no idea how to pull it off.

While Trent pondered his next move—and worried that his shifting loyalties were somehow apparent—the man himself stopped in the doorway. He looked authoritative in his crisp black suit with a cross pin fastened on its lapel, a gleaming golden reminder of past and purpose. Pretending to knock in the air, he half smiled down at Trent.

"Hey, there," he said in a deep voice suited to his stature.

"Hi." *Careful with every word,* Trent thought.

"No surprises today, right?"

Trent shook his head. "No, sir."

"I don't work with quitters."

"Sorry about that." He forced an apologetic smile.

"You're lucky that I have enough faith in you for both of us," Dopp said, turning to leave.

"Thanks." Trent hesitated and then called, "By the way, did you know the stem cell heart is still on display at the Natural History Museum?"

Dopp's head whipped back around. "No kidding. How do you know that?"

"A friend told me."

Trent felt his face grow hot—what was he hoping to accomplish? But part of him wanted to witness Dopp's reaction, to find out if there was any hope for redemption in the man he had long admired.

"It's truly despicable," Dopp said. "When you think about how many embryos they had to destroy to grow that heart . . ."

Trent nodded, knowing he had backed himself into a corner. "I don't know how they justified it," he said. "I guess they thought it might have helped people someday. . . ."

Dopp shook his head bitterly. "If you kill one person to save another, the sum is still zero. Put it another way: If a thief robbed a bank to give the money to charity, would that make it right?"

Trent dutifully shook his head, not daring to debate the semantics of personhood.

"Embryos are not just plain life," Dopp continued, "but the most sacred form of life—humans without sin, since they are not yet born."

Trent nodded, thinking sadly: *It's too late for you, boss.* Dopp was as steeped in religion as Einstein in physics; it was inseparable from his identity. Under the force of mysticism, his reasoning power had shriveled. Trent understood that Dopp was incapable of viewing an embryo as anything less than a full human being with rights. And Trent realized he had been on the same path. Once a person believes something long enough . . .

"*This* is why we have to fight for the department to exist," Dopp was saying. "We should all feel honored to come here every day. I know I do."

"So do I." Trent cleared his throat. "Of course I do." His lie felt laughably transparent, as if he had just stated his allegiance to Mars. Dopp was watching him with a displeased look—could he suspect anything had changed?

On Trent's desk, his cell phone shivered. The emergency.

"Who is it?" Dopp asked.

Trent had to answer, and there was only one person whose call was acceptable to take.

"It's her."

Dopp's face brightened. "Don't let me stop you."

He tried not to betray his urgency as he lifted the phone to his ear. An odd whimper escaped from the other end of the line.

"Hello?" Trent said. "Arianna?"

"Hi." The word tumbled into a sniffling sob that burst through his earpiece.

"Are you okay? What happened?"

From the doorway, Dopp eyed him with unchecked interest.

"Trent," she cried, "Ian quit. All because of you, isn't that the stupidest thing you ever heard?" She sniffled harder. "I told him you weren't a threat, but he's gone and now there's only two of them and they're furious. . . ."

"I'm sorry to hear that," he said carefully, his mind racing. "Where are you now?"

"Outside the lab. I'm going to have to cancel on my patients and go home; I'm a mess. . . ."

"Do you want me to meet you there?"

"I would hate to interrupt your writing—"

"Nonsense. I'll be right there."

"Thank you—thank you so much."

Trent closed the phone and looked up.

"What was that about?" Dopp asked immediately.

Trent looked somber. "She got some bad news about her MS. So she's skipping work and going home—I thought you would approve of me going to comfort her. . . ."

"Of course. Maximize the face-to-face time. And remember, no one is exempt from the law."

"Right." Trent rose, picking up his briefcase, eager to leave.

"Right," Dopp repeated more firmly, eyeing Trent's naked wrist. "Where's the watch?"

At home, he thought, *on the floor.* "At home; I didn't think I would be seeing her this afternoon. I'll stop by and get it on the way there."

"Fine. I want to see the transcript on my desk first thing tomorrow. Even if she says nothing pertinent."

"Of course."

Dopp stepped out without another word.

Dopp's skin alerted him first to the strange feeling that came over him as he walked down the hallway from Trent's office to his own. Heat seared his forehead, tinged with a shivery cool that made his hands clammy; it was the kind of unsettling instinct that demanded attention, the body's way of showing the mind what it already senses and does not wish to acknowledge.

He thought of the state budget that loomed ever closer; within weeks, it would be decided, along with the department's fate for the next year. He thought of Arianna's face at Christmas dinner, and the way she had stared at Joanie, disturbingly devoid of remorse for her past crimes. What other nefarious acts had she committed, or was she still committing, on his watch?

Trent was taking dangerously long to crack her. Dopp hated to cut it so close. He had assumed that after the dinner, Trent and Arianna's bonding would kick in, and her caution would unravel like a schoolgirl's braid. But apparently it had not. And what was this garbage that Trent spewed about the stem cell heart possibly *helping* people, the very heart that was the stuff of the dead? The thought revolted him. Perhaps he had misjudged Trent—maybe he was too inexperienced to be trusted with such a serious case. Not to mention his immature impulse to quit, as if he were pursuing Arianna for kicks and not out of a sacred duty to protect the Lord's youngest children.

But Trent had seemed so eager and capable, Dopp remembered. And he had managed to forge a closeness with Arianna that begged to be exploited. Well, now they were too invested to rethink that strategy. At any moment, she could confess to him. But it was possible to keep closer tabs on the situation.

A flick of his finger and a few words later, his trusted employee Jed White was standing before him. Like a sideways skylight, the sheer glass wall behind Dopp's desk ushered in sunlight, catching the copper in Jed's hair. The light bounced off the walls, highlighting the largest frame on the wall, one of ornate twisting gold, which held a photograph from a private meeting of Dopp shaking hands with the Pope. That had been before Dopp left the priesthood, but while his affair with Joanie was developing. Dopp still felt ashamed for having presented himself to the Pope as a servant of the church while lust festered inside him. He kept the picture front and center to remind himself not of the honored meeting, but of his deeply human failure.

"Jed, what do you think is the most important quality I seek in my employees?"

"Loyalty?"

"That's right. To the Lord and our mission. Those loyalties should outweigh any allegiance you feel toward a coworker."

"Of course."

"Are you friends with Trent Rowe?"

Jed hesitated, seeming unsure of the correct answer. "We're cool."

Dopp smiled. "I thought so. Given that, I need you to take over a special role for the department: integrity control."

"Integrity control?"

"Yes. What you will need to do is handle a private assignment that requires total confidentiality and discretion. A bonus will be arranged."

"I'm listening."

"Trent has been acting a little strange lately, so I need you to watch him and see if he is doing his job. See if he seems motivated to solve the case, or if he's slacking off. Spend some time with him and Arianna Drake together. Do they seem close or distant? Does she seem to trust him? And what does Trent tell you about her when she's not there?" Dopp paused while Jed scribbled notes on a pad. "Got it?"

"Yes, sir."

"Good. I saw them together at my house last weekend, but I bet she acts differently toward Trent when she's more comfortable, like around friends. And I bet Trent will share his attitude about the case more freely with you than with me."

"Makes sense."

"Fine, then I will suggest to Trent that you spend some time with him and Arianna again, so you can help reinforce his good image. The way we did it before, weeks ago. He'll buy it, no problem."

"Sounds like a plan."

Dopp smiled. "I know your paycheck is due in a week. I'll be sure to add a little something for your extra time."

"Thank you," Jed said graciously. "My pleasure."

"Seventy-third and Columbus," Trent told the cabdriver, hating that he had to pick up the watch before seeing Arianna. At home, he could at least change out of his suit.

Twenty minutes later, the same cab was speeding down Fifth Avenue toward Washington Square. Trent rubbed his palms on his jeans and looked out the window, ignoring the leather strap that felt too tight around his wrist. The glass face bore a scratch from being thrown at the wall, but the recording feature worked as well as ever. Outside the window, chic storefronts and fancy hotels sped by in a blur, until the cab stopped before the concrete arch at Washington Square Park. Trent ran into Arianna's building and climbed the stairs to her third-floor apartment. Before he knocked, he made sure to turn off the watch's ear, at least for now.

She answered the door with a tissue in one hand, wearing pajama pants and a tank top. Her ragged hair clung to her temples as if she had been lying down, crying.

"My God," he said, stepping inside and embracing her. She pressed her head against his chest, sniffling.

"What's done is done," she mumbled.

"It'll be okay," he said, aching to believe it. "There are still two men working practically around the clock, right?"

"Yeah."

"So we still have a chance."

She looked up at him, and a smile restored the beauty to her face. "We do."

"As bad as it is, this isn't the worst that could have happened."

She nodded, slipping a cold hand into his. "Come lie down with me. But let's not talk about this. I need a day away."

"I hear that."

She led him into her bedroom. Slanted light shone through the window, illuminating the dancing dust in its rays. Her red comforter sat on the floor in a fiery lump. On the bed, the white sheets were tangled.

"Looks like my bed most days," he joked.

"We should have slept here last night. Sorry I fell asleep on you."

"We can still make up for it." He kicked off his sneakers and slid on his stomach onto the mattress. Then he unhooked the watch-strap and put it on her nightstand behind a lamp so he couldn't see it. She climbed onto the bed and curled up next to him, slipping a hand around his waist. Her face burrowed into the warm crevice between his collarbone and chin, and he wrapped his arms around her, chuckling as her eyelashes tickled his neck. He wondered if she felt the same thrilling tingle where their bare skin touched: her forehead against his neck, her hand on his lower back, her shoulder against his biceps.

Her lips caressing his neck told him the answer. A flush of heat rushed to meet the spots where her lips touched him, as she moved up his throat to his jaw, over the tip of his chin, landing finally on his mouth. His lips burned to taste hers. They kissed hungrily before she drew back, pulled her tank top over her head, and unhooked her bra. Her breasts were sculpted ivory, exactly as he had imagined. He cupped them one by one with his mouth, feeling an aching yearning in his groin.

She ran her fingers through his hair and then down his back, pulling up his T-shirt. He yanked it over his head and she smiled at the parallel ridges on his torso, brushing her fingertips down the middle line from his chest to his waist, and then unbuttoned his jeans. As she touched him, he let out a little moan and pulled the drawstring of her pants untied. Her naked body was all curves bound by flat smoothness, no sign of its trauma within.

"You're beautiful," he murmured. With a demure smile, she reached over to the top drawer of her dresser and handed him a condom. He slid it on and then rolled on top of her, supporting himself with his elbows.

"I've wanted you this whole time," she whispered as he pushed into her slowly, so as not to hurt her.

Their eyes met as their bodies joined, and he knew that no words could express the desire he had been suppressing. Instead his body told her everything he wanted to say, with every move, it told her, as he lost himself in its rhythm, watching his own pleasure reflected in her open mouth, her pink cheeks. She writhed underneath him, hoisting her hips off the bed to receive every bit of him, faster and faster they moved, until, together, their bodies protested in one violent burst; she moaned, throwing her head back in fierce joy. As the pleasure dispersed, he watched every twitch of her face, overcome by a sense of awe and intimacy he had never before experienced.

She opened her eyes to catch him gazing down at her, and grinned.

"Wow," he murmured.

"Indeed."

Gently, he rolled off her and rested his hot cheek against his arm, inches away from her face. She reached up to stroke his bristly chin.

"Trent," she whispered. "I think I'm falling in love with you."

As if without permission from his mind, his throat grew a massive lump. He strained to gulp past it.

"What's wrong?" she asked.

He shook his head, unwilling to confront the reality in spoken terms: *I can't imagine life without you.*

"I don't ever want to get up," he said.

Her face relaxed. "You don't have to. Not today."

He closed his eyes, forcing himself to forget the vicious hourglass and the world it came from. In a later moment, he would fret about her; in a later moment, he would reach for the watch and revive his skilled deception, as well as the private suffering that came along with it. But for now, he would concentrate only on the delicate fingers stroking his face.

THIRTEEN

Trent reached for Arianna's hand across the kitchen table at his apartment. His right hand, which could easily palm a basketball or play a ten-key interval, dwarfed her left one. He closed his fingers over hers.

"How do you do anything with these little things?"

She chuckled. "It's brains not brawn, baby."

Baby. Embryo. Dopp.

And his lightness was shattered. Such inadvertent connections to his other reality had crept up often in the last several days. It was as if he lived with a chronic hacking cough that would abate—allowing him a few moments of bliss—but then return at the slightest trigger. The most mundane encounters would do: a gold cross necklace on a stranger; a headline about the stalled state budget; a glimpse of a classy brown watch.

"What?" Arianna said, noticing his slackened lips. "What did I say?"

"It's just hard," he said carefully. "To forget everything for a few minutes, but it's worse to remember. How do you stay positive?"

"Stress decreases my immune function." She smiled dryly.

"I'm sorry about Ian."

"It's not your fault. But Sam and Patrick are still giving me the cold shoulder."

Trent shook his head. "Wouldn't I have reported you by now?"

"You would think. When I brought them new embryos this afternoon, Sam literally turned his back on me and didn't even say good-bye. And I thought he and I were close."

"Weird," Trent remarked, thinking of his own fallout from the night he had seen the lab. Thrilled as he was to find hope and clarity, he was increasingly nervous at work—but the steep cost was one he would continue to pay as long as her life hung in the balance. At times, it struck him as absurd that his office looked the same when so much about his purpose there had changed. The painting of the Crucifix still hung on the wall, now a reminder of a different kind. As he passed familiar faces in the hallway, he wondered: Would they ever understand the cruel irony of their work—the actual lives suffering from disease because of them? He had to banish thoughts of Arianna to summon a cordial smile for his colleagues.

There, he was still one of them, and no one needed to be more certain of it than Dopp. So when Dopp had demanded the transcript and audio file of his visit to her apartment, Trent handed it over like a competent employee. Only it was the cut-and-pasted version, less the incriminating parts about the lab. He had uploaded the audio file from the watch to his computer at home, and then spent two hours deleting and chopping their conversation into a logical, safe flow. With a professional musician's software, he was able to match Arianna's tone and pitch to any words he improvised on her behalf. What remained was the requisite talk of her worries about her worsening condition, coaxed out by Trent's questions: "How do you feel?" and "What has your doctor been saying?"

Trent had placed this typed transcript on Dopp's desk with a sigh, his best portrayal of disgruntlement.

"Nothing?" Dopp asked.

"I'm sorry. That time with her was useless."

"Not good. She needs a push, a reminder of your trustworthiness."

"What do you suggest?"

Dopp's response was one Trent thought of now, as he caressed Arianna's smooth hand. The plan needed to be made; it was dangerous to procrastinate. He asked about her plans for New Year's Eve, the following Saturday night.

She shrugged. "I don't have any yet."

"Well, do you want to go to dinner with Megan and maybe my friend Jed again?"

The words felt like a dirty solicitation.

"Sure. I know she wants to meet you. And Jed seemed nice. Maybe they'll hit it off." She looked pleased at the idea.

"They might." *Sure,* he thought, *right after Jed brings flowers to your sickbed.*

He caught her staring past him, looking wistfully at his Yamaha keyboard.

"Can I play it?" she asked.

"Of course."

They rose from the table and squeezed onto the tiny leather seat in front of the keyboard. She picked out a few white and black keys before stumbling over the first few measures of Beethoven's "Für Elise."

"That's all I know," she said.

"Did you ever want to learn?"

"Always. I just never got around to it." She looked down for a moment and then back at him. "What do you like to play?"

"Would you like to hear 'Für Elise'?"

"Show me how it's done."

At the touch of his fingers, Beethoven's melody sprang from the keys, flush with tension and nuanced by careful dynamics. Trent's hands swept over rapid passages without compromising the pace. Each note lured his hands into the next chord and the next theme; the memory of the piece lived in his callused fingertips, crowded there with dozens of other pieces he had studied and loved. She applauded when he rested on the final chord.

"I knew you played piano, but I had no idea you *played.*"

He laughed. "It's just a hobby. Thank you, though."

She seized his hands, inspecting his fingers. "Who knew that these hairy hot dogs could pull off something like that?"

He laughed again, returning to that shifting, precious interval between bouts of anxiety. But the relief began to erode as soon as he became aware of it, like the edge of consciousness that splinters dreams. Trying to hold on to the feeling, he kissed her, and an idea struck him: it was one that would help enrich her days and, as a result, maybe help assuage some of his duplicitous guilt.

There was only one thing on Arianna's mind as she rushed to the lab the next morning, black case in hand: the progress of the research. But as she passed Washington Square Park, she saw a little boy a few yards ahead of her walking awkwardly next to his mother. His right foot twitched and stomped with each step as he held his mother's hand to stay balanced. As Arianna observed the pair, she noticed an orange rubber bracelet around the mother's wrist: the awareness-raising accessory of the MS Walks Foundation, a nonprofit that sponsored charity walks to raise money for research. Arianna's heart sank for them both—it was one thing to face the disease as an adult with access to a possible cure, but it was another to be a child or a parent staring down a lifetime of suffering.

"Can I play with them, Mommy?" the boy asked, pointing to the park, where a handful of kids were kicking a soccer ball.

The mother glanced at the kids with unmistakable longing. "Not today I'm afraid, sweetie."

Arianna yearned to rush up and put her arms around the woman, and to tell her son that one day, he might be able to play any sport he wanted. They just had to hold on a bit longer . . . hopefully not too much longer. . . .

The pair took no notice of her as she hurried past them, forcing her numb ankle to cooperate. It seemed she could not reach the lab fast enough. As she knocked on the door to deliver embryos, it felt like a relief to be so close to the source of her obsession.

Patrick opened the door and smiled for the first time all week. Her heart fluttered; progress?

"How's it going?" she asked.

"Better, now that we have more embryos."

She walked in and saw Sam peering into a microscope, his shoulders hunched. He did not look up.

"He's checking cells he altered the other day," Patrick explained.

Arianna's eyes widened. "So this could be it?"

Patrick looked hesitant. "It could be. But we test cells all the time."

"But eventually you'll hit on something. Statistically, you have to!"

A kind smile flickered on his lips, but Arianna could not read the emotion in his eyes. Was it hope, she wondered—or a tacit recognition of naïveté, a lament of idealism?

"You guys have come a long way," she said firmly. "It could happen any time."

She thought of the progress the scientists had made in the six months since they began researching: They had already coaxed the stem cells—total blanks—to differentiate into neuroprogenitor cells, the necessary first step before the cells could specify further into oligodendrocytes. These were the golden ticket, the crucial cells that could regenerate her spinal cord. But what would precipitate their occurrence remained a glaring unknown. They had to stumble upon the right combination of growth factors to coax the altered cells to differentiate the proper way. The growth factors were some series of molecular cues that would be injected into the cells to stimulate genes to make certain proteins that biologically spelled *oligodendrocytes*.

It was like mashing up all the languages of the world and then attempting to pluck the correct letters of the right alphabets to spell a specific word.

Arianna eyed Sam more closely. He was using an inverted microscope, which held a petri dish with cells. He lifted his head. She held her breath as he turned around.

Despite the face mask covering his nose and mouth, Arianna could tell that his eyes were solemn. Her heart felt as if it were bleeding out into her stomach.

Patrick put a hand on her shoulder. "It's a good thing you brought supplies."

She nodded, afraid to speak. But one thought prompted her to ask.

"What about the embryos Ian was working with? What happened to those?"

"Sam and I split them, but took out a few to make clones for the clinic."

Arianna frowned; it was already the last Friday of December, which meant that there would be an inspection Monday. And the freezer was missing dozens of embryos that still needed to be stocked.

"Don't tell me you're behind schedule."

Patrick smiled. "In fact, we're a step ahead. We already have the right amount for Monday all prepared and frozen. So, we're using Ian's batch to get a head start for January, since we're always rushing to make all the clones at the end of the month. Ian usually did the cloning, so I figured I would take over."

"Can't Sam help you?"

Patrick shrugged. "He'll throw a fit if he has to do anything mildly bureaucratic. It's easier for me to do it alone and let him research."

"I don't blame you." She rubbed her temples, feeling a sudden darting pain near her eyes. "I can't wait to get another month's inspection over with."

She glanced over at Sam, wondering if he was finally ready to come over and speak to her again. He had stepped into the tiny bathroom in the rear of the basement. The door was ajar, and through the crack, Arianna could see him leaning over the sink, vigorously scrubbing out the glass petri dish.

A copy of Saturday's *New York Times* lay discarded on their table at the restaurant, a noisy bar and grill place that Trent had suggested for its dependable chaos. Trent elbowed the newspaper aside as he sat down in the booth across from Arianna and loosened his shirt collar. Jed and Megan had yet to arrive. Not far from their table, a crowd of rowdy patrons sat around the bar. It was as far from the suffocating quiet of fine dining as he could take them.

The deception he would have to pass off tonight was troubling him: as far as Arianna knew, Jed was simply his college friend and a freelance reporter. Jed was also not supposed to know about her MS, so Trent could say nothing about that. And what was the name of the fraternity he and Jed were supposed to have been in? Had they even invented a name? Trent planned to say as little as possible, for if he and Jed contradicted each other at any point, it could be disastrous.

Trent looked into Arianna's watery blue eyes, desperately wishing they could share the night alone. Thin red veins stretched like map roads across her corneas. She was in a terrible mood: the scientists were getting nowhere, and she had just made the crushing decision to stop treating patients full-time because her strength was failing. Trent tried to reassure her it was only temporary, but her anger and frustration ran too deep.

She seized the newspaper on their table and flung it to the floor. "Screw the news."

"What's wrong?"

"This old OB-GYN on the Upper East Side is getting sued by the DEP for misplacing embryos. The man's been in practice for forty-two years!"

Trent winced, looking behind her to make sure Jed wasn't approaching.

"That's horrible," he said.

"Those DEP scum thrive off using scare tactics at the expense of good doctors like him."

"What's his name?"

"Brian Hanson."

"Brian Hanson? On the Upper East Side?"

Arianna frowned. "Yeah, you know him?"

"No," he said quickly. "I think I know someone who went to him once."

The response satisfied her, as Trent's mind reeled from the connection. He thought about the day Dopp had disciplined the doctor in his own waiting room, how privileged Trent had felt to witness the chief in action. Now he wondered how gaunt the doctor's face had become—and whether he was idealistic enough to fight or resigned to lose. Guilt seeped into Trent's conscience like a foul mist, and he fumbled for a distraction.

"By the way," he said, "how is Sam treating you lately?"

Her face fell to sadness. "Still ignoring me. You're obviously not a threat, but whenever I say so, he gets even angrier."

"You can't blame him, though. It's a tremendous risk to even refer to what you're doing at all. You really shouldn't talk about it."

"I know. Sometimes it's just hard for me to believe that there are people who don't support what we're doing, and not only that"—from behind her, Jed's figure drew closer—"they are actually doing everything they can to—"

"It's disgusting," Trent interrupted. "But, hey, look who's here."

Arianna turned around.

"Hey, guys," Jed said. His reddish hair was slicked back, oily as his smile.

Trent scooted over in the booth to make room for Jed, ignoring his own rising hostility. Then Arianna's face lit up and Trent followed her gaze across the room. A pretty woman with auburn ringlets was walking toward them. Arianna jumped out of the booth unsteadily and limped over to hug her.

"How's it going?" Jed whispered to him. "Any headway?"

"Nothing much," Trent muttered. "She's tough as a brick."

The women walked back to the table with linked arms.

"Jed, Trent, this is my cousin Megan—"

Megan gasped.

"Wait a second," she said, squinting at Jed. "You're that reporter who was outside the clinic!"

Trent's mouth dropped open: These two had met?

Jed looked just as shocked to see her. "Wait, wait," he said, looking at Arianna as if for the first time. "*You're* one of the doctors at that clinic? I had no idea you worked there!"

A true professional, Trent thought.

"It's *my* clinic." Arianna looked sharply at Jed. "What were you doing there?"

"I was researching a tip. I interviewed your cousin here when she walked out one day. But nothing ever came of it."

"I told you nothing would," Megan said as she and Arianna sat down.

"Sorry," Jed said. "I didn't mean to bother you."

"Such a small world," Trent marveled. "Anyways, nice to finally meet you, Megan." He extended his hand to her, hoping its shaking was imperceptible.

"Hang on," Arianna said, still frowning at Jed. "You got a tip about my clinic?"

"Yeah. That you had record numbers."

"According to whom?"

Jed did not waver. "A well-placed health source."

"I see." She paused. "I can't imagine why anyone would tip my numbers to a reporter. Yes, we've been getting more popular, but who cares except for the patients on the waiting list?"

Jed shrugged. "A lot of times these things mean nothing, but you have to check it out for the hell of it."

"What a coincidence," Trent remarked.

"Yeah, dude," Jed said, watching Arianna. "And when we went to dinner before, I met you and still had no idea."

"That's funny." Arianna looked thoughtful. "So what are you working on now? Now that you're done bothering my patients?" The defensiveness in her tone watered down her attempt at sarcasm.

"I've got a few leads," Jed answered evenly. "A lack of cleanliness at a certain hospital, a virus spreading through Bronx schools."

God, you're quick, Trent thought.

A waiter came up to their table and took drink orders: soda for the women, vodka martinis for the men. Trent silently thanked the bored-looking man for appearing, and for every second he took up reciting the list of specials.

Afterwards, Megan looked at Trent and Jed apologetically. "I hope you don't mind if I steal her for a second," she said, turning to Arianna. "Before we order, I need to ask about one of the drugs you prescribed—and trust me—" She turned back to them. "—it's not very appetizing."

"Go ahead," Trent said. "By all means."

"We'll be right back."

"That's my life," Arianna joked. "Always on call." She got up to follow Megan, whose hand closed around her arm. Trent watched their receding figures until they were out of earshot.

• • •

Arianna felt Megan's fingers clamping her biceps as they walked away from the table.

"What's up?"

Megan steered her toward the back of the restaurant, past the raucous bar, to the restroom. She said nothing until the door closed behind them, sealing out the din of the restaurant. Then she scanned the bottom of each of the four stalls, verifying that they were the only occupants, and leaned hard against the door.

"This is all so bizarre," she finally said. "I never expected to see that guy again."

"I know," Arianna agreed. "It's a weird coincidence."

"How do they know each other?"

"College. Trent told me they met in journalism class and then joined the same frat. I guess it's not strange in that way—it makes sense that they both became journalists, although now Trent is writing a book."

"And you met him at a book signing."

"Right. The coincidence is really the fact that Jed covers the health beat, which somehow led him to my clinic. I just wonder who his source was."

"Do you think Trent knows?"

"I doubt it; otherwise, he would have told me. But whoever it was had access to my numbers, so the person must have an in at the DEP."

"Which makes me wonder—"

Arianna nodded. "How did Jed get to this person? And what else does he or she know?"

"Exactly. But you can't ask Jed directly."

"Plus I don't want to seem concerned."

"Should you be?"

"What do you mean?"

Megan's thin eyebrows knitted. "What if he wants to reopen the story about the clinic? Now that he knows Trent has access to you, maybe he'll pump him for details—I knew it was a bad idea to tell him!"

Arianna shook her head. "Seriously, Meg, what do you think means more to him? Helping his friend get a scoop or my life?"

"You haven't known him that long, Arianna. And he's been friends with this guy for years."

"He's not going to say anything. You sound like Sam."

"Maybe Sam has a point. We can't take any chances!"

Arianna sighed; why did no one trust her judgment anymore?

"You just don't know him like I do," she said. "He would never hurt me. If anything, confiding in him has widened my support system. You, Sam and the Ericsons, and now him—you guys are it for me. And I don't even know about Sam anymore."

"I hope you're right. And what about Jed? Are you worried?"

"Well, I wasn't that worried the first time you ran into him, and I'm not that worried now, for the same reason: If the DEP had any clue, they would have been all over me by now."

"But what if someone there is still suspicious about your numbers?"

"So what? I've passed every inspection and audit." A cunning smile tugged at Arianna's lips. "So really, they've got nothing to go on."

Trent and Jed both sighed as soon as Arianna and Megan disappeared into the back of the restaurant.

"Shit, man," Jed said. "That was *close*."

"You're pretty fast on your feet."

"Thanks. I can't believe that chick is her cousin. Is she even allowed to treat family?"

Trent shrugged, feeling his gut tighten again. He wondered if there was any way Jed could tell. "Yeah, why not? Plus I'm sure she's doing it for free."

"Oh. So what do you make of the case so far? Do you think she's going to tell you anything soon?"

"I think she would have by now. We've been hanging out for quite a while, so I don't know why it's taking so long. Maybe there's nothing to tell?"

"Maybe. But she did seem to get kind of defensive about her numbers, like she had something to prove. Or maybe I'm reading into it."

Trent shrugged again, aiming for subtle doubt and a hint of detachment. "Who knows? I've just got to do the job as long as the boss wants to. I hope we're not wasting our time, though. For the department's sake."

"Yeah, me, too. So you're not as eager about it as you used to be, huh?"

"I just don't know if it's been worth it. All this effort—for what?"

"I hear you, man."

The waiter returned to deliver their drinks. As soon as Trent's vodka martini touched the table, he picked it up. "Cheers," he said. "To effort paying off."

Jed lifted his own. "I'll drink to that."

Their glasses clinked. The clear liquid stung Trent's throat and dulled to warmth sliding into his stomach. When he set the glass down, he scanned the room and saw the women moving toward them, whispering to each other.

"They're coming back," Trent muttered. And then, louder, "So what neighborhood are you looking to move to?"

"I'm thinking about Murray Hill," Jed replied without missing a beat. "The rent is more reasonable over there."

Arianna and Megan scooted into the booth as Trent answered, "Yeah, prices are so crazy. I don't know how long I'll be able to stay in my place on my savings. Unless I sell my book."

Arianna smiled at him encouragingly, but before she could speak, the waiter appeared again to take their orders. The waiter's presence was comforting, and when he disappeared, Trent took another generous sip of his martini. He set the glass down with renewed energy.

"Let's talk about something happy," he declared. *Off topic,* he thought.

"I have something," Arianna said. "My piano lessons!"

"Oh?" Jed asked. "You play?"

"Well, thanks to Trent, I'm taking lessons now. He surprised me with them!"

The previous night, Trent had invited Arianna over to meet a Juilliard piano professor for private lessons using his keyboard. He knew she had regretted never learning to play, and his thoughtfulness had thrilled her. When she sat down to play a scale, Trent had been surprised at the poignancy of the simple notes under her fingers—like a warrior's call to battle, they sounded plaintive yet proud, the emotion of a symphony condensed into a scale. It was perhaps the greatest gift he could have given her—an outlet to express her exultant sense of life, which was precisely what had drawn him to her.

"Cool," Jed said. "That was nice of you, man. What made you do that?"

"It means she has to come over to my place and practice," Trent half joked.

"No wonder I haven't see you much lately," Jed teased.

Perfect opening to reinforce my good-guy image, Trent thought. "Do you miss me?" he joked.

"Of course," Jed responded. "What's Friday night without my brother?"

"I guess I have been taking over your guy time," Arianna admitted.

"Don't worry about it," Trent replied, smiling sadly. *I have my whole life to make up for it.*

The group parted an hour later after a dinner that segued into peacefully irrelevant conversation about sports, pop culture, and movies. It was well before midnight, but Trent could tell that Arianna was exhausted, and he was glad to turn in early. They starting walking back to his apartment.

But just as he indulged a sigh of relief, Arianna grabbed his forearm.

"Are you okay?" he asked, assuming she had lost her balance.

She looked intently into his eyes. "Did you have any idea before that Jed was snooping around my clinic?"

"Not at all. He never mentioned anything to me—we didn't realize the connection until tonight."

The air outside felt chilled, like the physical manifestation of dread.

"So," she said, "you must not know who his health source was, then?"

"I have no idea."

"It had to have been someone with access to the DEP, since the person had my numbers. Could you find out?"

He hesitated. "You want me to ask Jed?"

"Do you think he would tell you?"

"Doubtful. You know that keeping sources confidential is a cardinal rule of journalism. It's the only way reporters are able to get access to inside people at all."

Arianna sighed. "I just wonder what else that person knows. But at the same time, it can't be much, since the lab is still safe and the clinic is doing fine."

Trent put his arm around her shoulders. "Try not to worry about it."

"Did Jed say anything when we went to the bathroom? Megan was worried he might want to reopen his story, now that he knows you could get information from me."

"I'm not going to scoop you, Arianna. And if you thought I would, then I don't think you would be here right now."

"True."

"We talked briefly about the clinic. I said that you're just a really popular doctor."

"Thank you. I told Megan you wouldn't give us away; it was ridiculous to even consider it."

Trent felt her shoulders loosen under the weight of his arm.

"I guess I took enough of a chance telling you. But I trust only you."

He resisted his urge to stiffen. "How come?"

"Because I know you love me."

"I do." Overcome by a sudden fervor, he stopped short on the sidewalk. She turned to face him, and her skin looked pallid in the moonlight. He took her cheeks with both hands, wishing he could rub some color back into them. "I would never tell anyone," he said. "I want to protect you however I possibly can."

"I wish you could."

He held her gaze for a moment—could she tell it was meaningful?—and then kissed her lightly. They continued to walk in silence. Her cane slapped the ground at regular intervals, a third footstep.

Trent's mind wandered to the lab in the church basement and its enormous potential just out of reach. While the public would no doubt see the lab as scandalous, Trent realized that its existence was actually their culture's greatest sign of enlightenment.

"Hey," he said, "I've been meaning to ask you something about the lab. What does 'sad face' mean? That password you used at the door?"

She chuckled. "I thought you would ask. It's an acronym."

"For what?"

"First I'll tell you how we came up with it. At my clinic, I need to separate the donated embryos from the ones that come from actual patients. But since I don't want the DEP inspectors to understand, I put the donated embryos in a separate cluster in the incubator, and label that area with a picture of a sad face. Whenever the inspectors ask why, I say that those embryos just aren't looking viable for pregnancy, so I set them apart until they're ready to be frozen. In reality, when those embryos are ready, I bring them to the lab. I started referring to them as the sad-face embryos, and the scientists got a kick out of it. Then one day, when we were complaining about bureaucracy, Patrick suggested that we coin an acronym for our group to go by, like an answer to the DEP. So Sam, always the snarky clever one, suggested we go by SADFACE. But of course, we all wanted to know what it would stand for. And then, totally straight-faced, he said, 'Scientists and Doctors Fighting Absurd Christian Edicts.'"

Trent laughed. "That's great. Sam is witty as hell."

Arianna grinned. "Just like my dad was."

Trent found her hand. The next words escaped him naturally, though he had shied away from discussing her father at all.

"He would have been so proud of you."

Arianna's smile faded as she stared reticently at the sidewalk. Trent inferred that there were no words available to express the complexity of her emotions: her enduring grief over her father's death; her love of his memory; and her gratitude toward Trent for understanding both.

Her fingers, thin and bony, tightened around his, rendering the tacit message.

Trent knew then what else she wanted to say:

No words were necessary.

FOURTEEN

"You're sure you don't want to leave now, Sam?" Patrick asked, standing at the door of the lab. His briefcase hung over his shoulder, stuffed with his folded white coat. "It's New Year's Day! You could go home for a change . . . take a walk. . . ."

Sam looked up from his microscope, focusing his strained eyes on Patrick. Contempt blistered his throat. He glared, pulling his face mask down around his neck. "A walk?"

Patrick shrugged. "There's more to the world than this basement. Like the sun and fresh air." He smiled. "Ring a bell?"

"No."

Patrick's smile faltered. "All right. Then I'll see you tomorrow morning."

Sam grunted and turned back to the microscope. The door closed softly and he heard one, two, three bolts lock. Then silence, except for the buzzing of the overhead lights. Or perhaps it was a ringing in his ear, the kind he noticed only in total silence. He glanced at the rat cages; even those little beasts were still.

He shifted his weight on the stool and heard a crack in his back—loud, like a pop. It felt good. Maybe he should stretch. His eyes were blurring, and the cells on the slide were becoming difficult to distinguish. He knew he needed to focus on an object far away for a minute to buy another few hours of visual clarity. So he stood up and rubbed his numb rear, leaning backwards against his hands, staring at the rat cages in the corner. They weren't that far away, but in one room, nothing was. He glanced next to the cages at the five metal folding chairs stacked against the wall.

Only a few hours ago, Arianna had been sitting on one of them.

Hers was the first chair, the one touching the wall. After the group's regular Sunday afternoon meeting, Sam had folded up the chairs, inadvertently noting hers. Only five members remained—himself; Patrick; the two doctors at the clinic, Gavin Ericson and his wife, Emily; and Arianna. But Sam was aware only of her. Even sitting, her movements had seemed stiff as she crossed and recrossed her legs.

He thought of the way she had glanced at him during the meeting—with the hurt and confusion of an abandoned child. He looked away and barely spoke for the rest of the meeting. But how could she expect him to just nod and smile, after she had brought that man here? That *dolt* who had the gall to kiss her in front of him? Of course, during the meeting, Arianna was so quick to point out that he had caused them no harm, that he meant no harm, excuse after excuse. And the infuriating part was that Patrick, Gavin, and Emily had nodded. Almost a week had passed, and they were in no greater danger that they could detect. Despite the premature loss of Ian, it seemed her carelessness was forgiven.

Sam bristled when she spoke of him. Each time, her face glowed. It was not the fluorescent lights. She acquired the semblance of health when his name rolled off her tongue, restoring that joyous dimple in her chin, as if it boosted her to say that single syllable: Trent.

But when she looked at Sam, sorrow. How could it have come to this? And how could he ever explain to her? The truth pained him like a physical ailment when he slept in his cot here at nights, his curved back sinking low to the ground in the darkness. Only then, without the mental distraction of his research, would his mind allow their glorious old times to replay. It was okay, he told himself, to bask in those not-so-distant memories, even if it hardened a flimsy hope; it was okay as long as it fueled him to continue his work. She would not care what fantasy he lived in, as long as he delivered results; that was all he meant to her now. So it did no harm to recall those times when he was the centerpiece of her world. Whatever suffering both of them might still endure, he had lived those times, and because of them—or perhaps in spite of them—he would continue to live.

He returned his tired eyes to the microscope. The slides still looked blurry. Frustration welled within him. He did not have time for petty optic nonsense. With Ian gone for good and Patrick for the day, the lab felt full of pressure, as if it were miles below sea level instead of only ten feet underground. Every combination of growth factors he had tried so far had produced a swarm of incorrectly differentiated cells, including some that would surely lead to cancer if implanted in Arianna's spinal cord. The resulting cells had to be pure oligodendrocytes if they were to have any real chance of saving her life. To be healthy, the body demanded perfection of its parts. But perfection was not yet the province of such nascent biotechnology. If only they had had the last twenty years to research, she might have been in no danger at all today, Sam thought. Her treatment might have been a routine outpatient surgery.

He stared harder down the barrel of the microscope. The cells looked like indistinct clumps on the slide. He blinked several times, his eyelashes brushing the lens. But the cell outlines did not appear to sharpen. He could not deny that his poor sight was due to lack of sleep.

With a sigh, he ripped off his mask and gloves, pulled off his lab coat, and left it all in a heap on the floor. He flicked off the lights and stumbled toward his cot. Just a few hours of sleep would do the trick, he thought, feeling his way forward. His hand hit an aluminum rod, and he felt along the nylon fabric to the pillow resting at one end. As he climbed onto the cot, it groaned under his weight and sank low. He could sense the concrete coolness of the ground below his back.

On the night she had found him in his apartment, a year ago, he had been lying in darkness, coming out of an intoxicated stupor. The memory of those first few minutes was vague: a haze pinpricked by the sound of a doorbell he did not realize he had. He had picked himself up off the couch and staggered to the door, cursing the doorman for allowing an unannounced visitor to drop by. Damn tax collector, he had thought. But hadn't he paid the bills? Or was that last month?

He opened the door. The sight of a beautiful woman standing there made him shut it. Wrong apartment. The bell rang again—a sharp note, like a dog's cry. Hesitating, he opened the door a second time.

"Sam Lisio?" the woman said tentatively, a hopeful smile on her lips.

And then she had shifted into focus: those long black waves covering her shoulders, the high cheekbones and the intelligent blue eyes, but now with tiny crow's-feet at the corners, the only testament to the intervening sixteen years. He wondered later how he must have looked to her then, with his thinning white hair and sallow skin, and the scent of whiskey permeating the air between them.

"Arianna Drake?" he ventured.

"Sam, I can't believe I found you!"

"After all these years . . . ," he mumbled, fighting the mental fog of alcohol and memory lapse to recall the last time he had seen her. It must have been at one of her staged rallies at Columbia, right before the DEP swept in and arrested him. Oh, how quixotic they had been at that rally—he, a respected professor, and she, his admiring student—to believe that logic would prevail. Only three months later, he had stepped into his prison cell, fifty-four square feet of helplessness.

"What are you doing here?" he blurted.

Her proposition, and the reason for it, had shocked him out of his daze. The risks involved did not bother him; returning to jail was not much worse than the way he was living, in purposeless, endless solitude. And the thought of having his own lab with fresh embryos—it was like handing eyes back to an artist so he could paint his masterpiece. Of course, he would have to study his neurobiology texts again, to be sure he remembered all the procedures correctly, and he would have to examine the pathology of multiple sclerosis in particular. Years before, his peers around the country had been starting to develop theories about MS and embryonic stem cells that could help him get started, and he knew just which scientific journals to consult.

"You'll do it?" she had gasped. "You really want to do it?"

"I want nothing more," he had replied.

As he lay asleep on the cot, Sam's lips moved to form the words in accordance with the memory. The image of her unbridled elation sprang to mind, on cue, as the familiar sequence progressed. How she had looked at him in tears, with so much gratitude, so much hope, as if he were the only person in her world worthy of a hero's reception. Only one other woman had ever looked at him like that.

Never did he think he would look back again. Shame and joy chafed within him, an inseparable pair, yet each dulled the other. A woman three decades his junior; a woman who had likened him to her own father; a woman whose life he had the power to save.

He almost told her once, a few months back when they had shared a steak dinner at her apartment. Though their lives flowed from the same high-pressured well of uncertainty, together they found reason to smile; together they laughed. With her, time simply slipped away. Sam remembered thinking that life used to be like this, that it still could be. It saddened him to say good-bye to her even for a night—and so, on that night, he had hovered outside her apartment, daring himself to chase his heart back inside. And even then, he knew he was fooling himself. As long as she did not know, he could keep clinging to the hope that perhaps one day, after he managed to solve the biological lock on those cells, she would see him as the man he really was—a man full of brilliance and passion and life. And not just as the old hermit he had become, the emotional coward who fended off human closeness with irritability.

A trilling noise startled him awake. His cell phone was ringing somewhere on the counter next to his microscope. He jumped out of the cot, swearing at the darkness. While the phone continued to jingle, he felt for the light switch on the wall, flicked it on, and then rushed to the counter. As the phone vibrated between his fingers, he fumbled to open it.

"Hello?"

"Sam, hi, it's me." Arianna. Sounding nervous.

"Hi," he said gruffly.

"Am I bothering you?"

"I was taking a nap."

"Right now? It's seven P.M."

"So?"

She paused. "Well, never mind, then."

His tone softened. "What's up?"

"I thought you might want to come over for dinner."

"Why?"

"I know I've been seeing a lot of Trent lately, so you and I haven't spent much time together. Let me make it up to you."

Despite the dreaded syllable, Sam plucked joy from her words: She had not forgotten him. But her voice sounded more subdued on the phone than he remembered.

"Sam? Hello?"

He cleared his throat, feeling aghast at himself. Given what she was facing, his jealousy was strikingly trivial.

"I appreciate the offer, Arianna, but I should be getting back to work." The crustiness in his tone was gone. "We can't waste time."

Dopp sat in his office, staring out at the dreariness of January. Skeletal treetops poked through fog in Central Park like hands reaching up for help. Charcoal clouds hung low in the sky, obscuring buildings.

Why was the Lord leading him on a path to frustration?

The current plan was not working. A week into the New Year, progress remained nonexistent. That manipulating abortionist had passed the monthly inspection, though her clinic's embryo count was still inexplicably high. And Trent continued to waste time with her. With lawmakers still leaning toward the wrong priorities, the department might as well be a sinking ship, Dopp thought. And they had no other leads.

He turned to his desk and once more scoured the transcripts

that Trent placed there each morning. Banal conversation dulled the pages. *How is your clinic?* Trent would often ask. *Fine. Busy.* Short and pat. Never a hint that something was awry.

Yet a drastic move could still be made. All week, Dopp had wondered if it was time; he had prayed, paced, squirmed, not slept. The move would be a gamble, an irreversible toss of the dice tied straight to his livelihood. He couldn't imagine facing his wife in the meantime, not to mention his kids. But his options were as slim as ever: to wait and hope, or to act and hope? At least the latter would give him a sense of control, while God formulated his fate.

The phone rang, filling the office with its sharp trill.

"Dopp, Windra here." The man's voice sounded rushed.

"Senator Windra! How nice to hear from you." Dopp cringed as he spoke. The state's top Republican, Senate Majority Leader Chuck Windra, called him directly only when there was trouble.

"Listen," Windra said, "I want to give you a heads-up about the budget. The buzz I'm hearing around here is that it's still not looking too good for you."

Dopp swallowed. "Because of the Department of Embryo-Fetal Protection?"

"Yes. The moderates are saying that's a bigger priority than the DEP right now. And, personally, it's hard for me to disagree. You know I support you, Gideon, but I don't have to tell you that pregnant women are a dime a dozen, and your bureau hasn't seen much action for a while. And yours is the biggest one in the state."

"But we just filed a class action lawsuit against a doctor—"

"Small change, Gideon. Frankly, it looks like you're grasping at straws."

"I can assure you that is not the case. We are every bit as productive as we've always been, if not more."

"I hope so, because there was some pretty ugly talk last week."

"What do you mean?"

"I wasn't going to mention it, but I guess you should know. Some are saying that DEP isn't even necessary anymore—that basically nobody today has the training to manipulate embryos anymore, so we should start to phase out the department altogether."

Dopp gasped. "Are you kidding?"

"I'm afraid not."

"But EUEs can still be killed!"

"They could, and that's why I'm still behind you. Although, what would be the point?"

"Why do any murderers kill?" Dopp retorted. "Just because they don't have a good reason doesn't mean we should abolish the police force!"

"It's not me you have to convince. Maybe there's something you could do to bring the DEP to the forefront of the conversation again? To remind us why it's still worthy of taxpayer dollars?"

Dopp fumed silently. If Trent had done his job by now, Windra would not be calling. But with or without Arianna, there was still a way to generate headlines. And if they could bring her down in the process, they would be set.

"Realistically, how long would you say we have until the budget talks officially start?"

"Well, the bribery investigation is set to conclude in a few weeks, and as soon as that happens, the governor will either be forced to resign or be cleared. In any case, the budget is going to be the first order of business. We're all anxious to get it sorted out."

A few weeks, Dopp thought. Plenty of time to reap a payoff if he could summon the courage to act.

"Windra," he said, "I'll get back to you. I think I have an idea."

As soon as he hung up the phone, Dopp swiveled in his chair and faced his glass wall, staring at the dissipating morning fog. His idea would require extensive manpower, thus stretching the department's already-thin budget. But, he reasoned, one must spend money to make money. If the department was to be a casualty of next year's budget anyway, it made sense to use every last dollar now to fight for its existence. The plan would sound extreme to his colleagues, but Dopp was confident they would trust his management. And sure, it would generate headlines for a few days, but talk would fade unless the momentum continued somehow. Since Arianna was their only lead, the goal was clear: If they could find a shocking reason to shut down her clinic, no one in Albany could assert that the DEP was irrelevant or inactive. The media storm around a scandalous shut-down and court trial would be God's ultimate blessing for the department's future.

And if anything else was clear, it was that Trent was useless. It was a shame; the zeal Dopp had recognized in Trent at the beginning of the case had plainly evaporated. The evidence had come in the form of Jed's integrity control report. The report concluded with a paragraph that was painful—and embarrassing—to read:

> Trent's lack of persistence is frighteningly apparent. He confessed that he hoped he was not wasting his time on a dead-end case, and then went on to reveal his own frustration about what he termed a worthless effort. At the same time, when the topic of Arianna's clinic was broached, she perhaps protested too much about its growing popularity. Together, these conclusions imply an unstable situation for our department, one that ought to be rectified before any serious damage is done.

Dopp reread the report on his computer screen, his agitation escalating with each word. By the time he finished, he could almost feel the rancid breath of Albany on his neck. No, he thought, there could be no more putting it off: the time to act was now.

Trent's stomach tightened when his office phone began to ring. He dreaded hearing that booming voice, but answered the call after the third ring.

"Come see me," demanded the voice. *Click.*

Robotically, Trent got up, brushed off his suit, and walked to the office he knew too well. The reason for this sudden meeting, and the icy tone, was no mystery: Dopp was frustrated with the case's inertia. Something had to change. Trent could already hear the words, and in his mind, he practiced his forthcoming lie, one that cast Arianna in an innocent light. Would it forestall the inevitable, if only a little longer? The chances seemed slim: Dopp was determined to find fault with her, even if Trent's hints appeared to indicate otherwise. And, worse, what if Dopp was frustrated enough to remove him from the case? How could Trent protect her then?

By the time he reached the office, his heart was pumping at the base of his throat. He opened the door, and was surprised to see Jed sitting in one of the two leather guest chairs in front of Dopp's desk.

Dopp was nodding and muttering something, but when Trent walked in, he grew stern. "Sit down."

Trent nodded hello and sat. Now, he told himself, *spit it out.* He smiled, lips stretching to reveal his teeth.

"I was about to come talk to you. I finally made some progress."

Dopp raised his eyebrows skeptically. "You did?"

"Last night, I asked her point blank where she's always going after work, since I never followed her anywhere interesting. I'm pretty sure she trusts me by now, so I thought it was about time to get to the point."

"And?"

"And you would never believe how disappointing the answer was: the doctor."

"The doctor?"

"She has a specialist in the East Village who she has to see regularly for treatment and monitoring."

Dopp looked unimpressed. "If it's as simple as that, why did she never mention it?"

"She doesn't like focusing on her MS," Trent replied. "She usually refuses to talk about it at all."

"I don't believe her. First of all, if she were sick enough to require such frequent doctor's appointments, she would not still be going to work, even part-time. Second of all, Trent, you are very gullible. Did you forget that she has lied to your face in the past? She told you she was a Christian, do you remember that? And then she admitted to doing abortions! She is a total manipulator, and you fell for it again."

"You think so?" Trent said helplessly.

"Give me one good reason not to take you off this case right now. You have done nothing to advance our agenda."

"I have," he protested, racking his brain. "I surprised her with piano lessons! To make her think that I really care about her, so she will trust me and open up to me. Even you said it would take time!"

"That did seem like a good move," Jed said, nodding at Dopp. "She brought it up at our dinner and seemed really happy about it."

Trent threw Jed a grateful look. "I don't want to let you down, boss," he said. "Please just give me a little longer to work on this. I'll keep following her to the doctor's or wherever. I'll do whatever it takes."

"This is the kind of motivation I should have been seeing for weeks from you, Trent. Not your wishy-washy apathy. I know you're bored."

"I'm not! I admit to getting a little frustrated here and there, but that was just my own inexperience, and I realize that now. You're the boss and you know what to do."

Dopp's face relaxed. "Look, Trent. I won't take you off the case, but I'm not going to let you do it alone anymore either. It's taking too long. We only have a few weeks until the budget talks start up again, and this case is too important to let slide on what you yourself called *inexperience*."

Trent chomped down on his lower lip to prevent himself from protesting. The taste of blood dribbled onto his tongue.

"I didn't think we would have to resort to this," Dopp went on, looking from Trent to Jed. "But we have little choice if we want results. I am going to authorize a quiet sweep of all labs within the vicinity of the East Village. No public announcements, because we don't want to give them time to hide anything."

Trent felt himself catch his breath.

"But that's not all. I am instituting a new policy for our bureau, which will cost extra manpower and money, but it's our last resort and I think it's a good one. Unless we do something to catch Albany's attention again, they could cheat us out of a lot of money. So, starting tomorrow, we will begin a quiet new policy of random surprise inspections at any fertility clinic in our jurisdiction—all five boroughs. So when Banks shows up weeks ahead of schedule, Arianna will have no time to cover her tracks—and if she is stealing embryos from her clinic, we'll catch her red-handed."

Trent's head felt as if he were submerged in a deep pool of water. He said nothing, thought nothing.

Jed was nodding his approval. "But I have a question, boss. Won't the clinics have to submit the records of their embryo counts more often than once a month, then, if we can inspect them at any time? We'll always need to know the most current counts."

Dopp smiled. "Yes. We will. Which is why we will now require them to submit daily, not monthly, counts of their embryo stocks. But we won't announce this publicly yet—instead we'll just let the news break naturally tomorrow after we start the inspections. And then we'll issue a notice to all clinics with our new regulations."

"But the inspectors won't have the most current counts when they start tomorrow, so how will they know if the embryo reserves are accurate?"

"That's very simple," Dopp answered calmly. "The inspectors will flash their DEP badges. It's not as efficient as the way we do it, but it will work: just like that, the doctors will have to open their own record books."

Numbly, Trent realized he needed to show interest in the plan. "How are you going to explain this to the rest of the department?"

Dopp's gaze shifted to him. Trent gnawed the raw flesh of his lower lip, hardly feeling the pain.

"I will circulate an internal memo to the whole department," Dopp said, brushing his fingertips against his chin. His eyes shifted to a spot on the wall above Trent's head. "Look for it in your in-box before the end of the day. The subject line will be: 'Crackdown.'"

FIFTEEN

Trent was staring at his computer screen when it happened: A box in the lower right-hand corner popped up with a ding. *One new message.*

TO: undisclosed recipients
FROM: gdopp@dep.gov
SENT: Monday, January 10, 2028 at 4:26 P.M.
SUBJECT: Crackdown

To my trusted colleagues,

Due to recent worrisome behavior at a number of fertility clinics, I am hereby instituting a new policy of random, surprise inspections. Every Monday, I will e-mail a weekly list of the targeted clinics and the agents who will be inspecting them. Starting tomorrow, these inspections will quietly begin. After the news inevitably breaks, we will announce to all clinics that we now require daily electronic filing of their EVE counts, rather than monthly, so that we can more closely monitor them. I regret that this means many of you will be working overtime, but let us pray this is a temporary measure until the situation improves.

The list for this week is as follows:

Washington Square Center for Reproductive Medicine—Inspector Banks
Family Fertility Center—Inspector Hodges
East Side Fertility Associates—Inspector Gordon
Infertility Solutions—Inspector Freeman

Queens Center for Assisted Reproduction—Inspector Jenkins
Family Beginnings—Inspector Laughlin

Please know that I will gladly address any of your questions or concerns. Lastly, please also note that this information is to remain strictly confidential within the department until further notice. I appreciate your full cooperation in this sensitive matter.

Regards,
Gideon Dopp
Chief Supervisor, New York City Bureau of the Department of Embryo Preservation

Behold, Children are a heritage from the Lord,
The fruit of the womb is a reward. —PSALM 127:3

CONFIDENTIALITY NOTICE: This electronic mail message contains information intended for the exclusive use of the individual or entity to whom it is addressed and may contain information that is privileged and/or confidential. Disclosure of any content herein will result in appropriate legal action.

Trent grimaced. For a time, he sat completely still, reading and rereading the e-mail, which he had dreaded receiving all afternoon. A single thought overwhelmed him: *Do I have to tell her who I am?*

He knew he had to warn her about the impending inspection before it destroyed all their hopes. But how could he explain without revealing his identity? It was like rafting on a river littered with boulders; there had to be a safe route somewhere, but all he could see was danger. *Tell her who I am,* he thought, *and risk her never speaking to me again. Don't tell her anything; risk the inspection ruining everything.*

He felt his desperation climbing. No, he thought, there had to be a third option, and if only he could focus his mind on strategy instead of fear, he might be able to think of something.

A copy of the *Daily News* lay on his desk, leftover from the morning's subway ride. The headline on the cover quipped, BED OF MALES! The mayor of Newark had been caught having an affair with his male secretary; it was shocking and scandalous, exactly the stuff of tabloid newspapers. Trent turned back to the e-mail glowing on his computer screen. It was not exactly sexy, he thought, but it screamed *scoop,* and it could have a far greater impact on the public than some politician's seamy affair.

The pieces of a plan were coming together on the horizon of his mind—vague at first, and then sharper, integrated, whole. He grabbed the newspaper off the desk and stuffed it into his briefcase. For the idea to work, he could not enact it here or at home, where his computer was too easy to trace. A quick search online pointed him to the perfect anonymous office.

On the wall, the clock hands pointed to 4:57 P.M. Trent jumped out of his chair, turned off his computer and lights, and headed out before any of his colleagues could stop by to speculate about the new policy.

Ten minutes later, he walked into the Broadway Cyber Café, an Internet café in Times Square that accommodated both phone conversations and privacy; thick plastic slats separated the rows of computers. Tucked between a massive toy store and a famous theater, the café was narrow inside, but long. The place hummed with the patter of typing and the whir of an espresso machine. About ten people sat dispersed throughout the room, sipping coffee and staring at their screens. It cost $8.50 for a half hour. Trent paid cash and then selected a computer near the back of the café, on the end. No one was next to him.

He signed in to his work e-mail and brought up Dopp's note, even though he had unintentionally memorized it. Then he pulled out his phone, checked around for eavesdroppers, and dialed Arianna's number. What if she was too weak to deal with this? The phone began to ring in his ear and he closed his eyes. What if her body couldn't take the stress?

"Trent!" her voice exclaimed. "I was just going to call you!" Exuberance burst through the line like champagne from a bottle.

"You were?"

"I just talked to Sam—and it sounds like they're getting close to a breakthrough!"

Trent felt himself gasp. "No!"

"Yes! They might be almost there!"

"How do they know?"

"Remember I told you how they need to add the right combination of these molecules, these growth factors, to get the stem cells to transform into this one type of cell that I need?"

"Right. The oli-somethings?"

She laughed brightly, clinks of a dozen crystal glasses. "Yes, oligodendrocytes. Well, the growth factors that they just tested spawned some oligos for the first time, as well as some other cells that weren't the right ones, but still—they're finally on the right track. Sam thinks they just need to tweak the combination now, and then once they manage to come up with pure oligos, we can transplant them into my spinal cord!"

The joy in her voice was unbearable.

"Arianna, wait."

"What's wrong?"

"Are you alone?"

"Yeah, I'm just bringing them new embryos. What's up?"

"I need to tell you something." He took a deep breath.

"What?"

"I just got some upsetting news about the DEP. Remember Jed's insider health source, the one who tipped him off to your clinic's numbers? Well, that person just landed him a huge scoop: The DEP is going to change its inspection policy starting tomorrow, when they plan to begin random surprise inspections at whatever clinics they choose. Apparently, there was a list of clinics in an e-mail sent to the whole department, and Jed's source sent him a copy of it. He immediately noticed that your clinic is on the list and called to let me know."

"What? Oh my God! Did you say starting tomorrow?"

"Yes."

"But there's embryos missing from the clinic's lab. . . . We weren't going to have the clones ready until the end of the month!"

"Is there anything you can do to get them?"

"Shit, I don't know—I can't believe this. . . ."

"There has to be something you can do."

"Wait, Patrick told me a while ago that they used Ian's embryos to make clones. But I don't know how many they made or how many we need."

"Go check your records."

"But I haven't filed our monthly count yet—how is the inspector even going to know how many we're supposed to have leftover?"

"I don't know all the details," Trent allowed. "But I bet those assholes will find a way."

"I guess they could make me open my books. I'm going to go check right now. You didn't tell Jed anything right?"

"Of course not."

"Where is the story going to run tomorrow?"

"The *Daily News*. He couldn't write it tonight, so he passed it along to his friend there."

"God, if it weren't for him calling you . . . I owe him big. But of course, he'll never know it."

"No, he won't." *And now,* Trent thought, *I'll have to make sure you never talk to him again.*

"But do you know what this could mean still?" Her voice quivered. "If the DEP fucks this up—"

"No," he said firmly, "you'll—"

Her voice cut through his. "Gotta go. Can't waste time."

Trent heard a click and the line went dead.

A box on the computer flashed in red on his screen: twenty minutes left.

He closed his eyes and pressed his forehead against his palm. Sweat smeared onto his hand and dribbled down his wrist, but he didn't bother to wipe it away. The clicking of keyboards around him faded as anguish set in. To know he could help her only to a degree; to watch her struggle alone, in her condition, against the relentless procession of his own department—it was no less than horrifying. Could it be that the force of the DEP was unstoppable, that despite the scientists' progress, there was no other realistic conclusion but the one he feared most? His stomach cramped. It was the first time he allowed the possibility to be real: She could actually die in jail.

Trent looked up, knowing he was losing time. Dopp's e-mail still filled the screen. Hastily, he created an anonymous e-mail address on quickmail.com, then copied and pasted Dopp's e-mail into a new message. The only section he still needed to fill in was the destination address. His briefcase lay at his feet. He pulled out the newspaper and looked inside for a number. By the time he had downloaded Trype, the free—and untraceable—Internet phone service, the computer screen was flashing again: ten minutes left.

The line rang only once before a man answered.

"*Daily News,* city desk."

"Hi," Trent murmured, his head bent close to the computer's speakers. "I work for the Department of Embryo Preservation, and I have a huge exclusive for you. . . ."

"Oh yeah?" The voice sounded perkier.

"A major change in policy is starting tomorrow: random, surprise inspections at any clinic, and more. The whole thing is in a confidential e-mail that the chief sent to the department just an hour ago. Give me your e-mail address, and I'll send you a copy of it right now."

Arianna stood inside the lab, leaning against its steel door for support. Her knees felt shaky, but whether it was from anxiety or her depleting nerve fibers, she did not know.

Sam and Patrick were both gaping at her.

"Are you sure?" Patrick asked. "It sounds pretty extreme. Couldn't there have been something lost in translation?"

Arianna shook her head, ignoring the twisting of her gut. *Don't fall apart,* she told herself. *This is not the time to cry.* She spoke steadily.

"Trent told me everything his reporter friend told him, which he got straight from the source. It's going to be in the paper tomorrow, so there's no sense in second-guessing it." Before the men could respond, a cold sense of pragmatism overtook her. She stepped away from the door and pushed against her cane, standing erect.

"We need to stop standing around and figure out what to do. I checked the records—to be current, we need twelve embryos in the freezer by tomorrow morning. How many clones do we have ready right now?"

Sam looked at Patrick, whose wide eyes betrayed his alarm.

"You took care of the cloning," Sam snapped. "Answer the question."

"We—well, I," Patrick stammered, "I only made ten clones."

"But we're twelve short!" Arianna heard herself shout.

"I wasn't rushing to make them—we weren't supposed to need them for weeks!"

"Why did you only make ten?" Sam demanded. "Why didn't you just make as many as possible?"

"I didn't want to spend all my time on it before I had to," Patrick choked out. "Maybe if you would have helped . . ."

"How dare you." Sam's lip curled up in a sneer. "I was doing both of our jobs."

"At least one of us was avoiding the backlog," Patrick shot back. "You know how we always spend so much time the week before an inspection on cloning!" He glanced wildly between Arianna and Sam. "You can't be mad—I had no idea we would need them this instant!"

"None of us did." Arianna shook her head, cursing under her breath. "But we're two short. What are we going to do?"

As soon as she asked the question, she felt, rather than thought, an idea so painful that a barbed rod seemed to twist inside her throat.

"Sam, what about the embryos I brought you a few days ago? Are there any you haven't used yet that I could—take back?"

He shook his head. "No. We've used them all. I thought you were bringing us a new batch today. . . ."

"I was going to," she whispered. "I have some ready at the clinic. . . ."

"We need them right now!" Patrick cried. "Now more than ever!"

"I'm sure she realizes that," Sam snapped. "Now, Arianna, what if you just changed a few numbers in the records? It's not as if you already filed the count. You're not even supposed to know about the new policy!"

As Arianna winced he continued, "If we were short a lot of embryos and you drastically manipulated the records, the numbers might jump out, but it's matter of two, Arianna. Two!"

She looked at Patrick. He did not appear to agree or disagree, but stood by silently, arms crossed over his chest.

"But it's still risky," she protested. "If they found out I underreported, they could immediately arrest me on felony charges. In fact, it's less of a crime to misplace two embryos. So we'd get a ten-thousand-dollar fine and probation, but I wouldn't have to worry about jail."

"How do you know?" Sam retorted. "You give them too much credit, Arianna. The whole department is running amok with power. Who's to say they'll just give you a ticket and walk away? How can you be so sure that the second they find fault with the clinic, they won't shut it down under the new policy?"

Sam's face pinched into taut lines—a dark rage that befitted his firsthand understanding of the government's transgressions against its citizens. "They're gangsters," he spat. "All of them."

"They are unpredictable now," she admitted. "I guess we can't give them an inch."

"So you have to change the numbers," Sam said. "It's the only way."

"I'll have to be very careful about it. Patrick, do you agree?"

Arianna turned to look at him and wondered if he might faint: the whiteness of his face was eerily similar to the color of his lab coat. He did not answer right away, and when he did, Arianna had to strain to hear the three words:

"I guess so."

Arianna sat in her office early the next morning holding a copy of the *Daily News*. The pages felt smooth in her hands, but the words on the cover may as well have been spikes: FERTILITY CLINICS IN FOR A SURPRISE—INSPECTION!

And on the line beneath: "DEP Cracks Down." Stamped at the bottom of the page was a rectangular box: "Exclusive! See Pages 4–5".

Barely breathing, Arianna flipped to the pages. A copy of the chief's infamous e-mail was blown up on the left page, with the accompanying article on the right page. She skimmed the e-mail, and then the article:

> A confidential memo sent from the chief supervisor of the Department of Embryo Preservation to his staff—and obtained

exclusively by the *Daily News*—indicates an abrupt, sweeping change in policy that will affect all of the city's 112 fertility clinics, starting today.

Under the new policy, surprise inspections may take place at any clinic that chief supervisor Gideon Dopp designates on a weekly list. Clinics will also need to comply with new reporting guidelines; instead of filing their leftover embryo count with the department at the end of each month, they will now need to do so every day. According to the memo, such frequent filings will allow the department to "more closely monitor [the clinics]."

When reached at his home in Long Island, Dopp initially demanded who had leaked the memo to the *News*. After a reporter refused to disclose the source, who had acted on condition of anonymity, Dopp said, "God has given me the sacred task of protecting the many EUEs in fertility clinics from abuse and neglect. I believe this change in policy will better accommodate that goal."

Just then, a high-pitched alarm sounded and the flat-panel screen on the wall lit up in red bursts. Shielding her eyes, Arianna found the remote in her drawer and clicked it off. It was barely 9 A.M. Someone had either just broken in, or held up a certain badge to the front door.

Her heart plummeted. She set down the newspaper and stared at the screen. It took about four seconds for the picture to sharpen. A stout, blurry figure appeared, and then focused into round edges, a dark suit with a glint of gold, a familiar solemn face. The snapshot captured the man walking through the door with one knee raised, as if on a death march. Arianna's breath caught in her throat. Even though she was prepared, she wondered if she could summon the politeness and calm she had always managed to show before.

The clinic's first appointment was not scheduled for another hour. Dr. Ericson was already in his office, prepping for the day's patients, including a few of her old ones, as well as a donor's egg retrieval surgery in the afternoon. Emily, the embryologist, was in the clinic's lab, checking on the growth of fresh embryos. Arianna swiveled in her chair to face the intercom on her wall and pressed a button: laboratory.

"Em, are you there?"

"Yeah, what's up?"

Arianna lowered her voice. "He's here. We'll be in soon."

"Already? Christ, those jerks are fast."

"Are you surprised?"

"Not one bit. Don't worry, I'll get out of your way."

"Why do you think I called?"

During a routine inspection a few months prior, Emily had rolled her eyes at the back of an inspector who demanded three re-counts. Although the man did not see the gesture, Arianna did. Both women realized then that Emily's contempt was too blatant, and her self-control too scant, for her to be trusted around anyone from the DEP.

On the flat screen, the inspector's picture still gleamed, his unsmiling face out of keeping with the pictures of sleepy newborns covering the wall. Arianna hit a button to clear the screen, and then rose gradually, willing her legs to carry her to the waiting room. By now, she was accustomed to the tingly, half-asleep feeling in her legs that bordered on total numbness. Instead she concentrated on where each foot was in space, and where it needed to go: out the door, to the left, into the hallway, forward.

But whenever she put pressure on her feet, the tingling sensation exploded into a furious, inside-out itch, and she willed her legs not to thrash. Soon, the sensation became too intense to ignore. There in the empty hallway she stomped and squirmed, feeling completely dissociated from her awkward body. She imagined watching herself from a bystander's perspective. *I must look totally crazy,* she thought as she wiggled her legs like a dancer without rhythm or sanity. She chuckled in spite of herself, and the sound skidded off the white walls and faded away.

Then she stopped short, grinding her cane into the linoleum floor. Her own laughter, she realized, had become a foreign sound. In the corners of her eyes, tears pooled.

No, she thought simply. No.

Left foot forward, plant. Right foot forward, eye on the prize . . . The waiting room door was within reach. She yanked it open.

Inspector Banks rose from the sofa and smiled coldly. She could not bring herself to smile back, or to show any emotion at all.

"Good morning, Dr. Drake," he said. "I take it you are not surprised to see me?"

"No. I read the paper this morning."

His lips tightened. "I see."

"It must be hard to have a traitor in the department."

He narrowed his eyes, as if trying to spot a smirk on her lips. But she remained blank. "Shall we?" she asked.

"I need to see your most current record count," he demanded.

"Of course. Follow me."

They walked to her office. He did not ask about her cane, or why she was walking so woodenly, as if on the sea floor. When they reached her office, she motioned for him to sit down across from her desk.

"I'll stand."

She shrugged and turned to her filing cabinet. After rifling through it, she pulled out a stack of records and dropped them onto the desk.

"There's all the patients' records in the days since your last visit."

He looked over the pages, signed by both doctor and patient.

"What's the total EUE count?"

"I will have the computer add it up. One moment."

She turned to her monitor, which faced away from him, and pressed her thumb on the upper right-hand corner of the screen. After a second, a box popped up that read UNLOCKED, which enabled her to navigate to patients' records. She opened a program that automatically studied the records from a specific date forward and then calculated the total number of embryos that ought to be in the clinic's lab. But before she hit the CALCULATE button, she checked the one record she had changed last night. It was of the most recent donor, not an actual patient. The woman—who was the daughter of a family friend—had given up nineteen of her eggs last week, but Arianna had changed the number to seventeen in order to compensate for the two they were short. Last night, Arianna had also called the donor and explained the change, so that in case the DEP ever contacted her to corroborate the record, her answer would be consistent. On screen now, the woman's record still showed seventeen, so Arianna hit CALCULATE and then printed out the total.

"Here it is," she said, handing Banks the paper. "Seventy-eight leftover embryos."

Banks flinched at her condescending term—*leftover*—but Arianna didn't care. It wasn't illegal to call them what they were, she thought. Let him go to hell.

Anyway, she knew the number was correct; late last night, she had counted the embryos twice herself and checked each one under the microscope.

"Let me just check that number against your paper records here," Banks said.

"Go ahead."

He leafed through every page of records in the stack, scanning the numbers with a pen-sized device that added them on an internal calculator. Arianna held her breath when he came to the altered record she had replaced in the file. He passed it without incident. Finally, he announced the sum.

"Yes, seventy-eight is correct."

Arianna nodded and led him to the lab. Inside, the freezer and incubator purred quietly, sustaining a veritable farm of embryos between them. Banks opened the freezer door, waited for the billow of icy mist to evaporate and then counted the embryos labeled JANUARY, including the ten undetectable clones. Then he turned to the incubator and counted the fresh ones growing there, including the donated ones that should have been in Sam and Patrick's able hands. The embryos languished in the incubator in the sad-face section as the cells continued to divide—and Arianna realized that they would soon grow past the early window that accommodated the extraction of stem cells. The precious donation—and the careful effort that went into recruiting the woman, preparing her body with hormones, and extracting her eggs—would end up in the freezer, a waste. Arianna looked away from the inspector's bent neck, gripping her cane. She tried not to think of it as a weapon.

After the bureaucratic exercise of viewing random embryos in the electron microscopes to check that they were being properly preserved, Banks turned to her, barely concealing a sigh. "They're all there, and they're being properly preserved."

She signed the form he handed to her.

Wordlessly, they left the lab and she led him back to the waiting room. It was still empty. He turned to her again, and she thought he was going to shake her hand. He did not.

"I suppose," he said, "since you're so caught up, you already know you have to start filing daily counts with us, starting by the end of today."

She nodded.

"An official notice will be sent to you this afternoon. See you soon, then," he said, flashing her a sinister smile.

Something about his words unsettled her, and as he walked to the door, she realized why: She had assumed that since the clinic passed the inspection, he would not be returning for another several weeks, per the regular schedule.

"Wait," she called out.

He turned around.

"What do you mean, soon? How often are these surprise inspections to take place?"

Banks shrugged maddeningly. "I really am not authorized to say. Hence, 'surprise,' Dr. Drake."

"But we passed it. This clinic has passed every inspection and audit. I'm sure we have one of the cleanest records in the city. Doesn't that count for something?"

He shrugged again. "Things have changed."

"So you're saying you could come back again next week?" She hoped her tone did not sound indignant.

"Or even tomorrow. Good-bye, Dr. Drake."

He turned and walked out without waiting for her to reply.

Stunned, she stood in the doorway of the waiting room, staring at the spot he had vacated. It was as if his words had stripped her of her ability to function. *Things have changed.* She knew she needed to call Sam, and her hand reacted appropriately, reaching into her pocket and pulling out her cell phone. He answered right away.

"Don't tell me the bastard already showed up."

"Yeah. We passed."

"Good!"

"Not really. He could show up any day—I didn't realize it was going to be a constant—"

"You're kidding."

"No. We need to have an emergency meeting tonight. I'll come to the lab with the Ericsons as soon as the day is over. But you and Patrick need to start cloning new embryos as soon as possible, because until we have replacements ready, I can't take any embryos out of here. He could show up again tomorrow."

"But we don't have any embryos left, remember?"

"I know. So tonight, I am going to bring you the batch I was going to bring yesterday—but only to clone. And then—" Her voice faltered. "—then I will have to take the originals back here right away to restock in the freezer before tomorrow, just in case he shows up."

"So we're not even going to be able to use those?"

"No."

"So when the hell are we going to get embryos again? We can't mess around here!"

"I know that, Sam." Her voice shook. "But I can't here either. Look, I have a girl scheduled this afternoon for her extraction surgery. The embryos from her eggs will be ready for research in five days. And by then, the clones you make tonight should be ready to stock."

"That puts us at Sunday!" He sounded accusatory.

"Yep. That's the soonest I can take any embryos out of here. Whenever I take them out from now on, I will have to come back right away with replacements. So that means a constant supply of clones. If we're ever short again, we risk wasting even more donations."

"Why can't you just change the stupid numbers again if you have to?"

"Because now I have to file the count every day. There's no room for that anymore."

"But we don't have time for this goddamn bullshit!"

Arianna couldn't speak past the lump in her throat.

"Hello?" Sam said.

"I'm here," she muttered.

"Sorry, I just can't believe those bastards." He paused, and Arianna knew what he was going to say, for the tears that coursed down her cheeks were already mourning the words: "We just lost five days."

From the head of the conference table, Dopp glared at each of the twenty-five faces around him. He pressed his palms hard against the table, turning his fingertips white.

"One of you," he snarled, "is a traitor. Not just to me, or the department—but to God. Unless you come forward and repent, *He will not forget it.*"

The faces around him looked solemn, even fearful. None had seen this side of their amicable boss before, the one who asked about their children's birthday parties and their sick spouses. But Dopp had never been publicly betrayed.

"I am shocked and disgusted by such an outrageous, deliberate effort to undermine my new policy. Until the traitor comes forth, all of you will suffer consequences—blame it on your colleague, not me. There will be no more honesty policy about clocking in and out of work. From now on, you must all have your immediate supervisors sign off on your timesheets before submitting them to me. And from now on, the tech support team will be closely monitoring all e-mail correspondence and all Internet activity. Anyone found sending personal e-mails, or otherwise slacking off, will be suspended without pay."

Dopp slapped his hands against the table. The woman on his right side jumped. "Also," he said, making eye contact with each person around the table, "if any of you know who the traitor is, and you do not come to me, you, too, will face God's wrath. Keeping silent is an equal sin to lying. Remember Proverbs, passage fourteen twenty-five, 'A truthful witness saves lives, but a false witness is deceitful.' If there are any witnesses in this room, come to me today, and you will be forgiven. Now, go. Get out of here. I don't want to see your faces anymore."

People pushed back their chairs and scurried out of the conference room with the urgency of a fire evacuation. Dopp waited until they had all funneled through the door before walking back to his own office. He felt chilled inside. Such treachery was unprecedented. What did it say about his own judgment that he had hired a person capable of it? He would have to beg the Lord's forgiveness for such a costly error.

Who could the offender be? There was Doug Anderson, whom Dopp had recently denied a raise. (Budget problems prohibited anything of the sort.) Perhaps he was feeling especially spiteful? There was also Marie Hunter, who had once lied about being hospitalized when Dopp sensed she had actually gone on vacation. But was she capable of duplicity of this scale? And why? Then there was Trent, who had been acting frustrated recently, but swore his attitude had turned around. Dopp recalled how eagerly Trent had pledged not to disappoint him, so this kind of stunt would not make sense for him to pull. Meanwhile, the tech guys had found no evidence on anyone's computers to suggest a culprit. Maybe someone would come forward.

In the meantime, Dopp's only hope was Inspector Banks—the man who could deliver news that would render the leak meaningless. It was 9:45 A.M. Banks was probably on his way back from Arianna's clinic already. While Dopp waited, he pulled out the Bible from his drawer. Yellow stubs protruded from the tops of the pages, marking certain sections Dopp had especially liked. He flipped to one tab randomly and read:

"Colossians 2:5: For though I be absent in the flesh, yet I am with you in the spirit, joying and beholding your order, and the steadfastness of your faith in Christ. . . ."

Dopp continued to read, feeling the Lord's words revive his soul and reinstill his humbleness. The betrayal of an employee seemed petty in contrast with Christ's ultimate sacrifice. Motivation filled him anew: no one would get away with killing embryos on his watch, for he would track down the sinners and bring them to justice in Christ's name. But it needed to happen before the state legislature mowed down the department, along with his job. . . .

There was a knock at the door. *Banks.*

"Come in," Dopp called.

Banks walked in, dejected. "She passed."

"No!" Dopp rose furiously. "How?"

"She said she read the paper this morning. I guess she could have had time to straighten things out before I got there, but we'll never know. I went as early as I could."

Dopp clenched his teeth, sending a sharp pain through his jaw. "Can you believe this?"

Banks shook his head. "In all of our years, I never . . . Do you have any idea who?"

"No. It doesn't make any sense."

"What now?"

"Well, for a start, I'm going to check out all the labs in the East Village myself. I know for a fact Arianna Drake isn't going to a doctor there, like she told Trent."

"How do you know?"

"I researched MS specialists in Manhattan. Since she's a doctor herself, I know she would only go to the best. Funny enough, all the top-rated people practice at big-name hospitals like Mount Sinai, New York Presbyterian, Saint Luke's. Nowhere near the East Village. You'd think that Trent, as a former reporter, would be able to figure that out. But no, he's a gullible fool, I'm sorry to say."

Banks clucked his tongue. "He's just inexperienced and idealistic. Some young people tend to believe that true evil isn't possible in the world. I used to think so myself."

"If it weren't, our department wouldn't need to exist."

"I know that. But maybe you should give Trent the benefit of the doubt. He hasn't seen what we've seen. After all, he's been a loyal employee for three years and he's the only one of us in direct contact with her. She could still open up to him. Who knows?" Banks gave a close-lipped smile.

Dopp frowned. "What are you saying?"

"I'm saying, if we were going to catch her in error, it would have been today. Now she's wise to us. She'll be prepared. And Trent's been trying to get her to talk, but he's stymied by the Devil's force in her. She's a master manipulator, and he's never been up against anything like that, so he needs us, and we need him."

"Go on."

"If we put more pressure on her and really intimidate her, she'll want to confess all her worries to someone. Like good cop, bad cop. And who will be right there listening, playing to her fears, and encouraging her to spill her guts?"

Dopp nodded, fingering the cross pin on his lapel that mirrored Bank's. "I like the way you think."

"I'm quitting," Patrick said.

No, Arianna thought, *not again.* The faces around her in the basement looked as appalled as she felt.

"What did you just say?" Sam asked Patrick, who hugged his arms close to his chest and looked away.

Arianna's foot twitched, egging on her urge to jump out of her folding chair and kick it to the ground. But her legs would not cooperate.

Gavin and Emily Ericson flanked either side of Arianna in the group's tiny circle, per the emergency Tuesday night meeting. All of them were gaping at Patrick.

"How do you dare," Dr. Ericson spat. "After everything we've done!"

Emily put a hand on Arianna's knee and said nothing, looking supremely disappointed.

"I have to quit," Patrick said. He rocked slightly back and forth on his chair. "I'm sorry, Arianna, I really am. This was a very hard decision."

"Just because of the crackdown? We got around the inspection, Patrick! They're not going to catch us. The worst part is just that we're losing time, so we need you even more now! Now that we're close . . ."

"I held out against my better judgment before, Arianna. I gave you the benefit of the doubt. But now it's gone far beyond that. The DEP is trying to bring you down, you and all the other clinics on that list. And once the government is hell-bent on destroying you, how can you possibly win?"

"We can," she insisted. "We have to."

"I wish I could believe that. But they're closing in. I don't want to spend the rest of my life in jail. What if someone followed you here?"

"They obviously haven't, have they? And what about the plight of science? What about Galileo, Copernicus, and Newton, remember?"

Patrick shrugged sadly. "Who was I kidding? I'm no genius."

Arianna opened her mouth to argue, but Sam cut her off. "Forget it. He's a lost cause."

"I'm sorry," Patrick said. "But Sam's made the bulk of our progress anyway." He looked at Sam. "I know you'll stay, and if there's a solution, you'll find it. You don't need me."

No one responded or moved. Looking down, Patrick rose and walked to the door. Before he opened it, he turned once to look at the furious group.

"I'm sorry," he said again, quietly. Then he opened the door and slipped out as a chilling wind swept in.

Arianna closed her eyes, willing herself to remain calm. It was easier this time because she was not completely surprised. Patrick had seemed strangely apathetic the day before, as if his will to fight had disappeared with his courage.

Emily patted her knee. "Don't think about him. We still have Sam."

Arianna looked up at Sam, expecting to see him seething. But he was watching her with concern.

"Are you okay?" he asked.

"I think so. I just keep thinking about how you said you were getting closer. Maybe you don't really need him?"

Sam shook his head. "I don't. I know what combinations I have to try now; it's just a matter of testing."

"And only five days to wait," Dr. Ericson chimed in. "And then we'll get back on track. We can make it."

Arianna looked at him gratefully. "I was so worried you would want to walk out, too, and then we'd have to close the clinic, since I can't practice. . . ."

"We would never," Emily interrupted. "We would rather go down with the ship than walk away."

Her husband nodded. "That's absolutely right. The clinic is everything to us, Arianna. We could never abandon it, or you. And if the only thing I ever did in my life was to help science even a little, then I would say it was damn worthwhile."

Arianna smiled, feeling tears sting her eyes. She was about to respond when she heard a scraping against the floor. Sam pushed back his chair and stood up. The ceiling hung low above his head.

"Two things," he announced. "First of all, none of you doctors should come here anymore. Patrick had a point—it's plausible that someone could start following you, especially now. Who knows the extent of the new policy?"

"Fine," Arianna said, "but we still need to get the embryos here when they're ready."

"Right, so we need someone trustworthy to step in and bring them to me."

"How about Megan? Or Trent?"

Sam's expression grew hard. "The former."

"I'll arrange it."

"Second of all," he went on, pacing across the concrete basement, "What we need to do now is plan for the transplant."

"Already?" Emily asked.

"We need to prepare for the best-case scenario, so that if and when a breakthrough happens, we'll be ready."

Gavin and Emily nodded, excitement visible in their eyes.

"Sounds good to me," Arianna said. "What do you need?"

"Egg cells. Five will do. I really need only one, but just to be safe, I want a few extra. Once I figure out how to make pure oligos, then the trick is to get your body to accept the cells, which is unlikely and dangerous if they are foreign matter."

"Right . . ."

"So the theory is that we will scrape some skin cells from your cheek, Arianna. And then I'll take a donated egg cell and remove its nucleus. In its place, I'll inject the nucleus of your skin cell. The hybrid cell will act like an embryo and start dividing and growing, except that it will be your exact DNA. When it gets to the five-day stage, I'll remove the stem cells, cue them to differentiate into oligos—by this point, I would have the growth factors down—and then we can transplant the cells into your spinal cord. Your body ought to accept them as its own. The cells should then travel up and down your spinal cord and replenish your lost myelin."

"It's genius," Arianna cried. "Brilliant."

"Theoretically, yes. But this technique has never been tried on humans."

Sam stopped pacing and their eyes met. He looked at her with the adoring worry of a father unable to conceal his distress. Arianna smiled, feeling any lingering tension dissolve between them. *Sam,* she thought, *you are my family.*

"Tell me one thing," she said. "What have I got to lose?"

SIXTEEN

The abrupt buzzing of Trent's doorbell startled him. It was only 5:35 P.M. Arianna's weekly piano lesson was not starting for another hour and a half. Who would be coming to see him this early? Surely not Dopp–it couldn't be.

As Trent walked to the door, he imagined the interior of a jail cell—dirty, cramped, and cold, with maybe a sliver of light to retain his sanity. Paranoia had gripped him since the media leak had gone public the day before. Over and over, Trent mentally retraced his steps to the Cyber Café, the phone call to the *Daily News*, the dummy e-mail address he had created. Impossible, he thought. There was no way he could be discovered.

He put one hand on the doorknob. "Who is it?"

"It's me," came a voice, higher-pitched than he expected.

"Arianna!" he exclaimed, swinging open the door. "I didn't—"

There was no beautiful face across from him. He stared blankly at the hallway wall.

"Down here," she said.

He looked down and felt his jaw drop. She was sitting in a wheelchair, staring up at him. Her characteristic smile was gone, and without that merry distraction to plump up her cheekbones, Trent noticed how drawn they had become. Below her lower lids, dark circles spread like smudged ink, underlining the fear in her eyes.

"It was time," she said, tapping the wheelchair's padded armrest.

"I—I'm sorry," he stuttered.

"I knew it was coming." She paused, and in her eyes, an ember of mischief caught flame. "The good news is that I can finally beat you in getting just about anywhere, including up and down stairs. This thing goes eighteen miles per hour at top speed."

Trent raised his eyebrows. This was sounding more like the woman he loved. If he closed his eyes, in fact, she would sound exactly the same, minus the troubling visual.

"You must be the fastest woman on earth now."

"Something like that." She smiled and leaned forward in the chair, propelling the machine into Trent's apartment. "It senses my movements," she called over her shoulder as she zoomed past him. She leaned backwards and it stopped.

"Not too shabby, huh?"

"That actually looks pretty fun," Trent said, catching up to her. He leaned down and kissed her, then grabbed her hand to pull her up. She staggered out of the chair and took tiny steps toward the couch, holding his forearm. He noticed that her hand did not close fully around his arm, though she was struggling to keep her balance. When she let go and sank onto the couch, her fingers remained curled, like the petals of a dying lily.

He sat next to her and covered them with his hands. "I'll cancel the lesson," he said quietly.

"Don't be silly. I came over early to practice."

"What?"

She withdrew her hands and wiggled her fingers slowly. "I can still play scales, even if the tempo is *molto largo*. And I'm pretty sure I can still pull off *twinkle, twinkle* at least."

Trent's lips stretched into a thin smile. "You don't have to prove anything to me."

She narrowed her eyes. "This isn't about proving anything to anyone. It's about living my life to the fullest, and right now, playing your keyboard is about all the living I can manage. So if you will now get up and please escort me to the keyboard, I can practice for a while before Molly gets here."

Trent studied her with awe. "That time outside the lab, you really meant it. When you said you were reclaiming your life."

She nodded. The subtext of his words hung in the air between them, but she did not flinch or even avert her eyes. It was he who looked away first, he who struggled to stand as he lifted her from the couch and buried a kiss deep in her hair.

Two days later, Arianna felt excited for the first time since the crackdown. It was Friday morning, and Inspector Banks was leaving her clinic for the fourth time that week. Each morning he'd arrived, demanded to count the embryos, and then departed with a look of vague hostility. She always regarded him blankly, concentrating on the wall behind his head or the deep crease between his eyes. But this morning she bade him good-bye with a smile, as if she were seeing off a patient.

"I'm sure I'll see you soon," she said, beating him to his line.

He frowned and nodded, tucking his paperwork under his arm. "Bye, then."

As soon as the door closed behind him, she scooted in her wheelchair straight through the hallway to Dr. Ericson's office. It was thrilling to arrive there so quickly, after weeks of labored effort to walk the short distance. Her wheels squeaked over the linoleum floor as she leaned forward, daring herself to lean farther, to move faster. She hardly pitied herself at all.

A new donor's egg-extraction surgery was scheduled for this afternoon. The woman's supply of eggs was especially crucial: Arianna would save five of them for Sam as he had requested, in order to be prepared for—and oh, how she willed for—a breakthrough. The rest of the donor's eggs would provide another batch of desperately needed embryos once they were mixed with donor sperm that the clinic had bought en masse from a sperm bank.

Arianna stopped in Dr. Ericson's doorway.

"He's gone," she announced.

"Good." Dr. Ericson set down a chart he was studying. "We have the young woman coming in at two for her extraction."

"How many eggs do you think you'll take out?"

"I would say we have a good shot at twenty. I saw her yesterday morning, and her ovaries were highly stimulated."

"Perfect," Arianna said. A typical extraction surgery yielded somewhere between fifteen and twenty eggs, and rarely varied from that range. As long as Dr. Ericson could take out twenty eggs, then Arianna could smuggle five of them to Sam, and record the extraction at the end of the day as a normal fifteen, without arousing the suspicion of the inspector, who was well aware of the typical range. Several months ago, in fact, a forty-two-year-old patient had undergone the same extraction surgery as part of the IVF process. When the woman's aging ovaries produced only eleven eggs, the inspector who reviewed the records that month had seized on the low number, demanding a medical explanation in writing, and then had called the patient to corroborate it herself. Shortly thereafter, the DEP subjected the clinic to a random audit.

"I'll tell Emily to separate out the five strongest eggs for Sam," Dr. Ericson said. "But who's going to bring them to him, and when, since none of us can go to the lab anymore?"

"Megan will. She's planning to go in a few days anyway to finally bring Sam embryos again, so she'll give him these egg cells as well. Then he'll give her clones he made this week so she can come right back here and stock them."

Dr. Ericson smiled. "I haven't seen you beam like this in days."

Arianna wished she could jump out of her chair and hug him, the man who was not just her colleague and accomplice, but her friend.

"We're finally going to get back on track," she said. "Once those embryos are in Sam's hands, I'll feel so much better."

"Me, too. And with the eggs from today, we'll have more embryos ready, let's see—" He counted five fingers in the air. "—next Wednesday. So Sam will have a continual supply again. No more gap days."

Arianna smiled, thinking of Sam's wry sense of humor. "It sounds like SADFACE finally found its slogan," she mused. "No more gap days."

• • •

Sam Lisio was terrible at waiting. With no embryos to research for several days, and thus, no means of productivity, he returned home after spending hours in the lab cloning replacements. The process was monotonous, constantly splitting embryos at the four-cell stage to coax out more and more clones. At last, when several hundred petri dishes of tiny embryos filled the incubator, Sam felt it was enough. That large a reserve would take months to deplete, he reasoned. Months they didn't have anyway.

The new clones would soon need to be frozen, but in the meantime, Sam had nothing to do. So he went to his apartment, which felt less like home and more like a temporary holding cell.

As soon as he opened the door, he dumped his duffel bag on the floor and went straight to the kitchen, stopping in front of a particular wooden cabinet above the sink. Its bronze handle was rubbed down to a dull yellow. He grabbed it and swung open the door, feeling a familiar heady anticipation. Inside the cabinet stood deliciously full bottles of liquor: whiskey, rum, vodka, and scotch. Hesitating only briefly, he seized each bottle and emptied them, one by one, into the sink.

He did not trust himself to be patient the right way; it was far too tempting to be alone in his apartment with nothing but pressure and worry as his constant companions. Once stripped of his only desirable means of escape, he let the hours wash over him, hoping their ebb and flow would begin to soothe him into sleep. Instead, time seemed to stagnate like a swamp, and he felt stuck in its dense muck. Fully clothed and awake on his bed, Sam pictured the blue eyes that had looked at him so tenderly in the lab. His heart began to race as the memory replayed: he pacing and talking, she sitting and listening.

"But this technique has never been tried on humans."

He'd stopped pacing, and at the moment he felt his own worry and longing burst forth onto his face—their eyes met.

In that moment, some kind of understanding had passed between them. Could she have read him, and mirrored his sentiment in a glance? Or was she simply thrusting all her hope upon the one man who could save her?

Could he?

To find the combination of growth factors that yielded oligos was the key, and he knew he was close. Yet so many critical hours were passing by, delivering no change except for the further deterioration of her spinal cord.

How much would these five wasted days matter?

It was the main question Sam obsessed over as he plodded through the time, alternately studying his notes long after he had memorized them, cursing the DEP, and thinking of her. When she unexpectedly stopped by with takeout on Saturday night, he had to hide his disproportionate joy at seeing her, and his devastation at seeing her wheelchair. He wondered if she might mention their charged glance in the lab; part of him wished she would. But she did not, and craven as he was, the topic was never broached.

Sunday's arrival felt like the landing of a trans-Atlantic flight: a thrilling moment, even though all he did to reach it was wait. At last the five days were over, although their damage done. But ahead lay an uninterrupted week of research, an hourglass dripping golden sand.

When Megan arrived at the lab that morning with the black case, he hugged her as soon as she stepped into the basement.

"That was out of character," she joked.

He only smiled and unloaded his precious red flasks, each one a vase cradling a rare seed of hope. One, two, three, he counted . . . nine altogether. A foreign feeling overcame him as he held each flask, and after a moment, he realized it was sentimentality. In the potential for life, he thought, there was so much promise for those already living.

Megan watched him carefully place each flask into the incubator. "There are also five egg cells in a special flask that Arianna labeled for you. She told me you needed them."

"We better."

"Do you think you will?"

Sam paused. He knew that the longer he waited to answer, the less legitimate his confidence would sound, but he couldn't lie either. "Whether we will in time, I don't know."

Megan lifted her chin slightly up and down, her nose twitching.

Aware that she might start to cry, Sam turned away and carried the now-empty black case to the freezer. Without speaking, he loaded it with flasks of cloned embryos that awaited their final destination in the clinic's freezer.

"Are you going to have enough clones after this to account for the next batch of embryos?" Megan asked him from behind. "Arianna told me they'll be ready in a few more days, on Wednesday."

Sam turned around and, seeing her composure, relaxed. "I made a few hundred clones last week, so I don't have to waste time on that BS anymore, or worry about shortages."

Megan sighed. "At least you're prepared. Arianna told me that same inspector showed up every day last week."

"I know. And the bastard will probably show up every day this week. If he could, I bet he would rent out one of her examining rooms and sleep there."

Megan rolled her eyes and reached out for the filled case Sam handed back to her. "I wouldn't speak too soon."

Sunday night, Trent reluctantly found himself on a train to Long Island at the behest of his mother to come home for a family dinner with a couple of special guests—none other than Dopp and Joanie. Trent could often count on his mother to interfere somehow—with only the best of intentions, of course—but this was beyond his expectations. And the worst part was that he could only smile and thank her, for she really did think she was doing him a favor.

"I know you've been struggling at work lately," she had told him over the phone, "and I've been wondering how to help. And then it hit me—of course! We could have your boss over for dinner!"

Trent had to hold back a groan. "Mom, you really don't have to—"

"Oh, please, he told us himself on Christmas that he wanted to get together, remember? I've already called to invite him."

As uncomfortable as the evening promised to be, Trent thought now that maybe his mother really would be helping. Spending an evening with Dopp outside of work would give him a chance to showcase his loyalty to the department and his solidarity with its mission. *Be who I was,* Trent told himself. Dutiful son, noble employee, and a guy who wondered why the hell any of it mattered.

His mother opened the door with a smile and greeted him warmly, telling him with one look that their guests were already seated inside.

"What's wrong?" She pulled back and stared at him.

"Nothing, I'm fine."

"Are you sure?"

He nodded breezily. Was his unease that obvious?

She put an arm around his waist and led him toward the dining room. "Greet them first, and then come help me serve."

As they turned the corner, a long mahogany table came into view along with a man's familiar profile, with its prominent nose and long chin—a man who turned to face Trent as soon as he stepped into the room. Next to him was his very pregnant wife, and across from them sat his father. All three smiled.

Trent forced a wide grin and gave a little wave. "Hey, Dad. Hi, boss. Funny seeing you here."

Dopp smiled good-naturedly. "Who were you expecting?"

Trent shrugged, not feeling up to witty banter. "Glad you both could join us."

"Our pleasure," Dopp said, putting an arm around Joanie.

"We'll be right back with dinner," said his mother. She pinched Trent's waist and they turned around, heading for the kitchen. "Isn't this perfect," she whispered. "Just what you need."

"Yeah."

In the kitchen, she handed him a platter with pot roast and a bowl of salad from the fridge.

"But, Mom," he said, "don't you think he realizes you're just sucking up on my behalf?"

She cocked her head. "Honey, that's how the world works. There's nothing wrong with it."

"You don't think it's too phony?" Not that he cared, but he couldn't help asking.

"You have to play the game to get ahead. Act like there's nothing you care about more than your job."

They walked back to the dining room single file, arms loaded with food.

"Trent," his father said as soon as they entered, "I was just telling them about all the cover stories you did for *Newsday* on Saint Mary's. How many was it again?"

Trent cringed at the name, once synonymous with disgust. Saint Mary's was the church near their home they had often attended during his childhood that had later been revealed to harbor lecherous priests and financial fraud. Trent had covered every ugly ripple to come out of the church: a wonder for his journalistic visibility, but not so much for his psyche.

"Seventeen, Dad."

His father's eyes widened. "That's right. Over just a few months, wasn't it?"

"Yep."

Joanie looked impressed, while Dopp gazed thoughtfully at Trent. "I remember when all that happened. What a nightmare that was."

Trent nodded. "It was a tough time."

"But," his mother pointed out, as she sat down next to him, "it did get you nominated for the Pulitzer."

"One of the reasons I hired you," Dopp said. "You can't turn down that kind of talent."

"Thanks," Trent said, forcing a gracious smile as he smoothed his napkin over his lap.

His mother said a quick grace and announced, "Bon appétit."

"Speaking of church," his father said dryly, "how was everyone's sermons this morning?"

Oh yeah, Trent thought. Sunday—and the rest of his world was the same.

Joanie nodded. "Fantastic. Our priest is really passionate about family values, so he's been talking a lot lately about that."

"Of course, we just eat it up," Dopp said with a smile. He turned to Trent. "What did your priest talk about? I always wonder what goes on at city churches."

The pasta in Trent's mouth seemed to wrap around his tongue. He held up a finger as he chewed, then swallowed. "Faith, mainly. The importance of faith, no matter what."

Trent heard the words and felt his lips moving as his face grew hot; the guilt was an equal and opposite reaction to his lie. But wait, he thought. What was there to feel guilty about? He had committed no sin; no angry God was going to strike him down. Yet his looking-over-one-shoulder reflex had not entirely ceased, as if he were a recovering addict grappling with relapses. With no drug to encourage his hopes and placate his fears, the world—however free of guilt—seemed much more dangerous, and more lonely.

He looked around the table at his mother and father, at Dopp and Joanie, the people who had not long ago constituted his network of ideals and support. Now what were they? His parents, talking so earnestly about the faith discussion he had begun—they were still good people, he reasoned. People who simply wanted the best for him, in their own misguided way. There was no evil in that.

And Dopp: he was stroking Joanie's hair as he leaned over the table, speaking about the issues facing modern-day priests. How recently Trent had watched him the way his parents were now, with rapt respect. Dopp's voice was mesmerizing—commanding in volume but subtle in inflection, the mark of a true ex-priest. As Trent studied the man he had once considered his mentor, he was surprised to feel the tiniest bit nostalgic. Dopp was a man of passion and conviction, a man who inspired action, whose judgment was keen and his lifework important to him.

From Trent's seat at the head of the table, he glanced over at his father, who sat with his chin on his fist, a humble listener, mustering only enough interest to follow, never to challenge or to lead.

Suddenly Trent realized he was grateful to Dopp. If it were not for him sparking the motivation, Trent never would have done his job well enough to uncover the suspicion in Arianna's numbers, which had led him to her. . . .

". . . is why our current case depends on it." Dopp turned to him, rubbing the rim of his water glass. "Don't you think, Trent?"

He wasted no time. "Absolutely."

"I hear what you're saying," his mother cut in, "but to us on the outside, the crackdown seemed very sudden. We should have known it was part of the plan."

She smiled at Trent, and only he understood the craftiness in her eyes: she had noticed his mind wandering and found a way to catch him up. He smiled back, grateful for reasons she would never know.

"It was a policy trick up our sleeve," Trent said.

"Though it has yet to really pay off," Dopp said, looking at him.

"It will. I'm doing whatever it takes to make sure of it."

"I'm sick of hearing about that woman," Joanie said. "By the time this baby comes, I hope I never hear her name again, unless it's in reference to a court date."

Dopp chuckled. "From your mouth to God's ears."

Wry smiles flickered around the table, hyenas united over their prey, Trent thought. Any trace of nostalgia and goodwill vanished. He wanted nothing more than to be sitting on the train heading back to Manhattan, to her. How much longer would he have to keep up this farce?

"So who wants dessert?" his father asked.

Everyone nodded, even his mother, who never ate sweets. "There's a fresh apple pie in the oven," she said.

"I'll go get it," Trent replied, jumping out of his chair.

"Thanks, sweetie. It's so good to have you home."

He smiled as he turned away. Never had he felt more alone.

When he walked into his building's lobby a few hours later, he was startled to find a young woman crying, hunched over on the bench near the elevators. Trent recognized her as a neighbor with whom he often exchanged pleasantries. No one else was around to help, so he approached her.

"Are you okay?" he asked. "Do you need something?"

She looked up at him with reddened eyes, her shoulders heaving. "Oh God, I'm in such a mess. There's nothing you could do."

"What's wrong?" he asked. "If you don't mind me asking."

She wiped her hand across her face. "Well, I'm pregnant, which is the good news. Three months along. But my caseworker found out that I drank on New Year's, one glass of champagne, and now I have to pay a one-thousand-dollar fine."

"Jesus," Trent muttered. "Just for one glass?"

"I'm dreading telling my husband. We were saving up for a vacation. . . ." She broke into sobs again. "We haven't gone on vacation for two years."

"Fuck the DEFP," Trent said, his heart pounding with increasing rage. "What you do with your body is your own goddamn business."

"I wish."

Trent wondered how many mothers-to-be were crying all over the city, fined for similar so-called crimes, as countless more anxiously waited out their pregnancies. He remembered the woman whose MetroCard he had recovered in Washington Square Park, who had tried to conceal her fear of him. He thought of Arianna and the millions of sick people like her with no cure in sight, cut off from research that could help make it possible.

"Damn them," he declared. "I'll take care of the fine. Don't you worry about it."

A sob died in her throat as she stared up at him. "What? How?"

"I know people," he said. "There are ways." It was so simple, he thought. Of course, it was criminal, too, but that wasn't stopping the DEP and the DEFP. Trent could just go into their joint database, find this woman's case history, and mark the fine as paid. No one in their sprawling bureaucracy would know the difference.

She looked at him in disbelief. "Are you sure?"

"It's no problem. Really."

She jumped up and hugged him, and when she stepped back, her smile was full of relief and joy. Trent yearned to see the same expression on Arianna's face, worrying that he never would.

• • •

The next afternoon, Dopp sat in his office with a scowl. Almost a week had passed since the crackdown, and the department was no better off for it. Many agents were working overtime to process the daily influx of clinic reports, while other agents were neglecting their regular duties to conduct random inspections. In turn, the general atmosphere in the office was one of chaos mixed with silent resentment, and Dopp knew it was all directed at him. Up in Albany, he was not gaining fans, either. He had just hung up the phone with Senator Windra, who personally called to report the capitol's response to the crackdown.

"Well, it *has* gotten people talking about the DEP again. . . . But not in the way you want, I'm afraid."

Dopp balked. "I thought there was no such thing as bad publicity."

"The liberals are scoffing at you, Gideon."

"What do you mean?"

Windra paused. "They're saying you'll bankrupt the department before they even get the chance."

"That's outrageous!"

"Is it, though? What good is this crackdown doing? I know you can't afford to keep this up for long. And I would hate to think you're destroying yourself for publicity. Tell me you have some strategic reason in mind."

"I most definitely do. We have a very serious case under investigation, and the crackdown was designed to speed things up."

"Well, has it?"

Dopp cleared his throat. "It's helping every day."

"I hope so, for your sake. Let me be completely clear. No one here is going to negotiate for you if we think you're squandering the money you already have. We need to see some results that prove exactly why this crackdown was necessary. If we don't, well, you can start writing pink slips." Windra's voice hardened. "I like you, Gideon, but ultimately, I have to be practical. The DEFP could use every extra dollar possible. Are we clear?"

"Yes," Dopp murmured.

The line clicked off, and Dopp closed his eyes. Windra never said good-bye when he was upset, and it left Dopp feeling rattled, as if he had suddenly been tossed out of a moving car.

He walked to Trent's office with a purposeful stride so that no one would stop and question him. With his head held high, he could avoid indignant gazes. He ducked into the office and pulled the door shut behind him.

"Hi, boss," Trent said. "What can I do for you?"

Dopp leaned against the door and crossed his arms. After last night's dinner, he had come away feeling more sympathetic to Trent, though no less frustrated in general. Joanie had also thought well of him; it was clear that he came from a good Christian family like their own. Dopp sincerely wanted to like him, as he always had—and it was easier to do so when he recalled Banks's suggestion: Give Trent the benefit of the doubt.

"Albany just called," Dopp said. "It's not looking good."

Trent frowned. "I'm doing everything I can."

"It's still not enough." Dopp recounted his search of all the known labs in the East Village, which had yielded nothing. "You're supposed to find out what she's doing in that neighborhood."

"I know. But she hasn't gone anywhere except home and the clinic since she got her wheelchair."

"And I assume she said nothing significant?"

"No, nothing." Trent looked apologetic.

Dopp shook his head. "It just doesn't add up. She has an excellent motive, access to embryos, and a black heart."

"I'll keep following her and seeing her as much as possible." Trent reached into his briefcase and pulled out a thin file. "Here's the report of her comings and goings over the weekend and the transcripts of our conversations."

"So she hasn't said anything about Banks showing up every day?"

"No. She's really focused on her MS. The doctor told her he can't do much for her at this point, so she said she isn't even going to see him regularly anymore."

Dopp paced three steps forward in the cramped room. "She's young to be so sick. God must be delivering some kind of retribution, but *why*?"

Trent shook his head, baffled.

"Banks is supposed to be intimidating her," Dopp went on. "But it's not working. So obviously what we have to do now is increase his presence."

"Isn't he already going every day?"

"Now he'll start to stay there much longer than what she's expecting. No wonder she's not scared enough to talk. But think about Banks going there for hours, maybe even all day, just watching her. Shadowing her." Dopp's pulse hammered in his temples. "It's perfectly legal for us to shadow a doctor as long as we're not interfering with her patients' privacy."

"She stopped seeing patients anyway."

"Right, and there's no time limit on our visits. That ought to startle her enough to mention it, don't you think?"

"It seems like that would be pretty hard for her to ignore," Trent said slowly.

"Exactly. And then you can coax her to keep talking about her clinic, about why she might be worried about us being there. Everybody wants to confide in someone. You were a reporter, Trent. A darn good one. You should be a professional at getting people to talk to you."

"I am."

"Prove it," Dopp said, and walked out.

It was two days later, Wednesday at 5:15 P.M. Dopp believed Trent was loitering in Washington Square in order to follow Arianna's every movement once she left her clinic. But actually, Trent was sipping tea at a café nearby, writing up a phony report of her alleged activities to hand in the next morning. As he typed, his cell phone in his sweater pocket began to vibrate. Arianna. She spoke his name like a plea for mercy.

"What happened?" he asked immediately.

"I need a huge favor. Megan got held up at work, so I need you to bring the case to Sam ASAP. I don't know who else I trust enough to—"

"It's fine," he interrupted, relieved. "Is it at the clinic?"

"Yes. My colleague Emily is still there to let you in."

"No problem. I'll be right there."

"Thank you so much," she said. "If I didn't get this batch to Sam soon, it would be too late to use them."

"Don't worry, love. He'll get them."

"Thank you. I'm sorry it's so last minute. Megan had actually called me earlier today, but I couldn't call you until now, just after I left work, because that goddamn inspector has started staying all day. Just watching me!"

He coughed. "Why in the world would he do that?"

"I don't know! Yesterday he came for four hours. Today, for six. I could barely get out of his sight. It's bizarre. When Megan called, I knew I had to pick up, but then I could only reply with a word, and of course she couldn't understand why I was being so short with her."

"That sounds excruciating. I'm sorry you have to go through that."

"It's not your fault."

Trent's boiling tea scorched his tongue. "Did the inspector explain?"

"He called it Phase Two of the crackdown—this new shadowing of doctors. But I don't know what they're trying to accomplish."

"It sounds crazy," he muttered. "But he left for today, right?"

"Yep, he left when I did. That's why I couldn't take the case with me." A troubled sigh came over the line. "Do you think they're trying to kill me from stress?"

"No way," he said. *Then you would be useless to them.*

The black case felt oddly light in Trent's hand, even though he knew it was filled with eight glass flasks. He carried it protectively under his right arm, leaning headfirst into the cold wind as he walked from the clinic to the church, recalling an afternoon when he was a little boy.

For his seventh birthday, his parents had given him a new fifty-dollar bill. It was the most money he had ever held, and it made him feel astonishingly rich. He had belly-flopped onto his bed and smelled its distinct sweetness. Even now, he remembered the tiny date in the right-hand corner: It had been a series 1996. Little did he know then that he would one day be holding cargo countless times more precious than even the Hope Diamond, which could never repair a spinal cord, or save a life.

In spite of his awe, guilt clouded his mind. He not only knew about the inspector's stifling presence, but he had also approved of it. And now Arianna was worried that the added stress might kill her: What if it did? Would he be partly responsible, since he had done nothing to stop it? But what could he have done? If he showed any loyalty to her, it would destroy them both. There was nothing he could do, except continue to hand in phony reports and inaccurate transcripts, shrug apologetically at Dopp's growing frustration, and privately glorify Sam.

The power Sam held over Arianna's life—and thus Trent's own—was remarkable; if Trent were still religious, he would be inclined to pray to such a being. But it was both liberating and disappointing to know that praying was futile. Safely delivering the case was the most he could do. He looked over his shoulder every several blocks, worried that someone from the DEP could be trailing him, just as he had trailed her. But each time he glanced behind him, he saw mostly empty sidewalks and a few people who were not the least interested in him. To refocus his paranoia, he thought of Sam, flushing at the prospect of their meeting.

By the time he reached the dark alley and hopscotched over its filth, he felt privileged to be knocking on Sam's steel door, to hand a genius his tools.

"Well?" came a faraway voice.

"Uh—SADFACE," Trent called. It was the only password he knew.

"Who is that?" barked the voice, coming closer. "We don't use SADFACE anymore."

"Sam, I mean, Dr. Lisio, it's Trent. I have the case for you."

There was no response, and Trent wondered if he should repeat himself. But after a few seconds, he heard the three dead bolts unlocking inside. The door pulled back an inch, and Sam peered through the slit suspiciously, reminding Trent of their first—and only—meeting.

But this time they were alone.

"Hi," Trent said, holding out the case. He was torn between wanting to step inside, away from the alley's stench, or to step back, away from Sam's surly gaze.

"Where's Megan?" Sam demanded. Through the narrow opening, his pink cheek rubbed against the door's edge.

"She got stuck at work. Arianna called me at the last minute."

"Sure," Sam snapped. "She calls to tell you but not me."

"I'm sorry," Trent replied, wondering why he was apologizing.

"Never mind." Sam opened the door just enough for Trent to enter. "You better come in and wait while I exchange the clones."

"Thanks." Trent walked in and handed him the case, surveying the lab for a place to sit. Besides the stools that lined the counter in the back of the room, there was only a nylon cot on the floor. He decided to stand. While Sam emptied the flasks into the incubator and replaced them with clones from the freezer, Trent tried to come up with pleasant small talk. But his lips would not form the words, sensing that Sam would not play that game, at least not with him. Could he still be angry that Arianna had brought a stranger to their sacred grounds? But that wasn't Trent's fault, and he had obviously not reported them, so what was the problem?

Perhaps Sam had been antisocial for so long that his interpersonal skills had atrophied like a useless muscle. Trent wondered if he was lonely. The old man did not exactly seem to yearn for company. Did he have anyone to confide in, or wish he did?

As Sam transferred new flasks into the case, his gnarled hands moving with precision and grace, Trent was overcome by a strange feeling of kinship. Here they were, two men, as isolated from the world as from each other, united in the fight for one urgent goal, each doing his part the only way he knew how.

"I'm glad I could help you," Trent blurted.

A sound like a grunt escaped Sam as he leaned into the freezer for another flask. Trent looked around the lab, trying to think of something else to say. Judging from the look of the place, Sam was certainly eccentric. Next to the cot on the floor, an open duffel bag was bursting with purple sweatpants and frayed T-shirts. Strewn on the floor were notepads, crumpled balls of paper, and old, heavy-looking textbooks. One book near Trent's feet read in block letters: *Genomics, Proteomics, and Systems Biology, 2006.*

"Do you sleep here?" Trent asked, even though he realized the answer was obvious. Sam did not turn around.

"Yep."

"Oh. Well, can I bring you anything else?"

"The less anyone comes here, the better." Sam turned to face him while he snapped the black case shut. "I bet you didn't even look twice before you walked into the alley."

"You're right," Trent said. "I was too busy thinking about how honored I was to be helping you."

Sam stared at him stonily. Trent stared back, determined to thaw his hostility, well aware that he risked worsening it. Outside, he heard fierce wind whipping up the air and barreling through the alley. From miles away, it seemed as if the clinic were howling for him to return. Inside his sweatshirt pocket, he rubbed the key Emily had given him to go back and stock the freezer's vulnerable shelves.

He reached out for the black case. Sam handed it to him.

"Thank you," Trent said. "I won't bother you any more."

Inspector Banks stood before Dopp on Friday morning like a prisoner before a judge: humble and ashamed.

"You're supposed to be intimidating her," Dopp said through gritted teeth. "She has hardly mentioned you to Trent all week!"

Banks grimaced. "What did she say, at least?"

Dopp grabbed the thin transcript off his desk, which Trent had handed him only minutes before. "Here," he said, bringing the transcript close to his face. "Yesterday, Trent asked her, 'How are things at the clinic these days?'

"And she said, 'Okay. Frustrating that I'm not seeing patients. I've been seeing more of that inspector lately, though.'

"'Really, how come?'

"'It's part of their new policy to monitor doctors now.'

"'That must bother you, doesn't it?'

"'Yeah, it's annoying. But not that big a deal. By the way, I wanted to tell you about this book. . . .'"

Dopp sighed in disgust and slammed the page onto his desk. "Why doesn't she seem to care that you're there, *watching her,* all day?"

"She doesn't *seem* to care," Banks said. "But she did change the subject right afterwards, like she didn't want to dwell on it."

Dopp seized the transcript again. Rereading it, Arianna's words seemed both flippant and circumspect, as if a secret lurked between the lines.

"That is strange," he agreed. "She didn't appear to react at all. It's unnatural. She must be holding back for some reason. Lying."

"She just needs to be broken down," Banks said. "I'm telling you, Gideon, she has the Devil's force in her. If you had to be with her, you'd know."

"Trust me, I know. Now, today's your last chance this week, so go and stay by her side all day."

To witness time passing, those in the outside world looked up at the sun and the moon; Sam looked down at his petri dishes. Eight of them lined a shelf in the incubator, all injected with the slightest variances of molecular growth factors. Since Wednesday night, when he had extracted stem cells from the embryos Trent brought him, and then altered the cells with injections, he had not slept for more than an hour and a half. Every two hours, he carried the dishes, one by one, to his inverted microscope to check on the progress of their growth. Every two hours, he jotted down notes, checked them against previous attempts, and returned them to the incubator. Each dish was carefully labeled, one through eight, with a corresponding chart of which molecules he had injected in each. After an injection, it took about thirty-six hours for the cells to differentiate into their final form. To Sam, it was always a period of time both hateful and exhilarating, thirty-six hours of pacing and nervousness brought on by renewed hope. And despite hundreds of attempts, it was always followed by a thirty-seventh hour of gut-wrenching disappointment.

His stomach was rumbling when the two-hour alarm on his cell phone went off again, near his head on the cot. For this batch of experiments, it would be the last time he needed to get up, open the incubator, and carry the dishes to his microscope. It was during these final two hours that the cell development had often faltered, spewing mistakenly differentiated cells like a malfunctioning vending machine. But recently the cells had been tantalizingly close to the goal, developing as astrocytes or microglia instead of oligodendrocytes, like Cokes instead of Diet Cokes.

Sam's eyelids drooped. Even though he would never admit it, part of him longed for the days when Patrick and Ian were here, and the three of them switched twelve-hour shifts to monitor the cells. And then, after Ian had quit, he and Patrick had each taken on eighteen hours—exhausting, though not unthinkable. But to handle thirty-six hours alone was close to disorienting. He did not know if he was hungry for breakfast or dinner, or which was even appropriate. And his circadian rhythm was disrupted. Was he dreaming that he was opening the incubator, cradling the warm circular dish in his palm, walking to the inverted microscope on the counter? Had he even fallen asleep at all? He squeezed his eyes shut and opened them wide. They felt dry and scratchy. Yes, he was awake.

He consulted the label on the dish in his palm: number one. The first of eight chances, he thought as he slid the dish under the microscope's indifferent lens.

The flat-panel screen on Arianna's office wall let out a screeching whistle, followed by bursts of red light. Unfazed, she barely glanced up as she hit the OFF button on her remote. Inspector Banks's prompt morning arrival was as consistent as the numbness in her legs. She no longer bothered to wheel herself to the waiting room to greet him. Oppressive though his presence was, together they had slipped into a tense routine—first, he would walk unescorted down the hall to her office, and then they would silently proceed to the laboratory at the rear of the clinic. After his inspection, she would sign the same bureaucratic form and then he would follow her back to her office, where he would plant himself in a chair across from her. Arianna hardly ever initiated conversation, and neither did he. As she updated patients' files and accounts, she tried to avoid his gaze, but she could always feel his empty-looking eyes feasting on her, like a vulture waiting to swoop upon a dying animal.

While she found him nearly unbearable, she sensed that he somewhat enjoyed the hours. He never sighed or made a point of checking his watch, but rather leaned back in the chair, the epitome of patience. The other day, she had deigned to ask him if he was bored.

"No true Christian is ever bored," he had replied. "There's always a passage from the Scriptures to think about."

Great, she thought, *all I need in my office is a Sunday school.*

Now she heard his shoes slapping down the hallway.

At least—at the very least—it was Friday.

Trent nodded at the towering presence in his doorway. Dopp's voice filled the tiny office with a suffocating fullness.

"Make sure," Dopp said, "that you are in the park at four forty-five today to watch her leave. Banks will be with her until then. And then if she goes straight home, call and tell her you want to come over. Spend as much time with her as possible tonight and this weekend, and try to talk about her fears."

"I will." Trent hesitated, thinking about the Manhattan judge who had recently turned down Dopp's application for permission to bug Arianna's cell phone. Given a judge's order, a phone company could remotely install a piece of software on a person's cell, which activated its microphone even when the phone was not in use. To a listener nearby with a radio interceptor, it was the perfect bugging device, especially since it was undetectable. To Dopp's frustration, liberal sentiment was so strong in New York that he had to obey the letter of the law, following established channels of legality to obtain a judge's permission. But the judge assigned to review Dopp's application had decided there was "no clear-cut indication of criminality" in Arianna's case. Although it was a setback for Dopp, Trent feared it was insignificant. He knew Dopp was not about to back down.

Bracing for the answer, Trent pressed on. "By the way, are you going to file an appeal?"

Dopp smirked. "Are you kidding? That judge was some kind of feminist nut. I'm already working on getting some friends in Albany to help me speed things along this time."

The words assaulted his ears. "Good," he replied.

"But as of right now," Dopp went on, "until we can intercept all of her conversations, our only hope is a confession to you directly—unless, of course, she goes back to the East Village and leads you somewhere important, or mishandles embryos under Banks's nose. But I don't see either of those things happening at this point."

"Me either."

"So you have to *sympathize* with her as much as possible."

"I am, boss. I am."

With a great sigh, Sam pulled the fifth dish out from under the microscope and set it next to the other four failures on the counter. His spine ached from hunching over the lens, attempting to identify the pure cells he longed to see. Yet improperly differentiated cells had popped up in every petri dish, mixing dangerously with oligodendrocytes. That was unacceptable; the cells had to be pure oligos in order to form myelin sheaths and repair Arianna's spinal cord.

Sam consulted the chart to remind himself which growth factors he had injected into dish number six: the nuclear thyroid hormone receptor, T4 (L-thyroxine) at 40 nanograms per milliliter; the antioxidants selenium and vitamin E; thioredoxin reductase; bone morphogenic protein; and retinoic acid—along with the other standard culture ingredients of nutrient supplements, insulin, and antibiotics.

He went to the incubator and removed dish six, holding it with both hands as he brought it back to that mercilessly objective judge, the microscope. He slid the dish under the lens and peered down into it.

He squinted.

The landscape of the petri dish transcended that of a cell culture. It was a field of flawless diamonds, sparkling and scintillating under a master jeweler's knife. It was the bottom of the hourglass, where the golden droplets of time had accumulated, pure and precious and waiting to be found.

It was one oligodendrocyte next to another, and another, dozens of like cells jostling for space in the modest dish.

Conformity had never looked so beautiful.

In the tense silence, Arianna's cell phone vibrated loudly on her desk. Inspector Banks eyed it as if it were an annoying fly that needed a good swat. Arianna pressed a button to turn off the vibration and then glanced at the caller ID. It was Sam—the one person whose rare calls she hated to postpone. In a flash, she thought about wheeling herself out into the hallway, to the bathroom—but then Banks would wonder why she had never made such an effort for privacy for any other call. To downplay his suspicion was key.

She looked down at her phone, at Sam's name insistently lighting up the screen.

What if there was another emergency and he needed her right away?

Temptation tipped her decision, even as Banks watched her.

"Excuse me," she said to him, lifting the phone to her ear. She willed herself to remain expressionless, no matter what. Calm and cool.

"Hello?"

"Arianna." The word sounded strained, as if Sam were struggling against a barrage of emotions. She hardly recognized his voice.

Her heart leapt into her throat; she could almost taste its frenzied pumping. *Calm and cool.*

"What's going on?"

And then his voice broke.

"I did it."

SEVENTEEN

Arianna gasped. "You *did*?"

"It's flawless," Sam choked out.

Tears slipped down her cheeks, draining from a pool of desperation deep within her. Even as she fought to contain them, the droplets escaped from the corners of her eyes in a free fall of euphoria, gaining momentum as they coursed down her face.

Through her blurry eyes, she saw that Inspector Banks was watching her intently, his eyebrows arched in surprise.

She shielded her face with her hand, unable to speak or think.

"Arianna?" Sam asked.

"I always knew you could," she whispered.

Finding her voice again launched an ecstatic swell within her, this time in her vocal cords, and she had to repress the urge to scream.

"I want to see you," he said.

"I'll come over right now!"

"Don't you dare."

"But I want to see you, too!"

"We should meet at the clinic to extract your skin cells. I want to start the process right away."

She paused, wondering how to communicate the impossible.

"The bastard is right there, isn't he?" Sam said.

"Yes."

"How can you stand him right now?"

She laughed freely, thinking that Banks did not matter anymore, nor did her fear. She laughed still at the fact that such things had mattered minutes ago, and now they did not. Oh, the energy she had wasted—all along, a farce, a cruel one, but that was all.

"Let's meet somewhere," Sam suggested. "We need to talk and plan. Your place?"

"I'm leaving right now."

"Good. I'll see you there."

She tore the phone from her ear. Wetness from her cheek had dribbled onto the mouthpiece, so she wiped it onto her pant leg, slipped the phone into her pocket, and then looked up. Involuntarily, she felt herself beaming.

"Some good news, I take it?" Banks asked.

"Yes."

"You look stunned."

She shook her head slowly and took a sidelong glance at her office. "I am." The left wall looked like a checkerboard of pink and blue, adorned with contiguous pictures of her patients' babies.

"My sister just had a baby. A girl. It was an unexpected early delivery."

Banks's face relaxed. "Well, isn't that nice."

"She's seven pounds four ounces. Sophia Roxanne."

It was the name she had always wanted for a daughter.

Banks nodded. "What a blessing."

She smiled, turning her wheelchair toward the door behind her. "I'm off to go meet her now. See you next time."

Leaning forward, she propelled her wheelchair to the door and pushed it open without waiting for Banks's reply. The hallway gleamed white, no longer sterile and monochrome, but dazzling. For a moment, she thought about going to tell the Ericsons, but they were busy with patients. As soon as the workday ended, she would call them. Instead, she dashed to the waiting room, waved to a few regulars there, and then flew out the door onto the sidewalk. The air was chilly and nipped at her face as she rode jubilantly through the park, savoring the scent of cool freshness after rain. When she flew over a puddle and it splashed up to her blouse, she laughed and went faster, speeding past the fountain, under the glorious arch, and veering left, straight into her building's lobby.

In the elevator, she took her cell phone out of her pocket and called Trent, drumming her fingers excitedly on her armrest. If only she could see his face. She wondered if he would scream or stay silent, or even cry.

One, two, three, four rings passed before his voice mail picked up. Undeterred, she tried again. One, two, three four, voice mail. Growing frustrated, she tried once more. But his phone continued to ring, unanswered.

Dopp worked quickly, rewriting the department's application to bug Arianna's cell phone. This time, he thought, they'd better be assigned a good old-fashioned judge who could smell something foul when it stank up the room. Senator Windra ought to help land them the right judge, if he was sincere about wanting to support the department. But Dopp was putting off making the call to Albany. Part of him worried that the senator would lose respect for him for asking a favor, that it undermined his own leadership skills to rely on political connections. But then again, that feminist judge had not given their application a fair review. It was up to Dopp to set it right. He knew he needed to shun that worst of human sins—his own pride—and just make the call.

At that moment, his phone rang. No way, he thought, it would be too lucky. He waved his hand over the desk phone's speaker to answer.

"Gideon Dopp," he intoned.

"Boss. I have an update."

Dopp recognized Banks's throaty voice immediately. "Yeah, what's up?"

"She left. Said her sister just gave birth, and took off. She was happier than I ever saw."

Dopp's skin prickled. "How did she find out?"

"She got a call on her cell."

"If only that idiot judge had approved our application already!"

"I know."

"So you don't know where she went?"

"No." Banks's voice wavered. "I guess to a hospital. I just thought you should know."

"Obviously. Thank you." Dopp said good-bye and waved his hand over his desk phone's speaker to turn it off.

For a few moments, he sat completely still, wondering why the hair on his arms was taut and his skin cold. His intuition was a precise instrument, as reliable as a compass, and he knew never to ignore it. On a hunch, he reached into his filing cabinet for a manila folder labeled, ARIANNA DRAKE/WASHINGTON SQUARE CENTER FOR REPRODUCTIVE MEDICINE.

The thick folder held all the information Trent had compiled about her over the past several months, complete with transcripts of their conversations, notes about her moods, and sly observations of her comings and goings.

Dopp turned back to the records of their earliest conversations, when she and Trent had talked during breaks in their bike rides. He skimmed the mostly boring pages, flipping through them quickly. And then he gasped.

Her words were right there on the page, woven into a stock conversation about their family histories, an incidental revelation that held no meaning until this moment:

DRAKE: *You're an only child? So am I.*

Trent's cell phone began to vibrate as soon as Dopp rushed into his office. But a more pressing matter than the call confronted him: Dopp's eyes were wide enough to reveal the whites all around his dark brown irises. His lopsided lips were parted and moist, and a glint in his eyes signaled an alarming level of intensity.

"What is Arianna's sister's name?" Dopp demanded, clutching the side of the doorframe as if to steady himself.

"What's *what*?"

"You heard me."

"I—I don't understand. What are you talking about?"

In Trent's pocket, his cell phone began to vibrate against his thigh for a second time.

"What I am talking about," Dopp said, "is Arianna's sister. Do you know her name?"

"I thought she was an only child like me."

Dopp's face flushed, taking on a feverish tint. "You're right."

Trent felt his heart smack against his ribs. "What's going on?"

"Banks just called from her clinic. She had some sort of ecstatic outburst and then took off, telling him that her sister just had a baby. But isn't it funny—" Dopp paused, handing Trent a single sheet of paper that he remembered typing two months before. "She told you she's an only child."

Trent took the paper and skimmed it as his cell phone vibrated a third time. He realized then who might be calling . . . an ecstatic outburst . . . Could Sam have—?

"I don't understand," he said. "Where did she run off to?"

"That's the whole point! That woman is a liar, and now we've caught her in the act! If she doesn't have a sister, where in the world did she go? And *why*?"

Trent shook his head. "I wish I could tell you. I'm as confused as you are."

"Call her right now," Dopp instructed. "Ask her what she's up to."

Oh my God, Trent thought.

Nodding, he pulled out his cell phone and ignored the three missed calls on the display. Then he called his father's cell phone. He knew his dad hardly used the slim device, which stayed in his car's glove compartment. The elder Mr. Rowe preferred the old-fashioned bulkiness of land phones, which were easier for him to hold on his shoulder.

The cell rang five times, predictably, before voice mail picked up, and his father's voice instructed him to leave a message. Trent shrugged apologetically at Dopp as he spoke:

"Hey, it's me. Just wondering how your day's going. Hope you're doing okay. Give me a call when you get this. Bye."

He looked up at Dopp. "No answer. Hopefully she'll call soon."

"I didn't think she would pick up," Dopp muttered. "Are you seeing her tonight?"

"I was supposed to."

"Well, find out the truth. And if you don't, there will be consequences. We have the upper hand now, and I intend to use it before it's too late."

"How?"

"I have an idea of my own. But I may not have to go that far if you can make things easy for us. I'll be in touch tonight. If you don't have her voice on record saying where she was going and why, then you can expect consequences."

"But what if she won't tell me?"

"Then I guess you're pretty useless on this case."

Trent tightened his lips and did not answer.

"We have to do whatever it takes," Dopp said, reaching up to hold the back of his flushed neck. "This isn't about you, and it's not even just about her."

Trent nodded, ironically sympathizing with his boss's strength of convictions. Their motivation was the same: to stop something each saw as evil, because it was a threat to life. On one level, Trent wished that his onetime mentor could see him for who he really was—not an inept agent, but an equally fervent adversary. He hoped they were well matched.

Sam rushed to Arianna's apartment giddily. When his taxi pulled up to her building, he tossed the driver two twenties for a ten-dollar ride, and then bounded inside. He waved to the doorman as he ran across the tiled floor into the elevator. The mirrored panels inside showed him the dopey grin on his lips, and he chuckled, hardly noticing his five-day growth of silvery stubble. The anticipation of seeing Arianna's face carried him on light feet to her door.

When she opened it, he was thrilled to see her sunken cheeks flushed, her smile wide. In her rosy skin and bright eyes, it was as if the life left in her was already proclaiming its comeback.

"Hi," he said, grinning and stepping inside.

"Sam." The rogue dimple in her chin appeared when she said his name, and she reached out to him with both arms from the captivity of her wheelchair.

He bent down and hugged her, relishing their three seconds of physical closeness. He was acutely aware of the sweet smell of her hair, her warm cheek against his own, her deep exhale. When he pulled away and stood up, she held on to his hands. In her eyes shone unspeakable gratitude.

"Is this how religious people feel toward saints?" she asked.

He chuckled. "Are you saying you're going to worship me?"

"Something like that. Would you like a shrine?"

"Sure, I'll take it."

She beamed up at him. "I can't believe you did it. I mean, I can—but still . . ."

"I know. . . ." He trailed off, stymied by tightness in his throat.

"As soon as that idiot leaves tonight, we can go back for my skin cells."

"Good." He grew focused, creasing his brow. "If I can use them tonight to create a hybrid embryo, then we have to wait five days before we can take out the stem cells. That's next Wednesday night. Then it takes thirty-six hours for the cells to properly differentiate, so that puts us at Friday morning. But we need the equipment in your clinic to do the transfer, and it will take some hours for the cells to proliferate. So we ought to aim for next Friday night, once the bastard inspector leaves for the weekend."

"A whole week from now!"

"Yes. That's the soonest possible."

She squeezed his hands. "I can wait. I'll be okay."

He nodded.

"It's kind of like a starving person about to sit down to a feast," she said with a smile. "As long as you know it will happen, you can force your body to hold out."

"Your will is a powerful thing," Sam agreed. "And I mean *your* will, not just any old one."

"Thank you!" She grinned, wriggling her shoulders as if to a beat. "I wish we could dance right now."

"With me?" he teased. "I don't believe it."

"You'll do."

"What happened to—" *Trent,* he almost said, but then decided to bypass that topic. "—to me being a stiff old man?"

"No way you're as stiff as me!"

They both laughed, and in that moment, Sam wanted nothing more than to tell her he loved her. The realization of this desire shocked him—he never planned to confess. And yet, the way she looked adoringly at him and his newfound hero's confidence were combining in potent, unforeseen ways. *She has to know,* he thought with sudden certainty. *I ought to tell her right now, before I lose the courage. . . .*

It was a freedom from inhibition he had never felt, entirely unlike the predictable and transient pleasure that drew him to alcohol. This was like reaching for the highest rung in the ladder of temptation: the highest risk promised the highest return.

She was squeezing his hands again and moving her upper body to her own rhythm, pretending to share a victory dance. He laughed as he scuffed his shoe against her wheelchair in attempt to keep up the beat.

No, he did not dare to ask any more of this moment. But, he thought, she still deserves to know, and before the spinal cord transfer. No one knew for sure how risky the procedure was, even if the DNA in the cells was her own.

Was he really going to tell her?

He shivered as she pulled herself out of the chair, using his hands for leverage.

"Put my feet on yours," she instructed, wrapping her arms around his neck.

He obeyed, feeling surreal as he hoisted her up and onto his beat-up sneakers. The weight of her body rested on his feet, and their bodies were completely aligned—knee-to-knee, waist-to-waist, face-to-face.

"What song are we dancing to?" he asked over her shoulder.

"I don't know. But if we can just make it over to the stereo, I'll put something on." She nudged him backwards, laughing as they took an awkward joint step. "Hold on to me!"

"Don't worry," he said, clutching her tighter around the waist, trying to ignore her breasts pushed into his chest.

Life is so short, he thought. Too short to carry such secrets. Then, with a sinking feeling, he pictured the lab. In a week, they would no doubt decide to shut it down as a safety precaution. Without the ability to research, what was left for him to love, except for her?

But he knew how ridiculous he would feel blurting out his feelings, let alone if he ever worked up the nerve to do so. His lack of practice expressing himself did not help. It seemed there was only one way to get the words out, and to make them sound right. In his head, a letter began.

It was not until lunch, when Trent was safely away from work and headed to a fast food place two blocks away, that he finally called Arianna back. How he passed the remainder of the morning was a mystery, even to him, but he knew better than to risk calling her when Dopp could charge into his office at any moment.

She picked up and yelped his name.

"What happened?" he asked. "Sorry, I was working and didn't see my phone."

"Sam did it! He made the breakthrough!"

"Oh my God! Are you serious? What does this mean?"

"In one week, we're going to transfer new cells into my spinal cord that will hopefully save my life." She paused, and a man said something in the background. "They *will*, according to Sam." Her voice sounded euphoric, astonished.

"Oh my God. I could kiss that man. He's a fucking genius!" Trent leaped into the air and landed two yards away, almost bumping into a passerby on the sidewalk. The man shot him an angry glance. Trent laughed as his throat constricted. "Is this real?"

"It's real. I know. I still can't believe it. I don't know what to do with myself! We just broke out the champagne. You should come over and celebrate with us!"

"Tonight?" An image of Dopp's face intruded on his joy. "I—I can't. I wish I could." He stopped short on the sidewalk, oblivious of the frustrated people who wove around him. Tonight, he remembered, *Get the truth or face consequences.*

"Why, what's wrong?" Arianna asked. "I want to see you!"

"I would love to see you, too. I don't want to risk it, though. I'm not feeling too well. My stomach is a little upset. . . ."

"Oh, I'm sorry to hear that. But then you shouldn't come over. My immune system . . ."

"I know. Tomorrow, hopefully."

"Yes, feel better!"

"Thanks. Are you going to party later?"

She laughed. "Even better. I'm going back to the clinic tonight so Dr. Ericson can draw some skin cells to give to Sam."

"You have to wait for the inspector to leave first?"

"Exactly."

"Well, good luck, baby. Give Sam a giant hug from me, and I don't care if he squirms!"

Arianna chuckled as they said good-bye.

But the queasiness in his stomach that Trent spoke of was no lie. There was no way he could get her voice on record admitting to the major revelation that Dopp wanted. And there was no way he could face her tonight with appropriately rampant elation. As deeply relieved as he was, fear gnawed at him, muddying his clarity of thought.

She needed only seven more days. Once the transfer was over, she wouldn't need the lab or the clinic for her own personal use; the danger of catching her in action would be over. With his hands in his pockets, Trent kicked a street pole in front of him. His prudence had carried Arianna through the past several weeks, but it was not enough. How could he contain Dopp for one final week? It depended on his contingency plan, which Trent might not discover until it was implemented—until perhaps it was too late.

He cut his lunch break short, reluctantly returning to work, unable to think of food. What would he tell Dopp later? His mind swirled around the question throughout the rest of the day, unable to devise an answer.

Before he left work four hours later, Dopp instructed him to go to Washington Square and plant himself in a discreet spot to watch the clinic, in case she returned that evening. He was to switch shifts with Banks, who was leaving at five o'clock.

"We can't take any chances on missing her," Dopp said. "Just in case she might go back for some reason, since she's obviously sneaking around."

"Of course."

"Has she still not called you back from this morning?"

"No."

"That's not good. Remember, Trent, I'm counting on you tonight."

At 4:45 P.M., Trent arrived at the park to greet Banks as he left—ostensibly obliging Dopp's orders. The park was too sparse for Trent to wait discreetly on a bench, so he stood in the recessed doorway of the Catholic Center, one block west of the clinic. From there, shrouded by the arched overhang of the doorway, he could still see the clinic's brown door open and close. Soon, Banks walked out of the clinic with a man and a woman who Trent assumed were the Ericsons, the remaining members of Arianna and Sam's group. Trent watched the couple part ways with Banks, and as soon as they were out of earshot, he called out to the inspector.

Banks walked the one block over, shaking his head. "I wasted another whole day here. No sign of her."

"Let's pray I have better luck."

Banks nodded, and then hailed the first cab that passed. Twenty minutes later, Trent did the same. Once at home, he did something he had not done for at least a decade: He drew a bath. He hoped that being submerged in hot water, mimicking relaxation, would help him think.

He lay back against the smooth ceramic tub and wriggled his

toes under the running faucet. Trying to conceive of ways to outwit Dopp, he watched the water fill up to his neck. The heat made him sleepy, and he twirled his finger on the surface of the water, creating tiny whirlpools. Eventually, he turned off the faucet and closed his eyes, and in the silence of his bathroom, he could pretend to himself no longer. This time, he was entirely out of control; there was no way to get around Dopp tonight.

He visualized himself on a crashing airplane, the recurring nightmare of his childhood. When he once admitted his fears to his mother, she told him, "God is in control, even if you're not. Whatever happens is in His hands, so don't worry."

The words had been adequate consolation for a ten-year-old.

But who could comfort him now?

He knew it was only a matter of hours before he received the dreaded call. At 11:07 P.M., it came. The chiming ring filled his silent apartment, quickening his heart like a crank. For a second, he thought of ignoring it. But that would only hasten his boss's wrath.

"Hello?"

"Are you with her?" Dopp prompted without a greeting.

Trent swallowed. "No, I'm sorry. I didn't see her tonight. And she hasn't answered any of my calls."

"Well, well. Son of a gun. I expected more from you, Trent. You said you didn't want to disappoint me."

"I know, and I don't. It's just that I can't get hold of her."

Dopp's tone was brusque. "You're obviously incapable of doing this on your own. Whether that's because of your incompetence or her manipulation, I don't know."

"I'm sorry. . . ."

"And she never returned to the clinic?"

"No, I waited for hours. And I tried to call. . . ."

"When did you leave?"

"Around ten. I know she can't stay up later than that." Trent also knew that Dopp could not expect him to work more overtime hours than the department could afford to compensate.

Dopp sighed irritably. "Meet me in the office tomorrow morning at ten sharp."

Trent's heart palpitated. He had never known Dopp to work on Saturdays, which he referred to as a "sacred family day."

"Okay."

"When I told you there would be consequences, it wasn't an empty threat. This has to be a 24/7 effort from now on. Starting tomorrow, everything is going to change."

"Oh, really?" Trent cleared his throat. "Like how?"

"You'll find out tomorrow. I expect to have everything ready by then."

The line clicked off. Trent dropped the phone onto the table, wishing he hadn't picked up the call.

Late that night, Sam walked alone from the clinic through the East Village, making his way back to the lab. He strode quickly, hunched forward into the wind, with his balding head exposed and ears chilled. Tonight, he found the cold air refreshing. He passed a line of boisterous clubgoers behind a velvet rope and did not resent their carefree partying. He passed a stumbling man swigging a drink from a flask, and did not feel the urge to grab it away. Curled tight in Sam's fingers was a glass tube containing certain crucial DNA.

The group's private rendezvous in the clinic—an hour after Inspector Banks's departure—had safely yielded the two things Sam needed: Arianna's skin cells and more time with her. He marveled at the fact that they had spent almost an entire day alone together, in a joint state of ecstasy. He had even allowed himself a glass of champagne, knowing that her presence had already lifted him to the height of intoxication.

Now, alone again, he returned to the lab to carry out the procedure he had prepared for and dreamed of for months. When he unlocked the door and entered the basement, an unanticipated wave of nostalgia hit him. He surveyed his precious microscopes on the counter, his incubator and freezer, pipettes and centrifuge, and even his box of rubber gloves—all old friends who had rallied around him night and day, helping to execute his mission. Together, finally, they would finish it.

After slipping on his lab coat, gloves, and face mask, he carried the stored tube of five egg cells from the incubator over to the counter, where there waited a sterile laminar flow hood and an electron microscope. Using the microscope to view the cells, he separated each one into its own dish. Then, he switched on a polarized light to view the chromosomes in the nucleus, and—for the trickiest part—he carefully plucked each nucleus out of each egg cell. Only five shells remained. Then he repeated the procedure with all five of Arianna's skin cells. With these cells, however, he saved each nucleus—like a computer's hard drive, they were the microscopic nuggets that held all her genetic information.

Moving with a robot's precision and steadiness, Sam injected each nucleus into each empty egg cell to form five single-celled hybrids. Each step he performed tapped into distant memories; more than two decades prior, in a Columbia University lab, he had learned this innovative procedure. As he worked now, it still awed him that he could seize on a brilliant theory and then coax it into reality, into life. How many people today knew that this was even possible?

When each of the five egg cells contained Arianna's nuclei, Sam completed the final step: he shocked each cell with an electric generator, which would stimulate each to begin dividing. Watching the tiniest of magic shows with his microscope, he saw the moment that each cell split into two. It was such a basic, simple action—the crux of all life—and yet, he thought of how astronauts must feel watching Earth from space. As a teenager, Sam had wondered about such a surreal experience, but now he grasped how they felt watching that blue orb glowing against the blackness of the universe. He understood that his own experience happened at the same fundamental juncture as theirs: whether minuscule or vast, it was where man, through the force of his mind, was able to view the horizon of nature's power—the most spectacular beauty imaginable.

Sam looked up, profoundly satisfied. All the cells were growing. He deposited them into flasks prepared with nutrients, and then put the flasks into the incubator set at 37 degrees centigrade. Inside, a controlled amount of carbon dioxide would help the cells grow into embryos. After five days, stem cells would be ready to be extracted. There was nothing left to do but wait.

Sam pulled off his gloves and mask, and went to his duffel bag on the floor. Inside, buried under a pile of socks, was a lined notebook. He dug it out, grabbed a pen, and sat on the edge of his cot, placing the flimsy notebook on his lap. Toward the back, past pages of his scientific scrawls, was the first blank page.

"Dear Arianna," he wrote, in his neatest cursive. He paused. Was he really going to tell her? What about Trent—what was the point? But he thought about the adoring way she had looked at him all afternoon, the way she had tightened her arms around his neck and thrown her head back with pure elation. It seemed impossible that any other man could make her as happy as he had today. She and Trent had known each other only a few months, anyway; how attached could she be? Besides, in a week, what else would he have left in the world to treasure? If he yielded her to Trent without even trying . . . No. He was ready to be done losing women he loved.

He held his pen to the page again, letting a blot grow before beginning to write. "There's something on my mind that I—" No, he thought, and ripped out the page. Another clean one was waiting behind it. "Dear Arianna," he wrote again. "It's taken me a long time to realize I want to tell you this, but—" Definitely not. How the hell was he supposed to say this?

He ripped out the page and started over for a third time. "Dear Arianna," he wrote, in his own messy print. "I hope this is the last weekend of your life that you have to suffer."

The next morning, Sam arrived at Arianna's apartment for the group's scheduled meeting to discuss the transfer procedure. She looked rested and happy as she welcomed him inside, moving in her wheelchair with adept grace. Dr. Ericson and Emily were already sitting at the kitchen table, helping themselves to a spread of bagels, cream cheese, and lox that Arianna had arranged.

"Wow," Sam said. "We should have always met at your place."

"Help yourself. I bet you haven't eaten since we ordered lunch yesterday."

"You know me too well." As he sat down at the table, he felt the crunch of folded paper in his jeans pocket.

"So how are the cells?" Dr. Ericson asked.

"Perfect. Four of them are growing according to plan. We lost one overnight to the stress of the procedure, but the others are stable. And we only need one, so I'm not worried."

"Good," Dr. Ericson said. "So let's get down to business. I want us to get all the details straight."

Sam smiled. He had always liked the doctor, a man who got right to the point and never worried if he was too abrupt.

Arianna wheeled herself between Sam and Emily, who picked up her hand and squeezed it.

"This is so exciting," Emily whispered.

Sam wrung his hands under the table. "Bottom line is that the cells should drain intravenously into her spinal cord between vertebrates four and five."

"That's what I was thinking," Dr. Ericson agreed.

"So a lumbar puncture, then," Arianna said. "How long do you think it will take?"

"Well, we'll have to put the whole solution containing the cells into a sterile bag and let it drain," Sam said. He looked at the doctor. "What do you think?"

Dr. Ericson was nodding. "We'll have to make sure to squeeze the bag very gently, so as not to increase the pressure in her spinal cord too quickly." He looked meaningfully at Arianna, who was already wincing.

"I know," she said. "I'm going to wind up with the migraine of my life."

"How come?" Emily asked.

"The change in pressure. But that's fine—trust me, I'm not complaining."

"So how long do you think it'll take?" Sam asked.

Dr. Ericson considered. "How many milliliters?"

"About three hundred," Sam said.

"Then the bag should take about forty-five minutes to drain. I'll have to hold the needle completely steady in her spine." He held up his hands so they were level with his nose. "No shaking yet," he noted proudly.

"I would hope not," Sam said. "So what's the plan, then?"

"Come to the clinic Friday night, and we'll funnel the solution into the bag and set up the rest of the equipment before Arianna gets there."

"Fine."

"What about anesthesia?" Emily asked.

Sam looked at Arianna, who was spreading cream cheese on a bagel as if she had not a care in the world. "I don't know what effect that would have on the cells," he said.

"It's fine." She barely hesitated. "I can deal."

"We can have it on reserve if you decide you really need it," Dr. Ericson offered. "It should be safe to use an IV sedative at least."

"Okay," she said. "But pain isn't the worst thing ever."

"Technically, they're your own cells," Sam pointed out. "So I wouldn't expect any bad reactions, would you?"

Dr. Ericson shook his head. "But we are moving into uncharted territory."

"I think we're pretty much in it," Emily said.

Arianna smiled at her. "In the best way possible."

"So you're not scared?" With her girlish sloped nose and widened eyes, Emily looked much younger than mid-forties. Sam wondered how much younger he looked than sixty-seven.

"Honestly? Not in the least." Arianna chuckled at Emily's surprise. "Okay, maybe slightly. But it's the kind of fear you get when you're climbing a roller coaster. A fun fear, if that makes sense."

"An anticipation," Sam clarified. "Of something dangerously thrilling to come."

"Exactly."

He thought: *I know just what you mean.*

• • •

When the meeting was over, and everyone had cleared the table and placed their dishes in the dishwasher, the pummeling in Sam's chest signaled what was near. The Ericsons were saying good-bye, walking toward the door and wishing Arianna a restful weekend. Sam lingered behind them, dawdling in the kitchen just to the right of the foyer, with a hand in his pocket. He fingered the edge of the paper folded there.

"You guys go ahead," Sam called as Emily held the door open for him. He wished he could think of a convincing reason to stay behind, instead of nervously waving.

Emily shrugged and waved, and then the door closed. Arianna reached up above the doorknob to lock the bolt, and it clicked loudly into place.

They were alone.

She turned her wheelchair around to face him. "What's up?"

Sam sat back down in one of the kitchen chairs and motioned for her to come over.

How do I do this? he thought, panicking. Hadn't he rehearsed this moment all of last night? Hadn't he lost sleep over it, imagining exactly what he would say?

"Are you still hungry?" she asked, wheeling up in front of him. "I have a lot more food you could take."

"No, thanks, I'm fine." He cleared his throat. "I just wanted a moment with you."

She nodded as if she understood. "I'm glad."

"You are?"

"Yeah. I've been thinking about something that happened a while ago between us. It was kind of an unspoken thing, and I was planning to talk to you about it, but then we got so distracted—"

"Yes," he interrupted. "I think I know what you're talking about." His heart raged against his rib cage. In the lab, that look they had shared, loaded with meaning— Now, finally, she was acknowledging it. . . .

She sighed. "So it's bothering you, too? I should have talked to you about it sooner. I knew you were mad at me and I just ignored it until it seemed like you were over it, and that was wrong of me.

So I'm sorry. And I never apologized properly for upsetting you either."

Sam frowned, feeling disoriented. He saw her lips moving and her remorseful expression, heard the strange words that pelted his eardrums. When was he mad? And then he understood. This was not about them; it was about the outsider who had invaded his lab and her heart, and in doing so, threatened all that Sam held dear.

He grimaced, not trusting his voice. In his pocket, his hand closed tightly around the folded piece of paper; its edge pierced his skin, a thin but stinging blade.

"I'm sorry I didn't consult with you before I took him there," Arianna continued. "It was impulsive and potentially dangerous, and I admit that. I guess I got so swept away by how badly I wanted to show him that I didn't think of you or Patrick or Ian, and how you guys would feel about it. I should have shown you more consideration."

Sam nodded. He pulled his hand out of his pocket and noticed tiny beads of blood across his palm.

"Are you still mad?" she asked. Worry spread across her face, rendering it even more innocent, and more lovely.

"Not anymore," he said.

"I should have apologized a lot earlier."

"Probably."

She bit her lip. "Better late than never, right?"

"Yeah." Sam paused. "So how are things going with him?"

She ventured to smile. "Amazing. He's so supportive. I don't think I could ask for more."

Sam glanced behind her at the front door. It had never looked so welcome; and yet, he glanced back into her dark blue eyes, compelled by a savage impulse to watch the end of the crash, the final horrific moment of combustion.

"Do you love him?"

Eagerness crept into her smile—there was no mistaking such a look, one that Sam knew well from his days of teaching: It was the recognition of an easy question.

"Definitely," she said.

He felt strangely detached, as if he were following a script written as punishment for his foolishness.

"Good," he murmured. "I want you to be happy."

It was the gut-shredding truth.

She grabbed one of his hands with both of hers. "Oh, Sam, I'm so glad you feel that way! I was worried you didn't approve, and your opinion means the world to me. I've always felt . . ." She looked down, smiling almost shyly. "Well, that you're like a second father to me. I know you hate being sentimental, but it's true. Even beyond saving my life, which is—well, there are no words for that . . . but I'm so lucky just to have you *in* my life. I see us as family, don't you?"

Sam nodded, smiling at the sheer irony of his idiocy.

"And, I know this is impossible, but if there is anything I could ever do to repay you at all, you have to tell me." She shook her head, looking stunned. "I still can't believe it. And beyond me, what this could mean for so many more people . . . You should be all over the news right now! Like the next Pasteur!"

"Galileo's more like it," he muttered.

"Except you're not under any kind of arrest."

"No. But if I were, it would be by the same people."

She shivered. "Scary."

"It's goddamn infuriating is what it is."

"We ought to find a way to tell the world what you've done."

He nodded, though glory was the furthest thing from his mind.

"But, hey," she said, "what was it that you wanted to talk to me about?"

"Oh, we already covered it."

"So you also wanted to get that off your chest?"

"Yep."

"I'm honestly surprised you stayed behind to talk about it," she said, throwing him a teasing look. "But I'm glad you did. It's so much better to clear the air."

"Yeah. I should be getting back to the lab." Sam rose, letting go of her hands.

"Okay. And call me if you need or want anything. I can have someone bring stuff to you."

"Thanks." He thought: *I'd rather starve than have your boyfriend visit me again.* He walked to the front door, careful not to rush.

"See you soon," she called from the kitchen.

He could not bear to turn back around and see her radiant face. But he did it anyway, smiling. And then he was out the door, alone in the quiet sanctuary of the hall. His face began to burn, as repressed shame flowed upward. All he wanted was to escape this building that housed the truth—now so painfully obvious, like a hidden blister exploded upon chafing.

He hurried out of the building. The folded paper crinkled against his right thigh, but he ignored it, refusing to acknowledge any reminder of his folly. Outside, the cool air felt moist, as if the gray sky was preparing to shed its clouds. He stood on the corner, with one limp arm raised, until a cab pulled up. Once he settled into it, he craved something to dull his mind: the sting of vodka or the warmth of whiskey or even just the relief of a cigarette.

By the time the cab dropped him at Avenue C and Tenth Street, it had begun to rain, and he sprinted, groaning, to the alley. Bolts of pain shot through his lower back. He reached the threshold, looked all around the desolate street, and then headed into the alley. Puddles of muck were lapping up raindrops and oozing outward in all directions. He could hardly avoid them as he rushed to the concrete stairs, then down the short flight and to the steel door. He fumbled with his keys before unlocking all three bolts and then bursting inside, pulling the door shut behind him.

Cool droplets slid down his forehead as he caught his breath. He looked down; the cuffs of his jeans were soaked. He had no choice but to take them off. After tossing his keys onto the cot, he removed his cell phone from his left pocket and his wallet from his back one, and threw those onto the cot as well. When he crouched down to untie his sneakers, he felt the folded paper stiffen against his thigh. Exhaling, he stood back up and looked around the familiar room that had become his home. The microscopes waited loyally on the counter; the incubator and freezer hummed; the cot and flannel blanket promised warmth, if not comfort. Here, at least, he was guaranteed total privacy, however poor a consolation.

He hesitated. Then he reached into his pocket and pulled out the rectangle of paper. He knew he could simply toss it into the wastebasket under the counter and never look at it again. But some masochistic force drove him to unfold the page, to read the words he had written, if only for the sick pleasure of seeing exactly what humiliation he had avoided:

January 21, 2028

Dear Arianna,

I hope this is the last weekend of your life that you have to suffer. You have no idea how hard it's been for me to watch you get sicker these past few months. But what happened today will change everything—of course it's unknown, but I have every reason to believe that it will work. Theoretically, it's perfect. I can't wait for this week to pass. And when it does, you'll be the bravest patient your clinic has ever seen. All I want is for you to live, Arianna. The world can't afford to lose you.

You have no idea what you saved me from when you showed up at my apartment all those months ago. I hate to think what would have happened to me if you hadn't come. That day, I think we made each other's wildest hopes come true. And then I started to see you as the woman you are, and not just as a former student who needed my help. Why do you think I could never imagine quitting like the others? I know you've never seen this side of me. I bet you're surprised. Well, so am I.

It's funny sometimes how life works. When I thought everything was over for me, you found me, you breathed life back into me, and now I will do the same to you. Maybe one day we'll walk in the park together, hand in hand, as if it were the most natural thing in the world. Forgive me for this fantasy, if that's all it is, but I've had stranger dreams come true. You might agree that it is audacious to fantasize about something against all odds, but I know you of all people can sympathize with the joy—and the horror—of our kind of hope. The kind that drives you mad and keeps you up and keeps you going.

Together, Arianna, we are pioneers. Eventually, I think we'll be united in history's eyes, like Lewis and Clark, or Watson and Crick. And none will know the truth between our names except for you and me; the truth I would take to my grave, were it not for the tiniest chance that you might feel the same. For the truth is this: I love you.

Yours, always,
Sam

Sam stared, unblinking, at the scribbled piece of paper in his hand. The words were as embarrassingly honest as he had ever been with himself, let alone with her. He cringed, feeling his soul curl up on itself.

In one swift movement, he crumpled the page into a ball and hurled it into the wastebasket.

EIGHTEEN

On Saturday morning, Dopp rushed down the sidewalk to the office. The streets in Midtown were much less crowded than he had ever seen, and for once, he was able to keep up his natural pace. He wore a beige trench coat and boots, and kept one hand ready on the handle of his umbrella. Dark clouds portended a storm at any moment. There was a certain piece of paper in his briefcase that he had worked hard to obtain, but his briefcase would protect it from rain.

All his trouble was going to be worth it. He could feel it. Even though Abby had cried when he left the house this morning and Joanie was furious with him. With a cringe, he recalled her stomping into the computer room late last night. Her eight-months-pregnant belly had entered the room a foot ahead of her. Luckily, he had just hung up the phone.

"Gideon," she whined. "When are you coming to bed? It's eleven thirty!"

"I know, I know, I'm sorry. Just give me a few more minutes."

"You have to let go of work! It's too much!"

He had sighed. "Look, try not to get too upset, honey. But it looks like I'll have to stay in the city for a little while. I just got off the phone with the hotel." He held up a hand at her scowl. "I'm sorry it has to come to this. But I need to do everything I can right now."

She made a disgusted sound in the back of her throat and rubbed her protruding stomach. "You've got to be joking."

Dopp shook his head. "I'm doing this for us. If I lose my job, then what would we do?"

"How long is a little while?"

"Maybe just a day. I don't know. As long as it takes."

"I can't believe this! How do you expect me to manage the kids alone when the doctor said I'm barely supposed to get out of bed?"

"We'll call your mother. No, I'll call her and arrange it. Just go back to bed and relax. I love you."

Joanie shook her head, muttering under her breath as she turned around.

"What'd you say?" Dopp asked. He watched her trudge down the hall, planting heavy steps, one hand on her lower back.

"This better be worth it," she seethed over her shoulder.

He thought of those words now as he rushed inside the sleek black skyscraper that housed the department's headquarters. Windra had told him the same thing: *This better be worth it.* But it would be, since God was in control. He always came through, and always had a wise reason for Dopp's struggles in the meantime. Besides, the fact that Dopp had been able to secure permission from Windra's judge friend on such short notice was a clear sign of the Lord's cooperation.

When Dopp walked into the appointed meeting room, he saw that Trent, Inspector Banks, and Jed were already waiting for him at the rectangular table, wearing ties and black suits as if it were a normal workday. They stopped chatting as soon as he came in.

"Good morning," he said, nodding. "I'm glad to see you're all on time."

They chimed hello, a bit stiffly, Dopp thought. But it was early on a Saturday. He took off his coat and sat at the head of the table, with his briefcase at his feet. Trent was sitting on his left, Banks and Jed on his right.

"So you're probably all wondering why you're here," he said. "As I told Trent last night, some critical changes are starting today. For you, there's good news and bad news. So which do you want to hear first?"

"The bad," Banks mumbled. Jed and Trent nodded, looking anxious. Trent fiddled with a rubber band on the table, rolling and unrolling it with his thumb and forefinger. Better to give it to them straight, Dopp thought.

"You're all going to start working real overtime. And I'm talking overnight." He turned to look at the two surprised men on his right. "You two are going to switch overnight shifts, monitoring Arianna's apartment building outside, in an unmarked car. I know it sounds painful, so you're going to cut back your day shifts to just a few hours so you have time to sleep during the day. I'll have another inspector monitor her at her clinic full-time starting Monday. But starting today, we can't let her out of range."

"For how long?" Jed asked.

"As long as it takes. I hope not longer than a few days or a week. I'm also going to be monitoring her during the day, which means I'll be out of the office from now on." Dopp turned to his left. "So Trent, from now on, you will be staying here and catching up on everyone else's paperwork, while we're out in the field. And I mean a thorough analysis of all reports. I'll need updates throughout the day."

Trent nodded, expressionless. A lock of hair fell into his eyes, but he did not appear to notice it. Dopp coughed, unexpectedly feeling sorry for him. He really was quite young; Dopp had to admit that it had been his own mistake to think Trent could handle the case alone, with no proven experience as an undercover agent. But he had seemed so promising, Dopp remembered. And now he just looked pathetic.

"I know it's a bit of a demotion," Dopp acknowledged. "But it's not personal, you know that."

"Boss," Banks said, and then wavered. "I thought the department couldn't afford overtime?"

"We can't," Dopp replied. "As it stands now. But on Monday, I'm going to let a few people go."

Banks's lips fell slack, but he said nothing.

"But not me?" Trent blurted.

Dopp turned to him. "No, you're still our only direct link with Arianna. Who knows if that will end up coming through after all?"

"So we're just going to sit outside of wherever she is and wait for her to come out and then follow her?" Jed asked.

Dopp smiled for the first time that morning. "Well, yes, but now we finally get to the good news." He lifted his briefcase to the table and rummaged inside for a white laminated folder. "Here we go," he said, opening it. Inside was a single sheet of paper, stamped and signed in all manner of judicial formality. The three men peered curiously at it.

"This piece of paper," Dopp said, "is our key to solving this case. I finally got us permission from a judge to tap her cell phone. It came through early this morning. I was on the phone pretty much all of yesterday working it out."

"Thank God," Banks sighed.

"That's fantastic!" Jed exclaimed. "Just what we need."

Trent nodded, looking amazed. "But didn't you just resubmit the application?"

"I got Senator Windra to pull some strings for us. He let me send the application directly to one of his judge friends. And Arianna's little lying episode yesterday gave us reasonable suspicion, so it was a no-brainer for the judge to sign the form and fax it over to me this morning."

"Wow," Trent said. He leaned back in his chair, then forward. "Helps to have friends in high places."

Banks was bobbing his head. "Impressive."

"Very," Jed said.

Dopp smiled, thinking that he had done the right thing by exploiting his connections in Albany. Not only did he make major progress, but he had also gained the admiration of his employees. How absurd it was to remember that his ego had almost stopped him from asking for help.

Trent put his elbows on the table and clasped his hands. "So how exactly is this going to work?"

"Well," Dopp said, "I'm about to call her mobile carrier and relay the judge's permission over so that they can bug her phone as soon as possible. First I wanted to get all the details straight with you three. Whoever is on duty will wait outside of wherever she is, in a car equipped with a radio interceptor. The interceptor will pick up any sounds near the microphone of her phone, even when she's not using it. So whenever she drops the bomb to anyone—it doesn't have to be Trent now—we've got her right then and there."

"It's perfect," Jed said. "It's practically over."

"Finally," Banks agreed.

"That's the hope," Dopp said, turning to look at Trent, who was nodding eagerly like the others. "Oh, and one last thing. Trent, I have a note about her cell phone number, but I just want to double-check it with you. Can you imagine how stupid it would be to go to all this trouble for the wrong number?"

For a brief moment, Trent did not appear to have understood. And then he reached into his pocket to pull out his own phone. "Sure. One second. Here we go." He cleared his throat, staring at his phone. "Ready?"

"Yeah, yeah. What is it?"

"It's 212-723-3223."

"Good. Thank you. That's just what I have here."

When the meeting was over, Trent harnessed all his self-control and managed not to race out of the room. Instead he plastered on a smile and nodded while the others wished Dopp luck during his first monitoring shift, which was to begin immediately. As the four men walked to the elevator, Dopp explained that he had ordered a car to be waiting for him downstairs with all the necessary radio equipment. It was to be a gray electric sedan, a few years old, and utterly indistinct. All Dopp had to do was drive it to Arianna's building, park it across the street, and wait for the phone company to remotely install the wiretap. Then they would be "in business," assuming, of course, that she was at home. If not, the surveillance would have to wait until she returned. And if she happened to be out, it would be for the last time with privacy.

When Dopp noted this fact, he smiled. Trent's skin crawled.

At that moment, the elevator doors opened and the four men walked inside, single file. They each took a corner of the small space, but Trent's sleeve brushed against Dopp's as they stood still, feeling the elevator's measured descent. There was no room to move away. Trent wondered if this was what prison was like: crammed in one room with your least favorite people. A feeling of constriction crept into his collar, then his throat. He wondered if he'd ever have to find out.

At last—or maybe within seconds—the doors parted. Trent stepped out first, inhaling deeply. The other three followed. Outside, it had begun to rain. As they approached the glass lobby door, Trent saw a gray car idling in front of the building. It looked dreary and plain, just like the sky. The windows were an even darker, tinted gray.

"Ooh," Jed called. "That must be the one."

"Our new office," Banks said, slapping Jed on the back. "If it even gets that far."

Dopp was beaming. As they walked out the door, everyone opened up umbrellas, except for Trent. He had forgotten to check the weather.

An official-looking man in blue blazer got out of the car as Dopp approached the edge of the sidewalk. Banks, Jed, and Trent hung back. The cold rain slithered inside Trent's collar and down his back, but he hardly noticed as he watched his boss shake hands with the man. Dopp nodded as the man spoke and gestured, pointing to devices inside the car that Trent could not see. After a minute, Dopp signed a form—probably an expense report for the department, Trent thought—and then took the keys.

Dopp thrust them into the air like a trophy.

Banks and Jed clapped, and Trent had no choice but to mimic them.

"See you at eleven tonight, Jed," Dopp called. "Outside her building unless I call about a change."

"You got it," Jed hollered back.

Dopp waved, jingling the metal keys, and then disappeared into the car. Trent heard the engine rumble and saw the headlights turn on, projecting parallel beams onto the slick street.

As soon as the car jerked away, Trent knew what he had to do. He said good-bye to the others, ran up to an empty cab sitting at a stoplight, and jumped in. He squished into the leather of the backseat, feeling his wet shirt and pants clinging to his skin. The driver eyed him crossly.

"Sorry," Trent muttered. Dopp's car was already out of sight, on its way downtown. With little traffic on Saturday morning, Arianna had at most ten minutes until he got there.

"Well?" the driver snapped.

"Seventy-third and Columbus, please."

The cab sped ahead, and Trent looked away from the rearview mirror, where the driver's brown eyes were watching him with dismay. Then he called the number he had been forced to give his boss. The phone rang only once, giving him no time to decide what to say or how.

"Hey!" Arianna answered.

"Hi."

"Are you feeling better?"

"Umm, yeah. Look, Arianna, you have to come to my place right now."

"What? Why?"

"Just trust me. Leave right now."

"But Sam just left, and I was going to lie down. . . ."

"Listen to me. You have to leave this minute. And don't bring your cell."

"Why not? You sound panicked."

"Just come over and I'll explain. Don't make any calls. Hurry."

With a sense of dread, Arianna tossed her phone onto the kitchen table, grabbed her purse, and wheeled herself out the door. She felt woozy, as if she were high on the most disparate drugs. One moment, Sam was here and they were marveling at his achievement, at the extension of her life, and then the next, Trent was shattering her newfound peace with some strange crisis of his own. And what did her cell phone have to do with anything?

All she wanted was to hoist herself out of her sedentary jail and lie down on her bed. At this time of morning, the sun would be slanting through her window, bathing her red comforter in warmth. She had been looking forward to resting with the gentle light on her face, as soothing as chamomile tea.

But as soon as she left her building, she saw that it was pouring rain. With a sigh, she wheeled to the street corner to wait for the rare van cab, which could accommodate her chair. As raindrops pelted her and cars zipped past, her irritation toward Trent mounted. Why did he have to go and upset her now, of all days, and drag her out into this mess? She wanted to be there for him, of course, but it was difficult enough to manage her own situation right now, let alone his. *And, seriously,* she thought, *why couldn't he have come to* my *apartment?* It was so much easier for him to hop on the subway than for her to wait in a downpour for the right cab.

Finally, a yellow van taxi pulled up, and she wheeled up its ramp into the roomy backseat. She instinctively felt for her phone to call and tell Trent she was on her way, but then she remembered it was on the kitchen table, that he had bizarrely told her to leave it at home. Something in his voice had warned her not to disobey his instructions. Her heart thumped against her chest. She hated the anticipation of bad news, which was often worse than the news itself.

Trying to discard her mind's wildest scenarios—her cell phone was somehow an explosive device or spreading radiation—she stared out the window at the raindrops zigzagging down the glass, blending together into larger drops. As her eyelids drooped, she realized she was exhausted. Last night, instead of sleeping, she had talked on the phone to Megan about vacations they had always meant to plan—Hawaii, the Grand Canyon, Napa Valley, Switzerland. To be able to swim, hike, climb, and snowboard again seemed a miracle. At 4 A.M., she had hung up the phone and spent the next four hours grinning into her pillow, twirling atop the apex of happiness. And now, she felt herself crashing.

When the cab arrived at Trent's building, she hurried up to his seventh-floor apartment and rang the bell. He must have been waiting at the door, for it opened instantly. She gasped, forgetting both her annoyance and fatigue. Adrenaline shot darts of fearful energy through her veins.

He was crying.

"Oh my God, what's wrong?" she asked, reaching up to him.

He shook his head and closed the door behind her. He wept quietly, sniffling and wiping his cheeks with the palm of his hand. It was distressing to see any man cry, but especially him; Arianna had never seen him so distraught.

"Baby, what's going on?" she asked gently, as catastrophic thoughts took over: he was ill; a family member was dead. "I came as soon as I could."

"Thank you," he mumbled. He drew a deep, shaky breath. "I don't know how to tell you this. But I can't hold out any longer. You have to know."

She felt her eyebrows knit together. "Know what?"

He grimaced.

Louder, she asked: "Know what?"

"I'm not a novelist," he choked out. "I'm a DEP agent."

A buzzing. That's all she heard in her ears, as if her brain were reverberating from a solid whack, and all logic and sense and order had been upended. She clutched the cushioned armrests of her wheelchair, feeling insane.

"Huh?"

Trent fell on his knees to her level. She backed away. He bent over the ground she had cleared, elbows planted on the floor, as a silent sob shuddered through him.

"What the—what the hell is going on?" she sputtered.

He snapped back up, and his reddened eyes widened. "It's not what you think. I'm working against them now, but they don't know it. Just let me explain."

She backed away farther, nearly to the door. "I have to get out of here."

"No, please, give me two minutes. I've been helping you for weeks, please just let me explain."

"Do it fast before I get the hell out of here."

"I'll tell you everything." He barely paused as the words began to tumble out. "For the past three years, I've been an agent there, but I hated my job and all of its damn paperwork and I only did it because I thought it meant I was doing something good with my life. I was trying to be a good Christian, even though I never felt like one and I hated myself for that.

"Then back in October, my boss got suspicious of your clinic because you were reporting these incredibly high numbers that went against all precedents. So he had me do some research, and when we found out who your father was, and about your rallies in college, we got even more suspicious about what you might be doing with all those embryos. But you had never messed up an inspection or audit. We knew you were smart. So my boss assigned me to go undercover and try to get to know you, so that you might eventually let me in on what you might be doing, and then we could take you down. The whole point was to come at you from the side, where you weren't expecting it."

Arianna was breathing heavily; the words were coming faster than she could process as her mind connected certain events from the recent past: the random audit she had passed in October and, mere weeks later, meeting Trent at the book signing.

"How did you know I would be there?" she demanded. "At Dakota's signing?"

He looked sheepish. "That message online was from me, not the publicist." He stood up to pace, avoiding her dumbfounded gaze.

"For a while," he said, "I felt like I was doing a good job getting to know you, with the bike rides. And I kept asking you about science and your work to see how you would react, not because it was for a book. And then, that night you kissed me, everything started to change. I felt weird, but I ignored it. Then after your accident you told me you were sick and we realized that you had a motive to steal embryos. Knowing I was tricking you and you were so sick made me feel even worse, but I ignored myself again. It was for a good purpose, I kept thinking, though even then I found it hard to place so much more value on embryos than actual living people. Something about that seemed off all along, but I didn't understand what. Then after you told me you went to church, it just went against how

I thought of you, and my boss agreed that he thought you might be lying. So he wanted to observe you himself. Our thoughts were pretty much confirmed when we went and had dinner in Long Island, and you admitted to doing abortions. See, those were my parents, but Gideon, well, he's actually my boss, Gideon Dopp, director of the whole New York City Department of Embryo Preservation."

Arianna's jaw dropped as the memory of that night came into focus; the hostility of those people had taken her aback at the time, but Trent had hardly seemed one of them.

"Why didn't you tell me earlier?" she whispered.

"I needed your trust to protect you. Let me just explain the rest. Jed, my friend, is also one of them." She gaped and Trent winced. "He came along to talk up how loyal a friend I was, so you would start to trust me. I know; it's horrible. But anyway, after that night at Dopp's house, I felt this crazy urge to protect you from all of them, and I realized that I actually did want you to open up to me. It was so insane, because it went against everything I knew was right and moral. I got it in my mind that I was going to quit the case, and I told Dopp so the next day. But then he convinced me that you were worthy of suspicion, because of the abortions, and that I was just being impatient. And I didn't know how to defend you then. I didn't realize there was another way of thinking, though I knew you couldn't really be evil. Then right after that, you showed me the museum and the lab. And, you know this part, the whole world just fell into place for me. It was amazing. Everything you said and believed reflected the conclusions I was starting to come to on my own. I finally understood that it was religion that was the problem all along; I had been trying to believe something that didn't make sense in order to do something that didn't make me happy. No wonder I was miserable for so long.

"So it was done; I knew I loved you and I was completely on your side from that night on. And you don't know how much I wanted to quit my job! How guilty I felt for lying to you! But I realized that I couldn't quit or tell you the truth. My job gave me the power to keep them away from you, and I needed your trust to be able to do it. Plus you've been getting so weak that I couldn't risk upsetting you. The truth is that if they catch me, we'll both go to jail. But all I've wanted was to keep you safe, to keep you ignorant of all of this, until you were okay again. And now that you're so close, I hate that I have to do this to you now, but I have no choice."

Arianna blinked, still gaping. "Why not? And wait, what about the crackdown? You were the source all along! You leaked the news!"

Trent nodded. "I had to find a way to prepare you. Jed had nothing to do with it. After you passed that surprise inspection, Dopp was furious, and he started sending Banks there every day to intimidate you and corner you into wanting to spill to me. And every day, I told Dopp that you weren't talking. He's been getting frustrated with me. So he applied for a warrant to bug your cell phone, but the first time, the judge turned it down. I was so relieved.

"Then, yesterday, with Sam's breakthrough, you unwittingly tipped them off. In the beginning, I had given Dopp records of our earliest conversations, when we discovered we were both only children. After you told Banks about your 'sister,' Dopp went and found that conversation, and caught you in the lie. So now he's closing in. See, he's under all this pressure from the state to justify the crackdown with some major fallout, like a shutdown or an arrest, before the lawmakers cut our budget for next year. So he's freaking out that we'll lose our jobs unless we make a big move. And you're the only lead we have."

Arianna swallowed, trying to comprehend that her relative safety was a sham—perpetrated by the man she thought she trusted and loved. No tears came; only blankness.

"Why are you telling me now?"

Trent's wretched gaze met hers. "Because the warrant finally came through."

She closed her eyes.

"By the time you get home," said his hollow voice, "your phone will be tapped, and Dopp will be waiting outside your building in an unmarked car with a radio interceptor. It can pick up any sound near your phone, even when you're not using it. From now on, they're going to monitor you and follow you until they get what they want, and I don't know how much more I can do about it."

Shocked silence. She gawked at him as a sliver of her consciousness marveled at how fast the situation had deteriorated.

"So what you're telling me is that right here, with you, is the last time I'm going to have total privacy?"

"Yes."

"And what if they don't catch me? Are they going to give up?"

"I don't know. Not soon."

"So you're telling me that I'm going to be under government surveillance indefinitely?"

"Yes."

"Do they know about Sam?"

"No. Nothing about him or the lab or the group. We just need to keep it that way for one more week."

"We?" She turned her chair toward the door. "I have to get out of here."

"Arianna, wait." He looked desperate as he ran up to her side. "What about us?"

"What *about* us, Trent? Is that even your real name?"

"Yes . . . please . . ."

"Please what? Our entire relationship was based on a lie!"

"I'm sorry. I've done everything I could. I love you. . . ."

"Just open the door. I need to get out of here!"

He obeyed and she zoomed past him into the hallway.

"When can I call you?" he yelled.

"Don't," she snapped over her shoulder. "I can't lie as well as you."

She propelled herself forward, bumping over the uneven carpeted floor to the elevator. The doors opened and she whisked inside.

"Arianna, wait," he called, running after her. There was a kind of madness in his eyes, that of a man who has gambled everything and lost. "I'll do anything!" he cried. "When am I going to see you again?"

She kept her eyes on the lobby button, jabbing it hard. An undeniable part of her yearned to answer him, to pretend that she was still safe, and he a writer, and that they were two lovers, in love with life and each other, with time at last on their side.

The doors closed before she looked up again.

NINETEEN

At 1 P.M. the following day, Trent was still in bed, with his head buried under the pillow and the comforter tangled around his legs. His body slept long past its needs, as if gripped by an innate survival tactic to protect his mind from pain.

Just to his left, sunlight streamed through the window's maroon drapes and illuminated the dusty wooden floor. For such brightness, Trent's pillow was too weak a fortress. Light glared against his eyelids. He opened them, squinted, felt his stomach clench a second before his mind recognized why. And then he moaned. He shut his eyes to retreat again into sleep, but the harder he tried, the further away it seemed, like a sailor chasing the horizon.

He threw the pillow off his head, sat up, and grabbed his cell phone from the dresser. Two missed calls. His breath caught in his throat; could they be from her? He flipped open the plastic lifeline and saw that both were from his mother, ten and fifteen minutes ago. Frigid disappointment rushed in. He sighed and listened to the single voice mail: "Trent, where are you? Your father and I have been waiting here for twenty minutes. We're starting to get worried."

He moaned again, remembering it was Sunday—brunch with his parents. He had never canceled before, let alone stood them up. But his remorse was halfhearted. He wished he could communicate directly somehow with Arianna. A phone call was out of the question, and a text message was risky, since Dopp could intercept any message that passed through her phone. The phone company would quickly retrieve any text message and then bounce it to a special electronic transmitter in Dopp's car. Anything Trent wrote to her now would be read. But he worried that their prolonged—and obvious—lack of contact could be dangerous. And he desperately hoped that once her outrage subsided, she would come around to understanding why he had lied.

Trent typed her a careful message: Missing you. I know you're not feeling well, but try to call when you can.

He sent it and waited, phone in hand. A suspenseful minute passed before two notes rang out, not from his phone, but from his door.

He grimaced, inferring what must have happened. There was no putting off two worried parents, especially when both made a habit of fearing big-city crime. He slid out of bed, pulled sweatpants on over his boxers, and went to the door to look through the peephole. His parents were standing there, wearing their fancy church attire and looking concerned. He opened the door with gritted teeth.

"I'm really sorry," he said immediately. "I just woke up."

His mother's brows knotted in surprise, revealing that this was the one possibility she had not considered.

His father checked his watch. "It's one eighteen," he snapped. "We waited for forty minutes. And just because you decided to sleep late?"

Trent took a deep breath, unprepared to deal with their anger.

"Walter, wait a second," Mrs. Rowe said, stepping inside and pulling her husband with her. "Trent, your eyes are all swollen. I knew something was wrong."

He reached up and touched his lids; they felt puffy. He nodded. "Yeah, actually, I've been kind of stressed."

Mr. Rowe's irritation evaporated. "What's going on?"

"You can talk to us, honey," Mrs. Rowe said, touching his arm.

Trent felt torn. They looked so sympathetic, but at the same time, he knew he could not elaborate.

"Is this about that case?" Mr. Rowe asked.

He nodded. "But I don't want to talk about it."

"Are you sure?" his mother prodded. "We might be able to help."

"No, I don't think you could."

"But—"

"Mom, please. Just leave it alone."

"You can do this, honey. We have so much faith in you."

"I hope so," he mumbled.

"You will!" she declared. "And then we'll celebrate all your hard work, and—"

"Becky," Mr. Rowe interrupted. "Just let him be."

"I'm sorry. I just see so much greatness in your future, and I know God does, too."

"Thanks," Trent said, feeling as if his hypocrisy was as obvious as his mother's pride. They all sat on the couch.

"What did Father Paul say this morning?" he asked to distract them. "In his sermon?"

"He talked about forgiveness," Mr. Rowe said, "because the whole congregation has been bad-mouthing one of the clerics who was found stealing from the donation box. But Father Paul said we have to forgive, and that God will take care of sinners for us."

Trent's heart gave a lurch. "Yeah, what about that? Aren't we supposed to just turn the other cheek when people sin?"

Mrs. Rowe eyed him. "Are you talking about *her*?"

"No, I mean criminals in general. Or whoever is doing something immoral."

"Well, you should forgive them in your heart," Mrs. Rowe replied. "Just like Jesus would."

"But the law still has to have its way," Mr. Rowe added. "Otherwise, we'd have anarchy."

"Fine," Trent said. "So let's say, hypothetically, we're talking about a case like mine; what if it turned out the suspect *was* stealing EUEs? Could you guys forgive in your hearts?"

He looked back and forth at them. His mother fumbled with her gold cross necklace, while his father studied his knees. Both seemed to be waiting for the other to answer. Finally she spoke.

"I think if there was anything I couldn't forgive, it would be murdering babies."

His father put an appreciative hand on her arm. "I didn't want to say it, but same here. That's about as low as you can go."

"Put it this way," Mrs. Rowe said. "If I ever could, it would take a long, long time. Are you worried that you can't?"

Trent could only nod.

"Well, don't," she said, waving off the subject as if it were a nasty mosquito. "I think God has to understand if we have a hard time forgiving certain things."

"Yeah," he mumbled.

"You look so pale, sweetie. Come let me give you a hug."

She put her arms around him, and he inhaled her trademark gardenia perfume. If ever there was a scent associated with safety, it was her fragrance. Countless times she had comforted him as a child, whether it was after he had fallen off his bike, been teased, or stayed home sick from school. And always, her sweet scent was a reminder that everything would be okay.

Trent had never doubted his parents' love until this moment. With her arms tight around his back, he pondered whether it was unconditional—and realized that they had just unwittingly told him the answer. His throat tightened; he breathed in gardenia, yearning for that simple antidote to his troubles, but the scent only heightened his sadness.

The truth was bound to come out; he could not always live a lie.

And then? It was all too clear: their hard line against criminals, their faith in God and their loyalty to the Church.

So he let his mother hold him, wondering if it was for the last time.

Arianna looked at each of the four faces in her living room—they were wrinkled and smooth, male and female, old and young, and yet each wore the same expression of total shock.

Sam opened his mouth first.

Arianna put a finger to her lips. "Don't yell."

He closed his mouth and shook his head furiously. Next to him on the black leather sofa, Megan held her knees to her chest, the fear stark on her face. Dr. Ericson and Emily sat in two straight-backed kitchen chairs that they had dragged into the living room for this emergency meeting, or rather, revelation. Emily was gaping. Dr. Ericson, usually the paragon of composure, was biting his knuckle. Arianna sat back in her wheelchair, letting all of them digest the news of Trent's identity.

She herself had spent a full day alone after his disclosure, painfully rehashing her memories to find all his lies, tricks and setups. The extent of his subterfuge was striking, and yet she understood why she had been sucked in: She had been operating under a false assumption—that he was a writer. Once she believed that opening line—and why wouldn't she?—her fall had been scripted. As foolish as she felt, she could hardly berate herself. Only the most cynical of people would ascribe ulterior motivations to such an appealing stranger.

Conflicting thoughts plagued her: Yes, he had repeatedly lied, but yes, he had helped her. How to deal with him at this point was a question she seemed unable to answer. When she had returned from his apartment yesterday, passing a suspiciously drab car parked along her building's sidewalk, she put her phone on silent and did not touch it all day or night. Dopp's presence in her apartment, invisible yet relentless, made her feel as though the hair on her neck was standing permanently on end. Could he hear when she flushed the toilet? When she sneezed? When she cried?

This morning, she knew she had to inform the group. Aware that any private use of her phone was impossible, she slipped out of her apartment to her neighbor's, across the hall. She was an elderly woman, with a bad back and a blind eye, who always had kind words and a prodigious supply of baked treats. Arianna could picture her as none other than a beloved grandmother. So she knew that when she knocked on the door and asked to use the phone—hers had broken, she explained—the woman would accommodate her. Ten minutes later, everyone was notified to come over (without ringing the doorbell), and Arianna was holding a Tupperware bowl of chocolate-chip cookies. Back at her own place, she stashed her phone under her pillow, turned on the television in her bedroom, and closed the door.

And now, an hour later, all was told. But despite everyone's dumbfounded horror, it still did not feel real. Arianna looked around her living room at her wooden bookshelves, flat-screen television, glass table, leather couch, and white fur area rug. Only two days prior, the table had held a bottle of champagne, and she and Sam had clinked glasses, toasting "to life and to progress." It seemed impossible that today this same room could be the backdrop to whispered fears and worried looks.

Megan finally spoke first, her voice low. "Ar, it's not safe for you here anymore."

"What do you mean *here*?"

"I mean, in this apartment, in your clinic, anywhere they can get to you. They're not going to stop pursuing you until they get what they want. Isn't that what Trent told you?"

Arianna nodded. "He said it didn't look like they were going to stop anytime soon."

"She's right," Sam said. "You can't stay here. It's only a matter of time before they find some reason to arrest you on a technicality, and then that's it, once they have you, they'll never let go." He gestured wildly, the veins in his forehead bulging. "To hell with freedom! This is post-liberal America, the renaissance of the Dark Ages!"

"Shhh, Sam," Arianna whispered. "You're getting too excited."

"You should be this excited!" he whispered back loudly.

She nodded at Sam and Megan on the couch, while speaking to the Ericsons, whom she could always count on to balance Sam's outbursts. "They might have a point. But I would hate to leave home. What do you think?"

She braced for their response.

Dr. Ericson removed his knuckle from his clenched jaw. "I think they're absolutely right."

Her heart plummeted. "You do?"

"If you want any hope of recovering in peace, you've got to get out of here. And I think we do, too." He turned to look at his wife.

Emily nodded sadly. "Once they manage to pin you down, they'll turn to us. But I hate to abandon our patients. . . ."

"We won't be," Dr Ericson said. "The DEP will find a reason to shut the clinic down anyway. I've been thinking that our days there are numbered, ever since that inspector started showing up every day. I just didn't realize how seriously they had it in for you."

"Apparently there's a lot at stake for them," Arianna explained morosely. "They're in danger of losing state funding unless they pull off some major disciplinary action, and I'm their only lead."

"Then the three of us should seriously consider making a run for it." Dr. Ericson looked grave, graver than she had ever seen. "I don't know how else to avoid the inevitable."

"What about me?" Sam piped up. "I'm not exactly beyond liability."

"But they don't know about you," Arianna pointed out.

"No. But what the hell am I going to do here? I want to be able to see the results of my work!"

"Okay, Sam, keep it down," Arianna whispered. She looked at Megan wistfully. "I don't want to leave you."

"Just because I'd stay behind doesn't mean I wouldn't see you, right?" Megan said. "Anyway where are you planning on going?"

Arianna sucked in a deep breath, forcing herself to abandon emotion for pragmatism. "I don't know. We have a lot of logistics to figure out now. First of all, if we're really going to leave, the soonest we can go is after the transfer on Friday night."

"We could leave straight from the clinic," Dr. Ericson suggested. "But where to?"

The group looked at one another in silent bewilderment.

"It would have to be somewhere nearby," Emily said. "At least, accessible by car. So we don't leave a paper trail."

Arianna nodded, yearning for the days of relative anonymity, when one could board public transportation with nothing but a ticket; it was becoming hard to remember that she used to get around without showing her U.S. identification card, a magnetic log of her subway, bus, train, and plane trips.

"Do we know anyone trustworthy who has a vacation home that they would let us use for a while?" she asked.

Megan held up a finger with sudden eagerness. "My friend has a cabin in the Catskills. Belleayre Mountain. It's about three hours north of the city. She used to go skiing there, but after she had knee surgery a few years ago, she stopped going."

"How rural is it?" Dr. Ericson asked.

"Very. I don't think that many people live there. It's mostly a resort town."

Arianna shook her head. "Then we would stick out too easily, especially once they started to look for us. Which brings up another major problem. How are we going to get Dopp off my trail long enough for me to have the transfer and then flee?"

"Good question," Sam noted.

"What if you could just do the transfer here?" Megan asked the doctors. "Then we wouldn't have to worry about Dopp following her anywhere."

"I wish," Dr. Ericson replied. "But we need so much equipment: the heart and blood pressure monitors, the IV drip machine, the bag drainage stand. Not to mention the sterile environment of the clinic."

"All of our supplies are on hand there, too," Emily added. "Every drug and emergency tool that we need for surgery. It would be impossible to move it all."

"Plus we'd still have to get rid of Dopp afterwards," Sam grumbled.

Megan looked dejected, and Arianna shot her a resigned look; she had known from the start that there was no way to get around using the clinic.

"First, let's figure out where to go," Emily said. "There has to be someplace where we can blend in, especially in a city with nine million people!"

"You could be on to something," Arianna mused. "The best place to hide might be in plain sight."

"Like a different part of the city," Megan said. "Another borough, maybe."

Sam cleared his throat, and then gave a long sigh.

"What?" Arianna prompted.

"Well," he said, "it's not in another borough. But almost."

"What is?"

He looked both apologetic and uncomfortable. "I never told you this, but I still own an apartment in Harlem. On 123rd and Amsterdam. It was where I lived with my wife when I was teaching at Columbia."

Arianna opened her mouth. "Why didn't you ever tell me?"

He shrugged, reddening. "I—" He cleared his throat again. "Well, all of her things were there, and I meant to clear them out, but it was just—I just never . . . and then somehow I got in the habit of going up there . . . and it became impossible to move anything. . . ."

The group looked at him with sympathy, and he scowled. "I'm fine."

"Have you gone recently?" Arianna asked gently.

"Not for a few years."

"How big is it?" Megan asked.

"A one bedroom. First floor in the back of a dirty old town house."

"I bet it's worth a fortune now."

He shrugged as if the thought had never entered his mind.

"It sounds fine for us," Emily murmured. "If you're okay with that."

He nodded listlessly. "But I don't think it's livable."

"Because her stuff's still there?"

"Yeah." He looked down at his hands; ropy veins crisscrossed wrinkles like a contoured map. "Anyway, I have to stay in the lab all week."

"I have an idea," Megan said. "Sam, it's your call, but I'm used to going and inspecting old properties, and it would be a cinch for me to get the place set up, so you don't have to deal with it. If you'll let me?"

He looked relieved. "Fine."

"But I'll have to get rid of stuff," she added.

"Just do it," he muttered. "It's about time."

"Thank you so much, both of you," Arianna said, meeting their gazes. She hoped that her expression could convey the depth of her gratitude that words could not.

"We can't stay there forever, though," Emily said. "They'll be looking for us. . . ."

"It'll be fine for a little while," Arianna said. "We can probably hold out there until things settle down, and then we'll have to think about—about leaving the country."

Megan looked as if she wanted to cry.

"I'm all for it," Sam said. "Let's get the hell out of here and go somewhere where we can live in peace. Canada?"

"It is the closest," Emily said. "We could get fake passports and just slip over the border. . . ."

Arianna felt too overwhelmed to take in the idea of being a forced fugitive, of leaving the only city she had ever called home. "Let's go back for a second," she said. "We still have so much to work out first."

Dr. Ericson cleared his throat. "Like how we're going to get up to this apartment, and how to get Dopp off your back long enough to do everything."

"Too bad none of us have cars," Emily said. "And finding a cab would be too unreliable. Plus what about GPS tracking? We have to be careful about that."

"I could rent a car for the night," Megan said softly. "It's cheap and they wouldn't know to trace it to any of you. Then after the transfer, I could drive you there and drop you off and then return the car."

"Perfect!" Arianna exclaimed, and then remembered to lower her voice. "God, Meg, I should pay you for all this. What would we do without you?"

"Don't be crazy," Megan responded. "I know you'd do the same for me."

"Okay," Dr. Ericson said. "So what about Dopp? We're looking at about forty-five minutes to an hour for the transfer."

Arianna felt her relief dissipate just as quickly as it had come. "That's a long time."

"And if he sees you go into the clinic after hours," Dr. Ericson said, "won't he want to follow you inside?"

"I know. But I don't know what we're going to do."

"What about Trent?" Megan asked.

"What about him?" Arianna demanded, feeling heat in her cheeks.

"He has access to Dopp."

"So?"

"So don't you think we could use his help?"

"I knew it was going to come down to this," Arianna said. "But how am I supposed to face him?"

"He's a traitor," Sam spat.

"Well, in a way he is, and in a way he isn't," Megan said. "If it weren't for him warning you about the crackdown, you would not be sitting here right now."

"But I just don't know how I can bring myself to talk to him. It's worse than a breakup. It's like I never knew him to begin with."

"Be practical, Arianna." Megan shifted on the couch and gave her a severe look. "He might be the only person who can help us. And it seems as if he was only trying to protect you."

"Are you defending him?"

"I'm just saying I can understand what happened. I know you, and I know that you would have cut him off long ago. And then he wouldn't have been able to help you at all. It's too bad, but he had to lie."

"No one has to lie," Sam snapped. "It's a choice."

Megan frowned at him and then looked back at Arianna. "Look, I understand why you're mad and hurt, but would it have hurt you *more* if he'd told you the truth a month ago?"

Arianna sighed, wishing she could get up and pace. Yet the lower half of her body remained as inert as her desire to face Trent. Just before the group arrived, she had ignored a text message from him. But what troubled her more—what she had not dared to announce—was that a tingling sensation, the specter of paralysis, had begun in her forearms.

"I'm tired," she mumbled.

"You should take a nap," Dr. Ericson said. "Definitely conserve your energy as much as possible before Friday."

"And take the day to think," Emily added.

"But not much longer," Megan said.

Arianna nodded, grimly wondering where she would be in a week: Sam's old apartment? A prison cell?

Her deathbed?

TWENTY

Dopp felt cramped. His long legs were sprawled across the empty passenger seat, with his feet pressing up against the door and his knees bent. His head rested against the tinted window and slid down the glass at intervals. In between the two front seats was a digital dashboard with the radio interceptor and speakers, and on the glove compartment lay a solar-powered laptop. Attached to his belt, in a holster, was his tougher-than-steel pistol, for when the time came to make an arrest.

But until that moment came, Dopp dreaded his twelve-hour stretches in this vehicle, and it had been only two days. Two completely fruitless days. As much as he turned up the radio interceptor to full volume, listened and prayed, he was privy to nothing but blaring television programs, routine calls for food delivery, and updates on Arianna's health, as friends called to ask how she was feeling.

Last night, Sunday, she had spoken to Trent for the first time all weekend. Their brief exchange came through the car's speakers:

"*Hi,*" she had said.

"*Hey!*" came Trent's eager voice. "*I miss you. How are you feeling?*"

"*Not well. I've been sleeping for days. I don't think I can see you tonight.*"

"*Oh.*" Pause. "*Okay. Well, I hope you feel better. I'll call you tomorrow.*"

"*Okay. Thanks. Bye.*"

That was all. So much for her "sister's baby," Dopp thought. If anything was true, it was that this woman's existence was pathetic; she had hardly any visitors, unless the Chinese deliveryman counted. Neither Jed nor Banks had reported a single phone call during their overnight shifts. Arianna had slept or watched television the whole weekend, never once leaving her apartment—never going to church, despite the fervency she had once asserted to Trent. Simply another lie confirmed, Dopp thought. Not that he expected her to be religious, but he found it stunning that she would use something so sacrosanct as a pretext for her own misdeeds.

Nights he was spending at the Washington Square Hotel, a third-rate place that was desirable only because of its proximity to Arianna's building. It was strange to have his own bed, especially one with uneven springs and a synthetic comforter that felt inadequate, like a one-armed hug. The sheets resembled wax paper, and as he tossed over them, he thought of Abby, Ethan, and Joanie, and of the child to come. What he was doing here was for them, he thought; everything always was, even if they hated him for it. And above all, it was for God. To rectify the damage he had done all those years ago, in whatever way possible. It seemed he could always be doing more, trying harder, praying longer. As Dopp drifted to sleep, he thought that if only he could see this mission through to the end, it might somehow, at last, be enough. . . .

Now, Monday morning, he was back on duty, putting in a third shift at the familiar curb; the car was parked along the last straight section before the sidewalk curved in and wound along the circular driveway to Arianna's building. A hedge of thorny-looking bushes lined the curved sidewalks on either side of the building, forming a half circle of shrubbery. Dopp pulled the car forward just enough to peer around the bushes and keep his eye on the front door, about thirty feet away. At any moment, he knew she would be leaving for the clinic.

Dopp concentrated on the glass lobby door to distract himself from guilt over the severance notices he had sent out that morning. Of the three least important employees he let go, only one really hurt him, and that was Mark—his good old loyal driver. But how could Dopp justify keeping him on the payroll now?

The glass door opened and closed with frustrating regularity as residents left for work, briefcases in hand, overcoats buttoned to their chins. And then one man held the door open for several seconds, and a woman in a wheelchair passed through. Dopp recognized her mane of black hair, but her face had changed since that Christmas dinner. Protruding from a sallow sheath of skin were two eye sockets, cheekbones, a nose. It was the cast of her familiar bone structure, lacking tissue and color and warmth.

Dopp bolted upright, swinging his feet to the floor, his right foot hovering over the gas pedal. Arianna moved swiftly, hunched forward, with her chin tucked into a navy blue shawl, and her gaze fixed on the sidewalk. She wound along the sidewalk's curve until she reached the street and made a right, turning her back to Dopp. He watched her chair pass under the Washington Square Arch and recede into the park, toward her clinic at the opposite end.

Once she was fully across and out of sight, Dopp drove around the perimeter of the park and stopped on a side street a block away from the clinic, knowing that the radio interceptor would cover a range of up to two hundred feet. Soon Arianna's voice came crisply through the car's speakers as she greeted patients in the waiting room, and then introduced herself to the new inspector that Dopp had assigned to take Banks's position. Dopp reclined, pushing down the lever on the chair's left side, trying to find a comfortable position for the next eight hours. The chair hummed just as he heard another vibration coming from the glove compartment.

It was his cell phone. His heart kicked.

No, he thought. *Please, God, not now.* Recently, Joanie had been complaining of cramps in her lower abdomen, but the doctor assured her it was only a false alarm. Dopp yanked open the glove compartment and seized his phone. But instead of his wife's name, he saw a strange number blinking on the display, one with a 518 area code—Albany.

"Hello?"

"Dopp, it's Windra."

"Oh, hi," he drawled with relief. "How are you?"

"Listen, I can't talk long, but I wanted to tell you the news before it gets out. First, though, you got the warrant?"

"Yes, thanks to you. We're on her 24/7. Shouldn't take long now."

"Good, because the lieutenant governor is going to be sworn in tomorrow morning, and then we're getting right to the budget."

"*What?* Already? What about Vance and the investigation?"

"That's why I called. The results just came in. He'll be resigning in a press conference later today."

Trent rose from the chair in his office and closed the door. The only good thing about being confined to this place was the fact that Dopp wasn't here anymore. No chance of him bursting in now. Trent looked at his watch: it was just after 9 A.M., so he knew Arianna must have already arrived at the clinic. Their short, awkward conversation on the phone had only increased his desire to talk to her, to really talk to her—and to discover where their relationship stood after two days of distance. Whether it was on a bridge or a precipice or free-falling, he did not know, but he was desperate to find out.

He called her office phone, knowing that at least his side of the conversation would be private, since an inspector would surely be sitting with her.

"Arianna Drake," she droned.

"It's me. Don't hang up," he said, and held his breath. "You there?"

"How can I help you?" she asked stiffly.

"I just want to know how you're doing," he said. "And how you're feeling about everything. I know you can't talk, but just tell me in a word."

"I can't."

"Can't what? Talk? Or talk to me?"

"Both."

"I'm sorry. But I can't stand this! I miss you like crazy."

She coughed. "Well, sir, if there's nothing else I can do for you—"

"Let me see you tonight."

"No."

Trent paused; her tone was inarguable.

"Fine," he said. "But I still have to call you later on your cell. He needs to hear us talking normally. Okay?"

"Yes."

"Good," he replied, but the line was already dead.

By Wednesday morning, Arianna was more exhausted—both emotionally and physically—than she had ever been in her life. She was sleeping thirteen hours a night, and still struggled to consciousness when her alarm clock beeped. Always, in her dreams, she could walk, and always, in the morning, she woke to a half-lifeless body. It was enough to make her want to pound sensation into her legs—even pain would be a victory. *Someday I will feel it,* she told herself during random moments: brushing her teeth or dragging herself into her wheelchair or sitting at her desk in front of the new, equally hostile inspector.

She felt mechanical most of the time, as she played it cool in front of him, and on the phone to Trent, and as she passed Dopp's shark-gray car, pretending not to notice it. During these minutes, her mind was nothing but a receptacle that held a single number—how many days until the transfer. This awareness had become as innate as her body's need for water; she never had to stop and think to know if she was thirsty, or to know how much time was left until Friday night. It stood now at two and a half days.

Even spurts of nostalgia had been coming on less and less. She hardly recognized the clinic anymore as her own, and her apartment was just a familiar space. It was privacy and peace she craved, and each day her eagerness to flee grew. Especially now that she was sitting at her desk across from the new inspector, a skinny, fifty-something man whose mouth appeared to permanently taste sourness. He wore the requisite gold cross pin, at least two inches long lest it go unnoticed on his lapel. In its sheen, Arianna could see the reflection of her own pupil. Her lid hung tiredly over her eye, whose usual bright blue seemed gray.

The inspector reached up to stroke the pin. On his face was the hint of a smirk. "You like it?" he asked.

She looked away, at her computer. *Fuck you,* she thought. If she ever decided to make small talk with him, that would be the gist of it.

Her office phone rang sharply and jolted her.

"Arianna Drake," she answered, hoping it was not a professional call. Everyone in the group knew that her office line was not bugged, and called it to speak privately to her.

"Hey," came Megan's quiet voice.

Arianna tried not to display any relief. "Hi, how can I help you?"

"So Sam's old apartment is cool now," Megan said. "I cleared out a bunch of junk. His wife's entire wardrobe was still in the closet, filled with mothballs. But I threw everything out. It's still pretty dusty but livable enough. A bit small for four people, but the two rooms are decently sized. I'll put in a few air mattresses and a bunch of dry food. And I just got off the phone with the electric and cable companies, so that should be up and running on Friday."

"So nice to hear from you," Arianna remarked. "I just love to hear from former patients. And how is little James?"

Megan continued softly, her tone unchanged. "What I need now are everyone's suitcases, because I doubt there'll be enough room when we're all in the car. So I'm going to call Sam and tell him to drop his off at your apartment later today after you get off work. First I'll make a stop at the Ericsons' place down in TriBeCa tonight to get their stuff, then I'll stop at your place and get yours and Sam's, and then I'll schlep everything uptown so it will be ready and waiting in the apartment. Okay?"

"Glad to hear it."

"And please, please, tell me you've made progress with Trent."

Arianna cleared her throat.

"Arianna!" Megan exclaimed sternly. "You have to figure something out. Or am I doing all of this for nothing?"

"No . . ."

"I seriously want to believe you. I'll see you tonight. Around eight."

"Thank you so much for calling," Arianna said. "Take care."

She hung up feeling chagrined. Here was Megan, going to great lengths to help her and the others escape; then there was Sam, toiling away over the cells in the lab; and the Ericsons, both tirelessly keeping up the practice, as long as they had to; and then there she was, contributing nothing.

But she dreaded facing Trent.

Part of her wondered about that, though. As much as she hated their phone calls for the sake of Dopp's listening pleasure, those moments made her feel most alive. Her heart pumped harder at the sound of his voice, like an addict sneaking a hit. That she derived any enjoyment from these brief conversations was a source of shame. And yet, she was starting to glimpse the logic behind Trent's lies. In order to do so, she had to view him as an entirely different person from the one she thought she knew: not as an uninvolved writer, but as someone who had endured an ideological reversal at her hands, which had then resulted in a moral dilemma.

Maybe, said a small voice in her head, maybe keeping her ignorant had been a prudent decision after all. She thought about the night she took him to the lab. She had put herself in a dangerous position, while showing him the extent of her trust. The truth would have shattered everything between them at that point. Her vulnerability would have been too fresh, his betrayal too cruel. Megan was right. Maintaining a façade was the only way he could have protected her from Dopp, and from herself.

Whether she could ever love him again was another story. How could she regain trust in him after all that had happened? But that was the least of her worries. What mattered now was his access to the other side. In merely two and a half days, they needed a plan. How she wished they could speak face-to-face. But she was cornered, here at the clinic with the inspector and anywhere else with Dopp, who would certainly notice if Trent entered her building.

Tonight, she remembered, was Wednesday, the night of her weekly piano lesson at Trent's apartment. Although it was nearly impossible for her to play anymore, she had insisted on keeping up the lessons. The teacher had been gamely cooperating, although they all knew it was becoming futile. Arianna looked down at her fingers and wiggled them; they moved slowly, as if in a vat of viscous fluid. There was hardly any point in going tonight, unless just to hear the teacher play. And then she gave a little gasp.

"What happened?" the inspector asked.

She coughed. "I just got a sharp pain."

"Oh."

"It's okay, it went away."

The inspector's eyes glazed over.

She took her cell phone out of her purse and, without hesitation, called Trent.

"Hello?" he answered after only one ring.

"Hi, it's me."

"Hey! How are you feeling?"

"Eh. Tired. I'm calling about my lesson tonight."

"Oh yeah?" His voice let on disappointment. "Should I cancel it?"

"Actually, no. I thought you might, but I still want to try," she said carefully. "So I'll be there around six thirty."

A moment went by as he processed surprise. "Great!" he said. "See you then."

She closed her phone with amusement, thinking how baffled he must be. But tonight was the only opportunity, in spite of Dopp's phantom ear, that they could talk in person without worrying about being overheard.

When Sam arrived at Arianna's apartment later that night, duffel bag in tow, he knew better than to ring the bell. Instead he twisted the doorknob, and as he expected, the door opened. Anticipation gripped him as he walked into the foyer. He looked left, to the kitchen and right, to the living room, but she was nowhere to be seen. A loud laugh track sounded down the hallway from the television in her bedroom. He set down his bag on the wood floor, wondering if he ought to turn around and leave, rather than risk bothering her, but his desire to see her was too strong. Now that she was no longer sucked in by that traitor—that greatest of blessings in disguise—Sam was allowing himself to dream again. As fraught with danger as the future was, there lurked romantic undertones that thrilled him. With the cells growing to plan, Arianna would soon receive the transfer, and then they would escape and live together, in perhaps the most unexpectedly desirable outcome possible: He was going to spend every day with her, watching her health improve, and rejoicing from both his brilliant success and her constant company.

Of course, Sam knew there was still a considerable hurdle they needed to overcome, namely how to evade that bastard outside. But it was outrageous to think that a nosy bureaucrat might prevent her from receiving the transfer that ought to save her life, the transfer that would be the culmination of months of dogged work and risky maneuvering. No, that possibility was incomprehensible. If Sam could make a major scientific breakthrough, then the rest of the group ought to be able to handle some tactical planning.

"Sam," came a whisper. He looked up. Arianna was wheeling down the hallway with a tired smile, her bedroom door closed behind her. He broke into a grin.

"Hi," he whispered back as she stopped in front of him. He motioned to his bag on the floor. "It's all ready to go."

"Good, I was just packing, too. How long have you been here? I didn't hear you come in."

"Well, that was the idea. Not long, maybe a couple minutes."

"So how are you?" she asked. Sam smiled—that was one of the things he loved about her. What was a common throwaway remark, she meant as a sincere inquiry.

"I'm pretty excited," he said. Up close, her skin looked as thin as cheesecloth over her bones, and it made him want to shudder. The transfer would not be coming a day too soon. "How about you?"

"All I can think of is two more days."

"Same here."

"How are the cells?" she asked.

"Four perfect embryos so far. I'm just about ready to extract the stem cells and then inject the growth factors."

"Tonight?"

"As soon as I get back."

She beamed. "So you think this is really going to work?"

"I have every reason to think so."

"It's just so incredible." Then her face darkened. "All we need is a way to throw off Dopp."

Sam's pulse quickened in defiance. "I could kill that asshole."

"Luckily, I don't think you'll have to. I'm going to talk to Trent about it tonight and see how he can help us."

"You're going to give that liar the time of day!"

"We can't afford to cut him off, Sam. Plus, it does seem like he only meant the best for me."

Sam felt himself panicking. "So what does that mean?"

"What do you mean?"

Sam shook his head. "He's not going to flee with us, right?"

"No, I don't see why he would. Dopp isn't after him, and I'm pretty sure he wants to keep it that way."

"Fine."

"Look, I know you don't like him, but—"

"No kidding," Sam muttered.

"But try to think of it from his point of view," she said. "He took risks to protect *both* of us. The lab is still safe, isn't it?"

"So you've forgiven him, then?"

"Enough to cooperate."

Sam scowled. He could still hear laughter flowing in muted bursts from her bedroom.

"I know you're a hard sell," she said softly. "And I understand, especially when it comes to the DEP. But I need to get going now."

"Where are you going?"

"To his apartment for my piano lesson. I think it's the only place and time that we'll be able to talk privately."

"Why?"

Her lips spread into a mischievous smile. "Because of the music."

Trent and Molly were both waiting at his apartment when Arianna arrived. The sight of her, after four days of separation, was both heartening and alarming; she had returned, but when had her illness become so obvious? Was it possible that in the short time they were apart, her face had thinned—or had Trent not noticed before? Either way, he tried not to reveal his dismay as he let her in. Unsure how to greet her, unsure in fact why she had even come, he ventured to lean down and kiss her on the cheek. She didn't turn her lips to him, but she also didn't stiffen against his touch.

"How are you, dear?" Molly asked, standing behind Trent. "I'm glad you decided to come tonight."

"Me, too. Even though these things are pretty useless." She lifted her hands. "But I still want to try."

"As you should," Trent encouraged.

She wheeled past both of them to the keyboard. He followed, and moved the bench out of her way. "There you go," he said, gesturing to the empty space. "Park and play."

She nodded with a small smile and pulled herself up to the keyboard. Before he walked away, he leaned his head close to hers and whispered, "What's up?"

Wait, she mouthed.

Confused and intrigued, he walked across the room to the couch and sat down. A slab of plastic bounced in the pocket of his sweatshirt, but he had to gauge the right moment before taking it out. For now, he would have to wait. Molly sat on the bench near Arianna and instructed her to warm up with a scale. As the notes rang out, Trent thought of Dopp, and wondered where he was parked. Dopp had called him at work earlier in the day to check up on the office, and to confirm that he had correctly overheard Arianna say she would be coming tonight. Dopp's words were clipped, his tone urgent. It was obvious that his confidence had vanished, and Trent did not have to ask why.

Everyone was talking about the governor's ignoble fall, and the state's pressing business that would finally be dealt with. But while the newspaper editorials were heralding Albany's emergence from inertia, Trent's coworkers were sweating. Dopp had laid off four people in the last three days. More cuts were sure to follow. But Trent was detached from the office's collective anxiety; all it meant to him was that Dopp was growing progressively intent on finding a reason to arrest her. She had to know it, too. Trent yearned to ask her about Friday night's scheduled transfer and its logistics, and to implore her to be cautious. It seemed cruel for her to be so near, like an ocean taunting a parched sailor.

Trent listened to her stumble over Bach's "Minuet in G." The tempo was painfully slow, and the notes jerked together as if they were bumping over a dirt road, staccato and uneven.

And then in the middle of a phrase, the notes stopped. Trent heard her sigh. She leaned her elbows on the keyboard, creating a dissonant splash of sound. Molly put a hand on her back and said nothing.

Arianna turned to her. "I'm sorry to waste your time. I just can't do it anymore."

"Don't apologize. You've made a valiant effort."

"Thank you. That means a lot."

Molly smiled sadly and rubbed her back.

"I hate to leave things on such a depressing note," Arianna said, pausing. Then: "Maybe you could play something for us?"

Molly's smile brightened. "Well, I haven't given a concert in years, but I suppose I could try. What would you like to hear?"

"Something inspiring."

Molly nodded. "Let me see. Come to think of it, there's a piece that reminds me of you."

"Really? How so?"

Molly made a gesture with her fist. "It's got a real oomph at first, an intensity, but then it turns out to be very gentle and beautiful."

Arianna looked pleasantly taken aback. "Well, thank you, I can't wait to hear it."

"I played this with the New York Philharmonic a long time ago. Let's see how much my fingers remember."

"Great," Arianna said. She casually let her black pocketbook slide to the floor next to the keyboard. "I'll get out of your way." She turned in her chair and grinned at Trent.

He shook his head with an amused smile. When she reached him, he helped her out of her chair onto the couch and whispered: "You are one smooth woman."

A powerful chord boomed, followed by rapidly descending triplets. Trent recognized it right away; it was the Grieg Piano Concerto.

"I hope Dopp enjoys the concert as much as we will," Arianna whispered back. Trent snickered softly, and she smiled, putting a finger to her lips. Being so close to her again elated him, and he barely hesitated before pulling her into his arms.

She resisted slightly. "I'm not fully over it," she whispered, but Trent could tell she was well on her way. "You still lied to me."

"And I'm not even that sorry," he whispered back. "Or else you wouldn't be here."

"I get that," she said. "And that's why I am here."

Arpeggios rolled up the keyboard with magical fluidity as the melody began to dance in the upper register. For a second, Trent was mesmerized by the teacher's mastery of the music, and awed that his amateur instrument could produce such a rich sound.

"We need you," Arianna said into his ear. "To help get rid of Dopp on Friday night."

Trent grimaced. The concerto's uplifting tone suddenly sounded incongruous, the wrong soundtrack to such a meeting. "Do you have any plans so far?"

"We're going to flee. Me, Sam, and the two doctors. It's not safe for us to stick around. And I refuse to live my life being constantly monitored."

Trent stared at her in shock. "To where?"

"Sam still has an old apartment up near Columbia that he never got around to selling. Megan's been nice enough to prep it for us. We should be able to lie low there for a while."

"For how long?"

"I don't know. I guess until they stop actively looking for us."

"But—you're going to make yourselves fugitives!"

"It's a step up from prisoners."

Trent nodded. "So how long do you need to lose him for?"

"The transfer should take about forty-five minutes. And then Megan will be in a car waiting outside and we'll hightail out of there."

Trent swallowed; his mouth was dry. "That's a pretty long time. And if he sees you go into the clinic after hours, he'll definitely follow."

"I know. That's why we need you to help us distract him somehow."

"But—he's so intent right now, you can't even imagine. For him to leave you alone would almost be a miracle."

Arianna frowned. "There has to be a way!"

Trent studied the desperation in her eyes, the total unacceptability of failure, and he knew that he had to come up with an answer. This was not a time to bemoan his lack of cunning, to pass on the torch and wipe his pitiful hands clean.

"I'll figure something out," he vowed.

"We only have two days."

"I know that. I just need time alone to think."

"I should have come to you earlier," she moaned softly.

"I wish you had."

She sighed, and Trent's heart tightened.

"Wait," he said. "Before I forget, I have something to give you."

He reached into his pocket and pulled out a slender black cell phone. The front display was covered with a piece of adhesive clear plastic.

"It's clean," he said, handing it to her. "I bought it today, after you called to tell me you were coming."

Her mouth hung open. "Thank you so much!"

"No problem. It's for emergencies only—don't use it regularly or he'll get suspicious about why you stopped using your real cell. And keep it on silent always, so he never hears it ring."

She nodded. "Is it under your plan?"

"No plan. It's a TracFone with sixty prepaid minutes. You can always buy more time and it's anonymous."

"Thank you, thank you! I feel so much better having this."

"I thought you would."

She leaned her head back against his arm and closed her eyes. The concerto had reached the eye of the melodic storm, the passage of gentle beauty that Molly had described. But between the quiet notes, a harmonic tension lingered. Trent closed his eyes and pulled Arianna a little closer.

TWENTY-ONE

Dopp peered out of his driver's-seat window. In the middle of a snowing Thursday afternoon, the side street next to the clinic was deserted. Icy brownish slush, marked with tire imprints, coated the asphalt. Dead trees lined the sidewalk, their spindly branches reaching for warmth long forgotten.

Dopp pushed open the door and thrust his cramped legs out into the freezing air. How much longer would he have to stand this confinement? Arianna was the one who was supposed to be sitting in a tiny cell, not him. But she was still saying nothing to anyone.

Even so, he had to keep faith. God was testing his patience and wanted him here for a reason. God would not make him wait here, day after day—while his wife was about to burst and while the department was on the verge of extinction—without bestowing a worthwhile payoff.

With his feet hanging out of the car, ice-cold snowflakes settled on his ankles and soaked into his socks. He drew his legs back inside and pulled the door shut. Still no sound from the radio interceptor, except an occasional cough or sneeze. He hoped that Stewart, the new inspector who was also the dourest of his remaining employees, was giving Arianna one of his professionally dirty looks.

Dopp had never doubted his intuition about people before. It had been scarily accurate his whole life. The first instance had been when he was a boy and his gut feeling had tipped him off to his father's infidelity. Then as he got older, Dopp realized that he had an uncanny knack for spotting liars. Along with a strong sense of ethics, he had the perfect prerequisites to become a cop, as friends and relatives used to tell him. But he saw his talent differently: his intuition was evidence of a spiritual connection between him and God, who had granted him this sacred link for a reason—to enter the ministry. And so he did, and stayed, until Joanie came along and changed everything. Thrown from his calling, Dopp had lost his way for a while as he struggled to make sense of the urgency that drove him into her arms. He knew he needed to find his way back to God, but how to do it was a mystery.

When the DEP bureau formed in New York City, he had his answer. There he could apply his talent for intuition in a direct, practical way: weeding out sinners to protect innocents. So he had ended up in a branch of law enforcement after all, but one whose mission was straight out of the Bible. There was no way, then, that God would let him down at the most crucial moment of his career.

Reminding himself of this, Dopp inhaled a slow breath. The smell of new leather had begun to nauseate him. He cracked the window a tad, just enough to get a whiff of cold air, and subconsciously started to gnaw on his hangnails. It was a habit from his childhood that had cropped back up in recent days.

But what if, just this once, he had been wrong?

He spit a torn cuticle out the window's narrow slit.

What if she was just a very ill lady with some sinful ideas?

No embryos had ever gone missing. There was no evidence of a lab anywhere. Could she have been going to the East Village regularly before to see a doctor, as she had told Trent? Dopp had been so sure that was another one of her lies. But could there have been a little-known specialist who practiced there?

No. The tip of doubt was the first crack of faith; it was the Devil beckoning to him; it was the weakening of his divine link. At all costs, he could not ignore his intuition about that woman. It could not be wrong. His connection to God could not be slipping after fifty-seven solid years.

He spit another hangnail out the window and then rested his left hand on his gun, secure in its holster around his belt. The barrel was smooth and reassuring. He was still in control, still the director of the DEP: the noblest of all government agencies, despite any questions about its necessity.

If only Windra would call again, even to prod him. But Dopp had heard nothing from the senator since Monday, and the budget talks had begun by now. Dopp checked the news on his laptop like a fiend, but there was nothing noteworthy yet about their progress. The talks were behind closed doors, so he—and the news—could not follow them. Could Windra have stopped calling because he had written off the DEP as a lost cause?

Dopp would prove him wrong yet.

"I will," he pledged aloud to no one.

But his boldness sounded forced, even to him. He turned to his laptop and navigated to the website of an online Bible. Reading some of his favorite passages in Colossians and Revelations would at least keep his self-doubt at bay.

The five stacks of papers on Trent's desk should have overwhelmed him: they were printouts, separated by borough, of the daily electronic reports sent in by all the fertility clinics in the city. Yesterday's reports. He was supposed to be reviewing each one and checking it against past records, then sending a summary to Dopp, who was continuing to assign random inspections from his car.

But with an understaffed office consumed by apprehension, Trent could tell that the department's efficiency was sliding. So he wasn't too worried that his own productivity was about the same level as Dianne's, his notoriously lazy colleague who had been the first person Dopp fired this week. Trent's own employment status meant nothing to him. Not today. Not with one day left before the transfer.

Arianna was counting on him, one last time: it was a huge moment of truth. He hated to think of it that way, but the phrase sneaked into his mind like the slogan of a pressure-mounting campaign. How the hell was he going to distract Dopp for *forty-five min-*

utes? He sighed, blowing off the top report in one of the stacks on his desk. He could hardly imagine luring Dopp away from her for even forty-five seconds.

What could possibly take up his attention for that long?

Trent knew that his wife was heavily pregnant. How that could work to Trent's advantage, though, was unclear. Unless Trent could somehow suspend communication between the two, and then tell Dopp to rush to Long Island for an emergency delivery . . .

No, impossible. Besides, even Dopp's seven-year-old son had a cell phone, and was fond of calling his father during business hours to report the most mundane details, like the fact that Joanie had forgotten to cut off his sandwich crust. So there was no way that the boy would fail to communicate with his father if his mother went into labor.

What else might draw Dopp away? Trent scrunched up his eyes, summoning an image of his exacting boss. What might scare him enough to drop everything and run to another site? A fire in the department's headquarters? Too dangerous. A break-in at his own home? Possibly. Trent did have a gun, courtesy of the department, and knew where his boss lived. But the timing would be risky—what if the family wasn't even home? Not to mention that it was a heinous stunt to perpetrate on his wife and kids. But was Dopp's stakeout of Arianna any less vicious, any less undeserved?

It might work, though Trent was uncomfortable with the idea. There had to be a lure that was both surefire and nonviolent. Preferably not involving others. He tried rephrasing the question in his head: What did Dopp *want*?

And then he gave a start, and reached for his phone to call Arianna on her private cell. It was so obvious, and so simple—Dopp was desperate to find the secret place he had suspected and hunted for all along.

Friday. The day finally arrived, and more quickly than Sam had expected. It was early evening when he looked up from his microscope for the last time, feeling immensely proud. The cells had differentiated into perfect oligodendrocytes, all containing Arianna's unique DNA, and they had proliferated in the petri dish. There was no logical reason for her body to reject them.

Sam had outdone himself: out of the four batches of stem cells he extracted, all had differentiated into the correct cells, proving that his hit-upon combination was no fluke. But he needed only one batch for the transfer, so the other three would remain behind, lost testaments to his breakthrough.

He had flawlessly—if obsessively—executed the whole procedure, checking on the cells every hour instead of every two, for the past forty-four hours. Fatigue had come and gone, a momentary phase, as nervous excitement took hold. The only sign of his marathon of insomnia was droopiness in his eyelids, but he hardly noticed it. When Arianna's life depended on it, staying on task was easy.

All he had to do now was transfer the cells into a flask, load it into the black case, and head to the clinic. Dr. Ericson would be waiting for him there to drain the cells into a sterile bag attached to a tube with a long needle at one end. And then, if all went according to Trent's plan, Arianna would be free to meet them at the clinic shortly thereafter. At least the traitor had come through with an idea and even guaranteed it to work, since it would exploit Dopp's deep desire for his suspicions to be vindicated. In just a few hours, then, both those bureaucratic swine ought to be left far behind, as Sam, Arianna, the Ericsons, and Megan disappeared uptown.

It was hard to believe that the transfer was almost here, after so many months of trial and error, hope and disappointment, and the depletion of scientists, resources, and time. Sam took a final look around. The lab looked the same as it had on any other day—or night, for that matter. The microscopes sat on the counter, soon to be unplugged, like the freezer and incubator. Already it was equipment of a past era that would be left behind to rust. But all of it had served him well. He would miss this place, rats squeaking and all, this hidden room that could not mesh with the outside world, though within it had so much to offer.

A protective scorn rose in Sam's chest as he thought about the unseeing eyes that were soon to enter. And then suddenly he was overcome with tenderness. This private lab was going to serve them one last time, like a dying dog faithfully wagging its tail; *I'm here for you,* it wanted to tell its master, *until the very end.* And so it was with this basement, this chamber of progress and loophole of the world. In its dying role, playing the distraction, it was going to serve up their tickets to freedom.

At 7 P.M., Arianna was sitting in her kitchen, alone. She thought of Sam, who ought to be on his way to the clinic with the cells. A thrill tingled the hair follicles on her arms. Her apartment was completely quiet, so no sounds could interfere with the plan. Even the dishwasher was turned off.

She reached for her bugged cell phone on the table. In her hand, the slab of plastic felt light, even insignificant. She rubbed her thumb over the tiny microphone slit that served as both her mouthpiece and Dopp's earpiece. For the first time, she hoped he was listening.

Clumsily, she dialed Trent's number.

"Hello?" he answered.

"Hi, it's Arianna."

"Hey, I was just thinking about calling you. How are you?"

"I'm okay, I guess. Are you doing anything?"

"Not really. How come?"

"I was wondering if you wanted to come over, actually." Her voice dropped, growing serious. "I want to talk to you about something in person."

"Oh, well, sure. Is everything okay?"

"Kind of. I've just been thinking a lot and I want to talk to you."

"Okay, I'll come right now."

"Thanks. See you then."

Arianna snapped her phone shut. She hoped they had sounded natural. She checked her watch: 7:07 P.M. In the time it would take Trent to arrive, she knew that Sam and the doctors would be arranging for the transfer procedure: preparing the cells in the bag, checking all the monitors, concocting the IV sedation, just in case. How badly she wanted to be there with them!

She wheeled herself to the window above the kitchen sink. The view faced east, over Fifth Avenue and the front circular driveway of her building. She used to love standing at the sink and watching the cars fly down the street, all the way to the Washington Square Arch. But from her wheelchair, she could no longer reach the window. Channeling her lingering strength, she pulled out a stepstool from the nearby pantry, flattened it open, and set it down in front of the sink. Its highest step was level with the countertop. With every ounce of determination, she hoisted herself onto the lowest step of the stool, and then pulled herself up to the next one, and the next, until she was able to crane her neck to see out the window. Immediately, she spotted what she had come for: Dopp's gray car was parked on the curb.

Sam hugged the black case close to his chest as he walked briskly to the clinic. It was dark out, the air frigid. The streets were still piled with slush from the recent storm, but he hardly cared if his sneakers were soaking wet, as long as he didn't slip. Inside the case, the atmosphere was completely different; it was a toasty 98.6 degrees Fahrenheit, an incubator writ small. Sam thought of the glass flask inside, and conjured up the last image he had seen of the cells under the microscope. Could he have missed any problem cells? No, they were all pure. He was sure of it. He had checked so many times. But hadn't he been much more tired than he realized? No, unless his eyes had deceived him dozens of times, the cells were fine. He could allow himself to breathe; his part was nearly complete. All he had to do was make it to the clinic. Step by step, cross the street. Washington Square Park came into view, shadowy and grim. He could see the outlines of trees, their branches quivering in the wind. There was no moon. He tightened his arms around the case as he walked along the park's perimeter. The clinic's door was two blocks away.

"Sam!" yelled a female voice.

He stopped short and turned toward the voice, which had come from a street perpendicular to the park, one block over from the clinic.

Megan's auburn head was sticking out the window of a black four-door sedan parked along the sidewalk. He hurried over to the car.

"Just wanted to wish you guys luck," she said. Her eyes searched his as if for reassurance.

"Thanks," he replied.

"You sure she'll be okay?"

"I have every reason to think so."

Megan nodded, biting her lip. "I'll be here waiting."

Seeing her worried face unnerved Sam; didn't they have this situation under control?

"I have to go," he said. He could see the translucent puffs of his own breath in the air. The next time he'd be outside, he would be with Arianna, helping her into this very car.

"Okay," Megan said. "Be careful with her."

He nodded. Then he turned on his heels and headed toward the clinic. The black case had grown heavy in his tired arms.

Trent made sure to wait a few minutes before leaving his apartment, just to allow Dr. Ericson, Emily, and Sam extra time to prepare. He paced back and forth across his room, holding a sheet of paper and muttering the words he had so painstakingly typed. The plan had to work; it hinged on Dopp's Achilles' heel. If Trent understood his boss at all, they would be safe.

He ran through the words on the page again and then stuffed the paper into his coat pocket and ran out. A withered part of him had the urge to pray, but he reminded himself that no safety net had ever even existed. Courage had abruptly become more difficult to summon.

The subway ride passed quickly as he concentrated on what he needed to say, while remembering not to come off as rehearsed. As he emerged from the West Fourth Street station, inhaling the cold air, the imminence of the situation struck him. It was too late to second-guess anything; in the next few minutes, the plan would be set in motion. His heart hammered as he approached Arianna's building. *Don't look nervous,* he told himself. *You can't look nervous.*

He turned the corner at Fifth Avenue and saw Dopp's car parked on the curb, right before the sidewalk curved in along the driveway. Squinting at the windshield, Trent could make out the shape of his boss's head, but not his face. He hurried over to the car, composing his features into a look of anticipation.

He waved at the tinted window, and Dopp pushed open the passenger-side door. His eyes were bloodshot, but he looked alert.

"Hi," Trent said, stepping into the car. He had never seen its interior, with its dashboard panel of interception devices, buttons, and speakers.

"Why do you think she wanted you to come over?" Dopp demanded in lieu of hello.

Trent widened his eyes and shook his head. "I don't know. But I'm about to find out."

"Well, what are you waiting for?" he snapped.

Trent shrugged and jumped out of the car. "Text me if you need to," he said before closing the door. Then he turned and hurried inside the building.

Good, he thought; Dopp was still his eager self.

Inside the elevator, he rummaged in his coat pocket for his script. He hoped she had her copy in hand. It had taken them twenty-two e-mails during work yesterday to finalize it. He wished they could have practiced it live. As the elevator opened onto her barren hallway, he coughed. There was barely any saliva on his tongue.

He walked to Arianna's door and knocked loudly. A few seconds later, she opened it with a small smile and raised eyebrows, a tacit: *Are you ready?*

He nodded back: *As ready as ever.* "Hi, how are you?" he said, stepping inside.

"I'm okay. Thanks for coming over."

"Sure. So you got me all curious. What's going on?"

"Well, why don't you come sit down."

She motioned to the kitchen table, and Trent followed her there, then pulled out one of the wooden chairs and sat. On the table were two items: a printed sheet of paper that mirrored his own, and her cell phone. Against the sink, under the window, stood a stepstool, and Trent understood right away why it was there.

Arianna wheeled herself up to the table's edge and cleared her throat. He could tell she was nervous, as she kept licking her lips and glancing at her own script.

"So," she said, looking at the piece of paper. "I wanted you to come over so we could talk about something very close to my heart. I've been considering discussing it with you for a long time, but I just needed to feel completely ready. It's the kind of thing I don't want to regret telling you." She took a deep breath and exhaled.

"Okay . . ."

"The thing is that I realized today, finally, that I do trust you. And it's taken me a while to get to this point, a long while. But I do."

"Well, that's good news, though I thought you already did."

"I've been getting there slowly. And now I think I'm ready to take you somewhere very important to me."

"Really? Where?"

"Hang on. First I owe you an apology. Remember when I told you I went to a church in the East Village?"

"Yeah . . ."

"Well, I lied. Kind of."

Dopp leaned forward so that his nose was nearly touching the car's speakers. Every muscle in his body was taut, except his pounding heart.

"What do you mean, kind of?" came Trent's perplexed voice.

"Well, it's true that I was going to a church in the East Village. But not for the reason you think."

"Not for prayer services?"

"Right."

"Why else would you go to church?"

"It's not any old church. It's very unconventional. For starters, it's in the basement of the actual church. And in a back alley that's pretty filthy, so consider yourself warned about that."

"Umm. Okay. Is it in a bad neighborhood or something?"

"Well, it's Alphabet City, what used to be Saint James Church of Christ."

"Used to be? Can you just tell me what's going on?"

"I would much rather show you."

"Why?"

"You'll see."

"Okay, but please tell me one thing: You're not part of a cult, right?"

Moron, Dopp thought. *Just go along with her!*

He flipped open his laptop and typed, "Saint James Church of Christ, East Village, NYC" into a search engine.

Arianna was chuckling. *"No, nothing like that."* Then she let out a sudden, low moan.

Dopp frowned and turned from his computer back to the speakers.

"What's wrong?" Trent asked.

"Hang on."

Dopp waited impatiently, wishing he could see what was happening. About ten seconds of silence passed.

"I'm sorry," she said. *"I have to go lie down."*

"What just happened?"

"Shooting pain in my head. I'm—I'm getting dizzy. It's been happening out of the blue."

"Oh, I'm sorry."

"This wasn't supposed to happen. . . . Damn it."

Dopp winced.

"Well, don't feel bad." Trent sounded disappointed. *"It's not your fault. You can show me another time, right?"*

"Yeah, well, how about if I go lie down for a bit, and then see if I'm up to it?"

Dopp felt his spine stiffen.

"Sure. Can you get into this place whenever you want?"

"Yeah, I have the keys. I'm just going to go in my bedroom now, sorry. I need to take something."

"Do you need help?"

"No, thanks. Come wake me in a half hour, okay? Sometimes the pills take a while to kick in."

"All right."

"I'm really sorry. You can watch TV out here or whatever you want."

"Okay. Are you sure you'll be all right?"

Her voice sounded lower, as if she had moved away from him. *"Just give me some time."*

Dopp heard a door close, probably to her bedroom, and then silence. With trembling hands, he turned back to his laptop and clicked the link that had come up first in his search. The link led him to a map of the East Village, with a tiny green arrow focused on a certain intersection. It was near Avenue C and Tenth Street. Above the square map, a precious line of text popped up: 150 Avenue C.

He closed his eyes for a second. *Thank you, God.*

Then he grabbed his cell phone and typed a text message to Trent as fast as he could: I have the address.

Trent smiled at the text message and nudged Arianna. She had wheeled down the hallway toward her bedroom and pretended to close the door. But actually she was lingering in the hallway with Trent at her side, trading uneasy glances with him: *Did it work? What is he thinking?*

Trent held the phone up for her to see the message. She raised her eyebrows and mouthed, *Now what?*

He held up a finger and typed a message back to Dopp: Hang on—I got this.

Then he went into the living room and turned on the television. A news channel came on first, and he flipped through the channels for something more boisterous, settling on a live broadcast of a concert at Madison Square Garden, featuring a punk band he had never heard of. The guitars screeched along with the singer's growling voice, and in the background, the drummer crashed cymbals with glee. Trent turned the volume up.

Arianna remained in the hallway, expecting him to leave. But he mouthed, *Wait,* walked back to her side, and picked up her hand. She frowned in confusion. "Not yet," he whispered, hoping she would understand that it could only help them to further aggravate Dopp's temptation and curiosity. Sure enough, a second text message soon fired back: What's going on??

Trent knew it was time. He typed back: Found her keys. Be right there. Then he nodded to Arianna. She pointed to a little table in the foyer, by the front door, and he saw she had left her keys there for him. As he leaned his face close to hers, a few strands of her hair tickled his lips. "Wait until you see our car leave before you leave," he whispered.

"I will," she whispered back.

"Are you sure you can you make it up to the window?"

She nodded.

"Okay. Good luck. I love you."

He grit his teeth as his face hovered by her ear; the words could not help escaping him. He took her cheeks in both hands and gently turned her face to his. She looked away from him, hesitating.

"I understand," he whispered. Then he leaned in and kissed her on the cheek. The moment was fast, just a hurried peck, but in that split second, the world condensed the way it always did when they were together and alone. And then it was over, and he was hurrying to the door, snatching her keys from the table, and waving a final goodbye before running out to meet his boss.

When Trent reached the car, he could hear the faint rumble of the engine. A good sign. He yanked the passenger door open and jumped in, dangling Arianna's keys like bait.

"Look what I found!"

Dopp stared at them as if mesmerized, his lips parted, cheeks flushed red. He snatched the keys away. "I think this could be it," he said.

"I do, too," Trent lied. The televised punk concert was leaking through the speakers. "Let's go check it out, hurry, before she wakes up!"

Dopp balked, shaking his head. "You go back inside and keep an eye on her. I'll go myself."

Trent felt a cool shiver scale down his back. "But she's sleeping," he protested. "I want to see this place, too!"

"I don't care. We shouldn't leave her alone."

Trent sulked, dangerously pushing the limit. But he was supposed to draw out their time away as long as possible—so what good would he be if Dopp went unescorted?

"Get out," Dopp barked. "Let me go!"

Reluctantly, Trent got out. As soon as he slammed the door, the car screeched away from the curb. He stood still for a moment, watching the car turn out of sight at the first corner. Then he raced back into the building, took the stairs to the third floor, and burst into the apartment.

Arianna was perched atop the stool, clutching the edge of the sink. She stared at him in surprise. "What happened? I was about to leave."

Trent threw his hands up. "He wouldn't let me come! He wouldn't let me leave you alone! But you were 'sleeping,' so he wasn't supposed to care. Damn it!"

Arianna watched him calmly. "It doesn't matter. He still left, and by the time he goes there, sees the place, comes back, and then realizes we're gone, the whole thing should be done. So come help me get down, and let's get out of here!"

Trent hurried over and lifted her down into her wheelchair. "But now he's going to know I was in on it. He was never supposed to find out!" Trent shook his head in disbelief as his plan of returning with Dopp to find Arianna's apartment empty—an apparent shock—faded into oblivion.

"So you'll flee with us," Arianna shot back. "Now you have to. But as long as we're safe, who the hell cares where we are?"

Trent gulped, nodding. "Let's go, let's go. We already lost five minutes."

She reached up her arms to him. "Just carry me."

"And leave the chair behind?"

"There's too much slush outside. We have to run."

He scooped her up as if she were a fragile bird and raced out the door.

TWENTY-TWO

Dopp drove as fast as he could, following the directions of the car's built-in GPS system. Crossing over to the East Village, he hit traffic made slower by the slick roads, which forced him to keep stepping on the gas and then the brake, jerking forward in frustrating bursts. His left hand gripped the steering wheel, and his right clutched the keys that Trent had produced. On the silver metal ring hung eight keys of different sizes and ridges, and Dopp rubbed his thumb over all of them, wondering which one he needed. Maybe Trent was not so useless after all. It must have taken some kind of quick thinking to look for her keys, though Dopp hadn't asked where they were. But who cared? For once, finally, Trent had done a good job.

Dopp's head whipped back against the headrest as he slammed on the brakes for maybe the ninth time. He pounded the steering wheel with his fist. The keys stuck out between his fingers like a weapon. Even a siren would not get him very far in this. Reminding himself that God was in control, he tried to let go. The avenues past Broadway were less clogged, and he started moving east in longer spurts, crossing Fourth Avenue and then Third, Second, First, all the way to Avenue C. Then up two blocks, to Tenth Street.

"Your destination is on the right," the car's automated voice announced. He stopped at the curb and jumped out, keys in hand. A tall, magnificently constructed church rose in front of him, pockmarked with troubling signs of abandonment: On the landing above the front steps, an arm stuck out of a makeshift shelter of cardboard boxes. The rest of the body was hidden under blankets, either sleeping or drunk or dead. From the sidewalk, Dopp smelled urine. He grimaced and held his breath, studying the church itself. Oval-shaped stained glass windows on either side of the front door were smashed in, and a painted cross on the door was peeling. He squinted at the door and walked a little closer to the steps that led up to it, covering his mouth and nose with his hand, barely aware of the cold. A name was engraved above the peeling cross: SAINT JAMES CHURCH OF CHRIST.

Dopp read the words several times; *this* was the place Arianna had frequented?

She had talked about a back alley, a filthy back alley. Dopp turned and headed to the end of the block. To his right, sure enough, a few yards away, there was a narrow opening. He walked to it and leaned his head around to peer inside. A warning surge of fear swept through him—this was the type of place where he could be killed and the body could go unfound for days. It was completely black inside; he could discern only the two steep walls on either side, the backs of other buildings that were nearly contiguous, but not quite. He stepped inside, leaving the comforting glow of the streetlight. About a half block away, the steeple of the church rose high. He pulled out his cell phone and shone it on the ground. It was covered with debris sunken into yellowed slush, and right away he noticed curious footsteps planted into the slush at regular intervals. Fresh, he concluded, since the storm had stopped only hours ago. He trudged forward, keeping his arms close to his sides, hoping it was too cold for rats. A metal railing came into view, directly under the church's steeple. As he came closer, he saw that about ten concrete steps led down to a door. A basement. He shivered as he descended the stairs, gripping the left railing; it was freezing.

At the bottom of the stairs, he opened his fist holding the keys. There were three locks on the door: one next to the knob, one above, and one below. Pretty high security for such a God-forsaken place. He thrust one random key into each lock, but it did not fit any of them. He tried again with another, and another, until the middle lock turned. It took two more keys to unlock the top, and the last key turned the bottom.

His heart was beating furiously. As he opened the door, he pulled his gun out of its holster and cocked it. Inside, it was pitch black, but he heard tiny feet pattering across the floor. Something ran over his foot, small and plump. He jumped back with a shriek, his scalp bristling with fear.

"Anyone here?" he called loudly. Gauging from the fading echo that the room was not so small, he inched forward, shining his cell phone on the nearest wall until he saw a light switch. He moved closer and flipped it on. Fluorescent lights buzzed to life overhead, and he could only squint at the floor as he tucked his cell phone away.

Little by little, he looked up, and what he saw first was somehow both astonishing and expected: a row of microscopes. Three stood on a counter in the back of the room. On the floor, he saw what had touched him: rats. Five hairy rats with long tails. Two of them were darting back and forth with ease, while the others barely moved. Several cages stood in the back of the room with their doors flung open. Disgusted, Dopp looked to the right: On a counter along that wall, there was other laboratory equipment, which he was trained to recognize from his days as an inspector: three sterile laminar flow hoods, a centrifuge, a shelf containing supplies—empty pipettes, glass dishes, rubber gloves.

Feeling as if he were in an alternate universe, he looked to the left again. Two black refrigerator-like containers stood side by side, and Dopp surmised what they were: an incubator and a freezer. He felt the force of righteousness pull him in their direction, and he replaced his gun in its holster as he walked up to one and swung open the door, expecting to feel either heat or cold emanating forth. But there was no temperature change. This machine was not even on. Inside, however, stood several glass petri dishes containing red fluid. Dopp gasped. They looked just like the dishes that held embryos prior to in vitro fertilization. Horrified, he reached for one, cradled it in his palm, and hurried to the row of microscopes. It had been five years since he was last an inspector, but his old laboratory training had been thorough. He switched on the microscope at its base, but nothing happened. Why was everything here unplugged? He placed the dish on the counter, crouched down under it, and moved a half-filled metal wastebasket to find an outlet. There it was, along with a limp cord. He plugged it in and stood back up.

Now the microscope turned on. He carefully placed the dish under the lens, and looked through it. Instead of a clump of cells bound by a spherical mass—a primitive embryo—he saw a spread of individual cells. It was, undoubtedly, the spawn of a destroyed embryo.

A violent roar ripped from his throat, abrasive against his vocal cords. He shook with outrage, filled with unparalleled fury: How many babies had died?

He spit onto the microscope's lens, wishing to inflict his horror onto anything that deserved it, anything that contributed to what was likely a massacre of unimaginable scale. A fighting urge snaked through his veins. He was in a branch of Hell, set up in a *church*. The energy in his arms reached an uncontrollable peak in his fists, and he lifted the heavy microscope and hurled it to the floor. It hit the ground with a noisy smash as parts broke off and glass shattered near his feet. He kicked the bulk of plastic that remained and it struck the wastebasket under the counter, knocking it over. A stream of empty soda bottles, a half-eaten apple, and paper garbage poured out. Dopp stood with his shoulders heaving, catching his breath, still shaking.

Then he noticed a crinkled piece of paper on the floor, in the midst of the broken mess, on which was scrawled a very familiar name: *Arianna*. He crouched down and snatched the paper, smoothing it out.

"Dear Arianna," it read. "It's taken me a long time to realize I want to tell you this, but"

The rest of the page was blank. Dopp's interest was piqued. On the floor, mixed with shambles of the microscope, were a few other crumpled balls of paper. He reached for one of them and unfolded it. This one was much longer, an entire page of scribbled blue ink.

"Dear Arianna," it started again.

> I hope this is the last weekend of your life that you have to suffer. You have no idea how hard it's been for me to watch you get sicker these past few months. But what happened today will change everything—of course it's unknown, but I have every reason to believe that it will work. Theoretically, it's perfect. I can't wait for this week to pass. And when it does, you'll be the bravest patient your clinic has ever seen. All I want is for you to live, Arianna. The world can't afford to lose you.

Dopp's mouth hung open as he quickly skimmed the rest of the page, with particular words catching his attention: *walk, fantasy, hope, pioneers, I love you, Sam.*

Who was Sam? And what had happened today that would "change everything"? Dopp glanced at the upper right-hand corner of the page: "January 21, 2028." That was exactly one week ago. *One week ago* was the day she had lied to Banks about her "sister's baby," and then rushed out of her office—could that event be connected to this? He studied the letter again, feeling his eyes drawn back to the page; and then two entire sentences jumped out as if they were blazing red: "I can't wait for this week to pass. And when it does, you'll be the bravest patient your clinic has ever seen."

Dopp bolted into the air, stuffed the letter into his shirt pocket, and ran out of the lab, bounding up the stairs, tripping blindly down the alley. He reached the street and turned left, then around the corner. His car was waiting on the curb, and he jumped inside and wrenched on the ignition. A feverish pulse throbbed in his head, and his breath pinched in his throat as he slammed on the gas and fumbled to grab his cell phone from his pocket. He started to drive with one hand on the wheel as he called Stewart, the sullen inspector who had monitored her all day at the clinic.

It rang several times before his monotonous voice came on the line. "Hello?"

"Stewart," Dopp said. "Did you see Arianna do anything unusual today at the clinic?"

"No, like what?"

"Like get any sort of medical attention?"

"No, she was in her office all day with me."

"You're sure she didn't receive any kind of treatment?"

"How could she? I was there the whole time. What's going on?"

"I just found her secret lab," Dopp breathed. "Underneath an old church."

"Holy Jesus. Where?"

"Avenue C and Tenth. Gotta go."

Dopp hung up and called Trent. After four rings—*four rings*—he answered.

"Are you still at her apartment?" Dopp breathed.

"Yeah, why, what happened?"

"Is she still sleeping?"

"Yes . . . what's going on?" Trent sounded worried.

"I think she might try to go back to the clinic tonight. Make sure she stays put until I get there. Whatever you do, don't let her go *anywhere*!"

"What happened?"

"It was a lab, just like we feared." Dopp's voice quivered. "And there are more people involved. Someone named Sam."

"How—how do you know that?"

"I found a letter. I'll explain later. But just make sure she stays *put*. Don't let on that you know anything. I'll arrest her as soon as I get there."

"Where are you now?"

"Avenue A and Eighth. I'll be there soon."

For a second, silence, then: "Okay."

Dopp hung up, not caring to say good-bye. He tried to keep his mind on the road, but all he could see was the destroyed embryo in the dish. It was the kind of awful image that he knew he would never forget—a crime scene that would have made even the most seasoned DEP agents recoil. *This* was why he needed to keep his job. And it was exactly what was going to make that possible. The hidden lab was sensational—it would be all over the news, as soon as Arianna's arrest was made public. He couldn't wait for the moment he told her the words.

Never had he felt so validated; in a flash of epiphany, he understood that his whole long career at the DEP, his journey to fully re-establish himself as a servant of God, was just now peaking. Of course, God had known it all along, had offered the guiding hand and the patience to help him get here. What a terrible fool he had been to doubt his intuition, even for a second. Relief dawned on him, weighty and comforting, as he realized that his divine link had been secure all along. He would never worry again that he was alone with guilt, for there was always the Lord leading him to redemption.

"Amen," he breathed.

In a blur, he managed to make it safely back to Arianna's apartment building and parked askew next to the curb. With a hand on his gun, he ran inside, flashing his DEP badge to the doorman.

"Arianna Drake," he demanded.

The doorman looked flustered. "Is everything okay?"

"She's under arrest," Dopp said. How satisfying to finally speak the words!

"Apartment 3R," the man sputtered. "Third floor, make a right."

Dopp ran into a waiting elevator, jabbed the button for the third floor, then raced out into the hallway and made a right, skimming the numbers on each door until he reached 3R. He turned the knob; the door was unlocked, and he pushed it open, expecting to see Trent waiting there for him.

But the apartment was dark.

"Hello?" he called, flipping on the light switch next to the front door. A living room to the right and a kitchen to the left were both empty. Holding his gun forward, he walked down the hallway toward a closed door. He knocked.

"Trent?" he yelled.

There was no answer.

He pushed open the door and saw an unmade bed, a dresser, and a night table. A whistling breeze blew in from the window, billowing out the curtains.

No one was there.

He swung open the door to the closet and was surprised to find it practically empty, with just a few fancy-looking dresses hanging inside. About two dozen wooden hangers hung bare on the rack.

Dopp shook his head in confusion. How could they be gone? Hadn't he just spoken to Trent?

And then he felt a glimmer of understanding—and the deepest betrayal.

There was only one other place they could be.

By the time Dopp reached the clinic, he was breathless and sweating despite the bitter air. He whipped out his DEP badge, the key to the sensor on the outside of every fertility clinic, and waved it in front of the door. A green light flashed, and he opened the door, stepping into the waiting room. The lights here, too, were off, as if everyone had gone home for the weekend. He wasted no time rushing past the empty chairs to the door that opened into the clinic's nerve center: its hallway, flanked on either side by examining rooms. All the white doors were closed. Dopp cocked his gun as he prowled the hallway. A strange high-pitched alarm was emanating from one room off to the right. He reached its door and opened it slowly, expecting to see someone, but inside was just an empty office. On the wall, on a flashing screen, was a picture of himself, snapped by a security camera seconds earlier as he had stepped into the waiting room. In the picture, his face was dark red, and his hand was withdrawing the gun from its holster on his belt.

He gripped his gun tighter and let out an exasperated grunt; it was only a signal screen. Within two minutes, its alarm faded out. Back in the hallway, Dopp slowed his step next to each door, listening. As he walked farther down, he heard it: a quiet but steady beeping. It was coming from the last room on the left, which was labeled OR 2. He stopped in front of the door and turned the knob. It was locked.

"Open up!" he shouted, smacking the door with the side of his gun.

There was no response. Then he remembered he still had Arianna's keys. She owned this hell; surely she could open its doors. He pulled the key ring out of his pocket and steadied his hands enough to insert a random one into the lock. His fury mounted as the key refused to turn, as did the next one. But the third one fit, and turned the lock with a satisfying *click*. He leaned the side of his body against the door as he pushed it open, keeping his sweat-soaked gun close to his chest, finger on the trigger.

He craned his neck around the door. Five pairs of horrified eyes met his own, familiar and strange, male and female. About ten feet away, there was Arianna, lying on her side on a surgical table, with her knees bent, looking utterly appalled to see him. Under her stiff gown, a handful of wires stuck out from her chest area and led up to the machine that Dopp had heard outside: A beeping screen on top of a podium displayed a line of jagged peaks and dips, and green numbers that were spiking—155/95, 157/100, 160/105.

Dopp's gaze darted from the screen back to Arianna's ashen face and then to the strange man and woman behind her. The man was sitting down, eye level with Arianna's lower back, but Dopp could not see what he was doing. Next to the man, a frightened-looking woman stood holding a plastic bag of murky fluid that was hanging from a tube dangling from a pole. The tube was connected to a needle that disappeared behind Arianna's body, into her back, right where the man was focused. But now his face popped up over Arianna's waist, lips parted dumbly, and he was gaping at Dopp as if he were a monster only imagined, never expected to appear in the flesh.

Dopp looked to the left, and there was the traitor himself, standing next to an older, white-haired man who showed no fear; rather, sharp grooves cut his forehead and his eyes scrunched into slits amid a maroon flush of rage. Trent's face had drained in comparison.

"How could you?" Dopp roared, feeling power in the blast of his own voice. "You knew this the whole time and you let it happen! *You helped it happen!*" Dopp instinctively lifted his gun, knowing he was in a room of killers.

Trent's lips moved, but his face remained stricken. "Put the gun down," he commanded; his tone was an attempt at calm, hinging on urgency. "Put the gun down, boss," he repeated. "You don't need the gun."

Dopp let out a little gasp, lifting the gun higher, point-blank with Trent's chest.

"Put your hands up right now," he growled. "You're under arrest."

Trent obeyed, stepping backwards, slack jawed.

"Stand still!" Dopp shouted. He turned to the old man. "Hands up! You are all under arrest! You're all killers!"

The older man pursed his lips as if he were about to spit.

"Just do it, Sam," Trent implored.

"Aha," Dopp said. "So you're Sam, the author of this little gem." Still keeping his gun aimed, Dopp pulled the crumpled ball out of his shirt pocket. For the first time, the old man's eyes shone with terror. He raised his arms.

Dopp smirked and tossed the letter onto the floor, near Sam's feet. Sam bent down to snatch it up. "Stay still!" Dopp shouted, returning both hands to his gun. "Keep your hands up!"

Dopp turned to face the doctor whose hands were buried behind Arianna's back. "Hands up where I can see them!"

The man shook his head. "I can't—I can't move them!"

"You *can't*?"

"Please, sir, I can't take my hands off the needle or it will fall out. We're almost done, look." He nodded toward the plastic bag that the woman next to him was holding. It was almost fully drained, and she was squeezing it ever so gently.

"It's almost done," the woman pleaded.

"Both of you put your hands up *right now*," Dopp snarled, feeling the smooth trigger of the gun under his forefinger, cocking it in their direction.

"Please don't hurt them!" Arianna moaned from the table. The machine next to her was beeping wildly. "They're just helping me get the cells!"

The cells.

Dopp looked harder at the plastic bag, and then recoiled. He bristled, and his hands shook as he swung the gun toward her, the ringleader, the Devil incarnate.

"No!" came a man's shout off from the left side. "Stop!"

But Dopp was already narrowing his eyes down the gun's slick barrel, looking straight at Arianna's chest. Another voice shrieked, and then all of them were shouting together, a chorus of manically pitching voices. Dopp's finger dwelt on the trigger, sliding down a ravine of its own sweat; he eyed the goal, the heartless heart that in her was nothing but a muscle.

Then he heard a savage voice roar above the rest. In his peripheral vision, he saw two bursts of flesh charging at him from the left side, and his finger knew before his mind did, knew he could not wait a moment longer before squeezing the trigger.

The sound of the shot echoed in Trent's ears as he lunged forward, arms splayed, feet off the ground, suspended in the air a moment too late. Never had he acted so decisively, with no fear of man or God, no moment's hesitation, only the split-second knowledge that his own judgment was all that mattered and all that ever had.

Amid the blur of screams around him, he smashed into Dopp with the full force of his body's momentum and they crashed blindly to the floor. He landed on top of Dopp's chest, opening his eyes just in time to see the gun fly away from their bodies and skid across the floor, just out of range. Dopp writhed underneath him, reaching for it, but Trent drew back his fist and punched him in the face with an involuntary cry, and then again, harder, pummeling him with a degree of rage he had never before felt.

Dopp groaned as his squirming ceased. Still straddling him, Trent reached for the gun, stretching his arm as far as possible, leaning toward it, until he was able to pinch it with two fingers. He brought it firmly into his grip and turned back to face Dopp. Blood streamed from Dopp's nose, and he was coughing and gasping between breaths. His eyes widened at the gun in Trent's hands.

"You want me to die?" he choked out.

Trent's lip curled up in disgust. "It's either you or me."

Then he slid backwards on Dopp's stomach, knowing that what he was about to do wasn't so much a choice, but a forced action in defense of his own—and the others'—survival. Tightening his grip on the gun, Trent curled his finger around the trigger, aimed the barrel at Dopp's forehead, and fired a single shot. The gun kicked back as the bang resounded. Trent jumped to his feet, looking away from the blood that instantly burst from the hole between Dopp's vacant brown eyes. The sickening smell of burned flesh floated upward from his body.

Trent backed away with dread, suddenly aware of the sobs that were coming from behind him. His throat constricted as he turned around, not prepared to find Arianna in a similar state; and then he gasped.

On the floor, facedown, was Sam. Blood was pooling under his chest, spreading out at a frightening rate, and his arms and legs were strewn at awkward angles from his body. Emily was kneeling next to him, and she looked up at Trent in tears.

"He's dead now, too."

Trent dropped the gun. Her words matched the scene, but his comprehension lagged behind. "What?"

"It happened so fast," Arianna murmured. Trent looked up from Sam's body to see her, still lying on her side—intact—on the table; her face was stark white. "The gun went off, I closed my eyes, and then he was on the floor."

"He jumped in front of you," Dr. Ericson breathed. He was still sitting behind her, holding the needle in place in her spinal column.

She stared down at Sam's body in disbelief.

Trent shook his head, unable to speak. Emily was crying next to him. They said nothing, not knowing how to proceed from such a moment, for proceeding would involve accepting the reality of his death.

Dr. Ericson's anguished voice broke the silence. "It's our fault. He would have dropped the gun if we had put up our hands."

Emily's eyes met her husband's. "No, I don't think so. He wanted her."

Trent saw the glistening of tears spill over Arianna's lids. She said nothing, only squeezed her head and whimpered.

"The transfer, it's done," Dr. Ericson said quietly. Trent looked at the bag; it was empty. He watched the doctor remove the long needle from her back, and then covered the area with a gauze bandage.

"We have to get out of here," Trent finally said. It was the only thought that seemed clear. He looked over at Dopp, whose face was now drenched in dark red blood that slid over his chin and neck onto the floor. Trent knew the memory of the sight would haunt him as long as he lived.

"What are we going to do with them?" Emily asked, motioning to the two bodies.

Trent shook his head. "We have to go. What can we do?"

"How can we just leave Sam behind?" Arianna cried.

"It's not him anymore," Emily said sadly.

Arianna's face twisted in pain, and Trent found his legs and rushed to her side. He grabbed her hands and buried his face in her neck, feeling a cry rise in his throat. "But at least you're okay," he breathed. "You're going to be okay."

She did not respond, but clutched his hands; he felt her heart thumping against her ribs, strong and alive.

"We have to hurry," Dr. Ericson said, coming around the surgical table and intercepting them to remove the wires attached to her chest. "Come on." He turned to his wife and held out a hand. Before taking it, Emily gingerly reached inside Sam's pockets. She pulled out his wallet, keys, and cell phone, snatched the crumpled piece of paper near his feet, and then rose reluctantly, pulling on her husband's hand. When she took a step away from Sam's body, the sole of her shoes tracked his blood on the floor.

"I want to say good-bye," Arianna whispered. "Help me."

Trent slid his hands under her body and scooped her up under the knees and neck, careful to avoid disturbing the gauze on her naked back. She sank against his strength, her legs dangling limply over his arms. He lifted her over the table's edge and lowered her so that her face was nearly touching the back of Sam's head. She leaned in closer and planted a kiss on it, leaving her lips pressed against his thin white hair. Gently, Trent pulled her away.

"We have to go," he muttered.

Before she could protest, he swept her up and followed the Ericsons out the door. Their steps echoed down the hallway as they ran to the waiting room, and then out of the clinic and into the chilly black night, with Arianna's surgical gown flapping in the air, exposing her bandaged back to the wind. Trent's chest heaved against her side as he followed the Ericsons around the nearest street corner. Parked along the curb, a black car was waiting for them there.

TWENTY-THREE

The television in the apartment looked ancient—a hulking box about a foot deep, perched atop an antique wooden dresser. Trent, Emily, and Dr. Ericson were huddled in front of it, waiting for the Monday evening newscast to begin. Arianna was resting on the sofa out in the living room, having chosen to restrict herself from all news, lest the stress interfere with her recovery. Trent knew she was suffering enough guilt over Sam's death not to be able to cope with any further fallout from Friday night's events.

In the three days they had lived at Sam's old apartment, two vigils were ongoing: one over her and one over the television. So far, her body was showing no signs of rejecting the transferred cells, and Dr. Ericson was optimistic that she had cleared the first seventy-two hours, but said she was still far from safe. It was crucial for her to remain as relaxed as possible, since stress hormones could trigger an adverse reaction, so she was taking a daily regimen of antianxiety medication along with prednisone, an immunosuppressive drug. While Dr. Ericson monitored her health, Trent and Emily traded shifts at her bedside, trying to distract her from grief and worry.

But it was difficult for Trent to conceal his own struggle to adjust to the drastic changes in their lives: splitting two dingy rooms and one bathroom between four people, eating canned food, staying inside day after day, while wan sunlight poked through the threadbare curtains.

All his belongings remained behind in his apartment, which was now under government scrutiny. But it was too soon to risk leaving this apartment while the city searched for them, so Megan had generously brought him the basic toiletries, along with a hastily selected wardrobe of discount clothing.

To communicate with the outside, the group had Arianna's TracFone. Their own four cell phones, and Sam's—traceable by satellite—were floating somewhere in the Hudson River, flung there from the West Side Highway during their drive uptown after the transfer. Credit cards, also, were traceable, so the Ericsons had liquidated their bank account in advance and stashed hundred-dollar bills galore into their suitcases. Arianna had not been able to do the same under Dopp's close observation, and Trent had had zero time to prepare, so the money of both of them remained tied up in accounts; Trent worried that they would never be able to retrieve it without setting the Feds on their trail.

But most of all, he was striving to adjust to the new emotional paradigm of their lives. Sleep eluded him as he thought about Dopp's bloodied face and lifeless eyes. Trent replayed the scene in his mind over and over: the feeling of the sweaty gun in his hand, the loud bang of the shot, the sudden smoking hole in Dopp's forehead. This time, Trent thought, he really had become a murderer. Yet he knew he would do it the same way again. Dopp had fired the first shot—had escalated it to that level—and Trent was the only one who could fight back. Arianna had even called him a hero. Underneath his feelings of trauma and horror, there was no regret—only sadness.

And a constant, overshadowing worry about being caught. Paranoia was a powerful force: it was a vacuum that sucked away relief; it was a reason to wince at footsteps outside the door and to cringe before every news update on television. Would they ever be able to react any other way to the jarring beeps of a breaking news announcement? Yet the archaic television drew them in like campers around a fire, mesmerized by the flames they had sparked.

Trent felt a nudge in his side from Dr. Ericson, and looked up at the screen as a string of minor notes dinged. It was exactly 7 P.M., and the news anchor was staring into the camera, facing his audience with a palpable sense of dismay. The station's tense opening music faded out before the anchor opened his mouth.

"Good evening, I'm Michael Bradley, and welcome to Channel Seven *Eyewitness News*. First up, an update about the so-called Embryo Gang, the ring of people who allegedly smuggled embryos into an abandoned church basement-turned-laboratory and then destroyed them for research purposes. Gideon Dopp, the New York City Director of the Department of Embryo Preservation, was shot dead after he discovered the hidden laboratory on Friday night through a covert investigation, and confronted the gang in the fertility clinic from which they had been stealing the embryos. The confrontation also resulted in the death of one gang member, a man whom police are still working to identify. The remaining members—at least four people—fled the scene and remain at large as authorities continue the search. The fertility clinic in question has since been shut down.

"News of the violence and the revelation of the lab sent ripples through Albany, where state legislators reconvened this morning for budget negotiations, opening the day with a minute of silence for Mr. Dopp. Senate Majority Leader Chuck Windra released a statement calling his death 'a heinous murder' and the hidden lab 'deeply disturbing.' Mr. Windra said he believed the lab's discovery would 'give other lawmakers like myself an impetus to reexamine the state's law enforcement priorities before passing the budget, so that we can best protect all of the innocent citizens of the State of New York.'"

"I've had it," Trent snapped. He turned away from the screen, overcome with a nagging worry.

"We can't hide here forever," Dr. Ericson said, clicking off the TV and sitting down on the bed. "Once they figure out who Sam is, they'll be able to trace him to this apartment. . . ."

"I was just thinking that," Trent replied, looking at Emily, who nodded and plunked down on the bed next to her husband. "With DNA testing," he added, "I doubt we have long."

"Let's not discuss this in front of Arianna right now," Emily said. "But we have to figure something out."

"I'm sure we can." Trent furrowed his brow. "We've come this far."

"Fake passports," Dr. Ericson said. "We get them off the black market through Megan, and then she drives us up to Canada. We just need to get over the border."

"Sounds about right," Trent said, feeling a thrill go through him. *Over the border to freedom.*

"And then what?" Emily asked.

"Then," Trent said, "we live our lives." For a fleeting moment, he had an image of waking up in bed next to Arianna in the privacy of their own home. A home they could leave whenever they wanted. "I can't wait," he added.

"The sooner, the better," Dr. Ericson agreed. "We'll make the plans, and then we'll tell Arianna once everything is in place. It'll give her more time to stabilize."

Trent nodded. "I'm going to go check on her, and then we can get started right away." He walked toward the door that separated the two rooms.

"Trent, wait," Emily said. She traded a glance with Dr. Ericson, who nodded. Then she yanked open the top drawer of the antique dresser and pulled out a crumpled piece of paper. "Here," she said, handing it to Trent. "I've been thinking about giving this to her, but I wanted to wait until she was relatively stabilized. I think you should see it first."

"What is it?"

"A letter Sam wrote. It was lying near his feet after . . . after he was shot . . . and I picked it up. Look at it."

As Trent unfolded the page, he vaguely recalled that Dopp had thrown a ball of paper at Sam, who had tried to pick it up. As soon as Dopp turned his attention away, Sam had kneeled and furtively seized it. In Trent's mind, the action barely registered, and he had forgotten about it until this moment.

He smoothed out the page, whose creases felt soft, and skimmed the words.

Then, in amazement, his lips parted; it was a love letter to Arianna. Through the hope it projected, Trent saw pain and tremendous vulnerability. It was a completely unknown side of Sam—a side that showed he was capable of the kind of love that drove him to risk everything, and that proved he was not only a genius, but also human.

Trent looked up, feeling a profound awe. "So this is why he jumped with me."

Emily nodded somberly.

"And I guess this explains why he never liked me," Trent said. "Not that I blame him."

"And it explains how Dopp found us," Dr. Ericson pointed out. "Look at that line about her being the bravest patient in her clinic."

Trent read through the first paragraph. "No wonder."

"So," Emily said, "you know how guilty she feels, and I was thinking this would help her understand."

Trent blew a pinch of dirt off the page and smoothed it out again. "She will cherish this. And I think he would have liked that."

"I do, too."

He thought of the past few days he had spent by Arianna's bedside, feeling helpless while she moaned about wishing to talk to Sam one last time.

He looked into Emily's eyes, still clutching the letter. "Can I do the honors?"

"Sure."

He smiled and turned to open the door, slipping quietly into the living room. Arianna was sleeping on the couch, facing the worn cushions. A light cotton sheet was draped over her body, up to her neck. Waves of hair covered her cheek. Trent tiptoed to the couch and knelt down, wondering if it was worth waking her from a rare moment of peace. But then she stirred and opened her eyes.

"Hey," he murmured. "Did I wake you?"

"It's okay." She turned toward him and yawned, extending her arms, then stopped midstretch. "What is it?"

"What's what?"

"I can see it in your eyes. You want to tell me something."

Trent smiled. "Well, I happen to have something to give you."

"You do?"

He held up the letter. "Dopp found this in the lab, and it led him to us in the clinic. It's also the piece of paper he threw at Sam, and Emily picked it up from the floor on our way out. She just showed it to me. But it was meant only for you."

Confused, Arianna propped herself up on one arm, took the letter, and began to read. Trent watched the emotions play across her face: surprise, tenderness, sympathy, and in the end—heartbreak. In her eyes, tears shimmered.

"I had no idea," she whispered. "I must have caused him so much pain."

"But you did love him. You loved him in the only way you could."

She nodded, holding the letter close to her chest. She held it there for a few moments, thinking. Then she looked into Trent's eyes. "He was right that we shared the same kind of hope—extreme hope. And he succeeded for me, but I haven't yet for him."

"What do you mean?"

"I mean, he saved my life *twice*. I owe it to him not to waste my time now, not to just sit around and atrophy. If I did that, it would be the greatest betrayal of him possible."

"But what can you do?"

"I can still be productive. I have ideas—"

"You're supposed to be resting and recovering!"

"Just so I can die of boredom?"

Trent could not help but smile. The fervor in her blue eyes had returned, and it was the most reassuring sight in weeks. "Okay, so what's your next big scheme?"

"I'm going to spread the word about his breakthrough to all the people who will be able to appreciate it, and keep his progress alive, if only in their minds."

"And how are you planning to do that?"

She was sitting straight up now. "I'll type up all of his notes. Every last word that he saved in his suitcase, and then send them anonymously to every scientific journal and biology department at every major university."

Trent hesitated. "It's a good idea, but what if it's too late?"

"Too late for what?"

"For them to understand how moral his work really was. It's hard to see that when you're so used to the common attitude."

"Then I'll attach a letter explaining everything I told you. That worked pretty well, didn't it?"

He nodded. "But I happened to be already starting to think straight on my own."

"Well, I'm sure there are others like you, and they deserve to know what's possible. If only we can reach them."

She gently placed the letter on her pillow, then threw the cotton sheet off her legs and leaned forward to massage her kneecaps.

"I *will* walk again."

Trent did not smile, hoping his solemnity would convey his belief in her determination. "I know."

"And once I do, we should film it, and then put up the video for the world to see. I'll be literally living proof of what he did."

Trent smiled. "We should start filming you now, a documentary of your recovery."

"You're right! There's so much to be learned from my body. I should start to keep a detailed log. And that can be part of the film, along with his notes, so it's no mystery exactly how he did it."

"So no one can pretend it was a miracle."

"Exactly."

Trent felt himself growing excited. "It will be journalism on film. I can direct and you can star."

"But we know who the real star is. We have to make it clear that he deserves all the credit."

"Absolutely."

She smiled and motioned to Sam's duffel bag, which remained unopened in a corner near the front door. "Can you bring it to me? I want to start going through his notes."

Trent grinned. Part of him wanted to urge her to relax—doctor's orders—but the rest of him understood that her renewed vitality deserved only nurturing.

"Of course," he said. He rose and went to the corner to pick up the dusty bag. It was heavy from the weight of textbooks and paper, and he felt its contents shift as he lugged it toward her. She was sitting upright, waiting with flushed cheeks and outstretched arms.

ACKNOWLEDGMENTS

I am deeply grateful to the many people who helped me write and publish *Living Proof.* First, I owe tremendous thanks to my agent, Erica Silverman, for spotting promise in my project and becoming such a trusted partner; your hard work, wisdom, and positive spirit have made this publication possible. I am also very much indebted to my passionate editor, Bob Gleason, and the wonderful team at Tor, including Tom Doherty, Linda Quinton, Whitney Ross, Katharine Critchlow, Justin Golenbock, Patty Garcia, Aisha Cloud, Aubrey Lynch, Steph Flanders, Irene Gallo, Lisa Honerkamp, and Eric C. Meyer. Huge thanks also to M. J. Rose, John Brady, and Arnold Dolin.

Alex Steele and Matt de la Pena at Gotham Writers Workshop provided top-rate instruction in novel writing. Lisa VanDamme of VanDamme Academy encouraged my love of literature from a young age and taught me the technical tools I needed to become a writer, for which I will always be grateful.

For the medical and scientific elements, I am thankful to Dr. Jacqueline Berenson and Dr. Trace Jordan, and to Dr. Charles Ribak, who was kind enough to give me a tour of UC-Irvine's stem cell laboratory. I also consulted United States Patent 7285415 of Dr. Gabriel Nistor and Dr. Hans Kierstead, world leaders in stem cell research, whose work focuses on regenerating damaged spinal cords.

While tackling this project, I could not have had a more supportive network of friends and family—thank you, always, for your enthusiasm. Special thanks to Shea O'Rourke, Chris Shiota, and Ben Pomerantz.

My most profound appreciation is to my father, Leonard Peikoff, who encouraged me at age twenty-two to spend a year writing a novel, knowing it was my dream. Thank you for lending your support and guidance in so many ways and for not letting me quit early on. Equal thanks goes to my mother, Cynthia Peikoff, for your brilliant feedback and your unwavering belief in me.

Last, but certainly not least, thank you to Matt Beilis for enabling me to write about true love without doing any research.